WindLegends Saga
Book One

# WINDKEEPER

By

## Charlotte Boyett-Compo

Dark Fantasy Romance

New Concepts

Georgia

Windkeeper is a publication of NCP. This work is a novel. Any similarity to actual persons or events is purely coincidental.

New Concepts Publishing, Inc.
5202 Humphreys Rd.
Lake Park, GA 31636

ISBN 1-58608-836-x
© 2006 Charlotte Boyett-Compo
Cover art (c) copyright 2006 Eliza Black

NCP books are available at special quantity discounts for bulk purchases for sales promotions, premiums, fund raising, or educational use. For details, write, email, or phone New Concepts Publishing, Inc., 5202 Humphreys Rd., Lake Park, GA 31636; Ph. 229-257-0367, Fax 229-219-1097; orders@newconceptspublishing.com.

First NCP Trade Paperback Printing: July 2006

Be sure to check out our website for the very best in fiction at fantastic prices!

Visit our webpage at:
www.newconceptspublishing.com

## Chapter One

The three thieves looked at one another. They had not anticipated any trouble when they'd followed their mark to the stable. As a matter of fact, they had anticipated no trouble at all from this callow youth. They had thought him an easy mark as he sat drinking in the Hound and Stag Tavern, for he had appeared to be deep in his cups, his full attention on the jug of mead that sat before him on the rough-hewn plank table.

"You've time to turn around and leave before it's too late, you know," their intended victim warned politely.

"You ain't got nothing to be so confident about, boy!" the oldest of the three scoffed, coming closer.

"You might be surprised," was the roguish reply.

The oldest of the three men--a miscreant who appeared to be in his late sixties although his massive build could rival that of a man half his age-- seemed to be their leader.

He was a burly man with coarse, flat features, and a beaked nose that dripped a constant stream of yellowish snot from its crooked, battered tip. The nose looked as though it had been broken many times, for it sat at a slight left angle along the man's unshaven and dirty cheekbone. Scratching at the stained crotch of his equally dirty breeches, the man narrowed his drooping lids over dull, lifeless, rheumy gray eyes. "Hand over your gold, boy," he sneered, "and we'll let you live to get back safe-like to your mama."

From the corner of his eye, the youth saw the other two robbers easing away from their leader. He feigned a shiver of fear. "My gold, sir? But if I give you my gold, how ever will I get home to Mama?" His gaze was merry, innocent; but then the regard changed--quicksilver-fast--and the innocent look became a hot glare. The full lips lifted with contempt. The amused voice turned cold and deadly as the smile faded. "If you men think you can take my gold from me, then by all means go ahead and try," he drawled. "I have no intention of giving you bastards anything of mine."

The leader's expression turned hard. Encouraged by the grunts of laughter from his two companions, he smiled a gap-toothed sneer. "Well, now, boy. If that's the way of it, then you have seen the last of your mama and she of you."

"Don't make us have to hurt you none, boy," one of the other men advised. "Or have to mess up that pretty face of yours."

The young man stiffened. He was very aware, and very sensitive, about his looks. He'd often considered his softly rounded face and pale blue eyes far too girlish. Despite the deep cleft in his chin--the only truly mature thing about a face that still sported a peach-fuzz growth of light beard--he thought of his face as a liability rather than an asset. The mop of thick, golden hair that fell to the right over his high forehead annoyed him even more, for he thought blond-haired men were too often considered effeminate and ineffectual.

He was just a tad over six feet and he'd often complained to his brothers that his lack of height made him feel more boyish yet. His shoulders were broad beneath the soft sheen of his leather jacket and his chest was developing nicely; but he had not been able to add bulk to his muscles yet. His long legs were tapered and well-proportioned in the tight fit of his dark brown leather breeches, but he wasn't all that good a runner. His hands were strong, though, and that--combined with the lethal expertise that governed his sword--gave him an advantage these men could not see.

"A scar or two on that lily-white puss might give the boy some character, huh, Tymmy?" one thief said and giggled. "Make more of a man of him, you reckon?"

The man's taunt brought another blush of anger to the lad's face. "You gods-be-damned bastards have bitten off more than you can chew this time."

"When we get through with you," the leader chuckled, "not even a diseased whore will look your way, son!"

The lad crossed his hands over the jade pommel of his sword and leaned on the weapon. Lifting one golden brow, he let a smile tug at the corners of his mouth. "Now is that so?" A wicked gleam entered his sky-blue eyes. "And I suppose the three of you are thinking yourselves worthy opponents for me and my blade?"

Snarling, the leader put his beefy hands on his hips and glared. "You're a bigger idjit than I thought you were, boy, if you don't think we can spit you and roast you 'fore we're done!"

"An idjit?" the lad repeated, clucking his tongue in mock dismay. "I've been called many things, gentlemen, but never an idjit!"

"You be one, that's a truth!" one man dared to chime in, puffing out his scrawny chest. "We're gonna roast you for a certainty!"

"Let's see you try," the young man scoffed. "The only idjit here is the man who thinks I'll let him take anything that belongs to me. What is mine, is mine. And mine it will stay."

"Brave words for a man alone and outnumbered," one of the robbers reminded him.

"That's because you men pose no threat to me."

The leader took a step toward the youth and raised a gnarled fist, a meaty chunk of scarred and rough flesh. "You just signed your death warrant, you crazy little bastard!"

A short, balding man with only a fringe of orange hair ringing his shiny pate, the third thief had legs that were badly bowed. He looked as though he sat astride a keg of ale. His lurching walk would have been comical if it had not been so pathetic to watch. As he'd waddled closer to his victim, his stench came rolling across the stables in waves of noxious fumes. His torn and greasy garments looked alive with vermin. "He's about to meet his maker, he is."

"Then let's do it," the blond lad said, shucking off his leather jacket. He threw away the jacket, spat into his left palm, then brought up his sword. Grasping the blade in his left hand, he bent and flexed the tempered Chrystallusian steel, his gaze never leaving the burly leader's face.

With a furious grunt, the leader drew a short sword from the belt of his pants and lunged at the young man, staggering by his victim as the youth had stepped easily away. The thief yelped as the flat of the sword struck his rump.

"You sorry little...." he gasped, rubbing his backside with his free hand. "You'll pay for that!"

The remaining thugs turned their own weapons on the youth, striking out with little or no expertise.

True amusement flitted across the youth's merry, grinning face at the robbers' clumsy efforts to impale him. He met their frenzied, ill-timed attack with offhanded skill; pushing one man away with his foot while sending the other crashing woefully to the ground with a well-aimed backhand.

With a snarl, the leader struck out with his sword while the youth was doubled over with laughter. He managed to slice a thin slit in the billowing cambric sleeve of the young man's shirt.

Looking down at the tear, the youth ceased to laugh and a heavy scowl came over his handsome features. Sighing heavily as he plucked at the rent, he slowly lifted his gaze to his attacker's face. "Well, hell," he said with exasperation, letting the words drop like heavy stones. "This was a brand new shirt." With a low hiss of spite, he lunged forward and engaged his attackers in a shrill clash of blades.

In the shadowed confines of the stable's loft, a watcher peered over the edge and took in the drama. As the one-sided fight lingered on, the watcher followed the exchange of swordplay; keeping a close surveillance on the young man as his opponents clumsily circled him. But then something just outside the watcher's vision nudged that sixth sense most people have when danger is lurking near, and the onlooker's attention turned from the fight to scan the partially opened side door leading to the tavern's kitchens. A search was made for what had caused the sensation of wariness. Seeing nothing immediately in need of attention, the watcher pulled closer to the edge of the loft and finally spied the stealthy approach of a fifth man entering through the sun-darkened doorway.

The innkeeper, no doubt anticipating a quick end to the objective he and his cohorts practiced on a regular basis, had ventured from his establishment as time lapsed onward. Taking in the situation in a glance, he reasoned his own brand of intervention was needed. Easing himself over to a pitchfork leaning against the wall, he crept up to the wicked-looking implement and grasped the handle in his flour-caked paws.

Grossly fat and squat, short legs waddling beneath his long, dirty apron, the innkeeper nevertheless moved with a grace and speed that belied his bulk. His pudgy face was creased in a scowl and shone with sweat as he sneaked up behind the youth.

The sentinel studied the situation with concern and growing anger. A man who would stab another in the back was a coward and as vile as they came.

"I don't think so," the watcher growled quietly through clenched teeth. Silently and swiftly, the watcher drew a thin black blade and expertly flipped it over in a practiced hand so that the sharp blade rested lightly along the palm. A callused thumb eased down the blade until the very tip was held firmly by the heel of a flexed thumb and crooked forefinger.

Intent on disarming--and disrobing--the man who had torn his shirt, the youth saw no real danger in a man advancing on him with only a doubled fist as a weapon. He glanced quickly at the man and then turned his attention back to the robber with whom he was sparring. He had felled the leader just moments before and that mischief-maker now lay huddled against a stall, his greasy red hair plastered with horse droppings from where he had skidded on the floor. A well-timed kick knocked the orange-tufted, bowlegged man's weapon from his hand and a look of shock passed over the robber's grimy face as he scurried after his blade.

With his back still to the lurking innkeeper, the youth now had only one obvious opponent: the man who was within boxing distance of him, fist doubled. Confident that he could take the robber, that no actual threat was forthcoming from those arthritic-looking hands, the young man laughed.

He was still laughing as dirt was thrown into his face, effectively blinding him. He twisted away from hands that grabbed at his shirt and felt the material rip. Less concerned now with his clothing, he stumbled back, shook his head to clear the watery vision that blinded him to the men around him.

"Oh, no you don't!" The thief who had thrown the dirt laughed. "You ain't getting away from us, boy!" He made another attempt to grab the young man's shirt, and then grunted as a lantern crashed down from the ceiling. He wobbled to the floor, unconscious, his eyes rolling back in his head.

Mouthing an obscenity, the innkeeper craned his head up to the loft. The dirty little bugger had an accomplice up there. With an intense scowl of hatred on his beefy face, he kicked out at the red-haired leader who was slowly, groggily coming awake. "Get that bastard in the loft, fool!" he shouted to the bowlegged man.

Hearing a voice so close behind him, the young man spun around, his blurring, stinging vision only able to make out the bulk of someone coming toward him. He shook his head once more to clear it and then his eyes flared as the tines of the pitchfork gleamed in a ray of sunlight peeking through the loft's planking. Losing his balance, he fell backward, sprawling to the ground at the mercy of the rapidly advancing pitchfork. Landing painfully on his tailbone--the stall in which his own steed was sequestered blocking his movement backwards and an upright keeping him from twisting to the left--he found himself wedged against the stall and a wheelbarrow filled with grain. His face paled with an unaccustomed look of fear and he swallowed hard. With a silent prayer on his taut lips, he took a deep breath and waited for the piercing agony he knew the tines would bring.

"You're a dead man!" the innkeeper said and chortled. He started toward the youth, the pitchfork aimed at the young man's chest.

With a suddenness that chilled the air, something hissed through the morning rays and the advancing innkeeper stilled, a look of astonishment on his pudgy features. He half-turned, rasping in a low breath, and raised his eyes to the ladder. He looked down at the youth sprawled at his feet and then cursed.

"You little bastard," he mumbled as he let go of the pitchfork, his knees giving way as he tumbled sideways, the handle of a black crystal dagger protruding from his chest.

The youth's blue eyes bulged; the sensuous lips parted as the pitchfork sprang forward with its own momentum, its sharp tines arcing downward. Light shone eerily on the lethal-looking spear; flashed in a bright sparkle of danger as the implement came down with a thud. The tines buried themselves in the hard-packed dirt between the youth's spread legs, just inches from his groin. The wooden handle bobbed back and forth.

"It missed you!" a voice spoke from the loft.

The young man's eyes were squeezed tightly shut. He could hear the handle squeaking as the pitchfork wobbled, but he didn't feel pain. He forced open one eye and swallowed loudly as he scanned the tool from top to handle, to tine, to the juncture of his open thighs. He didn't recognize his own voice as he let out a softly quivering, "Oh, shit!"

"Is the innkeeper dead?"

He opened his other eye and glanced at the innkeeper. One look told him all he needed to know. Frothy red foam had bubbled out of the innkeeper's slack mouth and was dripping to the ground beneath his head. The dead man was staring sightlessly at the loft as though in mute disapproval.

"Deader than a door nail," the young man whispered.

"Good! What about the others?" was the question from above.

Sweeping his attention to the man whose head had been dented by the lantern, the young man thought that robber no longer posed a threat, for blood poured from the wound in his greasy pate. Apparently the leader had awakened and fled when the innkeeper met his untimely end, for that one was nowhere in sight. That left only the bowlegged thief whose whereabouts were uncertain.

The youth pushed himself from the ground and cast a quick look around him.

"I don't know," the young man replied. He felt his shoulder nudged and absently reached over to pat his horse's nose. "I'm all right, boy," he said softly in answer to the steed's inquiring nicker. The youth gently pushed his stallion's inquisitive face from his own.

A muffled oath and a snarl of rage from the loft drew his attention upward and the blond lad leapt for the ladder. Just as he reached the wooden steps, the bowlegged robber came tumbling head over heels to the ground to land with a mighty thud at the young man's feet.

"Oh, there you are!" The youth laughed, smiling benevolently at his dazed enemy. Totally ignoring the man who was gasping for breath from his fall, the youth was about to climb the ladder to thank his accomplice when something sailed past his ear. He reacted with quick reflex by spinning around to the opposite side of the ladder, nearly breaking his ankle as he pivoted on the bottom rung.

He glanced down and could not credit what he was seeing. He blinked and looked again.

The man with the bloody head wound was clutching a wicked, double-edged dagger that he had obviously been about to plunge into the young man's exposed back. Now, his wrist was pinned to the dirt floor by the shaft of a gleaming crystal quarrel.

"Did I get him with the crossbow?"

"Aye, you did," the lad whispered. Whistling to himself, he glanced up with admiration and then turned with laughter to the leader of the thieves. "Merciful Alel, but I bet that hurts." The young man smirked. He stepped down from the ladder and nudged the pinned wrist with the toe of his dusty boot.

"Mercy, Milord!" the robber screeched as his free hand grasped the bleeding wrist of his injured one. "Have mercy on me, Sir!"

All amusement left the young man's face and his eyes took on the hard glint of steel. "Mercy such as you were about to show me?" He shrugged indifferently. "Don't worry. I won't slit your dirty throat."

"You ain't gonna kill me, Milord?" The thief breathed a too-hasty sigh of relief as the youth shook his head.

"Why should I?" came the terse reply. "I'll let the Tribunal see to you." He folded his arms across his broad chest. "I hear the Labyrinth is nice this time of year."

Fear blazed across the man's face and he jerked in horror. "Kill me, Sir!" he pleaded, his free hand going up in submission. "I'd rather die than go to Tyber's Isle!"

Stooping over his captive, the young man grinned. "Do you know who I am?" he asked pleasantly. He hunkered beside the man. "Have you any idea at all?"

The thief vigorously shook his head. "No, Milord," he said, his voice breaking.

"Well, I think I should tell you," the lad said with weariness. He leaned over and put his lips to the thief's ear.

As the name registered in the bowlegged man's befuddled brain, he blanched white as freshly fallen snow and moaned in despair. There was no doubt in his mind the lad was telling the truth. He looked away and shuddered. "The gods have mercy," he whispered.

"They might. I won't," the lad said with a harsh snort. "And now you know why you'll spend the remainder of your life in the Labyrinth," the youth told his captive and then stood, his eyes going to the opened doorway where there was sudden movement. He frowned. "It took you long enough."

One of the two men who came hurrying through the doorway wore the livery of a military captain. The medallion of his rank was pinned to his wide chest. He was tall, over seven feet in height, with a shock of gleaming, bright red stubble on his oversized skull. His forehead sloped dramatically downward over small black eyes and his mouth was large with rubbery lips that were set in a prim line of worry. His big hands gripped a broadsword that required both hands to wield. "Are you all right?"

With a shrug of disdain, the young man looked down his nose at the Captain of the Guard, not an easy thing to accomplish since he had to crane his neck backwards to do so. "Why wouldn't I be?" The blond youth snickered.

The captain let out a ragged breath and shook his massive head, glancing over at his companion, a man wearing the livery of a lieutenant. A look passed between them and both turned their attention back to the youth. "Me and Edan were worried about you," the captain said, closing his eyes in thanksgiving and relief that his charge was in one piece.

"There was, of course, no need," the young man said haughtily, sniffing at the tall man's concern. He pretended to dust an imaginary particle of lint from his torn sleeve. "I am quite capable of defending myself."

The second guard chuckled. "Didn't I tell you what he'd say?"

A heavy sigh of hopelessness gushed from the Captain of the Guard. He shook his head. "One of these days...." His rubbery face turned crimson with anger. "If you persist in going off on these forays by yourself, you're gonna come up against the one man you can't best!"

A disdainful lift of the young man's shoulders was his answer to the dire prediction.

"Oh, the demons take you!" the captain spat and bent over the bowlegged thief. "What's to be done with this one?" He gave the dead innkeeper a cursory glance then pointed to the unconscious thief. "Is that one dead, too?"

"Nope. Take them back to Boreas with you."

The captain turned his head and looked at the youth. "Aren't you coming?"

"Yes."

Another sigh as he and the other guard unpinned the thief's wrist, ignoring the man's shriek of pain. "Any time soon?"

Another shrug. "Maybe."

"Will you be riding with us?" the captain asked as he helped to support the thief's limp weight.

"I'll catch up with you."

One more sigh at the futility of dealing with this boy and the captain dragged the thief out of the stable, casting a hopeless look at the young man as he went. "You will be careful?"

There was a cluck of the youth's tongue. "Aren't I always?"

"Oh, of course, you are!" the captain mocked. He pushed the bowlegged thief ahead of him and shouted at his fellow guard. "Truss up this bastard like a feast goose!"

The youth walked to the opened stable doorway and watched the guards leading the thief to a group of horsemen milling around outside the tavern's entrance, and grinned. Rayle Loure, the Captain of the Elite Guard, had brought ten men. When would the man learn that he was fully able to take care of himself? He shook his head and then looked up. "You all right up there?" he asked, leaning against the upright nearest the ladder.

"Uh, huh."

"Well, then, I think I've made it safe enough for you to come down." The young man laughed, and then frowned fiercely as a loud snort came from the loft. His ego stung at the reminder that he had not been the one to save the day. He pushed away from the beam, his mouth set in a mulish line. "You coming down?"

"Aye." Straw rustled in the loft and a few loose shards fell through the gaps in the wooden planks overhead.

"Any time soon?" he mimicked in imitation of his captain's question.

"In my own good time." The voice that had spoken was youthful, indeed: not more than thirteen, fourteen, at most.

The young man was annoyed that the child in the loft, a stable boy, no doubt, had come to his aid. With the supreme arrogance of youth and masculinity, he thought he could have handled the threat of the pitchfork by himself if he had been given time to rationalize the outcome of his next action. That he had had no sense, and was at the mercy of the innkeeper, had somehow managed to slip his mind. He smirked, rather than smiled, at the thought of a mere stable boy coming to his defense, but then his frown tightened to speculation when he glanced at the dead innkeeper. No ordinary stable boy was this.

He shrugged. A stable boy that could throw a dagger and use a crossbow was worth talking to, he supposed. "You'd make a fine soldier-apprentice," he said begrudgingly.

A light guffaw of laughter came from the loft, followed by the sound of boots crunching straws.

The nicker of a strange horse broke through the youth's moody self-absorption and he stepped over to a stall at the end of the stable. A small gray horse stuck its velvety nose out to him, a soft snort of welcome coming from its nostrils as he put out his hand. He spoke over his shoulder.

"Does this mare belong to the innkeeper?" He put his hand on the sleek gray nose and patted the beautiful mare. She nuzzled the palm of his hand and laughed. "If she does, I claim her. She's a beauty."

"Mine," was the offhanded remark as the ladder to the loft squeaked.

"Yours?" The young man's eyebrows arched in surprise. Not a stable boy, then; a guest at the inn, perhaps. He nodded his head in understanding. The young one was more than likely a boy traveling with his parents or a nobleman's son on holiday. He nodded emphatically. That made sense. It would explain how the boy knew weapons such as the ones he had used. Sixteen seemed about the right age for a boy out traveling alone in this day and age.

A booted foot crunched dirt beneath it as the sentinel dropped from the last two rungs of the ladder to land on the stable floor.

"She's a fine one," the youth said, referring to the mare that was pushing her velvety head under his arm in immediate affection. He kissed her smooth muzzle. "What's her name?"

"Windkeeper."

The young man tightly compressed his lips to keep from laughing at the rather elegant name. He silently mouthed the regal name to himself and shook his head, his eyes twinkling with mirth. Out of respect for the ego of youth, he managed to keep the laughter from his voice as he asked his next question. "An unusual name, don't you think?"

"Maybe," was the short, miffed reply.

"Is she fast?"

"As fast as the wind, Milord, and twice as loyal. She can outrun any mare you put up against her."

The blond youth's back stiffened. There had been something in the speech pattern, the tone, and the inflection that didn't ring right. Turning slowly to face his companion, his brows shot up in shock. "You're a gods-be-damned girl!"

"It would appear so, Milord." A wicked grin spread across the girl's face and bright green eyes lit with humor. "I kinda like it that way. How 'bout you?"

"You're alone?" His eyes went to the loft in hope of seeing the male who had, without a doubt, wielded the weapons with such precision.

"Quite alone." She propped the wicked-looking crossbow she had wielded with such ease against the wall and laid the bag of quarrels beside it. With barely a look at the dead innkeeper, she went to him, pulled her dagger from his chest, and wiped the blade on the man's dirty apron.

With a growl of disbelief, the youth ran his sword hand through his thick gold hair. "By the gods, girl. If I had known...."

Grinning broadly at his look of exasperation, the girl covered the short distance between them and unlatched the gate of her mare's stall, leading the pretty little horse into the stable proper. "I'd say things turned out all right, even if I am a girl, Milord." She laughed.

He stammered, his mouth opening and closing as the girl hoisted the mare's saddle from the low partition between his horse's stall and her mare's. He was so stunned by her attitude and obvious experience with weapons that he stood gaping as she swung the saddle onto the mare's delicate back.

The snit was a girl, he thought with alarm. And a little girl at that! She could be no more than thirteen! His mouth snapped shut and he reached out to shove her, none too gently, away from the mare's cinch as she had bent over to tighten it. "Let me!"

With a suddenness that made him draw in his breath, he felt the tip of something sharp lodged against his flesh just behind and below his right earlobe. He stilled immediately, instinctively realizing the sharpness came from the dagger she now held to his throat. His blue eyes blazed with fury and his lips clamped tightly together over grinding teeth. The bitchlet could be an assassin--another of the robbers' cohorts--and he had walked right into her trap! His mind went to the dead innkeeper and he had to force himself not to groan.

"As you can see, Milord," she told him in a light voice, "I need no help. I thank you for your offer, but I must decline. No one saddles my mare except me. She won't allow it." Noticing the pallor bleaching his deep tan, she felt a wave of remorse sweep through her. She gently placed her free hand on the hard, tense muscles of his rigid back. "You have nothing to fear from me, Milord. I think I've proven that rather adequately." She patted his back as though he were a precocious child.

Letting out a breath he didn't even know he held, his eyes slid sideways to hers. He stared into the frank green depths, locking his gaze with hers, and knew she meant what she said. The blade's pressure eased from his flesh. He could have strangled her, until her lips quivered with amusement before she broke eye contact.

"You should be more careful, Milord." She slid the blade into the sheath at her thigh. "You have to watch your back at every turn this day and age."

His demeanor turned dark with fury at her cavalier attitude. "Do you know who the gods-be-damned hell I am?"

"Does it matter?" she asked as she adjusted the saddle on her mare. She put her hand on the young man's arm and gently pushed him aside, stepping around him. She bent over the dead innkeeper and withdrew her other dagger, wiping the man's blood on his apron before sheathing the dagger in the top of her right boot. She stood and took her mare's bridle from a peg.

He watched her every move as she hooked the bridle over the mare's head and buckled it. He said nothing until she began to lead the mare out of the stable.

"Wait!" he shouted. He covered the distance between them, put out his hand to touch her again, to force her to stop, but brought back his hand. He wasn't so sure touching her was wise. "There's safety in numbers," he said in a voice he knew wasn't at all normal.

"Do you wish me to travel with you to the capitol, Milord?"

"How'd you know I was going to the capitol?"

"Where else would you be going?"

Conar's hands itched to throttle her. Instead, he pointed a finger and snapped, "You wait there!" Spinning on his heel, he stomped back into the stable and saddled his horse with one eye cocked on the girl standing demurely in the stable yard. His stallion snickered softly, a warning, it seemed, to him.

"I know she's going to be trouble, 'Yearner,'" he growled as he led the big black horse into the bright sunlight.

"Are you always so slow to make ready, Milord?" she asked, having overheard his nasty comment to his horse.

He watched her swing expertly into the saddle and adjust the crossbow she had looped over the pommel. She pushed the quiver of quarrels slung over her mare's rump away from her leg for easier riding. She sat her mare like a seasoned soldier and stared down at him with cool patience.

Grinding his teeth to stop a nasty retort, he took a deep breath, held it a moment as he met her challenge and then let it out slowly, releasing it as he did the uncharitable thoughts he was entertaining. He cocked one tawny brow. "Are you going to be an utter nuisance if I let you go with me?"

"Are you going to be in need of saving every time I turn around?"

He stiffened with his hand on the pommel. "I don't think you know who the hell I am!"

"And I told you it didn't matter," she shot back. "You're just a man."

"Who the hell do you think you are, talking to me like that?" he demanded, his eyes glittering with rage.

"Liza, Milord."

"Liza what?"

"Just Liza." She cocked her head to one side and grinned. "And you are Prince Conar Aleksandro McGregor."

Already annoyed at himself for having lowered his guard enough for the silly chit to place a dagger to his throat, he bit his tongue to keep a furious bellow from escaping. He couldn't, however, keep the angry tone from filtering through his words. "And just how the hell do you know that?"

She shrugged one dainty shoulder. "Who the hell else would you be?" she asked, mocking his tone. "The Elite Guards who came to your aid wore the personal insignia of the Prince Regent of Serenia. Your attitude, not to mention your churlishness and massive ego, supplied me with your true identity, Milord."

"Churlishness?" he sputtered. He glared at her. "How dare you...."

"I know you think it your due for all your loyal subjects to protect you, life, and limb, if they can, but I, Milord, am no subject, loyal or otherwise, of yours!" She crossed her hands over the pommel of her saddle and arched her left brow. "Do we ride together or separate? It makes not a single whit of difference to me!"

He desperately wanted to slap the smirk from her face. Swinging himself heavily into his saddle--something his steed did not appreciate and let him know by sidestepping none too gently--he glared at her as he yanked on the reins to still his recalcitrant beast. "You think you can keep up with me, girl?" His tone said he intended to see that she didn't.

"You think that bag of bones of yours can lead a goodly pace?" she quipped, leaning down in her saddle to take a closer look at his horse.

"Seayearner can outrun any horse in the Seven Kingdoms!"

"Seayearner? An unusual name for a stallion, don't you think?" She clucked her tongue and pulled lightly on the reins, turning her horse's head.

"I'm going to regret this!" he breathed, thinking she hadn't heard.

"No doubt you will, Milord!" She kicked her mare into a gallop. "No doubt you will," wafted back to him over her shoulder.

Conar sat for a moment and watched the horse and rider moving away from him at a brisk canter.

"Okay," he told his steed. With a lethal grimace of malice on his handsome features, he put his boot heels to his stallion's flanks and laughed. "Let's see what they're made of, boy!"

The black horse sprang forward with an arch of its magnificent hindquarters and steed and master galloped out of the stable yard and after the mare and her mistress.

## Chapter Two

Conar wouldn't have admitted it even under penalty of torture or death that he lagged deliberately behind so the girl could catch up with him. He simply told himself it was too hot and that his stallion should be kept to a slow trot. He wasn't even aware of the wicked grin that lit his face as soon as he'd heard her mare's hooves closing in behind him. He didn't glance her way as she drew rein beside him and slowed the mare's pace to his steed's.

They traveled close to three miles in a silence that had begun to weigh heavily on Conar. Not accustomed to females who could hold their tongue, her silence was strange and irritating, and it bothered him immensely. He looked at her and could tell she was making a supreme effort to ignore him. She didn't seem at all eager to open the conversation and he was annoyed he had to do so himself.

"Just where are you going?" he finally asked.

Her relieved breath told him she'd been waiting for an opening. Liza turned toward him. "To Boreas."

"And just what is it you intend to do there?"

Her hair was midnight black, as shining as a raven's wing and just as soft looking. It flowed down her back in one long untidy braid with tendrils of escaping hair that teased her temples and neck. The forest-green eyes were clear and bright, sparkling with health and vitality. Long, thick eyelashes swept over those green depths and fanned the smooth ivory of her cheeks. The fullness of her lower lip was a deep coral and he wondered fleetingly if the tips of her breasts were the same shade of dusky color. She was slim with a tiny waist he knew he could span with his hands; her hips flared out beneath the fabric of her breeches and her legs, long and tapered in the snug fit of corduroy, appeared strong and capable. She was taller than most of the women of his acquaintance and her complexion a darker shade of ivory. He decided she must have grown up on a farm, for she was far too healthy looking to have lived in a city.

She was young; thirteen, fourteen, at the most, he thought. There were already definitive curves under her silk tunic top. Staring at the peaks under the material, he nodded. She was fifteen and not a day over, he corrected.

Liza felt his close scrutiny and it pleased her immensely. She winked at him to let him know she had been aware of his appraisal and she felt a giddy moment of triumph when he hastily looked away, a pink blush of guilt suffusing his firm cheeks.

"I asked," he snapped, "what you intended doing there."

"I go to seek my destiny."

He snorted. "To snare and marry some rich merchant, no doubt," he scoffed, all too aware of the heat in his face.

"Oh, I think not, Milord." She laughed and craned her neck to look into his face. "Not a merchant, anyway."

Conar snorted again. "A nobleman, then? Think you can find one with your dagger tip, Mam'selle?"

"I found you, didn't I?" she quipped and let her eyes linger on his neck to remind him. "I can take care of myself, Milord."

He shook his head. "I would think you'd need a parent or guardian looking after your interests. If not that, then a chaperone ... or nanny." He turned a vicious grin. "Or even a master."

Liza slid her hand to the leather sheath strapped to her thigh. Caressing the ebony-handled blade, her look was frank and direct. "I have no need for chaperones or guardians, and I am beyond the age for nannies. And no man is my master! Nor shall one ever be!"

"How old are you?"

"Older than you think."

Conar studied her. With all the arrogance of his position in life, and his budding manhood, he now decided she was sixteen and not a day over.

"And where the hell do you come from anyway? I know you are not from Serenia!"

"My destiny did not lie in my own homeland. I think I shall find it in Boreas, though."

"What kind of destiny, Mam'selle? Marriage? Work?" He narrowed his eyes. "Annoying people?"

"I am rather good at that, aren't I?"

"Professionally so," he said, refusing to smile at her. He shifted in the saddle and a thought flew through his mind, making him grin. He turned an innocent look to his traveling companion. "Perhaps you are going to try out for one of the palace guard positions they announced last week."

"I had not heard the guard was hiring. But I do have the abilities for such a position." Out of the corner of her eye, she saw his mouth drop in stunned surprise. "I am most proficient with weapons, Milord. My talents might be wasted with the Serenian Guard. If I were to audition for a place in the guard, it would be on your own Elite staff, though."

His snort startled both horses; they sidestepped away from one another. Both riders calmed their horses with gentle pats.

"You're being silly," he snapped.

"You don't think I have the cunning and swiftness or timing and skill to be one of your Elite Guard?" she asked, referring to the hand-picked warriors who guarded, or tried to guard, him. She pulled on her mare's reins, halting the little gray, and sat looking at him. "Did I not save your life, Milord?"

Conar reined in his steed as well. "The men who protect me are hardened men; lethal men; men whose lives are devoted to me. Only the finest and deadliest of warriors are even considered worthy to audition for the Elite. Those who win their spurs are extremely capable men; but most important of all, they are men!"

"You have a problem with me trying out for your Elite, Milord?" she asked in innocence.

"Oh, I have no problem with it at all." He grinned. "But my men might."

"Oh?"

"You remember the tall guard from the stable?" At her nod, he continued. "His name is Rayle Loure. He's Captain of my Elite. Go see him when you get to Boreas." He had to look away to keep from letting her see the extent of his maliciousness.

"I didn't find him that mean." She thought back to the red-haired fellow. "Ugly, maybe, but not mean."

He guffawed. "He's as mean as he is ugly, little girl." He leaned toward her. "I once saw him break a man in half with his bare hands."

"Oh? And why did he do that?" She wasn't at all sure that was physically possible.

"I was being threatened. Rayle is very conscientious where my welfare is concerned; as are all my men."

"I don't believe he'd be inclined to harm anyone unless provoked."

"You don't know him."

"I wouldn't want to show up the others who come to the try-outs."

"As if you could!" he scoffed and nudged his stallion with his booted heels. "You're a silly chit to even contemplate trying out for the guard."

If anyone knew her abilities with crossbow, dagger, and javelin, it was she, Liza decided. Her confidence was all that was needed in a fight, fair or not. Not that she would ever think of trying out for an armed guard position in any Kingdom. No matter how well-trained she was or how proficient she was with her weapons, she knew her sex would prohibit her from being taken seriously. But Conar McGregor's condescending attitude annoyed her and made her reckless.

"I just might teach your men a thing or two!" she shouted after him, setting her horse to a trot. "Is that what worries you, Milord?"

Conar shook his head as the girl came abreast. He glanced at her and one brow shot up. "You're baiting me, aren't you?" He was amazed that he liked her tactics.

Liza grinned. "I was always taught that you beard the lion in his den."

"This lion bites, Mam'selle," he warned. He was unaware of the gentle smile on his handsome face.

"So does this she-panther, Milord." She winked.

He laughed as his eyes traveled over her. "This should be an interesting trip, little one."

## Chapter Three

They entered the edge of a forest speckled with high firs and thick undergrowth. The path slowly began to ascend to higher land that formed the foothills of the Serenian Mountains.

Rolling fields, lush with springtime beauty, spread ahead of them. Purple and reds, deep blues and deeper greens, rose in peaks and ebbs against the early afternoon sky. Off to the west, a white patch of cloud was forming, lazily heading their way. Somewhere to the left of them, unseen, was a meandering brook, for they could hear the tumble of water.

Liza watched her riding companion edge his steed beneath a heavy archway of trees that shot off from the main path. She shook her head in exasperation. The least he could have done, she thought, was tell her they were not going to follow the well-traveled road.

"Fool!" she snapped.

"What did you say?" he asked, his eyes narrowing.

"You don't want to know."

Conar's face wrinkled with confusion. Had the girl called him a name? Surely she had not. He was the Prince Regent of Serenia. She wouldn't dare! Not completely satisfied with her innocent look as she gazed calmly at him, he dug his boot heels into 'Yearner's ribs.

Liza caught up with him where the pathway widened as it wound close to the stream they had heard. She refused to look at him and he didn't turn around to look at her.

Overhead, the trees arched into a high ceiling of thick greenery, shading the clover-flecked ground with shadows of shifting light and dark. Spreading willows opened lacy green arms over the banks of the silver-shot stream like a mother hen beckoning her wandering brood to her. The tall scented pines and firs on the opposite side of the serpentine roadway lent a perfume all their own to the sweet-smelling air. It was a heady fragrance ripe with musk.

Conar let his attention wander to the girl. He was annoyed he couldn't seem to keep from doing that. With a snort of disgust, he shook his head, flinging the golden mass from his eyes. He was acutely aware of a growing attraction to her that both angered and thrilled him.

She was different from any woman he had ever known.

She rode her mare as though bred to it. It smacked of professional training, and that was an absurd thought, he reasoned, since no one but the nobility had such luxury. But then again, her father could be a horse master. That was a strong possibility, he knew, for her hands were light on the braided black reins and she moved in such complete harmony to her mare's gait, he was positive she had been trained by a man who knew what he was about. Yet that way of riding was not an easy thing to teach, or accomplish, even for a male. You either had the ability or you didn't. This girl obviously had the ability.

He shook his head as he observed her. She was an enigma that truly puzzled him; puzzled and alarmed him; worried his male superiority.

"Why do you frown so much, Milord?" her teasing voice called to him, breaking his reverie. He looked into her smiling face. "It causes wrinkles, you know."

Conar blushed at having been caught staring so intently.

"Do you not have some kin somewhere who care where you go and what you do?"

She wrinkled her nose. "Of course I have kin. My parents know full well where I am and what I do."

"And they sanction this stupidity?" he asked with astonishment, amazed any parent would be so lax in their care of a girl-child.

"Not only sanctioned, but approved and recommended! And it isn't stupid!"

He pulled on his horse's reins. "What parents in their right mind would allow a girl to go off on her own?"

"One having faith in their daughter's ability to take care of herself! And fully capable of taking care of those she might need to help! Who do you think taught me how to defend myself?"

"Your father should have his head examined!" he snarled, his eyes jerking away from hers. He was getting tired of her rubbing it in that she had helped him back at the Hound and Stag. "Teaching you to ride was one thing; teaching you to fight was insane. The man should have known better!" He threw a leg over his stallion's neck and slid smoothly to the ground.

"And just who said it was my father who taught me to fight?" She cocked her head to one side as she watched the look of disbelief form on his handsome face.

"Well," he thundered, "I know it wasn't your mother!"

She shrugged her delicate shoulders. "You don't know my mother!" She raised one soft black brow. "Do you?"

Conar blinked. If the mother was anything like the daughter, she could very well have taught the girl. It was a ludicrous assumption, but he had to entertain the thought, nevertheless. That made him all the more furious. He turned his back and walked his steed to the slow-moving stream. "You still haven't answered my question."

"What question?" she queried, getting down from her mare with one quick, graceful move.

Sighing heavily, realizing that getting angry would not gain him an answer, he rolled his eyes to the heavens, took a deep breath, exhaled, and then spoke to her as though he were dealing with the village idiot. He stressed each word as he spoke--

"From … where … do … you … come?"

She turned and gave him a coy smile. "Not … from … Serenia," she answered and her grin widened at the blaze of fury that suffused his angry face. "I … am … a … foreigner."

"You told me as much, reminding me in the stable that you were no subject of mine!"

"I have not forgotten," she quipped.

"Besides, our women are not so bold or argumentative."

"And they know their place, eh?"

"Aye, they know their place! They are not as disrespectful as you."

"Nor as interesting." She sat on the edge of the stream and began to pull off her boots.

"Interesting isn't the word I'd use to describe you!" He stared at the top of her shining hair, liking the way a beam of filtering sunlight through the willow branches turned the black into a shimmering band of midnight blue.

Liza shrugged and leaned back on her elbows, something Conar wished she hadn't done, for the fabric over her high breasts stretched taut, accentuating the curves beneath.

"How would you describe me, then, Milord?" she said, craning her neck to look up at him.

Tearing his gaze from her bosom was one of the hardest things he had done of late, but he forced his reluctant blue gaze to the running stream. "Irritating."

"Well," she said as she brought down her elbows and stretched flat on the ground, "I need no guide to escort me about and no chaperone to hinder me once I have found what I am looking for. Perhaps your women need to be led about like geldings in training. Our women don't."

His pulse began to beat faster as her breasts became even more prominent. He licked his suddenly dry lips and then bit his tongue. She was deliberately enticing him, but he was man enough to ignore it. He sat down heavily on the clover beside her, raised his knees, and rested his wrists on them. He looked to the far bank across the stream.

"Comfortable, Milord?" she asked sweetly.

"What is it you're looking for?"

"I've already found it."

He turned to gaze at her pretty oval face, but his stubborn eyes dipped once more to the rise and fall of her chest. "What the hell is that supposed to mean?"

She shrugged and the fabric tightened again. "I think you know, Milord."

His hands itched to strangle her. Or caress her. He wasn't sure which. "If you think I would allow you to audition for one of my Elite, you've got another thought coming!"

She giggled, her breath exploding in a gush of hilarity. "Don't be silly! A woman's place is to care for a man, not fight him."

His face lit up with triumph. "So you are looking for a husband!"

"Husband, lover. Whatever."

"Whatever?" There was sudden shock in his tone.

"Whatever."

He stared at her for a long time. He was having difficulty imagining the *whatever*. She certainly didn't look, or act, like a courtesan, and decidedly was not a common prostitute. Her gaze was too direct when she spoke to be one of those women whose duplicity was part of their stock and trade. Her eyes were not bold and sassy, just teasing, but not like the professional teasing of a whore. He knew that type of woman better than he admitted to anyone--other than his eldest brother--who knew that type better than any man alive. His lips curled in disgust. He could be totally wrong about the girl.

"I'm not one of them," she whispered. "Loose women, I mean."

He flinched, amazed she had been perceptive enough to realize what he must have been thinking. "I didn't say you were! Did I say you were?"

"No, but you were thinking it."

"What else would 'whatever' mean?"

"Fiancé, maybe?"

"Ah, ha!" he shouted. "It is a husband you want!" His hateful tone was meant to insult her. "Someone with money and land and title. Someone who will give you a station in life."

"I have a station in life."

"But you want a better one, isn't that true? You seek a nobleman, a Lord even, to give you status?"

"I won't settle for anyone other than a Prince."

Liza waited patiently as he remained silent. Instinctively, she knew he was about to say something patently male and idiotic.

She wasn't disappointed.

"If you think I am your destiny, Mam'selle, then I will disabuse you of that notion here and now!"

"I didn't say you were, did I?" she asked innocently, mocking him.

"You didn't have to. I know how you women work!"

Her brows shot up. "Oh ... really?"

"Only royalty marries royalty, Mam'selle," he said with a superior smirk. "It keeps the bloodlines pure."

"But it doesn't necessarily guarantee intelligence, now, does it?"

He narrowed his eyes. "Have you forgotten to whom you are speaking?"

"The dimwit whose life I saved?"

"Be careful, girl."

"I can tell you're attracted to me," she said, sitting up and tucking her legs beneath her buttocks as she faced him. Her look went over him, but there was a sweep of pure devilment in the forest-green depths as she smiled at him. "You can't deny that."

"That's absurd!"

"Is it?" Her smile deepened. "Then why is it you can't keep your eyes off me?"

Conar flinched.

"Well? You are, aren't you?"

A muscle worked in his jaw. If anything, he was scrupulously honest. He could have lied, but he had never told a lie in his life. He could have skirted the issue, but that would have been cowardly. He could have changed the subject, but that would have been tantamount to admitting she was correct. He saw no way out. And he saw no real harm in admitting that he found her, if not attractive, at least companionable. His admission wouldn't mean anything.

"You're distracting," he finally answered.

"You find me distracting? A loud noise is distracting, Milord. A buzzing insect is distracting. A baby crying in the background is distracting!"

"Aye, that's you!"

"You conceited oaf! Why can't you just admit you find me fascinating? Puzzling? Captivating?" Her voice became a soft whisper of sound as she leaned toward him. "Alluring?"

He stretched out one long leg and lay back on the clover, propping up his head with one fist as he leaned on his elbow. "It wouldn't matter if I found you all those things and more, Mam'selle. I can't, and I won't, take advantage of the opportunity you are so obviously offering."

"Did I say I was offering you anything?"

He grinned. "You didn't have to. I've played this same scene with more women than I can count!"

"But not with a woman like me!"

"Maybe not." He shrugged. "But the invitation is the same."

"There is nothing about me that is like anything you've ever before encountered, Milord! I am more woman than you will ever see again!"

His look turned hot with speculation. "I don't doubt that at all."

"So why not take advantage of it?" she countered boldly.

His face changed. The soft lines of laughter around his mouth were replaced with a mask of blankness. It was as though a thick curtain had dropped over his emotions. "I have my reasons."

"Not that I am offering myself to you," she quickly added, "but why would you not want me if I were to do so?"

He lifted one brow. "It's a moot point, isn't it? I've already told you I'm not interested."

Her mouth turned stubborn. "I'd like to know why you don't find me to your liking."

"I didn't say I didn't find you to my liking, Mam'selle."

"Then you do find me to your liking?"

"I didn't say that either."

Her exasperated gush of air made him laugh. "I don't think you know what you feel, Conar McGregor!"

He shook his head. "Let it rest, little one." He winked. "You're very attractive, but I'm just not inclined to take you up on your offer."

"I didn't make you any gods-be-damned offer, McGregor!" she shouted.

He cocked his head to one side and reevaluated her. This one was different, there was no mistaking that. He would have given anything to be able to show her just what he was made of.

"I am betrothed." He thought that would end the conversation and the temptation.

"Oh, pooh! Is that all? What does it matter? You aren't chained to the woman, are you?"

Conar felt a shiver go down his spine. "I might as well be," he said beneath his breath.

It was a moment before she spoke to him. "You don't seem particularly happy about the situation. Don't you like the idea of marriage?"

"Not really, but it is my destiny to produce an heir to take my place."

"Then is this particular woman not to your satisfaction?" She watched his facial expression. "What's wrong with her?"

Conar looked away. "I didn't say there was anything wrong with her."

"You didn't have to. If you didn't want to marry her, why did you ask her?"

His self-contemptuous laugh was strident and harsh in the fading sunlight. "I didn't ask the bitch to marry me. I wasn't consulted. I was betrothed to her on the day of her birth. The promise was made between her parents and mine. It is an obligation I can't reverse."

"I see. And would you have agreed to the marriage if you had been consulted?"

Conar chuckled, an ugly sound full of self-pity. "It is what is required of me as first-born legal son. I wouldn't have been consulted and I have no say in the matter."

"And is she as unwilling to wed you as you are to wed her?"

"How should I know?"

"Well, if anyone should, it should be you! What is she like?"

"Like any other woman, I suppose."

"What does that mean?"

"It means what I said. The bitch is like every other female. She was bred to burden some poor man. Unfortunately, that man was me!"

"Don't you like women, Milord?"

His lips twitched. "They're the only game in town for me, Mam'selle."

"But you don't think much of us as a species, do you?"

"You have your purposes."

She quickly glanced up, not sure she liked the way he had said that. "Such as?"

Conar raised his hand and ticked off his answers. "They are good for riding; good for breeding; good for caring for a man's offspring; and good for serving his needs." He lowered his hand. "Other than that, women are of little use."

"What of love and companionship? Or sharing? Do you not want that in your wife?"

He out stretched his leg and flipped over to lay on his stomach, his head cradled on his right forearm. "I love my horse, Mam'selle and he is my greatest companion. I share my thoughts and my food with him. And he never talks back to me."

"But he can't give you the...." Her face burned scarlet as she swallowed hard, striving to say the word she could not.

"Pleasure?" he concluded for her. "I can ride him, too. On occasion I derive a surprise from the motion of his gait. It isn't exactly like bedding a wench, but you get the same pleasure."

"What of babes?" she stammered, shocked by his bluntness.

"Oh! Is that what this is all about?" He sat up. "You want me to get you pregnant?" He wagged his brows.

"I want no such thing!"

"I don't think you know what you want."

"I want to be taken seriously!" she shouted.

"There's no such thing as a serious woman." He tweaked her nose. "You've been proving that all afternoon!"

Liza swatted away his hand. "And you have proven that being a crown Prince doesn't necessarily make you intelligent, either!"

He laughed and lay down again. "I have more sense than to continue with this line of conversation."

Liza ignored him for a moment, her attention on a group of waterfowl thrashing in the shallows near the far bank. She picked up a pine needle and chewed on it. "Doesn't it bother you that you're being forced to wed someone you obviously don't love?"

Conar sighed. "What the hell does love have to do with anything? The marriage was contracted to ally our two families. It doesn't matter how I feel about it. To do anything less than what is expected of me would be dishonorable."

"And you are an honorable man?"

"I like to think so," he said as he stared at the ground beneath his cheek. "I have tried to do my duty to my father, my King, and my country."

"Despite the fact that it is not something you truly wish to do?"

"Aye."

"Perhaps you will learn to love your wife."

"The woman is deformed! She wears a heavy veil to obscure her face. She goes nowhere without it. She has a horrible limp and hops about like a … like a … like a gods-be-damned toad frog! Love such an ogress?" He impaled her with his hard gaze. "I think not!"

"She is that ugly, Milord?"

"She could be uglier than that, for all I know."

"You haven't seen her?" she pressed, studying his face.

Conar shook his head. "I sent Rayle Loure and he saw her. He came back and told me all I wanted to hear about the Princess Anya of Oceania."

"And this man told you she was deformed? Did he see her without her veil?"

"He told me he saw her at a public festival with her parents, the King and Queen, and heard her father telling her not to take off the veil for fear the crowd would stampede in horror!" He glared at Liza. "Does that sound like she's normal when even her own father can't abide looking at her ugly face?"

Liza covered her mouth with her hand. "This Captain of your Elite called the lady ugly?" She had to bite her lip to keep from laughing. "How would he know what ugly was?"

"That's not the point!" Conar screeched. He saw her struggling to keep from laughing and it infuriated him. "Laugh, if you like, Mam'selle! It isn't you who'll be tied to that cursed amphibian!"

"How old is this woman?" Liza asked as she stretched out beside him, her thigh nearly touching his.

He might have been bored with the conversation, but at least one part of him was paying close attention to the shapely leg beside his own.

"I think she's sixteen, maybe a year older. I was about two when she was born and I'm eighteen."

"You look so much older," she said, watching him smile with the compliment. "If your bride is that young, perhaps she wears a veil to hide pimples."

"Her face more than likely resembles the pimples on a pig's arse," he said viciously.

"And the limp," she said, cutting him off, "could have been a bad sprain."

"That's speculation and you know it. Even if she were a veritable goddess stepped down from the vault of heaven, it wouldn't matter how I felt about being forced to marry her, although bedding and humping her wouldn't be such a chore, I suppose." He felt her flinch and grinned, knowing she was furiously blushing.

"Is that all you think about? Sex?" Her leg touched the full length of his as she spoke.

He shifted slightly away so their bodies no longer touched. That part of him paying such close attention to her was starting to raise its head to get a better look.

"Sex is rather like pissing. It's necessary for a man."

"When is the wedding?"

"It is to be this fall after the harvest."

"That's a full six months away. Are you planning on remaining celibate that long?"

Conar ground his teeth. "The marriage contract expressly forbids any intimacy for the span of six months before the wedding. I suppose that is to safeguard the simple-minded twit from any illness I might give her that would offend her delicate sensibilities! Too bad the contract doesn't mention anything about her giving me warts, the slimy froglet!"

"Now I understand!" She laughed.

"You understand what?" he asked, frowning.

"Why you're so churlish!"

Conar's eyes were glued to the movement of her breasts beneath the fabric. His alter ego leapt in pleading and he ground his hips into the earth to keep the enemy down. "I'm so glad you find my pain amusing."

"I find it unnecessary."

"Oh, you do, do you?" He itched to fling himself on top of her and show her a different kind of churlishness.

"You haven't been celibate." She regarded him with humor. "But you've just recently decided to try it."

His sudden grin told her he had not been long in the ranks of the celibate. "I am a man," he said in way of explanation.

"Don't you think her parents would have taken that into consideration? After all, Milord, you do have quite a reputation throughout the Seven Kingdoms. Would they not make doubly sure you were healthy before they allowed you to wed their daughter? I would imagine they would postpone the wedding if you proved to be otherwise. You've thought of that, haven't you?"

"Not until this moment, I must admit, but it isn't a bad idea. Even so, catching a dose of the clap wouldn't stop my father from fettering me to the Toad."

"And I would imagine a dose of said disease would be rather unpleasant." She regarded him intently. "So, find yourself a virgin!"

"Not so easy to come by, Mam'selle."

"I know one."

His look fused with hers until she turned away from his regard. "Do you now?"

Liza clamped her lips together.

"Are you such a one, Mam'selle?" he asked softly. Conar touched the soft coral of her lips with one strong fingertip and watched as her eyelids fluttered. "Are you?"

She nodded, unable to speak as she gazed up at him. Her soul was staring at him from beneath dark, sooty lashes. Unconsciously, she flicked out her tongue and touched the spot where his fingertip had been.

Something moved inside him. He caught his breath as he watched her tongue lick the smoothness of her bottom lip.

"Even if you are," he told her, "I can offer you nothing."

"Are you sure?"

He felt a weight settle over his heart as her eyes locked with his. "Don't get me wrong, Mam'selle. A year ago, I would gladly have rushed to accept what you are so sweetly offering."

"And now?"

"Now, I can't." He wanted to pull her into his arms; to feel her body against his own; to taste the sweetness of her lips. He felt his body's need rising and his eyes went dark with passion, but he shook his head, denying them both. "Don't tempt me, Sweeting. It would be wrong."

She turned away, tears of shame entering her eyes. She had played the whore to him and had been rejected for her effort. "I understand."

"No, little one, I don't think you do." He hesitantly touched her chin and drew her face toward him. He groaned at the sight of a single tear easing down her ivory cheek. When she tried to pull away, to hide her shame, he wouldn't let her. Instead, he kept her face toward him.

"Please, Milord," she whispered.

"I will have you know why I can not accept you, Mam'selle." He gently caressed her chin between his fingers. "A year ago, I would have taken you with no thought. I have broken many a maid to saddle and you would have been just one more to me. Now, for a reason I can't explain, I couldn't do that."

Liza smiled ruefully at him. "Perhaps you've grown a conscience, Milord."

He shook his head. "I don't think that's possible." He let go of her chin.

"Or perhaps you view your obligation to your future wife as being sacred."

His smile turned hard. "I view my obligation as a burden."

"But you will fulfill it nevertheless."

"Aye. Almost all of it, anyway."

Liza looked at him. "There is something to which you will not adhere?"

"There is."

"Is that honorable?" she inquired, wondering what portion of his marriage contract would cause such a militant gleam in his eyes.

"Honorable or not, I shall not heed that portion of it regarding my children, Mam'selle!" His voice fairly quivered with outrage.

Her head came up. "You have children?"

"At last count there were ten or so," he answered with that air of detached male pride that said he had accomplished a great feat completely on his own.

"Ten?" She gasped.

"Or so. I'm not sure how many are actually mine and how many their mothers are trying to pawn off as mine."

Liza closed her mouth with a snap. Had the man never heard of restraint? She managed to ask him as much.

"Why should I?" he asked in an offended voice. "Their mothers don't."

"But do you not care how the world views these innocent children? Bastard offspring of the royalty are especially disliked, Milord."

"I care not a whit what other people think, Mam'selle. No one would dare belittle one of my children; not to the child nor to the mother. I love my children and everyone knows I do. I take care of them. They are housed and fed and clothed, as are their mothers. I share their birthdays with them and they never lack for my attention." A crooked grin stretched his full lips. "That may be why I have more children accredited to me than I could possibly have sired!" He puffed out his chest. "I take care of my own. Because of that, the court in Oceania wishes to punish me!"

Liza's brow wrinkled. "How so?"

"They wish to deny me the right to see my children. They don't want me to go near the ill-begotten seed of my misspent youth!" His voice turned cold. "But I will do as I please where my children are concerned. I will give up my mistresses, they are of no importance and never have been, but I will not give up my sons and daughters!"

"And you should not! Ignore that portion of the contract, Milord. If the King and Queen of your bride's homeland wish to take exception and press the point, I would imagine you have legal recourse to nullify the contract!" She nodded her head in conspiracy. "Let them see you are a man with honor!"

"Nothing can nullify that gods-be-damned contract!"

"Not true," she mused. Her gaze went to the far bank of the stream. "If they do press the issue, your own Tribunal can add an appendix to the contract on your behalf stating you have adhered to the other contractual clauses, but on this particular matter, must decline on moral grounds. Life for a bastard child is hard enough without having the additional stigma of being an outcast from his own sire. Let your future in-laws know you will not desert your children. They will think you more the man for it."

Conar stared at the girl with awe. Where had she come by such understanding? How could she possibly know what could and could not be done by his Tribunal lawyers? And could such an appendix be added to the contract?

"Aye, an appendix is always negotiable in marriage contracts between royal families," she said as though she had successfully read his mind once more. "It's done all the time with land and dowry and personal property items. How more personal can a property be if it's your own child?" She looked back at him. "I see no way your in-laws could object, providing you have not already signed the marriage contract."

"In three weeks, as soon as I get back to Boreas, I'll have to sign the final papers that state I will be a good little boy," he mimicked the words through clenched teeth. "It states I will adhere henceforward to the moral stipulations of the contract. I've put off doing so for as long as I dared, now my time is running out. I'll have to sign it this month."

"Then it's good you've waited. This way, you can have the appendix added."

"Do you really think I can?" There was hope in his voice.

Liza put her hand on his arm. "Aye, I know you can, Milord!"

He didn't hesitate. His hand came up to cover hers. "Who are you, Mistress Liza?" His voice was soft, confused.

"Someone obviously sent to help you, Milord," she whispered back.

Conar smiled at her. "You are an unusual woman, Milady."

"And distracting."

He surprised himself by answering. "But a distraction I am beginning to enjoy."

"Truly?"

"Much to my annoyance." He cocked his head to one side. "I wish I had met you long ago."

"Would it have changed anything?"

"Perhaps." He caressed her fingers as they held his arm. "I believe I might well have pledged the moon to have had you at my side."

"What of now, Milord? Now before you sign the contract. Before any wedding vows are spoken?"

Their gazes locked on one another, both taking the measure of the other. When he finally spoke, his voice was a soft as a caress. "If I offer myself to you, just for this journey, for the span of three days time, Mam'selle, would it be enough for you?"

"It will be all I will ever ask of you, Milord Conar, but will it be all you will ask of me?"

Conar knew he was making a mistake, but as he looked into the exquisite beauty of her face, he let go of the restraint he had always had on his wayward heart. The future and everyone along with it be damned, as he was.

"It will have to be all," he answered.

"I will not ask anything of you once your marriage vows are spoken. I will leave you before your wedding day and never return."

His heart thudded painfully in his chest and he wanted desperately to shout that he would never allow her to leave him, but he knew better. He could only have her for a short time--and despite however much pain it might cause the both of them--during the journey to Boreas Keep, she would be his. Lowering his face to hers, he sealed their devil's bargain with a whisper-soft touch of his full lips to hers.

"The gods help me," he whispered, "but I will make you mine. I have to make you mine!"

Thunder rumbled overhead and they both turned their attention to the sky. The fleecy white cloud that had been drifting their way was now an angry gray color and appeared to be full of moisture.

"There's rain coming," she whispered.

"It's another forty miles or so before we reach Boreas. I was on my way to my brother's keep at Norus to spend the evening. We can make it there by nightfall." He looked up as lightning flashed high above them. "I don't fancy getting wet."

Maybe, he thought, as they mounted their horses, the rain would cool his fevered flesh and hot blood; but one look at the lady who rode beside him dispelled that notion. He knew nothing would ever cool his blood where this woman was concerned.

## Chapter Four

A slight chill had crept down from the tall mountains to the north of them and with the setting of the sun the air was thick with discomfort for the travelers. Like a heavy wet cloak the humidity wrapped around them to bear down on their shoulders and feel cloying against their faces. Off in the distance, the flares of lightning were beginning to light up the sodden gray sky. A spring storm was coming and bringing with it a deluge of rain, if the clouds were any indication.

Liza turned a worried face to Conar as they left the stream and moved deeper into the forest. "Do you think it will storm?"

"It seems likely. All the more reason for staying the night at Norus." He watched her. "Are you afraid of storms, little one?"

Wetting her dry lips, she turned an embarrassed face to him. "My only weakness, I fear."

They rode for nearly an hour as the sun melted into the lowering sky. The air was ripe with the threat of rain, and wind gusted against the riders in ever increasing blasts of cold. With each boom of thunder, Liza jumped. "I don't like it."

"It's only rain, Mam'selle."

Liza wasn't reassured. She felt the hairs along her neck stirring and that meant something dark and unhealthy was close by. She scanned the thick copse of trees and strained to see past the deepening shadows. Her sixth sense was tingling; her palms itched. She put her hand on the crossbow slung over her pommel. Something wasn't right.

Conar led their horses through a thick cropping of firs, past a dark blob that became a large boulder. He ducked his head under a low-hanging branch, cautioning Liza to be aware of it. His steed snickered, sidestepped, and pulled on the reins. "What is it, boy?" he asked, patting the horse's neck. "The little one's nerves making you edgy?"

As they skirted a massive live oak, coming out into an opening in the trees where the forest thinned, a terrible howl rent the air.

"Were-tiger!" he hissed and reached for Liza's reins. Digging his heels into Seayearner's sides, he urged the horse forward. He wasn't prepared for the swiftness of his companion's actions as she jerked the crossbow from her saddle horn, reached behind her for the quiver of quarrels on her mare's rump. With practiced ease, she drew back the lever, nocked the quarrel, and brought up the black wood weapon.

A snarl of rage shot through the air, a blur of tan movement, and a shape dropped from the branches overhead. Before Conar could react, Liza fired a crystal from her crossbow and the quarrel sank into the were-tiger's chest. The predator's snapping yelp of agony startled the already frightened horses and it was all Conar could do to stay astride his mount. As it was, a heavy thud from Conar's left side made his stallion rear in panic. The Prince had to fight to get his beast under control and to stay seated on the steed's broad back. Deadly hooves flashed in the air, striking out with terror until Conar could force the horse back to the ground, drawing tightly on the reins, injuring the stallion's mouth before he could get the war horse to still.

Seayearner backed away from the corpse, his nostrils wide and flaring, sucking in huge gushes of air as his front hoof struck repeatedly at the ground. His rider manhandled the reins as the stallion tossed his head, shaking the great mane of black hair.

"It's dead," Liza said calmly.

Conar stared at the beast whose heart had been pierced by the shaft. He could not believe he had come so close to being fodder for the were-tiger's den. His heart was thundering in his chest as he gaped at the dead animal and he had to force his gaze from the spreading pool of crimson. He slowly raised his eyes and stared at the woman sitting astride her prancing mare. Not only had she reacted with the lightning speed of one of his own Elite, and hit her target dead center--killing it instantly--but she had done so with the light fading from the coming storm and in a brisk wind. Such conditions would have deterred even his best marksman.

"I always hit what I aim at, Milord Conar."

It took him a full minute to adjust to the flippant way she dealt with death: first at the Hound and Stag, and now, here. Who was this woman? What was she? Where had she been trained like that and by whom? From what set of loins had such a warrioress sprung? He looked once more to the dead animal and then back to the woman who was hooking her crossbow on the pommel of her saddle. He heard her words from an hour or so before: "I was trained to protect myself and what is mine."

He felt his stallion quivering beneath him and put a hand on the horse's sleek neck, patting him, but his eyes were still on Liza.

She knew he was watching her, trying to make sense of her, but she was scanning the coming storm. Her unease had lessened somewhat, but her sixth sense still sent out a warning. "The rain will be on us soon, Milord. Should we not move on?"

Conar uttered a low whistle of admiration, shaking his head at her cavalier attitude.

"Life is important to me, Milord," she said in her soft voice. "Your life, more so than my own. I hold you precious, Milord Conar. All else is as chaff in the wind." She tapped her reins against her mare's flanks and shot ahead of him, leaving him to stare after her.

"By all that's holy," he whispered. One more incredulous look at the were-tiger and he shrugged. He was beginning to think he'd bitten off more than he could chew.

\* \* \* \*

They left the forest and stream far behind and were on a flat, desert-like terrain that spiraled around and between high sand dunes that seemed to loom out of the gathering darkness. A few sparse cactuses rose up like sentinels to mark their passing, the spiny arms raised in mock salute. One huge dune appeared out of the darkness and it was toward this mound that Conar rode.

"How do you read this barren place?" Liza questioned. Even with the occasional flare of lightning and what little sky glow came with it, there was little she could see that would mark a trail. To her estimation, it was hard to tell one lump of dirt from another.

"Instinct, maybe," he answered. "That and the fact that there are some signs to look for: driftwood, a strangely shaped cactus. This was once a great sea. The sands blow and change the dunes, but the cacti remain the same."

"But how can you see in this darkness?" The man must have instincts like a jungle beastie.

"I can't." He laughed.

"Then how?"

"I know where I'm going. Trust me."

As they wound their way around the dune, Liza was taken aback by the sudden twinkling of lights in the distance. A huge, squat structure sat in the very middle of this vast stretch of sand and the twinkling lights were from torches on the battlements.

"Norus Keep," he told her.

The hair along Liza's neck stirred and she felt an unease that was even more intense than she had felt before the were-tiger's attack. She was totally unaware that she spoke. "It is one of the Pathways."

Her tone drew his immediate attention. He saw her flinch as lightning snapped overhead, illuminating her frightened face. "What's wrong?"

She was staring intently at the keep. "It is of the Old Ones."

A tiny trickle of his own fear ran down Conar's spine and he stared at her, squinting to see her through the darkness. "This keep has been in my mother's family since the Outlaw's time. My brother Galen is Regent here. We've never been on the best of terms, but out of courtesy, and fear, he'll lodge us for the night."

This place was something from her worst nightmare. The aura surrounding the tall crenellated walls was a deep scarlet red; evil beyond understanding. Her flesh crawled as she looked at it and a strange, unaccustomed metallic taste filled her mouth. She instinctively realized that no one outside those who knew its terrible secrets firsthand had ever experienced the doom she was feeling. In her mind, she could hear the agonized screams of the tortured and dying; see the blood splattering the dungeon walls; see the bodies rotting in mass graves within the outer bailey.

"Together, you and I," she told him, "we can keep the Portal locked." She stared at him. "You understand? You have felt it before. You have felt the Darkness here. That is why you rarely visit."

"I rarely visit because I can't stomach Galen!" he snapped, but in his heart he knew she had chanced upon his real reasons for avoiding Norus Keep. There was still great evil beyond the thick walls.

"It doesn't matter the excuse you give, Milord. It is best you stay as far from this unholy place as you can get."

His heart skipped a beat. Those had always been his sentiments. Each time he visited Norus, he experienced an unease he felt acutely this night. He knew the keep was partially responsible for the unease that always accompanied him to this Zone. He had never wanted to know why; had never allowed himself to do so. It was enough he knew the legend of the place and that made him nervous as hell each time he was forced to come here.

As legend told, the keep had been built over an underground passage into the very bowels of hell. The Brotherhood of the Domination, a sinister sect of warrior-priests dedicated to the eradication of free thought and the enslavement of humanity, had used this particular place to hold sacrifices and plan the dominance of the human race. It had been here that the Brotherhood was formed; here that the first victim fell beneath the hands of the Domination's priests; here that the evil of mankind had been born. The dungeon walls still bore rust-colored markings of ancient dried blood, and it was said the walls of the dungeon hid many a victim's tortured body.

Lightning zapped across the firmament with a ragged blast of molten fire. The spear of light came to ground only a few feet from where Conar and Liza sat their mounts. The air sang with the acrid smell of brimstone. The wind howled like the demons of the pit, shrieking through the night sky like the laughter of a madman. Both horses reared at the sound and the riders had a hard time bringing their slashing hooves back to the ground. With a drenching suddenness, the rain came with a pummeling fury as the thunder boomed, shaking the earth, setting it to trembling.

"Milord!" Liza cried.

"Ride, my lady! Ride for the keep!"

He smacked his hand on the gray mare's rump and sent the horse forward, his stallion close on her hooves. Rain came down in pelting shards of icy torment and the night blackened as dark as the depths of hell. He squinted to see the keep's moat in the deluge, calling out to Liza to watch for the cobblestones surrounding it.

As her horse sped toward the twinkling lights, Liza's mind ceased to function on an immediate level. Her primal instincts took over. Here was the stuff of her worse nightmares. Her body shivered with childhood terrors blending together with the fears of what was to come. A litany of age-old spells used to ward off evil tumbled from her trembling lips. Her small hand went up to caress a black rune stone around her neck. The stone pulsed beneath her questing fingers, letting her know that it, too, felt--and understood--the dangers here.

A challenging cry came from the keep's high walls. The dark outlines of archers queued along the walls--ready to do battle with their unknown visitors--were silhouetted against the flashing thrust of the storm.

Lifting his eyes to the walls, he cupped his mouth, calling out. "It is Conar. Open!"

On the battlements, stunned silence stilled the men. Conar was Prince Regent, heir to the throne. Overlord to all those in the keep. To deny him entrance would have been treason, a hanging offense, but their own Prince Galen had given strict orders that no one be admitted to the keep this night. The men looked to their Master-at-Arms, who stood with his arms folded across his massive, naked chest.

A deep scowl marked the man's already scarred countenance, and he frowned into the driving rain. Now was not the time for the young Prince to come calling on his brother. Letting out a wayward sigh of pure frustration, the burly Master-at-Arms cursed. If he let the Prince Regent into the keep, Prince Galen would have him flogged. That was a foregone conclusion. If he did not let the Prince Regent in, he would be hanged. That, too, was a foregone conclusion. He had to decide between a few hours of intense pain or an eternity of it, for he knew gods-be-damned well where he would be spending his afterlife.

When the drawbridge did not immediately lower and the portcullis raise, Conar cursed soundly. A full minute had passed while he sat his horse in the pouring rain waiting for his entrance.

"Maybe they did not hear you, Milord," Liza offered, shivering in the wet clothes plastered to her body.

"They heard! It's always the same, every time!" He stood up in his stirrups and cupped his mouth once more. "I have no intention of remaining here in this rain!" he yelled at the battlements. "Either open these gods-be-damned doors or spend the rest of your miserable lives in the Labyrinth!"

The Master-at-Arms raised his eyes to the flashing heavens. He put his big hands on his hips and turned to his second in command. "Lower the drawbridge, Jon. We dare not deny him entrance to his own keep. Prince Galen will have to alter his plans this night."

"He won't like it," the man muttered.

"I don't like it either!" the Master-at-Arms growled, "but what choices do we have?" He looked out over the battlement at the prancing horses in front of the drawbridge and groaned. Not one rider, but two. He could expect another ten lashes for the extra visitor. "Lower the gods-be-damned drawbridge! Now!" he thundered and spun on his heel to go below to greet this most unwelcome caller.

"He ain't got his guard with him," one of the archers hinted to the Master-at-Arms.

"You harm Conar McGregor and you'll feel the entire wrath of Serenia on your ass!" the Master-at-Arms warned.

Sounding like the dying moans of some giant entity, the wooden drawbridge slowly began to lower over the moat. The portcullis shrieked upwards, its toothy grin yawning into the lantern-lit interior of the outer bailey. Something snapped and jumped in the green waters of the surrounding moat and then hit hard as it returned to the sinister depths of the brackish waters.

"Alligators," Conar murmured.

Each time he traveled over the drawbridge and took a whiff of the waters surrounding this keep, Conar always wondered how anything could survive in the moat.

Waiting behind the portcullis, the Master-at-Arms stood nervously, shifting from one foot to another. He was not a coward, nor was he a man accustomed to fear of any kind; but he was as nervous as a green youth this rainy night, had been since the sun began to lower. As his Overlord's horse clip-clopped over the rotting wood, the burly man hoped against hope that horse and rider did not fall through the decomposing planks of the ill-kept drawbridge. That would be the last of the Prince Regent, but it would also be the last of this particular Master-at-Arms!

Liza frowned. "It is not a hospitable keep, is it?"

"It never has been and it only seems to get worse," Conar said under his breath. "With every visit, I hate it more and more. It brings out the beast in me."

Norus Keep had few visitors and even fewer repairs. It was Prince Galen's wish that the outside of the keep be kept as disreputable as possible to discourage the occasional traveler. He valued his privacy. Those who did not heed the keep's crumbling condition, and nevertheless asked for lodging on such a night as this, were usually given entrance, and little else. Supper would not be provided; a room, out of the question; and servants would not go out of their way to do the visitors' bidding.

Norus Keep had gained a reputation as being a most inhospitable place and few travelers stopped at its gates. But on this night, of all nights, the Prince had given explicit instructions that he was not to be disturbed by anyone.

Conar's stallion pranced over the drawbridge, his hooves causing the rotting planks to groan in agony. Liza's mare stepped over the wood with care, her hooves making little sound on the apparatus.

"You kept me waiting long enough!" Conar snapped as the Master-at-Arms hurried forward to greet him.

The Master-at-Arms went to one knee in the running waters of the outer bailey as he made fealty to his Prince. His eyes were lowered, his right fist clasped tightly over his heart. "Your Grace! We were not expecting you. If you would have sent word, we could have been awaiting your arrival."

"I wasn't aware I had to clear my itinerary with you. If my visit is not to your liking, I would remind you that this is more my keep than it is my brother's. If I have inconvenienced him, that's too gods-be-damned bad!"

Still not daring to look up, the Master-at-Arms ground his teeth. He had to steel himself not to bring up his hand and wipe at the trickle of rain running off his nose. "I certainly meant no disrespect, Your Grace! It is just that you usually travel with outriders, with your Elite. We were only protecting Prince Galen." As soon as he said it, the man knew he had blundered and he dug his nails into his fist.

"From me?" Conar inquired. "And pray tell why you should feel the need to protect Galen from me? That certainly makes me wonder just what he's done now to merit protection."

Without thinking, without realizing he was doing so, knowing only that he had badly insulted the Prince Regent with his unwisely chosen words, the man lifted his face. It wasn't Conar's eyes he met, though, but Liza's, and a groan came from his mouth as it dropped open.

Conar pursed his lips and glared at the man's averted face. Miffed that he was now being ignored as the beefy man stared up at his companion, Conar cleared his throat and smiled a wicked grimace of spite as the man's attention shifted slowly back to him.

"Well?" Conar snarled. "I asked you a question. Or has the lady's beauty so ensnared you that you forgot to whom you were speaking?"

"Your pardon, Your Grace," the man stammered as he swallowed. "Please forgive me. I meant you no...."

Conar held up a black-gloved hand. "I know. I know. You meant no disrespect. Obviously, though, you intend for me to catch my death of cold as I am forced to sit in this freezing rain."

It was as though the Master-at-Arms had suddenly become aware of the pouring rain. His gaze went to Liza once more and he saw her jump as a streak of lightning flared overhead. Another groan came from his white lips and he was about to leap to his feet, but he remembered, just in time, that his Prince still had not given him leave to do so. He turned his strained and apologetic face to his Overlord.

Conar was keenly aware of the man's predicament. Some devilish imp inside him reared its ugly little head and he simply sat with his hands crossed over the pommel of his saddle and stared at the man with one golden brow raised in challenge.

Liza was shivering with the cold and knew precisely what Conar was about. She wasn't amused, and as she gazed at the poor man kneeling before them in a puddle of mud, she was not pleased with Conar's unconcern for the fellow. "Milord. I am getting soaked!"

Shrugging, Conar inclined his head. "See to the lady." Throwing a leg over his horse's neck, he slid to the ground. His boot heels squelched in mud and he looked down, frowning. The instep of the brown leather was beneath the mud. Looking up, he saw the Master-at-Arms regarding him.

"You have ruined your boots, Your Grace." The man smiled as he put his hands up to Liza's waist and lifted her down.

Conar's eyes narrowed in speculation as the two gazed deeply at one another, grinning, before the burly man lifted her to the plank walkway that led into the inner bailey. "But you won't mind seeing to them, personally ... will you?" Conar smirked.

Cocking has head in obedience, the Master-at-Arms turned a solemn face to his Overlord. "It would be my pleasure to clean your boots, Your Grace."

Conar grinned. This man was sharp. He liked him. He might be one of Galen's toadies, but the chap had a wry sense of humor that matched his own. "Have I interrupted something?"

"No, Your Grace!" The Master-at-Arms jerked, his head snapping around to face his Overlord. "You have interrupted nothing." Guilt flared across the scarred face.

"That's good," Conar said and saw the man visibly relax. His thoughts went to Galen and he wondered just what the stupid fool was up to this time.

"If it pleases you, Your Grace," the man spoke, "I will show you to your rooms."

## Chapter Five

"What is your name again?" Conar asked the Master-at-Arms as they were led to the curving stairway that led to the sleeping chambers.

"I am Belvoir, Your Grace." The man's deep green eyes strayed to Liza and he answered her gentle smile with a reluctant one of his own.

"And I am Liza, Sir Belvoir," she told the man and held her hand out to him.

"*Mam'selle* Liza," Conar corrected, not liking Liza's easy familiarity with the knight. He followed Belvoir's lips to the slender hand within the knight's own.

"Mam'selle Liza," Belvoir said in a soft, throaty voice as he released the girl's hand. "It is my pleasure to serve you."

"And is it your pleasure to serve me?" Conar snapped.

Belvoir turned to face his Overlord. "It is my destiny to serve you, Your Grace." There was a direct and honest look on the man's face. "As was written long ago, Sire."

"It is your destiny, but not your pleasure."

Belvoir's chin rose a fraction in the air. "I didn't say that, Your Grace."

"You didn't have to," Conar replied and gripped Liza's hand. "I know where the chambers are. You don't have to put yourself out because of me." He started off with a startled Liza in tow.

"That was abominably rude!" she hissed as they climbed the stairs. "He meant you no insult, Milord."

"Galen's people never insult me directly to my face. They do it just by their looks and what they don't say."

Liza turned her head and looked down the stairs to where the Master-at-Arms stood. His gaze was on her and she felt a prickle of unease run down her spine. Every inch of the man spoke of consummate villainy, but she didn't fear him. If anything, his presence in this place put her fears to rest and she looked him over closely as Conar stopped to bark orders to a passing servant.

Belvoir was a tall man. His height certainly rivaled that of the Elite Guard Captain, Rayle Loure. His face was set in a grimace of humiliation, for he was no doubt upset with himself for being a problem for the one he was sworn to protect; his eyes on Liza were full of apology. A livid, red scar split his face from his right cheekbone, across a nose that had obviously been broken many times, down the left cheek, and ended in a thicker scar on the edge of his jawbone. It was the kind of wound a man would receive in a fierce battle. His hair was thick and as black as Liza's and was worn long in coarse waves to below his broad shoulders. One thin braid hung on each side of his face and each braid was adorned with silver wrappings of ribbon threaded through the hair.

He appeared to walk with the rolling gait of a sailor, his legs wide apart as though braced against a stormy sea. His stance was full of authority, his spine straight, his shoulders squared. He seemed to favor his left leg and Liza couldn't help but wonder if some old battle wound did not bother him in weather such as this.

Her gaze swept down to his boots and then snapped back to his face. She saw him slightly shake his head and she blinked, wondering at the man's carelessness. Her lips parted and she broke eye contact with him as she nervously turned her head to look at Conar. When she looked back down the stairs, Belvoir was gone. She craned her neck, but still she couldn't catch sight of him. Conar's angry retort brought her attention back to him.

"Now!" he shouted at a hapless servant who was scurrying away to do his bidding.

Liza frowned. "Why must you be so uncivil? And loud? You give me a headache with all your blustering, Milord."

Conar's left brow crooked. He was appalled the girl would dare speak so to him. Her sweet face, locked in a grimace, did nothing to alter his vicious mood.

"It has always been my experience with Galen's servants that, what I tell them, they pretend not to hear. What they do hear goes in one ear and out the other if they bother to listen at all. You have to shout to get their attention. What little they have!"

"Perhaps if you tried kindness instead of churlishness--"

"I am not churlish!" he bellowed. He lowered his voice to a grating whisper. "I am not churlish, Mam'selle."

Liza ignored his outburst. "They might hear you better if you were less confrontational. Did it ever occur to you that perhaps your brother's retainers are always treated the way you treat them? Men and women so abused have little to gain by being accommodating. You can catch a fly's attention better with honey than vinegar, Milord." She tipped her pert nose up in the air and walked away, her spine taut under his furious gaze.

"I am not churlish," he snarled as he followed. "Firm, but certainly not churlish."

"Churlish and rude," Liza admonished, not bothering to look back as she climbed.

Under the canopy of the overhanging balcony, the Master-at-Arms slipped into a rare smile.

"Like mother, like daughter," he said and chuckled. He shook his head, looked down at the black crystal dagger tucked into the top of his boot and frowned. He drew out the dagger, hid it inside his tunic, and then went about his duties, his mind on the coming punishment he expected.

Once they gained the semi-circular antechamber from where the sleeping quarters were positioned, Conar and Liza could see servants racing frantically about, carrying linens and water for the visitors. None of the busy servants glanced at either of them as they sped to ready chambers for the travelers. Their heads were bent, their eyes on the carpeted runners at their feet. Doors opened, doors closed, and the stomp of feet was the only sound the servants made.

There was no idle chitchat, no hushed, excited whispers commonplace in most keeps when royalty came visiting. There were no furtive glances at the Prince Regent, no curious side looks at the lady with him. It seemed as though the rushing servants were more concerned with getting the work done and getting away from the two people who had intruded upon them.

Conar felt his unwelcome more keenly than ever in his brother's home. He could sense the charged atmosphere his sudden appearance had caused. There was a tight, malicious, and somewhat hurt grin on his handsome face as he watched the servants ignoring him.

"They don't like my coming to call," he said, but even though the words were spoken with a lilting laugh, there was a current of pain in them.

"I can't imagine why," Liza sniffed, still smarting from his cavalier attitude on the stairs.

"I've put them out." There wasn't the slightest iota of contrition in his twinkling eyes as he turned to Liza. "I should be sorry."

"But you aren't."

He grinned. "No, I'm not."

"Then don't expect them to be happy when you disrupt their lives."

"Don't you tell me what to do in my own keep!" he snapped, his grin fading at her reprimand. "Don't."

Liza followed his gaze to a small set of stairs leading off one of the far rooms. She was completely aware of Conar's sudden stillness; his immediate pallor; his held breath. His pale blue eyes had glazed as though in terrible pain and she saw his hand go up to his chest as though something hurt inside. She was about to ask what ailed him when a swath of color began to float down the stairs toward them. Her attention once more on the stairs, she failed to see Conar shudder as though with the ague.

A man of medium build, thin and cadaverous-looking, dressed in the red robes of the higher orders of the priesthood of the Serenian Wind Warrior Society, glided on bare feet down the stairs. His thin, skull-like face was set in closed lines of disapproval as his pale gaze shifted over Liza. That penetrating perusal, coming from black-rimmed sockets, was shadowed with anger so intense it was palpable. His shoulder length white-blond hair was braided in one thick queue that fell from the crown of his head to below his waist. His lips, two thin, pale slits of flesh, were pursed tightly together and his hawk-like beak of a nose was held high in the air, seeming to quiver with disdain as his attention swept away from Liza and settled fiercely on Conar's bent head. Wide nostrils flared as though a stench had entered the keep.

"My Prince," the man said as he passed them. As he reached the turn in the semi-circular stairway, he glanced over his shoulder and his hateful stare met Liza's, going through, and beyond, her.

Liza shivered as though she had been blasted with a gust of frigid air. The rune stone around her neck pulsed against her flesh and she reached up to touch it.

"A friend of yours?" she joked, for Conar's face was devoid of color. She felt his hand tighten. She knew he had forgotten her presence, for he turned to her with a blank, stricken look on his face.

"What?" His face was gleaming with sweat.

"Are you all right?" she asked and when he didn't immediately answer, she put her hand on his arm. He jerked so violently from her touch, she took a step back. "What's wrong with you?"

He looked at her--really looked--seeming to see her for the first time. His brows drew together in puzzlement as he saw the lines of worry on her face. He shook his head. "I'm fine." He looked back at the staircase of the main hall where the High Priest had disappeared. "I'm fine, now," he whispered as though to himself.

"Who was that man? That priest?"

"Tohre," he answered in a voice so low she had to strain to hear. "Kaileel Tohre."

"What is …?" she started to ask but was shocked by the sudden rush of motion toward them.

A young servant girl fell to her knees before Conar, her head to the carpet, her arms straight out. She did not speak, but her breath came in loud gasps of nervousness.

Conar frowned at the girl and for some reason her position at his feet greatly angered him. His lips pulled back over his teeth and in a snarl of rage, he shouted at the already frightened girl, "Get up, woman!"

Scrambling to her feet, the young girl would not raise her head. Her hands were gripped tightly together in front of her, the fingers running over one another in agitation. She was trembling violently as she stood there.

"What do you want?"

"Milord!" Liza warned in a steady voice. "You are frightening her more!"

Conar would have bellowed at Liza, but she was looking at him with challenge and he felt like a fool. "I don't like people falling at my feet!"

"No more than they like doing it, I would imagine."

He clenched his jaw, but managed to lower his voice as he spoke to the servant girl. "Don't just stand there. Tell me what you want."

"With your permission, Your Majesty," the girl stammered in a husky whisper, "we have one of the rooms ready for you. Can the lady wait until her room is done or will you be giving her yours?"

"What are you bothering me with this for?" he thundered, calming only as Liza hissed another warning. He tossed the thick gold of his hair. "Let her have the gods-be-damned room. I'll use my brother's until mine is ready."

A wild look of intense terror passed over the young servant's face, and in her fright, she forgot her training and raised her voice to her Overlord to gain his attention. "He won't like you going into his room, Your Grace!" She opened her eyes wide with fear as the young Prince impaled her with the full force of his fierce, direct blue gaze.

Conar's voice wasn't a shade warmer than the glaciers of his homeland as he spoke. "I am just as much my brother's Overlord as I am yours, Mam'selle! If I wish to make use of his rooms, that is my right! Do you understand?" He took a step toward her, his hand fisted. "No one gainsays me in a keep that is rightfully mine!"

It looked as though the girl had suddenly turned to jelly, for she collapsed to the floor in a heap, her arms thrown over her head to protect herself from her Prince's wrath. With her slight form shivering so badly-- Liza could actually hear the girl's teeth clicking together--the poor servant huddled on the floor and began to sob hysterically.

"Now look what you've done!" Liza snapped.

"What did I do?"

Liza knelt beside the trembling girl and would have put her arms about the heaving shoulders, but with a leap of sheer terror, the girl jerked away, her hands coming up to cover her sobbing face. There were thin white lines on the girl's hands and forearms. Liza looked to Conar for help. "Look, Milord!" she demanded as she lifted one of the girl's hands for the Prince to see.

Something dark and painful crossed Conar's face as he stared at the marks on the girl's pale flesh.

"Milord, please! Do something!"

He seemed to come out of some distant reverie and shook his head to clear it of whatever vile memory had claimed him. He swallowed, tasting bile in his mouth.

"Conar?" Liza inquired.

He looked at Liza's pleading face and then at the girl's bent head. He seemed to gather himself and then let out a ragged breath. Hesitant to further upset the servant, he knelt on the floor beside Liza.

"Milord?" Liza's whisper was like a calming breeze after the roughest storm.

With infinite care, Conar held out his hand to the servant girl, but didn't touch her quivering body. "Mam'selle?" he whispered, his voice breaking. He cleared his throat and tried again. "Mam'selle, may I help you to your feet?" When she didn't answer, he took a deep, wavering breath and let it out slowly, speaking to her as quietly and as reassuringly as he could. "I am not angry at you, Sweeting."

Liza watched the girl shrink further into herself. Speaking solely to the girl, Liza lowered her voice to a conspiratorial whisper. "I don't think you realize what it is you've done, Mam'selle." She saw the girl flinch and hurried on. "You have done something no one ever has before. You have brought the mighty Prince Conar McGregor to his knees. You had best take advantage of his momentary lapse of churlishness and take his hand, else neither of us will ever hear the end of it."

The girl hesitantly raised her head and she briefly met Liza's smile, her gaze skipped away and then returned for a moment, searching, pleading. What she saw in those beautiful green depths, almost the same shade of green as her own, made the girl stop shaking. Moistening her lips, she held Liza's warm, gentle gaze.

Conar could feel the girl's intense fear like a sentient life form invading his soul. Towering rage welled up inside him, for he knew the girl was accustomed to ill treatment, probably at the hands of his own twin, that she expected blows and beatings with every sharp word. He felt a great pity building inside as horrible memories surfaced in his mind, and he leaned down, putting his lips close to the girl's ear, even though she tensed like a steel spring as he neared.

"If you persist in behaving as though I am a beastie from the pits, Mam'selle, how will I convince this lady that I am a sweet-tempered and malleable knight? How will I win her heart, then? If she will not have me, I shall surely pine away, and you will be the one to blame for my untimely demise. You will be the one who will cause my insomnia, my loss of appetite, my hair loss, my gout, my...." He saw a tiny, flickering smile on the girl's lips. "My admission to an institution for the terminally suicidal and perhaps, ultimately, my celibacy." He saw her flinch with astonishment.

"Not that, Milord!" the girl whispered, her lips twitching.

"Most assuredly that, Mam'selle," he informed her, his hand over his heart. His soft, deep voice broke with feigned misery. "Would you be the cause of that?"

"I would be hounded to death by every female in Serenia if that were to happen, Your Grace," she whispered back.

"And rightly so, Mam'selle, should you deny so many, so much!" He smiled broadly.

"Conceited buffoon," Liza snorted.

He glanced at Liza. "Don't belittle what you haven't seen." He grinned at the red flush that quickly spread over Liza's face.

The servant giggled, her lilting laughter sounding like summer puffs of wind; but a loud noise from below stairs made her cower again, her laughter vanish, and her trembling fingers cover her face.

Conar immediately reached out and drew down the girl's hands, holding them in one of his own. With his free hand, he raised her tear-stained face so he could get a better look at her. "What troubles you, girl?" he asked softly. "I am no ogre from Diabolusia."

There was such misery in the girl's face and in her quivering tone that her childish voice, husky as it was, seemed even more youthful. "He will be so angry, Your Grace. He will beat me after you leave." Her chin trembled. "I have not gotten over the last beating." She lowered her head, her face burning with shame.

Forcing down his temper, for he had seen the warning shake of Liza's head as she saw his rage flare, he firmly gripped the girl's chin and gave her small oval face a gentle tug. "No man lifts a hand to one who serves me and gets away with it. No man; not servant nor Lord nor Prince. If he does, he will have me to deal with me, and I can promise you this: Galen McGregor wants no trouble from me!"

The girl raised her head. "You would protect me from your own kin?"

"Aye, I would. I am his Overlord just as I am yours." He shrugged. "And I don't like him all that well, anyway."

"But when you leave, Your Grace--"

"Are you indentured?"

"Aye, Your Majesty," she said, lowering her head.

"To my family or to my brother as his own personal servant?"

"To your family, Your Grace."

Conar smiled. "Well, then, if you are indentured to my family, as guardian for you, you are indentured to me. You belong to me, do you not?" He carefully watched the girl's face to see if she was following him. He squeezed her hand. "I am the Heir-Apparent to the throne. When I take that throne, I will, in essence, be your parent. Right now, my father, the King, is your surrogate parent. Isn't that true?"

The girl nodded.

"And I am his Regent, am I not?"

"Aye, Your Grace."

"So, technically, you belong to me." He winked.

Understanding lit the girl's small face and she smiled. "I belong to you," she whispered in awe. "I belong to you." She turned to Liza. "I belong to His Grace!"

"Well, of course you do!" he snorted. "And because you do, and because I have been looking for someone to stand as chaperone for me as I take this lovely lady with me to our next destination, I think I shall require you to travel with us." He glanced smugly at Liza.

Liza raised one fine black brow. "Chaperone, Milord?"

"Nanny?" He grinned.

Liza gave him a warning look.

"Guardian?" He chuckled.

Liza stuck her tongue out at him.

"Lady's maid?" His lids fluttered audaciously.

"Companion," Liza stated firmly.

Conar nodded. "Companion, it is!" Getting to his feet, he reached a hand to both ladies and smiled as they placed their hands in his. He grinned into the servant girl's beaming face, happy he had calmed the girl all by himself. "How does that sound to you, Mam'selle? Will you hire on as companion to this lady?"

"At his expense, of course," Liza added.

He turned to Liza, saw her smug expression of counter-challenge, and winced. He frowned, knowing he had lost. He nodded in agreement. "I'll pay your way, Mam'selle."

"And give you your free-lot papers when we reach our next stop," Liza said.

Conar sighed, recognizing the fact he'd been out-maneuvered by a slip of a girl not taller than his shoulder blade. He glanced at Liza's uplifted face. "I'll sign them this very night," he said through clenched teeth.

"Plus...." Liza stopped at his warning growl, but her face was bright with humor. "Plus the promise of work at Boreas Keep, if you should ever need it."

The girl's mouth fell open. She took Conar's hand and brought it to her lips. "Thank you, Your Grace! Oh, thank you!"

"No need to thank me," Conar snorted, his face turned to Liza.

"And it will be free-work with pay, won't it, Milord?" Liza amended.

"Free-work with pay?" the girl gasped.

"Free-work with pay?" Conar groaned.

Liza raised her chin. "Naturally."

Out-maneuvered again. "Naturally," Conar agreed in defeat.

"I will guard your lady with my life, Your Grace!" the servant swore as Conar gently withdrew his hand. "I would give my life for you, too, Your Grace!"

Lightning struck near the keep and the loud accompanying boom rattled the windows behind them in the nearest room. Liza yelped and jumped closer to the servant, grabbing the thin girl's body in a death-grip of fright.

Conar laughed, shaking his head. "You just may have to. She doesn't care overly much for storms."

The servant drew Liza toward the closest room. "Come, Milady. We will shut the drapes against this storm and you will be safe."

Conar shook his head as the door closed behind the two women and he heard the tinkling sound of female giggles. Raising his eyes to the heavens, he shook his head again.

"Great Alel," he thought aloud. "What have you done now, Conar?" One woman to travel with was bad enough, but two? Insanity! Shrugging his broad shoulders for getting into such a predicament, he gave up the notion of going to Galen's room to change. At that moment, he wanted nothing more than to find his ill-begotten twin and throttle the daylights out of him! He pounded his fist against the wall as he turned the corner and headed down the stairs.

His feet skipped lightly down the first decade of steps and then he stopped, his hand going to the balustrade to keep himself from pitching down the remaining steps.

"Good eve, Sweet Prince," the man at the foot of the stairs greeted him. "I trust you had a pleasant journey."

Conar stared at the man. He could feel his heart thudding in his chest and he swallowed hard, forcing down the bile that leapt to his throat. He couldn't seem to find his voice.

A tight smile stretched the older man's thin, pale lips. One thin white-blond brow cocked. He folded his arms inside the billowing sleeves of his red robe and stared intently at the young man. "Have a good night's sleep, my Prince," the man suggested. "I shall pray for you, my dear child." The thin lips pursed together as though the man was trying not to laugh. He turned his back and disappeared beyond the turn of the stairs.

Sweat ran down Conar's sides, across his forehead and upper lip. His breathing was erratic, his hands trembling. He slumped against the stone wall beside him and closed his eyes. There was only one thing in this life he feared, and he had just encountered it.

* * * *

"His Grace prefers cinnamon oil, Mistress, but if you would prefer something else, I will have it brought to you." The servant girl smiled. "There is some jasmine from Chrystallus."

"The oil you have will be fine." Liza ran her hand across the steaming water in the huge copper tub. She was aching to immerse herself in the cinnamon-scented water.

A roaring fire chased away the chill from the tapestry-covered stone walls and the air inside the guestroom was heavy with steam and a sweet, musky smell. Plush white towels lay warming on a brass stand before the crackling fire.

"I will lay out your clothes as soon as someone brings them from your horse."

Liza blushed. "I'm afraid what I have on is all that I brought. I was not expecting to be a guest in such a fine keep."

The servant glanced at Liza and wondered what kind of keeps she was used to if Norus was considered to be fine.

"It is rather bad, isn't it?" Liza grinned, referring to Norus.

The girl put up a hasty hand to stifle the giggle. "It is awful, Milady!"

"Well, it will do until we leave, won't it?" Liza winked and relaxed.

Under the soft gaze of this lovely woman, the girl nodded. "Aye, Milady. Until we leave."

"Well, maybe my clothes will dry if I put them before the fire." She started to take off her tunic, but the girl rushed to her, easing Liza's hands away from the sodden fabric. The servant helped Liza remove her clothing and then handed her a thick robe. The bath water was a little too warm to utilize as yet.

"If I have your permission, I can obtain a gown for you from the storage room. Prince Galen had several dozen gowns commissioned for his lady-wife before she died. Some, she never even wore. Would it offend you if I were to fetch such a gown for you to wear?"

"Not at all." Liza smiled, relieved that she wouldn't have to put on her still-damp clothing again.

Although the servant was several inches shorter and darker in complexion, the two women might have passed for sisters. They both had gleaming, long black hair and oval faces, deep green eyes and coral lips. The servant's face was as delicate as a cameo portrait and her cupid-bow lips seemed hard-pressed not to smile often. When the girl did smile, she revealed even, pearly-white teeth.

"What do I call you?" Liza asked her.

"Gezelle, Milady."

"What a lovely name! It suits you, too."

"My granny named me after the pretty animals that grazed near her hut. On the day I was born, one leapt past the window. Granny said it was like an omen."

"So, you were not born here at Norus?"

"No, Milady. My mother had me there in Granny's hut." A sad and wistful look came over the girl's pretty face. "My mama died giving birth to me."

Liza's heart lurched. She stood and touched the servant's thin shoulder. "I am sorry, Gezelle."

Gezelle smiled. When she had lived in that hut near the game preserve of King Gerren, her old grandmother had thrilled her with tales of the keep at Boreas where she had been a maid for many years. She spun tales of the handsome knights and their ladies; of the daring escapades of the Serenian Guards; of the pranks for which the royal sons were forever being punished. She told her mesmerized grandchild tales of courage and valor, of loyalty and honor, of romance and great, undying loves; of the kindness of the lady-wives of the knights; and of the gentle and sweet Queen whose life had ended so tragically. The child had grown up thinking Boreas Keep had to be the closest thing to heaven found on earth.

But when her granny had taken ill one winter and died, leaving Gezelle without kin to care for her, the child had been sent to the closest keep: Norus. Indentured to the royal family since the old woman had been a faithful retainer to them for many years, Gezelle was sure she would know the same joy her granny had known at Boreas. What she had found upon arriving at Norus was nothing at all like those wonderful tales.

Norus was filthy and it smelled. Diseases of every kind ran rampant behind the crumbling walls. Its inhabitants were not loyal to their King, let alone to the Prince who lived within the stinking walls. What Gezelle found at Norus was abuse and neglect.

It was in her lowest moment at the keep, a day or two just short of her seventeenth birthday, only a few months past, that her old granny had come to Gezelle in a dream, speaking to her of the grand things that would come to pass. Gazing up at the smiling lady before her, the girl couldn't help but speculate on the things said to her in that dream.

Sensing a question, Liza cocked her head to one side. "Did you want to ask me something?"

Gezelle chewed her lower lip. Did she dare ask this lady? What would this lovely woman think of such an outlandish question? But never one to leave anything to chance, feeling at ease in this lady's presence, taking courage from the gentle and warm smile on the lady's mouth, Gezelle ventured a rushed inquiry.

"Are you a Princess, Milady?"

Liza blinked. "Why would you ask that?"

"I didn't m … mean any harm."

"Don't be a ninny!" Liza laughed, recovering her composure. "Your question startled me, that's all."

"I should not pry."

"You must have had a reason for asking."

"You will think me addled," the girl mumbled, looking away.

"I will not!" Liza crossed her legs beneath her. "Tell me!"

Gezelle fussed with the wet clothing spread out on the towel stand.

"Gezelle!" Liza laughed. "You have my curiosity up now!"

Finally making her decision, Gezelle looked at Liza. "She had the sight, my granny did. She was the granddaughter of a gypsy woman and she told me things that always came true. People came to her for herbs and potions. She delivered babes all over the Southern Zone until she got too old to make the trips and wait out the labor. Townsfolk from Iomal would come to her with sick animals or to get a rune to chase away insects harming their gardens. People with troubles came to her for help, too.

"She never turned away a single soul and she never took even one copper coin from any of them, although she would take meat and vegetables for the two of us. She was a gentlewoman, was my granny. She sang to the animals and talked to them and they would come right up to the door and eat out of her hand. Nothing ever harmed my granny; not animal nor man. She was protected, I think."

"Protected by the village folk?"

"No, Milady. She was protected by the things in the fire." Gezelle ducked her head.

Liza's eyes darkened. "She spoke to the fire-spirits?"

Gezelle's head snapped up. "You know of them, Milady?"

"I've heard tales of the creatures. Do you speak their language, too?"

"No, Milady."

"She would not teach you?"

The servant smiled. "She said I was too young to learn the art of magic-spelling." Her smile faded slowly. "She would have taught me when I was older. I was eleven when she died. I've been here six years."

Liza nodded. "So, you never learned anything from her?"

"Only a few spells to ward off danger and the like." Gezelle pulled at the waist of her gown. "I wanted to learn the future."

"Sometimes that is something none of us should know, Gezelle." Her face gleamed with a strange light. "What we do not know, will never harm us."

"I know what will happen to me."

"How so?"

"About three months ago, I had this dream. It wasn't truly like a dream because I was awake. My granny came to me in the night and she sat on the pallet next to me and smiled. She took my hand and I could feel her cool skin. She patted my fingers and said that soon I would be leaving Norus Keep, never to return. She said a Princess would come to take me far away and that I wasn't to be sad anymore. She told me the lady's life and mine would be forever entwined. We would love the same and hate the same and there would never be a better friend for either of us."

There was such hope and expectation in the sad eyes regarding her, Liza did not want to disillusion the girl. "You hope I might be this person?"

"I do," she said, her voice lost and sad.

"You are leaving the keep, aren't you?" When the girl nodded miserably, Liza laid a hand on her thin arm. "So at least that part of your dream will come true. I may not be a princess, Gezelle, but I believe you and I will become the best of friends."

A storm of emotions crossed Gezelle's face. "Truly, Milady?"

"Aye, but we will have our secrets, you and I. What I say to you will be for your ears only. Do you understand?"

Gezelle went to her knees in front of the lady and took the slender hands into her own, bringing warm fingers to her lips. "I will never tell another living soul!"

"Good. Now that that's settled, I have a question for you."

"I will tell you everything I know!"

"Then tell me everything you know or have ever heard about this Princess Anya from Oceania. The one Prince Conar intends to marry."

Chapter Six

A little more than an hour later, Conar met a glowing Gezelle as the servant girl came up the stairs from the storage rooms near the kitchen.

Her attention was intent on the gown draped over her arms, and in her haste to get the laced and ruffled treasure to her new mistress, she didn't see Conar walking toward her from the opposite end of the long balcony. Her mind was working furiously on how she would arrange the Mistress Liza's hair, so she walked right into the young Prince's outstretched arms as he stood smiling at her headlong rush. She bounced off his hard chest.

"Have a care, Mam'selle," he teased. "You could have crippled me!" He beamed at the girl. Such banter was second nature to the man and he fully expected to be rewarded with a dazzling smile: his usual due.

But that didn't happen.

"Your pardon, Your Grace!" she stammered and would have dropped to her knees before him if he hadn't gripped her elbows to prevent her.

"Oh, no, you don't!" He laughed, the sun crinkles deepening around his blue eyes. "If you persist in flopping on the floor every time you come into contact with me, I shall be obliged to fasten a thick board to your spine to keep you upright!" His smile broadened as he watched a heavy crimson blush spread over her cheeks.

"I didn't see you, Your Grace," she said, her ready smile returning as she watched him grin. "Did I hurt you?"

Conar frowned, looking down at his person. "I'm not sure. You're so fat and massive, you might well have dented me." He craned his neck to look at both sides of his legs. "No, I think I'm in one piece still." He swept her a mischievous glance. "No thanks to you, Mam'selle."

She giggled. "Are you sure, Your Grace? There might be internal damage."

He liked this girl. She wasn't flirting with him; he knew those looks all too well. She was teasing him, giving as good as she got. Her smile was genuine and she looked at him without a duplicative bone in her slim body. She wasn't inviting, or wanting, or asking, or desiring anything from him but his smile, unlike the oily women at court who constantly hounded him. Could two such women actually exist: Liza and this girl-child? Neither one seemed to fit the known patterns he had encountered over the years.

"Are you from Mistress Liza's homeland, Mam'selle?" he asked.

A puzzled frown came over the lovely face. "I am Serenian, Your Grace."

Conar's brows went up. "And she's not?"

"Well, of course not, Your Grace!" Gezelle smiled. "Anyone can see that!"

"Ah," he said, damned if he could. "And where is her home, then?"

"She's not from here, Your Grace."

Now he knew the two women were exactly alike! He wanted to throttle this one, too. He shook his head. If the chit knew from where Liza came, she wasn't going to tell him. He reached out to finger the rich silk of the gown. "This is lovely. Is it for Liza?" At the servant's nod, he smiled. "It will do the lady justice." He started to turn away when Gezelle spoke.

"The Princess Cyle would have liked your lady, Your Grace." She met his startled look.

"You think so?"

"Aye. She was a lovely lady, very open and warm. She never raised her voice to us or struck us. She tried to keep His Grace from doing so." She bit her tongue. Everyone in the keep knew how the two brothers felt toward one another, but one did not criticize the royal sons.

"She sounds like the kind of lady I would have liked to have known. I've heard nothing but good things about her from everyone who knew her." His wicked thoughts prodded him with intense jealousy. Indeed, the lady would have made him a far better wife than The Toad.

"You would have loved her, Your Grace," Gezelle told him. "We all did. Even those who were dead set against the Prince marrying her."

"And how did my brother feel toward her, Mam'selle?"

There was hesitancy in the girl's answer. "I am sure His Grace cared for her. He wept at her funeral."

He searched her face. "I am sure he did." The Princess Cyle's dowry had been returned to her kinsmen upon her untimely death; Galen wouldn't have liked that.

"Is there anything you need, Your Grace?" Gezelle asked, fearful of the sudden hard look on the young Prince's handsome face.

Conar shook his head. "Just take that gown to Liza." He turned and headed toward the stairs.

Gezelle began to walk away, but Conar's voice cut across the hall to her. She stopped and turned, a look of fright on her face, for his voice had been sharp, demanding.

He frowned, seeing how his unthinking tone had undone all his cheerful banter of a few moments earlier. It was obvious this girl had been wounded by too many harsh words in her lifetime. He would try to remember to be extra careful in his dealings with her.

"Where did my sister-in-law die, Mam'selle?" he asked softly.

"There, Your Grace. She fell from the balcony near where you are standing."

Conar glanced at the four-foot high wrought-iron railing. How did one go about falling over such a balcony? It was nigh impossible. He looked back at the servant. "Was she alone when she fell?"

"I truly don't know, Your Grace. There are those who say she was not. They say they saw a man disappearing from the balcony when they came to investigate the lady's scream as she fell, but no one could say who he was. No one admitted to being with her."

"Naturally not, eh, Mam'selle?"

Gezelle smiled sadly. "She was a good woman, Your Grace."

"I am sure she was. She will be remembered."

"Always, Your Grace."

* * * *

At the head of a long trestle table in the unkempt and shadowed dining chamber of Norus Keep, twin candelabras of scratched and chipped ebony sat along the stained white lace of a torn and tattered tablecloth. Once, rich gold plate and the finest Chalean crystal had graced the long cherry wood table and the candelabras had been polished and smooth, casting a warm, rich glow over the hand-tatted lace of the table covering. Now, the gold plate was nicked, heavily scarred; the crystal was chipped, the tablecloth, an eyesore of gravy stains and wine spills. Even the ice blue napkins of fine Viragonian linen were stained beyond cleaning; gray with time and discolored from rust stains. Dust lay on the massive sideboard behind the trestle table, and cobwebs and grime caked the chandelier. No candles were lit in the massive pewter chandelier and the room was cast in lengthening shadows.

Seated at the head of the table, brooding into his wineglass, a blond-haired young man swirled a rich red port around and around as he glared into the blood-red glow. The port sent sparkles of color over the tablecloth like a jewel casting its reflection as the liquid caught and held the candlelight.

The young man's thoughts were hot with an anger he found hard to control. His blue eyes were squinted in petulance, his lips pursed tight with annoyance. The last thing he had needed this night, of all nights, was to have his much-despised twin show up on the doorstep, unannounced, and with a guest, a female guest at that, in tow. Hasty commands had had to be issued to the gathering of men who had congregated in the dungeon rooms; plans had to be averted; precautions taken. As the gathering dispersed, so, too, did the storm brewing on the horizon. Drumming rain had stilled to a slow trickle, the boom of thunder reduced to an occasional weak clap. It was the storm's ending that angered the young man the most. It had been a storm destined to destroy Conar McGregor.

No matter how hard the man at the table tried to still his fury, it scorched his soul like the hissing kiss of a branding iron.

His hand tightened around the goblet's stem, his thumb, and forefinger pressing inward against the fragile crystal. His other hand held the arm of his chair with a death grip, his knuckles white and strained with the force of his hold.

"Damn you, Conar," he spat with fervent wrath. "Damn your soul to the Abyss!"

Prince Galen Nicolai McGregor had always vowed that he hated his twin brother with a passion that went far beyond the ordinary sibling rivalry. It went, he swore, past even the hatred reserved for one's worst enemy. It even surpassed the loathing one could have for a despised wife.

Or so Galen had said. It was sharp and hot to the touch, and it seared him. It was bitter in the mouth and resisted swallowing. It pierced the gut, disemboweled, and consumed the innards. It was, he was fond of telling his cronies, a hatred that had grown in leaps, and bounds since the two men were toddlers.

Not identical twins, Galen was paler than Conar, for he rarely went outside; he preferred the dismal, dark, and dank walls of his keep. There, he was not being constantly compared to his fraternal twin.

Galen's hair was the same shade of ripe wheat, but it was coarser in texture, more unruly. The blue eyes were the same shade, as well, but Galen's eyes were hooded, more conniving, and full of mistrust and contempt. His mouth did not have the same sensual fullness of the upper lip that Conar's did. It was a thinner mouth, straighter, set into a perpetual sneer.

Their noses were identical, their cheekbones high, their facial structure the same; but Galen's face was fuller than his brother's and lacked the cleft of Conar's. It was the look on Galen McGregor's face—one of disdain and scorn, insolence and haughty arrogance—that truly set it apart from his twin's. There was no ready laugh on Galen's lips and no twinkling humor in the cold blue eyes.

Neither did he have the temperament or the respectability that was Conar's. And he did not possess the love and adoration that was given to Conar, who had earned such loyalties. People instinctively mistrusted Galen McGregor; shunned him; gossiped about him behind his back in uncomplimentary terms, comparing him to Conar and finding him lacking. Galen felt those comparisons to the very depths of his soul, and although he would never admit it, they hurt him deeply.

But if truth were told, Galen loved his brother. It was a self-destructive love; a love filled with the taint of jealousy and envy and covetousness. He had learned to hide that love behind a facade of indifference and coldness when he was around his brother. It was a weakness, a flaw—this love—that Galen McGregor could ill-afford if he was to gain his objective: an objective that might well have become a reality this night if Conar had not come calling.

With a violent oath, he flung the goblet across the room where it shattered into fragments against the stone hearth with its blazing fire. The wine sizzled in the flames and sent up a pleasant, warm scent of plums.

"You missed," was a sardonic voice from the dining room entrance.

Galen half-rose at the sound of his brother's amused voice, but with a shrug of his wide shoulders, he sat down again.

"If I'd been aiming at you, I'd have hit you, Conar." His tone was curt with contempt as he ran his veiled glare over Conar's white silk shirt and dark gray breeches. Never had he seen his brother dressed in anything less than impeccable taste. He admired the cut of his clothing and glanced away. Conar was a handsome, virile man and his presence always seemed to underscore Galen's own sense of inadequacy.

"Not happy to see me, little brother?" Conar asked. There was a lazy, nonchalance to his step as he walked to the head of the table where his twin sat. By all courtesy and tradition, in honor of Conar's position in the family, Galen should have relinquished the position to his twin, but he never had and Conar knew he wouldn't unless commanded to do so. It didn't really matter to Conar and wasn't worth arguing over.

"You weren't expected," Galen snapped.

"I never am," was the laconic reply.

Galen stared at his brother, marveling at the way the man had filled out over the past year.

"I'd have made ready for you if I'd known you were coming."

"No doubt," Conar said. He pulled out a chair for himself, swung a long leg over the back, and sat. He leaned back and folded his arms over his chest. "Your servants taking the night off?" he casually inquired, looking about the empty room.

Galen took a long draft of a fresh goblet of wine. "I said you weren't expected." He drained the wine and immediately picked up the decanter to fill his goblet. "If you'd let me know when it is you plan on visiting...."

"Isn't that the point of my visits?" Conar grinned at Galen's offended stare. "Forewarning you wouldn't be nearly as much fun, Galen."

"I was told you brought a woman with you this time," Galen said, trying to change the subject. He could never tell if Conar was laughing at him or warning him. "One of your legion of whores, I presume?" He ignored the look of caution on his twin's lean face.

"I have a lady with me, aye. And I don't believe I should have to tell you she is to be treated as such." There was frost in the tone.

A burst of laughter came from Galen. "Conar, you wouldn't know a lady if she were to rub herself against your...."

Galen was distracted by the arrival of a slovenly servant bringing in two fresh decanters of port. Nodding his head in Conar's direction, Galen indicated to the servant to fill Conar's goblet first. The man did so, leaving one decanter beside Conar's plate and placing the other beside Galen's.

Conar glanced at the sullen look on the servant's face, meeting the man's bold eyes. There was such hatred and contempt lurking behind the heavy-lid stare, Conar lifted one brow in surprise. The lack of respect being shown him this night was even worse than usual.

"Is there something wrong with your wine, brother?" Galen asked, drawing Conar's eyes from the servant.

Conar looked at the goblet and then back to his brother. "Do I need to have this good fellow taste this for me?"

Galen threw back his head and chuckled. When he lowered his chin, the smile left his face and he leaned his elbows on the table and looked his twin in the eye. "Don't you trust me, Conar?"

Conar's wintry smile lifted the firm lips. "No."

Galen leaned back in his chair. "What reason have I ever given you to mistrust me? No harm has ever come to you within the walls of this keep."

"What reason, indeed?" Conar snorted. "My trip through Colsaurus the last time I left your keep was exhilarating. I assume those men who ambushed me were meant to see I didn't reach home in one piece." He raised his goblet and took a tentative sip. Nodding his head in appreciation of the port, he looked back at Galen. "I think they were doing their best to see I stayed in Colsaurus. Underground, perhaps?"

Shaking his head, Galen smiled. "I am not the only enemy you have, Conar. If those men were truly intent on killing you, you would be more than likely moldering in your tomb." He saluted his brother with his wineglass. "I have never once said I wished you dead, big brother."

"But it wouldn't bother you if I were."

"I would pretend great sorrow should something ill befall you, Conar." Galen tented his fingers and rested his chin on the tips, gazing at Conar with a mournful expression. "I would weep and moan and gnash my teeth. I would prostrate myself at your casket and tear my hair." He grinned. "Our people would know how beloved you were to me."

Conar nearly spat out his wine. "Our people are not fools, Galen."

"You think I have no affection for you?"

"You want the crown."

"I've never said otherwise."

"And it is something you will never attain, I fear." Conar blinked as the servant plopped a piece of roast beef onto his plate.

"Don't be so sure," Galen shot back as the servant laid a fat slab of beef on his plate with gentle care. "There are those who would rather see me on the throne than you." He looked at his servant and they exchanged a smile.

"I have no doubts." Conar picked up his fork and knife and began to score the beef.

"But if you were to abdicate to me, then I would be the one to marry that bitch in Oceania. I'd take that loathsome burden from you."

Conar laughed, nearly pushing the beef off his plate as he tried to cut it. "Now that would be worth considering."

"Would you?" Galen's voice was husky with hope.

Conar picked up his goblet, took a sip of the heady port, and set down the goblet. He wiped his lips on the napkin, leaned toward Galen, and smiled sweetly. "No," he said softly and then sat back in the chair to resume eating.

"Have you met the Princess Anya yet?" Galen asked, trying to calm his raging anger at being laughed at. "I hear she's as ugly as ever."

Stabbing a slice of beef with his fork, Conar took a bite before answering, chewing the tender beef with care. He inclined his head to compliment his brother on the excellence of the meal. "Not yet. It can wait. Perhaps she'll decide to join a nunnery."

"Ah, I think not, Conar," Galen remarked. "Papa will have you well and truly married; manacled hand and foot and member to her before the year is out. If you aren't tied to Shaz's ogress, then it will surely be to some other mindless chit. As heir, it is your place to marry and produce offspring to sit upon Papa's knee. I would wonder, though, what those little half-Oceanian, half-Conar things would look like."

Galen laughed at his own barb, for he could see his twin had not found the remark palatable. Conar was frowning, viciously attacking the beef. Smiling to himself, Galen took another sip of wine. His voice was beginning to thicken from the amount he had already consumed.

"Doesn't the thought of bedding that beldame bother you, Conar? I would think the thought of humping such a haglet would take the steel out of any man's sword."

Conar placed his knife and fork beside his plate and glared across the table at his twin. "Be careful how your tongue wags, Galen. Your remarks are tasteless and crude even by your own standards."

Galen sulked as his brother continued to stare at him. It had always been so: Conar would let that guileless blue gaze hold until Galen could stand the pressure no longer and would have to turn away. Never once in their lifetimes had Galen won a force of wills between them. This night was no different. He looked away from Conar.

"I only tell the truth," Galen ground out.

"You let the wine speak for you."

Galen's mouth turned bitter. "I fear it causes me to forget in whose august presence I am being allowed to sit. It does help to ease the monotony of my existence here in your mighty shadow. Sometimes I can't seem to control my insatiable hunger for it."

"Then perhaps it is time the wine was ruled by the man and not the other way around," Conar quietly reminded him.

Galen glared at him. "And you have no one and nothing that rules you, do you, Conar?"

"Everyone has rules they must obey, Galen. Even I." He took a bite of fresh steamed asparagus.

"Speaking of being ruled: did you happen to see Master Kaileel Tohre when you arrived?" Galen asked, his humor restored as his brother's face lost some of its natural ruddy coloring.

Conar laid down his eating utensils and pushed away his plate, his appetite suddenly gone. He cleaned his lips on the napkin. "I saw him."

"I'm so glad you did. He often asks of you while he's visiting with me. We have such long chats about you." Galen's eyes hardened with malicious glee as his brother glanced uneasily away. "We discuss your childhood. He told me...."

Conar looked up to see Galen staring open-mouthed at the dining hall entrance. Turning his head to see what had caused his brother such surprise, Conar found he could not swallow past the lump that had suddenly formed in his throat.

Galen got slowly to his feet, his heart hammering wildly. He felt as though he had been kicked in the gut by a mule. He swung his stare to his brother. "Is this the lady you brought with you?" he whispered in a hushed, awed voice.

Conar could do no more than nod. His eyes were locked on Liza as she stood in the half-darkened doorway, her gown and hair gleaming from the light in the main hall. He followed Galen to his feet, snatching up his linen napkin to wipe the wine stain from his lips. He tossed the square of linen back to the table where it landed in the gravy boat.

Never in his wildest, most fevered dreams, his most intimate moments of fantasy, could Conar have imagined that the young girl who had accompanied him to Norus Keep was the one who now graced the chamber with her delicate, breathtaking beauty. He was unaware of his own gaping mouth, his own thundering heart. All he was cognizant of was the woman at the other end of the room.

"Conar?" Galen whispered. His mouth was dry, his breath ragged. "Who is she?"

"Who?"

Galen reluctantly tore his gaze from the beauty before him and glared at his brother, viciously nudging him in the ribs. "Introduce me to her, you dolt!"

Conar turned to him, his face devoid of expression. "What?"

"Introduce her!" Galen hissed. He pushed past his twin and started around the table, his hand outstretched toward the girl. "My lady! Welcome to my home!"

It took Galen's movement to break the spell under which Conar had fallen. He snapped his mouth shut with an audible click of his teeth. He hurried to outdistance Galen, rudely shoving his twin out of the way and reaching for Liza's hand.

Liza smiled warmly at him, amusement coming through. Her dazzling smile was like a ray of sunshine in the dismal room, lighting the darkened corners and warming the dank chill pervading the stone walls. As her hand slipped into Conar's, she laughed, for he immediately brought her fingers to his lips, his eyes never leaving hers. "Good eve, Mam'selle."

Galen was transfixed by the woman's beauty as he walked toward her. Long black hair hung loose around her creamy shoulders, cascaded down her slender back to her shapely hips. One thick tress hung over her bodice and was braided with pale peach ribbon. Soft peach-colored blossoms nestled at her right ear, bringing out the rose blush on her high cheekbones.

The gown she wore was pale green, cut low in the bodice to reveal the budding cleavage of her high breasts. Gathered in the center beneath those upturned mounds of perfection, the gown fell in gentle folds and ended in deep, lace-edged scallops as it swept the floor. Peeking out from under the gold lace scallops, were mint green satin slippers studded with golden sparkles.

There was a hint of peach at her eyelids and her mouth had been darkened to a deep coral. Around the upper part of her left arm, a thin gold ribbon of serpentine chain banded the tender flesh. Tiny coral studs sat in the flesh of her earlobes. The only other jewelry she wore was a black rune stone on a thin silver chain around her slender neck.

Struck mute by the elegance and ethereal grace before them, neither man could think. They had both lost their hearts and souls. They had given them to the Lady Liza.

"Am I late?" she asked and her voice was a whisper of soft, throaty laughter.

"Never," Galen said courteously, reaching his brother's side, taking the hand Conar did not hold. "You could never be anything but perfection." He smiled the first genuine, true smile he had ever bestowed upon a female. He brought her wrist to his lips and planted a gentle kiss on the upturned flesh.

Liza felt a shock of revulsion run through her at his touch and she shivered. She tried to smile, but her flesh felt as though maggots were crawling over it. She had to stamp down the urge to wipe her wrist on her skirt when he released her hand.

"I am Galen."

Conar noticed the look on his twin's face and could not mistake the sexual arousal. If he hadn't known better, known in which direction his brother's interests lay, he would have been angrier still. As it was, he had the strongest urge he had ever had to slap Galen's face. An intense prick of jealousy raced through the Prince Regent. "My brother, Mam'selle," he explained to her in a clipped voice shot full of wintry chill. He stared at Galen's inquisitive eyes. "Her name is Liza."

"Liza." Galen made the name sound like the soughing of a soft breeze in the forest. He murmured the name again, silently, to himself, and his face took on warmth rarely seen. "It suits you, Lady Liza. It is a very sensual name."

"We're so glad you approve since it is the only name she has!" Conar snarled. Reaching for Liza's arm, he pulled her away from Galen. "I know you're hungry!" He pushed her to the table.

Stunned by Conar's proprietary manner, Galen could only gape at his twin as Conar seated the lady beside him, well away from the place where Galen had been seated.

"Aren't you finished with your meal, Conar?" Galen ground out from between tightly held teeth.

"No, I am not."

"I thought you were," Galen hissed, sitting down and laying his napkin in his lap with a snap.

"You thought wrong."

"You had pushed your plate away."

"I … am … not … finished …Galen!" the young Prince Regent growled.

"The table is...." Liza looked around her. "Lovely. The food smells delicious." She looked from one man to the other as they sat staring daggers at one another.

"To your beauty, Milady," Galen said, raising his goblet.

From his place beside his brother, Conar scowled, but he held his goblet aloft in salute. He was about to speak, but Galen began to compliment Liza; telling her extravagant stories of their homeland; uncomplimentary tales of Conar's exploits, and unbelievable lies of his own.

As Galen droned on and on with his effusive speech, Conar brooded. It was obvious the man was attempting to woo the girl. He was flirting outrageously. Never had Galen bothered to court a woman, any woman, for Conar had known for quite some time that his brother's interests did not include women as sexual partners. The fact that Galen leaned toward his own sex had never bothered Conar. Galen was Galen. Now, he found himself looking at his brother with loathing.

Whether it was to annoy him or was a budding recognition of his own true male nature, Conar didn't care. Galen's sudden interest in a female, and this particular female, was irritating the hell out of him. He clutched his wineglass and took a large swallow.

"I haven't asked from where you come, Milady," Galen said. "I know you are not a native of our land; no woman in Serenia could rival such beauty as you possess, or give birth to it."

Conar groaned and rolled his eyes to the heavens. By the gods, but Galen had gone around the bend.

"I have not seen you at court, either. I would have remembered such loveliness."

"You wouldn't have noticed her since your attention wanders elsewhere," Conar snarled beneath his breath.

Galen threw his brother a hard glower of warning, then turned his attention to Liza. "You are not one of the Ladies-in-Waiting, are you?"

Conar toyed with his wineglass, glaring sullenly at Galen, and only half-listening to Liza's evasions as to her origins. He tuned out Galen's spouted garbage. The goblet twirled in his tanned fingers, the wine swirling up the sides in red waves. As Liza's laugh rang out, a tight frown marred his handsome face and the sensual lips turned into thin, straight lines of disapproval. He drained the goblet and refilled it.

Everything Galen and Liza were saying and doing was rubbing him the wrong way. He found himself fighting the urge to jump up and throttle his twin then and there. From some inner resource, he drew on his resolve to sit still; but for a reason totally beyond his comprehension, his irritation soared by the moment. He mentally shook himself and paid closer attention to the conversation to take his mind away from his seething rage.

"But from where do you come? You still haven't told me."

"She's from Oceania," Conar snapped and could have bitten his tongue. He turned to Liza to warn her to go along with his outrageous remark.

"Oceania?" Galen pounced on the answer. One golden brow shot up in unconscious imitation of the way Conar's often did. "Isn't that the homeland of the Princess Anya, dear brother?"

"You know full well it is, Galen," Conar hissed, emphasizing his brother's name with a warning of his own.

Galen smiled at Conar. "You did know this fellow is betrothed, didn't you, Milady?"

"She knows!"

"And do you know the Princess Anya Wynth?" Galen asked Liza, but his eyes were still on Conar.

"I can't say she and I have ever been introduced, Milord. I have heard the lady is crippled and not so pretty to look upon, though. Or so Prince Conar tells me."

Conar nearly choked on the wine in his mouth. He glared at Liza's innocent expression. Swallowing with effort, he frowned at her. "I didn't say she was a cripple, Mam'selle. I said she had a limp."

Liza pretended to think. "Ah, so you did. But I do remember you saying she was as ugly as a toad."

"Liza!" Conar shouted. He would have taken her to task for revealing such a thing in Galen's presence, but his twin's uproarious laughter stilled his angry retort.

"By all that's holy, Conar, but I find this entire conversation enlightening! I can see now why you aren't keen on marrying the poor little bitchlet. I can't see you, of all men, shackled to an ugly lass, although I must admit I find it deliciously funny considering the bawds I have known you to tumble in your day."

"I'll not have you speaking like that in front of this lady!" Conar snarled, half-rising from his chair.

"I'm sure the Lady Liza understands you, Conar. Your reputation has preceded you throughout the Seven Kingdoms and even into

Diabolusia!" He winked at Liza. "Don't you agree that it is dreadful Conar is being forced to marry this ogress?"

He came to his feet, roaring, "You aren't the one marrying the stupid bitch, Galen, so I don't think your opinion matters! It is late, Mam'selle. If you ride with me on the morrow, I suggest you bid this jackass a good eve!" He turned and stalked away, his footsteps ringing.

"Milord! Wait!" Liza called. She scraped her chair away from the table, hastily getting up and moving from Galen before he could assist her. She looked over her shoulder at him. "Please, don't trouble yourself, Prince Galen. A pleasant good eve to you, Milord." Her slipper-clad feet made hardly any noise as she ran after Conar.

The Prince Regent had stopped as she called to him, but had not turned around from where he stood in the doorway. "If you are coming, I would prefer it be sometime before dawn, Mam'selle!"

"Such an ass, Liza-love," Galen called after them. "You would find me far better company."

Spinning on his heel, Conar took a step toward his brother, but Liza ran to him, blocking his path, her face pleading for peace between the two men. Her presence and actions did not stop the fury pouring from his lips.

"She has no need of another companion when she has me, brother! I suggest you look elsewhere for your own brand of entertainment." He gripped Liza's hand and jerked her after him up the stairs.

Taking the steps to their sleeping chambers at a brisk clip, Conar could feel Liza stumbling behind him, but his rage was towering and he was hard-pressed not to slap the girl for being the direct cause of it. He had always prided himself in not taking Galen's barbs to heart, ignoring the insinuations and cheap retorts Galen aimed his way. Letting the bastard see that he had gotten beneath his skin infuriated Conar even more. A vein throbbed in his temple and his lips were pressed so tightly together to keep from bellowing his anger, there was a white line around his mouth.

When they reached Liza's door, he spun around and took both of her upper arms in his hard hands, gripping them with enough force to bruise her. He soundly shook her. "I did not appreciate your remarks concerning my wife-to-be, Mam'selle! The lady may not be to my liking, but I will not hear insults directed toward her. She will be the next Queen of this land! Do I make myself clear?" Fury flashed in his icy blue eyes.

"I repeated only what you said to me."

"Aye! You women are good at repeating things, aren't you?"

"If you don't want people to know how you feel about the woman, don't tell them!" she protested, trying to free herself from his punishing grip, but he held her fast, dragging her up hard against his body.

His upper lip curled with distaste. "I thought you were different, but I can see I was wrong. You're just like every other female I've ever known. You open your mouth and nothing but crap comes out!"

Liza's eyes went wide. "I'm like no woman you have ever known and that's what you're so gods-be-damned angry about!" she shouted, incensed with the way he was manhandling her.

"All women are alike! They take and they take and they take until a man has nothing left to give and then they leave him for another man who can provide more! They lie and they cheat and they steal and they spread vicious gossip about like so much manure." He pushed her against the wall, holding her prisoner with his body and ground himself suggestively against her. "And they spread their legs for any man with the price or the title!"

"Let go." Her voice was low and deceptively soft; her tone was calm.

He snaked out his hand and gripped her chin. "I haven't decided what it is you want from me, woman, but when I do, you may be sorry you ever laid eyes on me."

"I said let go," she warned, green eyes glaring at his icy blue smirk.

"When I'm good and gods-be-damned ready."

One moment he was holding her against the wall, his lower body thrust hard against hers; the next, he was kneeling on the floor, his manhood cupped protectively in his shaking hands. He stared up at her, disbelief running rampant in his shocked eyes. He could only stare at her as she snarled down, "Are you ready now, Milord?"

She stalked to her room, slamming the door behind her and threw the bolt with a loud clunk.

Having a door slammed in his face was bad enough. Being kneed in his privates was worse; but being treated so by a woman was something entirely different. He knelt there, gasping for breath, squeezing his eyes shut to the ghastly pain in his groin, and could have strangled the bitch.

"Bitch," he mumbled as he painfully pushed himself from the floor.

He was so furious that nothing mattered to him but the slamming of his door with enough force to put a crack in the lintel. Hearing the wood split, he grimly smiled and stumbled to his bed, crawling into its soft protection much as a child would. He snatched a pillow and buried his angry face in the plump thickness.

### Chapter Seven

Conar jumped, sitting upright with a jolt in the bed. His mouth was dry and his heart thudded painfully in his chest. Sweat oozed from his pores and ran down his temples, from under his arms, down the center of his chest. He ran a trembling hand over his face and sighed.

It was the old dream; the nightmare; that god-awful memory lodged in the back of his subconscious. It came periodically to turn his nerves to mush and to remind him that something lay in wait for him just beyond his peripheral vision. It lurked there, ready to consume him if he ever once let down his guard. He could feel it hovering about him even now.

He flung away the bed covers and swung his legs over the edge, sitting there, his head in his hands, trying to calm his heart and nerves. He sucked in a wavering breath and slowly let it out. He could still see that horrible face glaring at him; feel the cold flesh of the man's fingers on him. Feel the pain; the helplessness.

Mentally shaking himself, he stood, closing out the picture, forcing it away.

He started to reach for the bedside tumbler of water, but a sudden heavy knocking at his door spun him around and flattened him against the four-poster of the bed.

"Your Grace!" a woman's voice cut through the night silence. "Your Grace! Hurry!"

He reached for his sword, a purely instinctive act, and jerked the door wide.

Gezelle flinched. With a will all their own, her green eyes traveled down Conar's naked chest, flicked quickly, all the way down to his bare toes. "Oh," was all she said.

"What?" he shouted. When she did not answer, he took her arm, his body fairly quivering with rage. "What the hell is it, woman?"

Her head bobbed back and forth as he shook her, but she couldn't find her voice. Only a squeak of mild protest forced its way from her gaping mouth.

Afraid the girl had been struck with some horror, his first inclination was to shout at her to come to her senses. But remembering Liza's stern reprimand, he knew harsh words and violence would only drive her deeper into her terrified shell. With great effort, he lowered his voice and shook her again, but more gently.

"Is it the lady?" he asked and got no answer. He started to go around the servant, but the girl found her voice.

"Milord! Your clothes!"

Glancing down at himself, he realized he wore nothing save the night air. His mouth snapped shut and he snarled in embarrassment. Spinning around, he stomped into the room, closing the door just long enough to drag on his breeches.

In the hallway, Gezelle couldn't move. Her mind was filled with the naked splendor of a man she had fantasized about so many times. Seeing the young Prince standing in the doorway, sword raised, face filled with fire and combat, had etched itself into her fertile imagination forever; seeing him without a stitch of clothing was etched into her very soul. She looked up as he flung open the door, buttoning his breeches as he strode forward, sword tucked under his bare arm.

"Is it the lady?" he asked again, more annoyed than ever at the beet-red flush on the girl's face.

Gezelle felt like fainting. She would have if he had not taken hold of her arm once more.

"Mam'selle!" he said with exasperation.

She blinked, feeling the warmth of his hand all over her trembling body. She could only nod.

"Show me!"

Gezelle found her voice and pointed a finger to Liza's door. "She's having a nightmare, Your Grace. She called out your name. I couldn't wake her."

Conar had nightmares of his own from which his family could not awaken him, so before Gezelle could say another word, he had the door to Liza's room open and was at her bed, flinging his sword to the floor, reaching down for her.

"The water!" she cried. "Conar, the water!"

He took her in his arms before his knee ever bent the mattress. "Liza!" he commanded in a soft, stern voice. "Wake up. 'Tis but a dream, Sweeting."

She clung to him in her sleep, her body pressed tightly to his. Her hands clawed frantically at his shoulders and she gasped for air as though she were drowning.

"Conar! Help us! He can't hold me much longer! We will fall!"

"I am here, Sweeting. Here beside you." Conar crooned to her, stroking her gleaming black hair, sweat-drenched along her temples from the horror in which she had been thrust.

"Conar! The ledge! The ledge is breaking away! Help us, Conar! Please, help us! I don't want to leave you!" Her hands griped him as though she were being torn from his embrace.

"Liza!" his said, his voice raising. He pulled her face away from his chest and planted a soft, insistent kiss on her forehead. "I am here, Beloved. You are safe, now!"

Her eyelids fluttered open and her green eyes focused on him. "Conar?" she questioned, unsure, her voice wavering.

"Aye, I am here, Sweeting." He touched his lips to hers in a soft caress of protection.

Galen's voice intruded, harsh, strident as he rushed into the room.

"What's happening here?" He gripped his own sword, his knuckles white as he advanced toward the bed. "Has someone done hurt to Liza?" He reached out a hand to touch her shoulder, but Conar knocked it away.

"Don't you dare lay your filthy hands on this woman!" Conar snarled.

Galen's face turned ugly with contempt and rage. "By what right do you give me such an order? This woman is not yours!"

"Nor is she yours! Keep your hands off her!"

He would have retaliated, but Galen could see how Liza shivered with fright, could see the deathly pallor of her skin. He turned hostile eyes to Gezelle. "Get my physician!"

"She doesn't need a physician," Conar told him, gathering the frightened girl closer as though he could keep anyone from ever touching her again.

"Aye? She only needs you. Is that it?" Galen shouted, all semblance of civilized behavior gone from his furious face.

"She has what she needs. She has me and you can get the hell out of here!"

"You know better, Prince Conar! She can't have you and you sure as hell can't have her!" His voice went low and dark and contemptuous. "The Tribunal will see to that!"

If he could have reached his twin, Conar would have gutted him, but the quivering girl sensed his anger and clutched at him, clinging furiously. He could feel her thundering heart beating against his ribcage.

"You are frightening her more!" Galen snapped.

"She had a bad dream," Conar thundered. "Nothing more. If you'll get out of here, maybe she can go back to sleep!"

"Milady, please," Galen pleaded, seeing how the angry words he and his brother were flinging at one another was upsetting her. He lowered his voice to a soft, caressing croon. "Please let my man look at you. Perhaps he can give you something to help you rest, if nothing else. I like not the paleness of your flesh."

Galen wanted desperately to take the girl into his arms. He wanted to hold her, kiss her, and keep her safe. When Liza nodded acceptance, his look turned hard with victory as he glowered at Conar. "I'll send for my physician."

"I've already sent for him," a voice spoke.

Conar looked past Galen and saw the burly Master-at-Arms standing in the doorway, his scarred face a study of deep worry. His gaze strayed to Conar, then slid slowly away.

"Thank you, Sir," Liza said quietly to the Master-at-Arms and the burly man nodded.

"That will be all," Galen snapped at Gezelle as she hovered near the bed. "You are no longer required here."

"She stays," Conar said.

Galen turned on his brother with a fierce glower of rage. "Is that so? And since when do you order my servants about this keep?" His spine was taut with challenge; his voice laced with contempt.

Conar smiled at his twin, and it was a smile so evil and so filled with promise, that Galen took a step backward. "The girl belongs to me, Galen, and I wish her to stay."

"She is my servant!" Galen screamed. "This is my keep!"

"No, Galen," Conar said in a reasonable, pleasant voice. "This is my keep." His voice was steady and calm, but shot with triumph. "All the people who serve here, and that includes you, belong to me." He stopped smiling and his eyes went glacial. "It is high time you remembered that, Galen McGregor."

Seething with rage, humiliated by being put in his place, especially in front of Liza, Galen stalked from the room, knocking aside the elderly physician who was just entering. "See well to the lady," he hissed as he thundered down the hall to his chambers.

Conar was ordered from the room, the door closed in his face, as the physician looked to his patient. Twice he would have opened the door if the Master-at-Arms, who stood vigil, had not stepped directly in front of him, silently reminding his Overlord that the physician did not want the young Prince in the room.

When the Healer was through, he came into the hall. "I have given the lady some sleeping powders to take if she should need them. She doesn't think she will, but they are there for her. Taken with a small amount of wine, the powders are most effective." He pinched his hawk-like nose between his thumb and forefinger and sighed. "The lady will need wine, in any case. It will help her relax."

"I'll see to it," Conar promised.

"Call me if she should need me," the physician said quietly. "May I suggest you get some sleep, as well, Your Grace? You do not look well." Bowing a head filled with a shock of thick white hair, the old man, his joints crippled and twisted with advanced age and arthritis, hobbled down the stairs on knees whose cartilages had been devoured with time and disease.

Conar was annoyed at the Healer's observation of the way he looked, although, if truth were told, he felt sick to his stomach. He looked at the Master-at-Arms. "Get the lady some wine."

"I will stand guard at her door."

"Belvoir," Conar began, suddenly remembering the man's name.

"I will stand guard, Your Grace." He folded his massive arms over his barrel chest, his face carefully blank. His eyes said there would be no discussion. Prince or no Prince, he meant to stay. "The girl can go."

Conar glared at him, realizing the man was not to be intimidated. He sighed. "You think she needs a guard in this keep?"

"I will stand guard."

Looking at the man's uncompromising face, Conar shrugged. He reached for the handle of Liza's door, but stopped. "Have it your way, Belvoir, but no one would dare harm the lady while she is in this keep."

"I know they will not, Your Grace."

Conar shook his head. He didn't doubt the man's answer for a moment.

"Thank you for your loyalty, Belvoir," he said and saw the man nod once before looking away.

Liza lay in the bed, her long hair fanned out around her on the silk pillowcase. She smiled wanly at Conar as he sat beside her. "I am sorry to have caused you trouble, Milord."

Conar caressed her cheek with his thumb. "No trouble, Milady. Do you think you can sleep now? No nightmare would dare bother you with Belvoir outside your door." He smiled.

Liza's eyes crinkled with merriment. "They'd be too afraid to enter the room with that good knight there to protect me."

"Aye." Absently, Conar's thumb smoothed down her cheek and across her lower lip. He scanned that lovely fullness and then slowly raised his eyes to hers. "I am only a heartbeat away from you, Milady."

Her face flushed. "I am grateful, Milord."

"You have had this dream before?"

She glanced up at him. "Many times."

"And called my name to rescue you? I am touched."

She blushed. "My knight of the realm to the rescue, of course."

"Of course."

"I will be fine now. Truly I will. Go back to bed, Milord."

He wasn't sure she was telling the truth. She wanted to be no bother, to be no cause of his own sleeplessness, but he feared she would be. For many nights to come.

Turning over his hand, he drew his scarred knuckles, knuckles that had encountered many a hard jaw and even harder wall, down her soft cheek. Speaking over his shoulder, he ordered Gezelle to fetch wine from the study.

"And bring me a tumbler, as well," he asked. He had a feeling it would be a long, long night.

After Gezelle had slipped quietly from the room, Liza turned to Conar. "Please go back to bed, Milord. I promise I will have no more nightmares this eve." Her sweet smile melted his heart with its beauty.

"You promise?"

She raised her hand and crossed her heart. "I promise, good sir."

He returned to his room, passing Belvoir, who stood against the wall beside Liza's door. He mumbled a good eve to the Master-at-Arms and closed the door to his room, leaning against the portal for a long while, wondering why he had not kissed the lady good eve. He had wanted to. Felt she would have liked for him to, but something had stopped him, had almost seemed to warn him away from her. He felt again the unease that always troubled him at Norus. His eyes narrowed into slits of worry. What was it about this place that set his teeth on edge? It was more than the old legends. It was more than the nervousness he always felt while visiting here. It seemed to spread over him this night with an all-pervasive stench that smothered him.

There was knock on his door. He jumped, his heart skipping a beat.

"Your Grace? I have your wine," the servant girl called.

"Damn it, you idiot!" he cursed under his breath. "Get yourself together, McGregor!"

He opened the door, grabbed the wine goblet, drained it, and handed it back to Gezelle. "I ordered a decanter," he snapped as he slammed the door in the girl's startled face.

Gezelle stood there for a moment and then shrugged. In her left hand she held the empty goblet that had been intended for the lady; in her right was the full decanter of port His Grace had asked for. Should she knock and give him the decanter or leave him alone?

"I'd leave him alone if I were you, 'Zelle," Belvoir told her as though he sensed her uncertainty.

Gezelle smiled at the big man. "I think so, too, Sir Belvoir."

Without removing his breeches this time, Conar stretched out on his bed and looked at the ceiling. His thoughts strayed across the hall. He thought of the intrusion this girl had brought into his life, and he smiled.

She was a distraction. That was a certainty. Her sweet smile and gentle voice, her angry and flashing eyes, her beautiful face enticed him. Her stubbornness and female logic confused him. Her expertise with the weapons she carried annoyed him somewhat; but her utilizing of them to save his skin made him proud.

She fascinated him as no other woman ever had. He could close his eyes and see her as clearly in his mind as he could the tall peaks of Mount Serenia that he had viewed nearly every day of his life. He could hear her lilting laugh and soft voice; feel the texture of her skin against his fingertips although a full twenty feet or more separated them. He could even taste the silk of her lips on his own.

Aye, he thought with some dismay. The girl had intruded into his life, not gently and insidiously, but like an avalanche.

"Conar's pretty little intrusion," he thought aloud and grinned, thinking that was the same phrase Rayle Loure used to characterize his wife, Aurora.

He supposed all wives were an intrusion into a man's life. They came; they stayed; they tormented you. But some, like his Liza, would never make life's journey dull. She would make him a most invigorating and challenging wife.

He jerked up as though stung by a wasp. Where the hell did that notion come from? Liza as his wife? The thought of her in that capacity shook him to his very core and he mentally tore his train of thought away from such a dangerous idea. Thoroughly aghast, he lay down and pulled the pillow over his face, groaning with frustration.

Within a matter of seconds he was fast asleep.

He never heard the panel across the room from his bed slide open on well-oiled hinges. Never heard the soft, urgent voices speaking as they bent over his unconscious form. Never felt the hands that lifted him and carried him through a secret passageway into the very bowels of Norus Keep.

Across the hall, Liza turned fitfully in her sleep, calling out softly. She had refused the wine Gezelle brought to her, instead, giving it to the servant girl who had never before tasted wine.

Gezelle tossed in her own sleep, smiling, thinking what a wonderful thing was this wine.

## Chapter Eight

His head ached with a blinding agony that reluctantly dragged open his eyes. He knew immediately where he was.

"Galen!"

He jerked viciously on the chains that bound him spread-eagle to the uprights on either side of him, but his wrists and ankles were banded with thick iron manacles. Jerking on the restraints broke open the flesh along his wrists and sent pain shooting up his arms.

Another howl of pure rage tore through the darkness.

To be stupid enough to be drugged was one thing. To wake up, trussed like a common criminal, in the dungeon of a keep that by all rights belonged to him, was something else. He screamed in fury and tore at the chains again, feeling a trickle of blood slipping down his left wrist.

"Galen McGregor! You're a dead man!"

His attention went to a glowing brazier filled with long-handled instruments that glowed in the bowels of the fire. He threw back his head and howled again. By the gods, he would cripple Galen McGregor!

He didn't feel fear as much as boiling, rigid anger, and then that anger bubbled over into humiliation at the realization that he, and he alone, was solely responsible for his own predicament. Arriving at Norus without benefit of his own personal guard had finally proven to be his undoing. His own ego and arrogance had put him in such dire straits.

Conar knew, without a doubt, that Galen intended to use everything at his disposal to see that his brother abdicated the throne to him. One more look at the torture instruments in the brazier and Conar wasn't so sure that, come morning, the crown would still belong to him.

And then what? His fevered mind asked. What happens after you've been forced to sign away your birthright? Galen could ill-afford to let him leave with visible signs of torture on his body to negate the document he would be forced to sign. Would he be kept at Norus? Caged inside one of the filthy cells that lay beyond the studded oaken door off to his right? He didn't think Galen would have him killed, but he wasn't all that sure. Dead men could not challenge a writ of abdication.

He glanced at the instruments again. He knew well how much torture he could stand. His memory had not failed him. He groaned. Maybe torture wasn't all that Galen had planned. A shadow of evil loomed within his inner vision, a cadaverous face grinning at him out of the darkness, and he shivered.

"Sweet Alel, no!" he whispered. That he could not stand.

He tugged helplessly against his bonds, groaning with fear. Death would be preferable to the things Kaileel Tohre could do to him. He tightly squeezed his fingers together and prayed, beseeching every god he had ever known to let him die before Kaileel could lay hands on him again.

"Good eve, Milord," a sweet voice spoke.

Conar swung his head and stared at the silhouette of a woman striding confidently toward him. Her back was to the burning rushes so he could not see her face, but he knew that voice. His blood ran cold as she neared the brazier with its red-hot tongs and pokers. The light cast from the brazier made her face look evil and deadly.

How could he have been so dimwitted? The thought of her being in league with his brother filled him with despair and he thought his heart would break. When she giggled, his despair turned to bleak and icy rage.

"I am glad you find this amusing, Mam'selle," he growled, stung by her duplicity, in agony over her betrayal. He strained at his manacles, the chains rattling.

Liza placed her hands on her hips and turned her face to one side. "You have this uncommon habit of getting yourself into mischief when you're around me."

"Aye, that I do," he spat. It was so hard to look at her beautiful face and not feel such terrible pain in his heart.

"Why do you think that is?" she asked sweetly.

"I thought with the wrong head!" he snarled, blowing an angry stream of breath through his bared teeth.

"Isn't that usual for you, Milord?"

"Normally I'd have better sense."

"But when you're around me, you forget yourself?" She giggled.

"Leave me the hell alone!" he shouted as he pulled against the bonds. "Haven't you caused enough damage? Galen will see that he gets the crown. What did he promise you for your part in trapping me?"

"He'll not get the crown as long as you live, Milord."

A deadly missile of fear ran through his heart. So, they did intend to kill him. He should have realized that. He would always be a threat to Galen if he lived.

"And you'll watch while they take my life, won't you?"

Liza smiled at his silly assumption. "Would you like some help getting free, Milord?"

"Don't play with me, woman!" he bellowed, pulling fiercely on his fetters.

Liza folded her arms over her chest. "You don't know a friend when one comes to your aid, do you, McGregor?" She sighed. "I am not one of Galen's minions, Conar. I was sent to help you, but if you would rather stay here at your brother's mercy...." She shrugged one delicate shoulder and started to turn away.

"Wait!"

"Aye, Milord?" she sweetly replied.

Conar shrugged helplessly, hating to admit he needed her help. "If it would not be too much trouble for you, Mam'selle, I would appreciate your help. 'Tis a most uncomfortable position in which I find myself."

"I can see that, Milord. I suppose I could help you, then. I shall have to...." She turned to stare into the darkness, her hand going up to the rune stone around her neck, her fingers caressing the smooth black surface. When he started to question her, she held up her hand to silence him. "It seems I have happened along just in time," she snarled. "They have miscalculated this time."

Conar frowned. "Who? What are you talking about?" Her face was shadowed with fire from the burning brazier and the deeper darkness of the room, but it glowed with an eerie incandescence that made the hair along his neck stir. The green of her eyes was chatoyant, like cat's eyes in the sudden glare of light. He watched as she knelt on the floor, her hands out in front of her as though she were searching for something among the rushes. "What the hell are you doing?"

"Come, my Little Ones," she whispered to the darkness. "I have need of you."

Something stirred in the rushes, mewed, hummed. From out of the darkness a soft, pulsing sound rose, rising and falling with husky, grating sighs. Tiny mews came from different directions at once; blending, harmonizing, echoing, and breathing long gusts of purring rhythm. The sound grew into one long, continuous purr of contentment.

"Come. Come and meet our master." Liza's voice was as soft as the gentle purring.

Small, darting shapes moved in the rushes, rustling across the stone floor, pushing aside whatever was in their way. A sniffing sound stopped somewhere near the large stone ledge on which Conar stood and then moved on to Liza. An inquiring purr came from close by and then the shapes converged, flung themselves at Liza's ankles, twirling around her feet, rustling her gown, pushing against her legs.

Conar couldn't make out what the shapes were, for they moved with a blur of motion, but he had the impression of small cat-like beings with green eyes that glowed as they regarded him. Something brushed against his own leg and he flinched, looking down as a shape darted away, its mewling voice raised in question.

"Aye, my lovely," Liza crooned to the mewling. "He is the one."

A slow, long purr filled the dungeon as though the beings were conferring and it seemed to Conar as though some unseen entity spoke his name.

"Aye, it is Raphian's familiars they send," Liza answered. "I can hear Them coming for him through the fire. We must protect him."

Conar strained his eyes to see what it was she was speaking to, but all he could see was the blur of rapid motion against her legs as she bent down to caress some flash of movement along the floor.

She stood, her arms raised to the heavens, her head tilted back, and her voice joined the loud purr of sound.

"Zheil les easnth neum. Abas et meinth bas. Castra hav Bastus. Hyal hav Bastus. Ni have Bastus, Zhad. Ilith dor gritia, Thesius."

Six times the incantation was spoken. Six times the cat-like entities stilled and became silent until the last word of the chant was spoken. Six times the glow from the brazier dimmed.

A vile stench slowly began to drift under Conar's nose. His nostrils quivered and he wrinkled his forehead. He had experienced that smell before. It was the acrid aroma of burnt flesh. He looked about him, but saw nothing.

"They are coming, Milord," Liza told him, never looking his way. "They are coming through the fire for you."

The hair on his scalp moved. He was helpless where he stood. "Liza! Unchain me."

"There's no time."

"Liza!" he called, for the purring was growing louder, the shapes darting about Liza's legs in agitated fury. "Don't leave me here like this!"

Around her legs the cat-like entities were moving with a whirring, growing speed until they were no longer individual shapes but one solid whirl of multi-colored light that sparkled. Her chant echoed once more, the incantation spoken in a language as old as time, and the walls shook, the chamber filled with the eerie beauty of her voice.

"For the love of the gods, Liza! Unchain me!" The stench was so bad he was beginning to gag. He could feel the damp and chill of the dungeon giving way to a fiery blast of heat that washed over him with cloying, smothering waves. Although no light had broken the dimness of the dungeon's atmosphere, he knew there was a vast furnace of fire close by.

"The doors of the Abyss are opening, Milord," she told him, lowering her head and turning to him. "You will feel Their anger soon." She began her chant once more.

Her voice was an awful incarnation of the Feminine Dark Forces that had walked the land centuries before man had ever drawn breath there. Its unearthly beauty stirred the soul and moved the sexual organs to arousal. Conar was amazed that he could be so aroused at a time such as this. His manhood strained against his breeches just as he strained against the manacles holding him captive.

"Unchain me, Liza!" he demanded, acutely aware of his passion rising like molten lava in his veins.

"We will protect you, Beloved. You have nothing to fear."

Wind came whistling through the dungeon, lifting, swirling the long white nightgown she wore; pressed it tightly to her body so Conar could see every curve and mound beneath the gauzy fabric. His manhood leapt at the sight and he had to dig his nails into his palm to keep from groaning, so intense was his desire.

Spinning around and around her feet, the cat-like beings spun a web of multi-faceted color as they revolved around the hem of her gown. Sparkles of light washed up and over the gown and turned it to a brilliant, shining silver mesh.

As Conar watched her with avid fascination, Liza seemed to be lost to the world in which she stood. Her face was radiant, her lithe figure standing tall and erect as the spinning mass of purring entities began to tunnel up her gown, covering her body in a wash of blinding multi-colored light. The mass shifted, expanded in diameter and height until soon she was engulfed within a shimmering, cyclonic band of phosphorescent light. Her long black hair, turning a glimmering blue-black color, whipped behind her in the wind as she raised her hands high to the heavens.

"Come and play!" she called to the heavens, her voice tight. "Come and play with us, Raphian!"

With a suddenness that caused Conar to gasp, something emerged from the fire of the brazier. Rising high above the smoking coals burdened with their deadly instruments of torture, a shape shot toward the ceiling. It pulsed a sickening blood color and settled, spreading along the rafters as it covered the entire ceiling. It bubbled and hissed and moved in waves as it ran along the ceiling.

Its odor was worse than anything imaginable and it slid down the stone walls in thick primordial ooze, dropping to the stone floor to run among the rushes. The smell of rotting and burned flesh filled the air; the ripe and noxious stench of brimstone blended with it. Within the smoky red haze, darting, darker crimson shapes began to leap apart from the blood-mass. Mounds of distorted and bloated shapes sprang from the ceiling and plopped to the floor with a sickening thud. Sharp, distinct faces formed on the mounds and became fat, wiggling, hairless bodies. Triangular faces, whiskered faces, with sharp, snapping fangs that ground with an eagerness to tear and chew.

"Sweet Alel," Conar breathed as one red, gelatinous lump skidded across the ledge close to his bare feet. He turned nervous eyes to Liza. "Uh … Liza?"

"Don't go near him!" she screeched to the gathering red shapes, her eyes defiant as she turned to face the brazier. The cat-like beings around her purred, then growled, then hissed.

Conar swallowed hard. Gone was the arousal of a moment before; gone was any thought beyond the fear that was insidiously creeping down his spine. Liza's face could be seen for only a fraction of a second as the cyclonic band of color around her whirled and parted.

Liza directed her full attention to the forces gathering around Conar McGregor. She had become One with the Dark Forces. She had become One with the NightWind. She was primed to do battle with Evil.

Her arms crossed in front of her--once, twice, three times. With the third crossing, her arms jerked far apart, her voice shrieked to the heavens. She spoke the incantation for the third time and the hem of her gown billowed in the rush of a great, keening wind that swept around her with all the violence of a hurricane. The whirling band surrounding her began to fling away in chunks of sparkling bursts of light.

"Go!" she shouted above the rising wind. "Go and protect your master!"

It was hard for him to look away from the awful glory of her beautiful face. Her flesh glowed like the brilliance of the moon and her hair framed her face in such an enticing way, he once more felt the strain in his manhood. But he tore his attention from her, following the chunks of light that had spiraled from her gown. The cat-like beings as they formed, claws extended, teeth bared in a hissing protest, long tails swishing with annoyance, spitting their own defiance to the red shapes changing among the rushes were a wondrous sight to behold.

A savage, chirping cacophony rose in the air as the red shapes began to take their own form. Bloated bodies with small, round heads; whiskered noses that twitched; little mouths that gaped open to show row after row of pointed teeth; long, sharp claws on short, squat legs; hairless tail whipping about with deadly purpose: the creatures looked like giant rats.

Conar eyed the rat-creatures with revulsion. He smelled the rancid odor of their breath and bodies as they neared. He inhaled the rat smell that was so easily recognized. Their sharp fangs snapped at him, their beady, sly eyes following his attempts to get free of his chains. He tried to twist out of their way to avoid contact with them as they slithered over the stone ledge and moved stealthily toward him. They were now close enough for him to see the deadly gleam in their piercing eyes and hear the click of their fangs.

"Damn it, Liza! Do something!"

The vile things were almost upon him. He turned his head, searching for the beings that Liza had called forth. He could see the flashes of light below the stone ledge, hovering, pulsing, and waiting to attack.

"Liza!" He found her eyes boring into his. "Do something, woman! Don't just stand there!" His wrists were beginning to bleed profusely from the effort to pull his hands free of the manacles. "Liza!"

Her voice, soft as a falling leaf, was a whisper of sound in his ear. "Command them, Conar." It seemed as though her words were inside his head. "They are yours to command. Use your power to command them."

"What the hell are you talking about, woman?" he screamed. He jerked on his bonds. "I have no magic!" He felt one rat-creature thump wildly against him and he shrieked.

"Command them, Conar!"

"I can't!" He was glaring at her, and as a result, did not see the being that flung itself at him, burying its wickedly long fangs into the tender flesh of his thigh. He yelped as much in disgust as in actual pain.

"Get away from him!" Liza shrieked.

With unrestrained fury, Liza looked to her own minions, giving them free rein, and the cat-like beings shredded the fire-pit monsters; crunching fiery red necks with strong black jaws full of vengeance and hate.

A terrible din rose above the dungeon walls as the heat from the fiery pit of the Abyss began to abate. The stench to dissipate. Thin wisps of smoke drifted about the room in cool currents of shifting air and the light from the brazier grew dimmer and dimmer.

Conar gawked at Liza, her face gleaming so proudly and defiantly in the face of her enemy's defeat. Her eyes were wide and glazed, staring with rapture as the demons she controlled devoured those that had come to harm him. Her long black hair was being whipped into frothy ebony foam about her head. The silver-shot gown was plastered to her body so tightly she might well have been naked.

He shuddered. His flesh had turned cold despite the heat still issuing from the brazier. He knew her for what she was and that knowledge terrified him.

She was a wild creature of the dark protecting what was hers, and somehow, he understood that, to her, he had become a possession worthy of protection. He belonged to her in a way he never would to any other woman. A bond had been formed; a chain attached to his soul this very night. Her words to the cat-beings, fading away on a long purr, removed any doubt in Conar McGregor's mind that he was, indeed always would be, hers.

Liza threw back her head and sent an ear-splitting war cry into the night.

"He is mine! I will protect this man with all that I am and all that I ever will be! By the Grace of the Great Lady, you shall never have him!"

Her shout rang through the stone walls and wound itself into the heavens and down into the deepest pits of the Abyss.

"The Domination is, and always will be, defeated by the Daughterhood of the Multitude!"

"Sweet, merciful, Alel," Conar whispered. "What have I allowed to begin?"

This was no mortal woman. He had worried that he could not let her go when their journey was done; could not give her up when he was forced to wed the Princess Anya. Now, his fear was that *she* would not let him go; that *she* would hold him in bondage to her forever.

What have you wrought, Conar? What terrible bargain have you made this time, you foolish, arrogant man? He shook his head, his soul quivering inside him. He had bargained with a demoness, his pride told him, and now he must suffer the consequences.

"They would have dragged you down to the Abyss if I had not stopped them, Conar. They would have eaten you alive."

He opened his eyes and stared at her. He knew full well what she had done. He was no novice to the world of evil. And he fully understood now the significance of the storm that had been brewing about Norus Keep when they had arrived that evening. He knew now what it was that he interrupted, now that it was over. Now that he was beyond helping himself out of this mess.

"I might have been caused great pain, Mam'selle, but they don't want me dead."

"You think not?"

He shook his head, lowering the golden mass of thick hair over his forehead, obscuring his face as his chin sagged to his chest. He was suddenly very tired.

"They wanted my soul, Liza. They were sent to ravage my very soul. I thought Galen brought me here. He is bent on wrestling the crown from me. It wouldn't have been terribly hard for any of his ill-begotten sorcerers to torture me into renouncing the throne." He raised his head and looked at her. "Galen wants my birthright; the Domination wants me."

"As long as I draw breath, Milord, they will never have you."

"I'm not so sure anymore."

"We will fight them, Conar! We will fight them together and win."

"How, Liza? How do you propose we do that?"

"You could have stopped them alone tonight, Conar. You have the power within you to command the forces of the night. You know you do. Why do you deny it?"

He fiercely shook his head. "I want no part of that kind of power. It destroys you."

She pursed her lips. "There are all kinds of power, Milord. Good, as well as evil. How you wield that power is up to you."

Not the insight he possessed as a child, nor the magic he used as he grew older, nor the power he understood he could now wield, would sway him. He had seen evil up close, had felt it touch him, and had lived with it. He knew intimately what certain kinds of power could do to you.

He feared it; loathed it; shunned it. He wanted no part in anything that dealt with the supernatural.

"You fear you will ally yourself with the Domination if you give rein to your power?"

No, he didn't fear joining the Domination. Nothing this side of the Abyss could make him do that. He had been exposed to their brand of mysticism and all-pervasive black magic in his early childhood. The men of the secret society had crippled him in ways he couldn't even admit to himself. His fear was not of becoming one of those men; it was in becoming something others would shun as most people did the magic-sayers.

"I want no part of it, do you hear me?" He pulled on his chains, mindless of the thin, steady flow of his own blood down his upraised arms.

"You aren't ready to accept what is, Milord," she said sadly. "You cannot change your nature by denying it. I'm tired. We will discuss it again someday, you and I. For now, you won't remember the events of this night anyway."

"I'm not likely to forget anything that happened here this night!" he spat, wishing with all his being that he could chain Galen here in his place. He watched as she walked slowly toward him and realized her face was pale. "Are you all right?" he asked, alarmed.

She smiled, her eyes warm and filled with what he realized, with shock, was love. "I draw my energy from my destiny. When you are in harm's way, so, too, am I." She picked up the hem of her gown as she stepped onto the stone ledge. "To fight that kind of evil is to know real fatigue." She laughed.

He flinched as she unhooked one of his manacles from the upright, freeing his wrist.

"Galen will pay for his part in this," he snarled as his right wrist came free and he gazed down at the torn flesh. "I'll never forgive him."

"But you will, Conar. When the consequences of this night have real meaning for you, you will." Her voice was growing weaker.

Conar reached out for her as she slumped, picking her up gently in his arms, cradling her against his chest. Her eyelids were closing in slumber and she nestled closer to him, bringing her arms around his neck.

"Thank you," he whispered to her sleeping face and lowered his head to place a soft, feather-gentle kiss on her forehead. He carried her up the stairs, vowing to her silent form once more that he would not forget what had occurred that night.

Chapter Nine

King Gerren Yuri McGregor of Serenia, the father of Conar and Galen, was a robust man with the passion and stamina of a man half his age. He had sired many illegitimate sons on the more than willing servants and free women of his homeland; and although he had sired no daughters, a failing he bitterly regretted, he was keenly proud of most of his offspring.

His wife, Queen Moira Marie Hesar, had given him four sons: one for each Zone, he joked; but his mistresses had given him nearly two dozen healthy and vigorous ones. Only one such offspring did not bear the unmistakable stamp of the McGregor line.

That man was Conar's second eldest brother, Jah-Ma-El.

No one ever referred to the man as King Gerren's son, for that man refused to claim his father. Neither did they refer to him as Prince Galen's brother, nor Prince Coron's, nor Prince Dyllon's. And the rest of the illegitimate sons allowed no one to call him their brother, either. If he was spoken of at all, he was simply referred to as Prince Conar's bastard brother. The reason for this was simple: Conar, and Conar alone, claimed the man as kin.

But once, long ago, he had nearly cost Conar his life....

* * * *

It was in the Monastery of the Domination, shortly before Jah-Ma-El's twelfth birthday, that he met the boy he was told to call the Chosen.

Coming into the sacristy late one afternoon, Jah-Ma-El happened upon a small blond-haired child who sat huddled in a corner of the room, his eyes red from crying. His thin little arms were clasped tightly around stick-legs and the boy was trembling violently beneath the coarse wool of his brown robe. A vivid streak of bright red was stamped on the boy's left cheek and Jah-Ma-El knew from personal experience such a mark could only have been caused by a man's large hand.

A great pity welled up inside Jah-Ma-El. He had seen other such boys about the Abbey, some, like this one, bravely trying to show courage they did not feel. Most had eyes that were dull and lifeless, accepting of their plight, oblivious to those around them, their pain turned inward; but none had the snapping fire in them that was evident in this little boy's tear-stained face.

"Are you all right?" Jah-Ma-El whispered, looking about to see if any adults were close.

"He slapped me," the boy said through teeth clenched.

Jah-Ma-El shrugged. "It happens to all of us," he said gently.

A brief flicker of resentment flitted across the boy's face. "I've never been hit before."

"You'll get used to it," Jah-Ma-El answered and had been rewarded with a miserable look of pure fear from the child.

"He should not hit me." The little chin rose. "Not me."

Jah-Ma-El shrugged again.

"They lied to my father," the little boy muttered.

"It's a way of life here."

The child started to say something else and stopped, his eyes going up, past Jah-Ma-El's shoulders. The blue orbs dilated with terror.

A heavy-set man, his shoulder-length brown hair swinging angrily around his shoulders, descended upon the blond boy with a mighty bellow of rage. "So, this is where you've been hiding, you little bastard!" He reached out a huge paw of a hand and grasped the little boy's arm in a punishing grip that made the child yelp. "The Master will see to you!"

Jah-Ma-El had been knocked out of the big man's way as he dragged the frightened little boy behind him. Standing helplessly by, watching the boy look at him as he was pulled viciously along the corridor, Jah-Ma-El had gazed into tearful, terrified blue eyes that sought his for strength. He willed courage to the boy, wishing with all his heart that there were a way he could help.

He mentioned the encounter to his instructor, Keil Jabyur, that evening. He had been unable to get the boy out of his mind and had worried about the child all day. As he spoke, he saw his teacher's face pale.

"Stay away from him, Jah-Ma-El." Jabyur ran a hand over his thick face. "The boy belongs to Kaileel Tohre, and Tohre doesn't want the child near any of his kin."

Jah-Ma-El had been sewing one of the priest's ceremonial robes, his nimble fingers making an almost invisible repair in the rent hem. At his benefactor's words, he glanced up. "Kin?"

Jabyur sat heavily on his cot and put his head in his hands. A thick shock of pure white hair, combed straight back from a high, wide forehead, was being threaded through with pudgy, strong-looking fingers. Jabyur shook his head. He was debating with himself whether to tell the boy who the child was. Finally, seeing no real harm in telling, no reason not to, he raised his head and looked into Jah-Ma-El's confused brown eyes. It was a mistake that ultimately caused the instructor's untimely death.

"The boy is the little Prince, Jah-Ma-El. He is King Gerren's firstborn, Conar. He's been brought here to train for the priesthood." A look of disgust spread over Jabyur's pleasant, florid face. "But Tohre has other plans for the child."

Jah-Ma-El laid down his sewing and stared at his teacher. "My brother?" he asked and saw Jabyur nod. Jah-Ma-El had seen, but never before met, let alone spoken to, one of his many brothers. He was both thrilled and worried. "Why do you look so upset, Master?"

"He should not be here, Jah-Ma-El," the man answered, getting up and staring into the dark outside his window. "He is the Heir-Apparent. If Tohre needed one of the royal sons, he should have taken the second boy, Galen."

"His father does not know he is here, does he, Master?"

"No, but I have sent a messenger to tell him. The little Prince should never have been brought to this vile place."

Sleep was long in coming that night for Jah-Ma-El. He lay on his cot and thought of the young boy, his brother, sequestered somewhere within the Abbey. He worried that the boy was well, feared that he was not. He willed his spirit to link with the boy's, but it was no use. The magic he had learned so far from Jabyur was not strong enough to detect the boy's whereabouts and he was positive his reassurances, sent out through the dark night, never reached the little boy.

About a week before Jabyur's untimely death, Jah-Ma-El saw boy once more. They were crossing, from opposite ends, an arched footbridge that led from the Training Rooms to the Temple. There was stiffness to the boy's walk as he neared Jah-Ma-El and the older boy knew without being told there were probably fresh bruises and welts beneath the brown wool robe that covered the boy from neck to bare toes. Jah-Ma-El halted in the middle of the footpath and waited for the little blond boy to reach him.

The boy was six, no more than seven, yet he walked with the slumped shoulders and lowered head of a man ten times that age. His attention was on the boards over which he walked and he was startled as Jah-Ma-El spoke to him.

"Are you all right?" he whispered.

"I'll live," was the tired reply.

Jah-Ma-El watched the boy's back as he kept walking. He had to speak, he had to let him know. "You aren't alone, Your Grace," he said a little louder so the boy could hear.

The boy stopped and looked over his shoulder. "You called out to me the other night, didn't you?"

"You heard me?" Jah-Ma-El was amazed.

"I needed your strength just then."

"You will always have it, Your Grace." Jah-Ma-El felt tears in his eyes as the boy tried desperately to smile his thanks, but the tired little mouth would not budge.

"Who are you?" the boy asked. "I would know your name, friend."

Jabyur had strongly cautioned him against telling the boy who he was, but Jah-Ma-El felt a need he could not verbalize to anyone, not even himself. It was an ache, a desire so strong, so clear in his mind; he was blind to anything save the need to reach out to this person who, through the will of the gods, was his brother. Every nerve in his body screamed against him answering, cautioning him, but Jah-Ma-El ignored the warnings. He felt a greater need than he had ever felt to know the warmth of kinship, the balm of brotherhood.

"Your brother," he said at last.

A fleeting smile appeared finally on the sad little face. "Another one?" he asked in a feigned, exasperated voice. "Papa leads a merry life, doesn't he?"

Jah-Ma-El answered the smile with a flash of happiness. "I'm afraid so."

A loud shout from behind Jah-Ma-El brought both boys to immediate silence. They turned away from one another and began walking again. Jah-Ma-El was startled when a soft whisper of words floated back to him from the far end of the footbridge: "Take care of yourself, my brother."

Spinning around, Jah-Ma-El saw only a blur of brown robe disappearing into the Training Room. His throat closed up with pain.

"My brother," he repeated softly, turning the word over in his mind, letting it flow around his lips. It was a wondrous word, a magical word to Jah-Ma-El that could chase away the very beasts from the pits.

Several days later, on a cold, wintry morning, with snow falling heavily about the Great Abbey, obscuring the tall mountain range upon which the massive black stone monastery sat, Jabyur took ill. His coughs were racking bursts of straining agony; his flesh was hot, his eyes filled with a strange yellow matter. He lingered on for two days, his belly cramping, his flesh becoming clammy and slick to the touch; and on the third day of his sudden illness, he took one shuddering breath and then laid still, his eyes wide and staring at the ceiling.

"Need we worry about some illness here, Milord?" one of the priests asked the Healer who arrived to sign Jabyur's death certificate.

"His tongue caused his death," the Healer quipped. He turned to Jah-Ma-El. "Let that be a lesson to you, boy."

Jah-Ma-El had wept bitterly over the man's cooling body as the priests prepared Jabyur for cremation. He sat in stony silence as another High Priest, a man named Felix Hebert, came to tell him that he would be sent to train under a new priest. He listened to the High Priest's smug words with little thought to what his life would be like from that day forward. He had no need to ask; he knew. His life would be a living hell.

He was not disappointed.

Late one night, as his body ached from the rough abuse he had suffered during the day, and shivered from the sadistic, vile attention it had received that night, Jah-Ma-El was awakened by a small hand covering his mouth. He came awake in sheer terror, relief flooding through his soul as he looked up into shiny blue orbs also watering with fear. When the little hand was removed, Jah-Ma-El instinctively reached for it, tightly holding the chill fingers in his own.

"You shouldn't be here, Your Grace," he whispered, more afraid for his brother than for himself.

"It doesn't matter," the little boy said. He squeezed the hand holding his. "And don't give me no gods-be-damned title. My name is Conar, but my other brothers call me Coni, so I guess you should, too."

"They will punish you if they find you here." Jah-Ma-El sat up in bed, surprised when the boy climbed onto the cot beside him, snuggling against the warmth of Jah-Ma-El's thin chest.

"What can they do to me that they haven't already done?"

No amount of reasoning could make the boy leave. He stayed for over an hour, his hand clasped snugly within Jah-Ma-El's larger one. It was as though he needed the same companionship that Jah-Ma-El had craved over the years: the need of brotherly loyalty and love.

Every chance he got, the boy would come to Jah-Ma-El's cell, creeping in late at night, snuggling close, and they would speak of things outside the Abbey's black walls. Sometimes the boy would have to be lifted onto the cot, for his body was bruised and battered so badly he could not climb. Sometimes he couldn't speak at all, for his throat would be raw and hoarse from his screams. At such times, Jah-Ma-El would carry the burden of the conversation, telling tales of their homeland and of their joint ancestry. Sometimes the boy would fall asleep and Jah-Ma-El, fearful of discovery, would gently awaken him and reluctantly send him back to his own cell.

It was during just such a night, a night when Jah-Ma-El had fallen asleep, that Kaileel Tohre entered Jah-Ma-El's cell and the blond boy had been jerked viciously from his protective arms.

"How dare you!" Tohre screamed at the top of his lungs, his heavy hand slamming painfully into the little boy's cheek.

Jah-Ma-El had leapt from the bed, his arms flailing at the tall blond man who abused his brother, the man who ruthlessly slapped the little boy so hard blood spurted from his nose.

"Let him go! Let my brother go!" He kicked at Tohre's shin and was rewarded with a slap that made him hear bells. Jah-Ma-El slid down the wall as Tohre's heavy signet ring connected with his jaw.

"Don't hurt him, Kaileel!" Conar cried, pleaded. "I'll be good. I promise. I'll do what you say. Just don't hurt my brother!"

Through a fog of pain, Jah-Ma-El heard Kaileel Tohre's roar of outrage. He flinched, not from any pain he expected to be visited upon himself, but from the hard hit Tohre gave his brother.

"Your brother? You have no brother, my Prince!" A heavy, sarcastic laugh rang out through the small cell. "You have nothing save what I grant you!"

Jah-Ma-El saw his brother thrust into the arms of another priest and he felt the toe of Kaileel Tohre's sandal dig painfully into his ribs. He doubled over, gasping for breath, his eyes blurring to everything around him. He flopped about the floor as Tohre kicked him, pummeled him with closed fists about his neck and shoulders. From a distant he could hear Conar's screams of pleading, but soon all he saw was a red fog of pain and heard nothing but his own whimpers of agony. So severely was he beaten, he urinated blood for nearly a week. He could not stir from his cot, could not lift his arms to feed himself, one having been broken during the beating, and could not lift his head to take a sip of water. He lay at the mercy of one of the Order's physicians until he could be moved to the stables where he was put to work among the animals to be slaughtered.

Jah-Ma-El's life became a living nightmare after he was well enough to return to the Abbey Proper for further training. Gone was the protection of Keil Jabyur. Gone was the cruel Trainer who had physically abused him every night. Gone, too, was any semblance of humanity. Tohre turned him over to the men of the Order for their insatiable pleasure.

Not long after, Jah-Ma-El tried to kill himself rather than suffer the horrible abuse visited nightly upon him and the petty tortures performed during the day.

Secreting a length of hemp from the stables, Jah-Ma-El managed to loop one end over a high peg set in the stone wall of his cell. Placing the other end around his neck, Jah-Ma-El thought of his brother. He whispered Conar's name, tearfully, bidding his brother goodbye, and then he stepped off his cot, kicking away from the wall, and tried to strangle himself. He would have succeeded if Conar had not come running in, having heard his name. Desperate to save Jah-Ma-El's life, he began to scream at the top of his lungs for help.

Gripping Jah-Ma-El's thrashing legs with his small arms, Conar managed to keep his brother aloft until help arrived. He watched helplessly as the men lowered his brother to the floor, pushed against the thin chest as they tried to get wind back into his lungs. His childish voice begged Jah-Ma-El not to give up.

"Don't leave me, Jah-Ma-El," he cried, tears flowing down his cheeks. "I don't want you to die, big brother. I need you. Don't leave me in this place all alone!"

Jah-Ma-El could hear the pitiful sobs as though from far, far away. He wanted to ignore the pain in those sobbing words, but he could not. He strained hard to hear, to breathe, to live, and he made a rash promise to the gods he regretted all his life.

"Let me live, Merciful Alel," he pleaded. "Let me live for Conar's sake. I promise to live for him if for no other."

Even during his initiation, when his soul was taken from him in a ceremony so evil and perverse Jah-Ma-El erased it from his mind, he kept his promise: he had lived for no other reason than because his brother had not wanted him to die. No matter how awful his existence, how horrible the abuse heaped upon him, Jah-Ma-El struggled through each day with the knowledge that his promise to Conar meant the boy would not be left alone with the evil that had become their lives.

Jah-Ma-El left the Great Abbey eleven years later at the age of twenty-three. In all that time, he never once saw his brother again. His last sight of Conar had been as the boy was being dragged away, his terrified face peering anxiously around Tohre's flowing robes as the door to Jah-Ma-El's cell had been slammed shut. He knew only that his brother had barely survived a harsh beating of his own for having saved Jah-Ma-El's life, but other than that, nothing else was said of the little Prince.

Having been warned by Kaileel Tohre not to mention Conar McGregor or what had happened at the Great Abbey under penalty of a horrible death, Jah-Ma-El would be circumspect in questioning the men of the Order about his brother's whereabouts. It wasn't until the day he left the Abbey to be sent as the Domination's representative at Norus Keep, that he learned his brother had left the Great Abbey five years earlier without being initiated into the Brotherhood. Conar had been there seven years.

Elation had filled Jah-Ma-El's soul, for he knew the little brother he had grown to love so fiercely would never have survived the initiation he, himself, had endured. He knew Conar would have made no pacts with the men of the Domination. He would have suffered the terrible tortures that Jah-Ma-El had experienced, but he would have died rather than sign away his soul to such men. Jah-Ma-El had wanted to die during the process, but his promise, his desire to live for Conar's sake, had kept him alive through the most vile of punishments, the most degrading rituals.

* * * *

Sitting now in the Conjuring Room of Norus Keep, a wide, circular room with blood-red walls and ebony floor with a crimson pentagram drawn upon its shining surface, Galen McGregor gnashed his teeth and glared at Jah-Ma-El. "How the hell could you not have known she was a sorceress?" he shouted, turning a hateful stare to the tall man kneeling beside his chair.

"She is most powerful, Your Grace," the man whined. "She hid her power well." He flinched as Galen drew back a hand to hit him.

"Cur! You are trained to sense these things! Did the Master waste his time with you at the Great Abbey?"

The Prince's palm connected with his unshaven jaw, slamming him sideways into the thick stone. Putting up a shaky hand to wipe away the blood from his torn lip, the thin man cowered before his half-brother. "I did not sense anything, Your Grace. Not even the Master realized--"

"Do not speak of the Master to me, you sniveling bastard! If it were not for your bumbling, he would have known who and what she was!" Galen shifted in the throne-like gilt chair in which he sat. "You have made matters worse. Conar will know we tried to steal his blasted soul this eve."

Jah-Ma-El lowered his eyes so his half-brother would not see the anger and rebellion written there. Despite his trembling body and wildly beating heart, the sorcerer did not fear Galen McGregor nearly as much as he feared what Galen had tried to do this night. That the Prince had failed, and failed dismally, lessened somewhat the quickening terror in Jah-Ma-El's weak heart.

"So," Galen sneered, "what can you do to correct this oversight?"

Jah-Ma-El eased himself from the floor and stood before his half-brother, his body trembling.

"I can try to neutralize her, Your Grace. I can try, but I can make no promises where the Daughters of the Multitude are concerned."

"I want no promises from you, Jah-Ma-El! I want results!" Galen leaned forward in the chair. "I want her unable to help him again. Do you understand?"

"I can try to kill her...." Jah-Ma-El jerked away as Galen leapt to his feet in rage. Crossing his thin arms over his face to avoid another hard slap, the sorcerer whimpered with terror.

"Fool!" Galen bellowed, grabbing Jah-Ma-El's robe in his fists, shaking him hard. "I would as much allow you to do that as I would allow Conar to be killed!"

Jah-Ma-El spoke before he thought. His own safety meant nothing compared to Conar's well-being. "My brother is in greater danger from you than from any other source."

Galen shoved the thinner man away, then wiped his hands down his own robe to erase the touch of Jah-Ma-El's clothing from his flesh. His lip curled in disgust. "I would be careful if I were you, Jah-Ma-El," he whispered. "Don't forget to whom it is you speak."

"You know They would murder him if the Master but gave the word," Jah-Ma-El cried, his eyes brimming with tears. "And there may come a day when the Master can not stop Them and Conar will die horribly."

Galen sneered. "I will not allow that to happen. The Master will not allow that to happen."

Jah-Ma-El shook his head, trembling, sick to his stomach. "What would you care if my brother did die? You want his crown. What do you care about the man?"

A wild stab of fury shot through Galen. "Aye, I want the crown, and I will have it; but I will have Conar where I want him, too. My revenge on him will best be savored with the man alive and knowing it is I who wields the power in this land!"

"He has never done anything to you," Jah-Ma-El protested, gathering courage from his devotion to Conar.

"He came first into this world! That is a sin I can not and will not forgive!"

Chancing a furtive look at his half-brother, Jah-Ma-El was struck again with the certainty that Galen McGregor was quite mad. "What would happen if I did nothing, Your Grace? Would it be so bad to let our brother live in peace?"

Galen's face turned as hard as flint. He reached into his robe and withdrew a black jade vial. Holding out the vial to Jah-Ma-El, he smiled and the smile was as evil as the slime beneath the pits of hell. "I have a guarantee here that you will do exactly as I order, you filthy bastard."

Jah-Ma-El made a feeble grab for the vial, but Galen snatched it out of his reach. He cringed as Galen walked to a burning cauldron of coals that sat in the center of the room and held the vial over it.

"Give me reason to deposit this in the fire, you cur, and I will do it!" Galen lowered the black cylinder closer to the burning coals and watched as Jah-Ma-El's face broke out in a sudden sweat, his skin turning red as though he, himself, were being held over the coals.

"Please, Your Grace," Jah-Ma-El begged, his body burning. He was suffocating, unable to breathe. His hair felt as though it were singeing. "I will do what I can!"

"You will do as I say!" Galen replaced the vial inside his ceremonial robe. "I can promise you that, Jah-Ma-El!"

Mournfully, the sorcerer watched his hated brother leave the room. Jah-Ma-El's very soul was housed inside that jade vial and he would never have it returned to him. It was the hold the Domination had over him, and every unwilling fool, who served Them. It was a guarantee that Their wishes would be carried out despite the conjurer's own desires.

Jah-Ma-El looked around the Conjuring Room with its black marble floor adorned with the seven-sided star of the god Raphian, the Bringer of Storms, the Destroyer of Men's Souls. His gaze went to the huge wrought iron cauldron on criss-crossed tripod legs before the low jade green altar. The hissing coals within the cauldron gave off the only light in the room, sending shadows over the dripping, moist walls. He didn't look at the altar, with its lifeless victim staring with sightless eyes at the horrors that had been done here this eve.

He groaned, sliding in a crumpled heap to the cold floor. He covered his face with his hands and wept bitterly, his thin shoulders shaking beneath the voluminous folds of his green robe.

His magic was impotent against a Daughter of the Multitude; as impotent as Galen's claim to the throne. There would be little he could do to neutralize this woman's great power. Had she not summoned forth Bastus' playthings? Those cat-like entities that sprang up from the cracks in the floor? Only a powerful conjuress could accomplish such a feat.

Jah-Ma-El was fair at his own craft but his heart had never been in the Conjuring of the Red. His strength was not in the black magic that traveled the darker paths and he knew it. What magic he possessed came from a lighter realm. His was the power of the Blue Way, but he, alone, knew that, and Jah-Ma-El used what power he did possess to keep the Brotherhood of the Domination from suspecting. His life depended upon Them never finding out.

He lay on the slick floor and curled into a fetal ball. He wedged his hands between his knees and stared into the blackness of the Conjuring Room. What could he do? Was there some magic he could spread over

Conar that would assure his brother's protection? Some talisman he could use to ward away evil?

If there was, Jah-Ma-El had not found it. Search as hard as he could, the only item that had worked so far against the Domination's incessant demand to weaken Conar had been the appearance of this girl, this sorceress who had come to his brother's aid. He had spent many a sleepless night conjuring, begging help from the gods. His pleas had at last worked and help had come from an unexpected source. He was stunned that help had sprung from the Multitude, but that was the gods' choice, not his.

But had he made matters worse? Had his calling forth a protection for his brother brought further harm upon Conar? If so, Jah-Ma-El could not live with it. All he had ever wanted was to protect Conar, to have his love and respect, and now he may have caused his beloved brother irreparable harm. If that were the case, Jah-Ma-El knew he could not live knowing he had brought more pain into Conar's life.

A year after leaving the Monastery, Jah-Ma-El was expected to help in the Domination's plan to destroy Conar McGregor. Ensconced as Chief Sorcerer at Norus, Jah-Ma-El was to carry out Prince Galen's plan. He never considered the man to be his brother, none of Galen's kin readily admitted their relation to him; but with Galen in possession of the vial that housed Jah-Ma-El's soul, the older man had little choice in the things he was forced to do at Norus Keep.

Galen took great delight in using Jah-Ma-El against Conar. He knew how the older man felt about the younger. Keeping them apart each time Conar came to Norus immensely pleased Galen, for he could see the wistful expression on Jah-Ma-El's thin face each time Conar's appearance was announced.

"You'll never set eyes on him in the flesh again," Galen had promised and had kept that promise.

But Jah-Ma-El smiled as he stared across the Conjuring Room at the burning brazier. The Chosen Child of the Sea had come now and things would begin to change. His smile faded. He hoped for Conar's sake the change was for the better.

\* \* \* \*

Liza lay awake in her bed. She could feel the influence of another magic-sayer in the keep. She was lost in concentration, fingering the rune stone around her slim neck. The man meant her no harm, she was sure of it. He meant Conar no harm, either. But someone at Norus Keep surely had meant the Prince Regent harm this night.

Her eyes opened wide as the unknown sorcerer's thoughts lightly touched hers. "Who are you?" she whispered into the dark room.

"A friend, milady," came the soft, gentle reply.

Liza relaxed. There had been truth and reassurance in that soft sigh.

She turned over and gripped her pillow to her. Somewhere Conar McGregor had a powerful and deadly enemy, else the man would not have been taken to the vile dungeon. She meant to find out who he was and just how powerful he could be.

"He is called Kaileel Tohre," spoke the gently invading voice.

"How dangerous is he?" she asked, her lips never moving.

"He is an evil beyond knowing."

Try as she might, she could not get the disembodied voice to speak to her again. Finally, she swept her thoughts into Conar's room, assured that he slept soundly, peacefully. She could hear his even breathing.

Content that he was safe, she closed her eyes and slept.

\* \* \* \*

Galen was not sleeping.

He sat staring into the fire. A full glass of brandy sat untouched where it had been placed on the table beside him. He had ignored it then and ignored it now, even though the strong vapors of the peach liquor wafted gently under his nose, beckoning.

For the first time in his life, Galen McGregor did not need alcohol, drugs, or voyeurism to excite him. He leaned back in his chair, crossed one bare ankle over the other, and stretched his legs toward the fire.

Tonight, everything had changed.

His thoughts confused him. Bewildered him. He wanted something he had never thought he would ever want in his lifetime--a woman. He felt something he thought to never feel--desire for a woman.

And not just any woman, he thought with wonder. This woman was special, unique. She was a powerful sorceress who he knew could rival the Master, himself. Had not the man left, an unaccustomed fear glazing his pale eyes? Her name was Liza. She was not only powerful, she was beautiful.

Beautiful and should be left alone to be dealt with by the Brotherhood, he thought fleetingly. Galen shuddered.

The thought of Liza at the mercy of his own kind sent a spasm of pain through a heart he thought was long dead to love.

He wanted her out of harm's way, unable to help Conar, but he wanted her unmarked by the same vengeance the Domination had planned for his twin. He knew only one way to accomplish that.

A hard shudder ran through him and he grabbed the brandy, gulping it down in one harsh swallow. The fiery brew scorched his dry throat, but he hardly noticed.

Yelling for his servant, he called for his horse to be saddled.

Chapter Ten

Liza woke early the next morning. She stretched, turned over, and snuggled into the fleecy softness of the down comforter. A teasing smile spread over her lips as she listened to Gezelle's soft snores.

Liza sighed and thought of the man sleeping across the hall.

He had been a most pleasant surprise at the Hound and Stag. His strength and agility with the sword had impressed her. His handsome face had certainly gained her immediate attention. His reluctance to marry, sight unseen, the Princess Anya of Oceania had amused her. His devotion to his duty had also impressed her. His avowal to carry out that duty despite grave misgivings and true unhappiness concerned her. She had looked at him with something akin to awe as he told her it was his honor at stake. Few men let honor get in the way of their personal happiness; especially so members of the royalty.

Honor was something Liza understood. And admired in a man.

Thinking of him as she had first seen him, made Liza grin. His blue eyes had been sparkling with some devilish humor and the corners of his sensual mouth were lifted in the most wicked grin she had ever seen. He looked like a little boy hiding, playing a prank on someone who was not going to like it.

There had been no mistaking the raw sexual power emitting from him as he leaned against the stall. That careless power had no doubt wrecked many a lady's virtue, she thought at the time. The negligent way in which he leaned had told Liza the man was as sure of himself as he was of the glistening blade he was doodling with on the ground.

He had fought just as she knew he would. She had as much confidence in his ability with his sword as he did. The outcome was a foregone conclusion on her part until the sneaky innkeeper had come along and her intervention became necessary.

What she had felt when she first touched him had surprised her with a tremor all the way down her arm, through her chest, and into her belly where it settled in a spasm of intense sexual arousal. Having felt that immense sensation, having touched him, she knew there was no turning back. He would be hers or never belong to another woman. She meant to see that he forgot any other woman had ever existed, including the bitch in Oceania.

The thought of the Princess Anya brought a frown to her lovely face. That was one problem that was going to have to be resolved on the way to Boreas Keep. She turned to gaze at the canopy above. Norus Keep was one problem; the Oceanian Princess was another.

Her face darkened as she remembered her first sight of Norus. When they reached the summit overlooking the keep, she had had a chilling premonition of an evil so consummate it seeped to the marrow of her bones. Her instincts had screamed at her that here was one of the Three Gateways to the Abyss; it was one of the portals through which the

Domination conjured its vile minions. She had let her ego get in the way of reasoning as she thought back on it. So confident had she been that nothing could hurt either her or Conar if they were together, it had almost ended tragically in the Norus dungeon. She had been forewarned; she had ignored the sixth sense that had kept her alive all these years.

The thought of something, anything, happening to Conar McGregor, sent a deep chill through her heart. She had to be more careful. She had to consider everyone and everything an enemy until they were proven otherwise.

Thoughts along that line brought her attention to Galen McGregor.

He had not fooled her with his politeness and manners. The shock that had gone through her when they touched had been nothing like the shock when she had touched his twin. Touching Galen had left her skin clammy and cold and needing washing. There was evil in the man and she was determined to keep as far away from him as she could. His aura had enveloped her with a black, sorcery-tainted stench that had left a strange metallic taste in her mouth just as her first sight of Norus Keep had. Such an experience was a sure warning that the keep was steeped in the mire being brewed by the Domination.

A noise from the hallway brought her attention back to the present. She laughed at Conar's loud demands and braced herself on her elbows. She looked at Gezelle, who was awake and stirring. The servant girl's sleepy eyes were puffy and glazed. Liza grinned.

"We'd better get up before his lord and master comes pounding on our door, 'Zelle."

"Aye, Milady." Gezelle yawned, reluctantly throwing aside the blanket covering her. "I'll see to your morning bath."

"No need." Liza tossed aside her own covers. She swung her long legs from the bed and stood, stretching. "I'll just wash my face and get dressed."

Gezelle nodded, another yawn being the only answer she could give. The girl bent over the glowing coals and stirred them, adding a log or two to the fire as she tried to come awake.

Liza was finished with her dressing when the loud pounding came at their door.

"Liza?" The pounding came again. "Get up! We don't have all the blasted day for you to primp, woman!"

"What'd I tell you?" Liza grinned. She tiptoed to the door and slipped her fingers around the knob with one hand as she gently eased back the bolt with the other. She waited a second and then yanked open the door.

Conar, his arm raised in mid-strike, almost tumbled into the room. His mouth was open with what would have been another loud demand, but seeing Liza's smug expression, sweeping his gaze down her already clothed form, and looking past her to Gezelle's merry face, he snapped shut his lips and glared at her.

"Are we ready to leave, Milord?" Liza asked sweetly.

Conar's eyes were stormy. "Aye."

"We're ready when you are, Milord."

He glared at her for a moment, not sure if he should say anything, thought he should not, and then turned on his heel, striding away with his shoulders humped in the confines of his brown leather jacket.

Liza looked at Gezelle and winked. It was going to be a typical Conar day.

* * * *

"Think they're glad we're gone?" Conar asked, his voice filled with anger.

Liza shrugged. "It certainly looks that way, Milord." She glanced across the road at him. "I know I am glad to be leaving."

Conar grunted, feeling in a like manner. He put up his hand to swat at a horsefly and noticed something odd on his left wrist. He stared at it, a frown on his handsome face.

"Is there something wrong?" Liza asked. Her lovely face filled with worry.

He held out his arm to her much as a little boy would. "I don't know how I did that."

Liza glanced at the raw, scraped flesh, a deep purple bruise circling the wrist. "In the fight. Remember? At the tavern." Her eyes drew his; held on. She could see a memory forming in his mind.

There was a slightly confused look on his face as he lowered his gaze to the wound. "I guess so," he said, trying to remember exactly how he had hurt himself. He remembered the fight; the wound just seemed to elude him for the moment. He shrugged and looked back at Liza. "I remember."

Liza smiled. "I'll give you some salve for it." She breathed a sigh of relief when he nodded absently and looked away again. The last thing he needed was to remember being chained in his brother's dungeon during the night.

Gezelle stifled a mighty yawn as she sat limply in her saddle. She still suffered the effects of the wine she had consumed the night before. Mentally reminding herself to never drink wine again just in case that was the reason she felt encased in cotton batting, she turned her attention to the passing scenery to keep awake.

Trees were swaying in a brisk breeze; the day overcast; the sky a gunmetal gray, heavy with the threat of rain. The air was thick and oppressive; the earth smelled of damp fertility. It was the kind of day when cows gathered in huddles and birds scurried to the closest trees.

They had left the dunes behind and were steadily climbing into the foothills of the Serenian Mountain Range. With every passing mile, the temperature dropped a degree or two.

"Are you still with us, Mam'selle?" Conar called as he turned in the saddle to see Gezelle nodding off, swaying a little on her small pony.

The servant grabbed for her pommel, pulling herself upright, opening her eyes wide in order to get them focused. "Aye, Your Grace," she called, her face one huge swatch of red.

"If you tumble off that nag, Mam'selle, you will stay where you land!" he promised.

Out of sorts, Liza thought with disgust. Out of sorts and taking it out on Gezelle. He had barely spoken to either her or 'Zelle since leaving Norus and now, when he did, all he could do was snap.

"I won't stop if she falls off that pony," he said petulantly as he caught Liza's frown of pique. His lower lip thrust out in challenge.

"I'm sure you wouldn't," she retorted and looked away.

"Be assured, I won't," he added with emphasis and cocked a stare at Gezelle who was sitting tall and straight and attentive in her saddle. He snorted at her pleasant smile and then jerked around.

He's just hungry, Gezelle thought as she stared at the back of his golden head. She giggled and looked down at the pommel. She wondered if the prince was at all concerned that she had seen him naked the evening before. His nudity might not have bothered him, she thought, but it was with her every mile they traveled. She could recall every vivid detail of his bronzed body and the memory made her blush. Forcibly tearing her mind from wicked thoughts, she looked up and could tell by the way the prince sat his mount he was angry. To Gezelle's way of thinking, he had every right to be, considering how he had been treated at Norus.

When morning had come, Prince Galen had not come down to see if they had spent a restful night. Nor had he come to wish them a pleasant journey to Boreas. The servants had not offered, indeed, had not prepared a morning repast. So thunderous had been Prince Conar's shout, the entire keep had all but come to a standstill. Even the surliest of servants had backed away from that royal anger with fear on their stubborn faces.

"If you will give us an hour, Your Grace...." one of the cooks had ventured before being shouted down.

"You think I have all day to wait for your fires to be stoked, woman?" he had howled.

"Well, no, Your Grace, but--"

"But, hell!" he had screamed before flinging his hand around the gathered group of retainers. Promising retaliation, he had shouted at a nearby servant to have their mounts readied.

The three had ridden out of the Norus courtyard with bellies rumbling in protest.

"Ignore me, will they?" Conar had mumbled as Liza and Gezelle ran to match his long-legged stride to the stables. "Keep me waiting? Not feed me?" His voice was a death knell of fury. "We'll just see about that! Oh, yes! Let's see Galen explain this to his King!"

The Prince had been mulish and sullen as the stable boy brought their mounts. Scowling the whole time, he had obviously been making a mental note to inform his father of both his twin's lack of respect and his servants' lack of fealty to their future King. Somewhat mollified to be able to cause his twin trouble, he swung into his saddle and waited for Liza and Gezelle to mount.

"Will you hurry?" he had snapped.

"Will you behave?" the Lady Liza had snapped right back at him.

Only the Master-at-Arms, Sir Belvoir, had nodded a farewell as they crossed the rotting drawbridge. He seemed to catch the Lady Liza's attention and she had smiled at him, nodding. Gezelle could have sworn a slight stretch had come upon the good knight's hard mouth, but he had turned away as the portcullis began to lower and Gezelle thought she had been mistaken. Sir Belvoir never smiled.

"It looks like we'll see rain before the day is out," Liza remarked now, gaining both Gezelle's and the Prince's attention.

Conar's head went back and he took in the lowering sky. "Aye, but no storm, if that's what bothers you," he snarled.

Liza felt like beaming the fool on his head. What bothered her most was his bruised ego. He was upset that his people had not bowed and crawled along on their bellies to him. Well, that wasn't exactly true, she thought with a grimace. The servants had been rude and sullen. They surely deserved whatever trouble Conar meant to give them; but she and Gezelle did not deserve to be treated with such disdain.

"No, I don't think there will be a storm, either," she said sweetly.

"Even if it does," he said, looking down his nose at her, "we will ride straight through!"

"Of course," Liza agreed, seeing him frown over her answer. "After all, we have cloaks."

Conar turned and glared at her, his face a study in frustration. It was obvious he was spoiling for a good fight. She could almost see the steam coming from his nostrils. If he was expecting the two of them to be a burden to him, he was going to be sadly mistaken.

They had traveled only a mile when the rain began. Still ten miles or so from the nearest tavern, a new establishment called the Briar's Hold, Conar informed the women that they would ride until they came to a more well-known tavern where accommodations might be better prepared.

"I've heard tell the place isn't even open yet," Conar said, remarking upon the new tavern.

"Whatever suits you, Milord," Liza answered and almost laughed at the jaundiced look he swept over her. " 'Zelle and I are just fine."

Their heavy cloaks were put on under the thick, spreading canopy of an old live oak. Snuggling into the oilcloth cloaks, they ventured once more into the steady cascade of cool water.

The roads were still passable, not yet the quagmires they would likely become. The air was warmer, not yet the frigid blast of arctic chill expected come nightfall. So, in the fading light, they traveled on, their heads bent against the onslaught of ever-increasing wind and rain.

A boom of distant thunder caught Liza's attention and she stretched her senses; probed; sought; evaluated. The rain was nature's way of cleansing the earth of man's foul corruption. This rain was nature-sent, not sorcery-induced. She relaxed with the knowledge and somewhat enjoyed the gentle rhythm of the rain's beat. Her main concern was Conar.

He was a miserable sight as he sat huddled on his big black destrier. His hair was plastered to his head and he looked fit to kill. She had a strong notion they would be stopping at the Briar's Hold whether the inn was ready to receive guests or not. As soon as that establishment was in sight, she was sure he would make some excuse to stop.

Conar felt like screaming. Having to travel with one woman was not to his liking; traveling with two was insanity; traveling in the rain with one woman was asking for trouble; traveling in the rain with two women was suicidal. He glanced at Liza and grinned wickedly.

The woman looked like a drowned cat. He turned to the road again. As soon as the sign for the Briar's Hold was in sight, she'd be begging for him to stop.

Conar's head snapped up when Liza sneezed. "Are you catching cold, woman?" There was challenge in his voice.

Liza ground her teeth behind a sweet smile. She shook her head in denial, not trusting herself to speak. He looked like a man with the burdens of the entire world on his shoulder and he wanted her to know it. She tried to stop it, but another sneeze blasted out.

"I suppose you want to stop at the Briar's Hold." He sounded disgusted, but Liza could see a gleam of hope in his blue eyes.

"Not unless you feel the need to, Milord. I am fine. Really."

"Gods-be-damned stubborn female!" he mumbled. He'd given her the opportunity to ask him to stop. Why the hell hadn't she taken it? He looked back at Gezelle. "How are you, Mam'selle?"

"Fine, Your Grace." Gezelle wondered why he looked so angry that she was all right.

Conar grunted with anger. He heard Liza sneeze and he pounced. "We can stop and get something hot to drink. That won't take long."

"Whatever you think best, Milord."

Hell! He thought. What was wrong with the woman? Gods-be-damned if he gave in first. He shouldn't have to. After all, they were the weaker ones, not him.

The only thing was, he was freezing to death in the rain, and he had to piss. He was light-headed from not having eaten much the night before, nothing this morning and he had to piss! Water was running down the back of his cloak and he was sitting in a cold puddle of it as it collected under the seat of his leather pants. The thought of that made his bladder throb. By the gods, he had to piss!

"If you're hungry, Milord," Liza ventured, "perhaps you could get something to eat at the new tavern." She looked into his hopeful eyes, knew he was waiting for her to plead with him to stop. She smiled, thinking she'd bite off her tongue before she did. "I know you must be very uncomfortable."

What the hell did she mean by that? He seethed. Were not she and the servant girl just as uncomfortable? He twisted around to look at Gezelle, confident the servant would ask him to stop. "Do you wish to stop, Mam'selle? Are you hungry?" Only Liza could see the expectation on his face.

"No, Your Grace. I can wait."

Conar spun around and faced the roadway. It took every ounce of his strength to bite back the angry remarks. Women were the problem with the entire world. They were more trouble than they would ever be worth. They wreaked havoc wherever they went so that a man could never have even one day's peace.

"If you wish to stop, Milord...." Liza paused as another sneeze came.

A wild gleam shot from Conar's triumphant eyes and he pounced again as Gezelle also sneezed.

"We will stop at the gods-be-damned tavern whether I like it or not!" he told Liza. "I need no sick females on this trip!"

"Whatever pleases you, Milord," Liza answered, hiding her face from him.

"Gods-be-damned sick females are worse than well ones and well ones are bad enough! It will delay us, but I suppose it can't be helped. If it were just me, I'd ride on, but you women can't be expected to have the same vigorous constitution."

Liza could have shot him through with her crossbow. "We are capable of riding out the storm, Milord."

"I will not have you sneezing and sniffling, woman! It is ... is...." He searched for the right word.

"Distracting?" Liza prompted, her lips twitching.

"Aye, very distracting!"

Liza glanced at Gezelle and winked. Like she had told the servant girl, you had to put a man in his place, and keep him there, if you wanted any peace in this world. But she twisted the dagger just a little so he'd realize it was he who was giving in, not her.

"I guess it will be all right if we spend the day at the tavern; wait out the rain," she said.

Conar puffed out his chest. "I said nothing about spending the entire day there, Mam'selle! We will get something to eat and then ride out!"

\* \* \* \*

No sooner had they entered the tavern than the sky opened up with a virtual torrent of rain that ran in thick rivers over the roadways and blew hard against the windows. The air turned as frigid as a deep, dark January night and the wind howled with banshee force among the eaves.

"Damn it," Conar snarled as the rain came harder. "Damn it, damn it, damn it!"

"When do you think we will be able to ride out?" Liza asked in the calmest, sweetest voice she could as the innkeeper and his wife set about preparing a meal for the travelers.

Conar turned stony eyes to her. "Does it look like we'll be able to ride out, woman?"

Liza shrugged. "If you'd rather stay...."

"What the hell choice do I have?"

He stomped away, his fists clenched at his side and Liza looked at Gezelle. The servant girl was hiding a wide smile behind her slim hand. She, too, knew they'd be spending the night at the Briar's Hold.

Not at all prepared as yet for visitors, the new innkeeper, and his wife did all they could to make their guests comfortable, but the linens were still damp as they were laid to the beds; no wood had been chopped; no food stored in the pantries. The candles had not been unpacked; the oil had not been poured into the lanterns.

What little food was available came from the innkeeper's picnic basket that he and his wife had brought with them as they worked at the inn making ready for an opening in two week's time. Cold fried chicken, tart apples, jars of dried peaches, and leathery biscuits weren't much of a meal for the three travelers who had had little for two days.

Linens brought into the stables to dry now smelled of horse droppings and damp earth. It was not an enticing aroma upon which to sleep.

The Prince Regent's temper started to rise. He was sorely tempted to lash out at the hapless innkeeper who obviously had no notion who his guest was, but Liza stopped Conar from making a fool of himself by pulling him aside to point out the tavern owner's predicament.

"Think, Milord. The man is already upset and embarrassed that he can provide no better for his guests. How do you think he and his wife will feel when they find out their very first guest is the future King of Serenia?"

"I don't give a rat's arse if...." he thundered, but she shushed him with her fingers.

"One of the things you should have been taught by your father was that your people come first, Milord. Before your own comfort; before your own needs, before your own sense of worth! Why shame this man who has gone out of his way to do what he humanly can? Has he not given up his own meal so that we may eat?"

"That's his problem," Conar said petulantly. "He's supposed to show me homage."

"Spoken just as your brother Galen would have, Milord," Liza said with a sneer. "Petty men think alike, I suppose!"

"I am not petty!"

"No? But you are ill-mannered, aren't you? You wish to make this good man cringe in fear of you because you consider yourself someone important."

"I am someone important."

"To yourself, aye. And if you should bluster at this man, tell him who you are, he will be mortified with shame. Is that what you want? You want to see the man on his knees to you, begging forgiveness for not having the foresight to know his future King would come calling in the middle of a rainstorm?"

Put in that light, he had no choice but to clamp down on his bitterness. He sulked, but at least the poor innkeeper did not suffer any more embarrassment that night.

When morning came, Conar was the first one up. One look out his window and he groaned with frustration. The sky was awash with dark, angry clouds, swooping and swirling in a wind that blasted his window so hard the panes rattled. With a snort of disgust, he shut the curtain and stomped from the room in search of the innkeeper, vowing if the man had no better accommodations this day, he'd strangle him and be done with it, Liza or no Liza! Seeing the downcast expression on the tavern maid's face made him sigh in defeat. He could hear Liza's words echoing in his ears.

"Good morn, Milord," the girl said, bobbing a curtsy. "I trust you slept well."

Conar shrugged. "I suppose." He swung a long leg over his chair and slid down, eyeing the girl's light sway as she placed a plate of biscuits on the table before him.

"Would you care for some hot cider?"

"Hot ale would be more to my taste if you have it," he answered and let his gaze sweep down the girl's curving body.

A dimple formed in the girl's cheek as she blushed at his heated look. The man was handsome, no arguing that. The tavern keeper had told her the man had two women with him, but she knew he had slept with neither. Perhaps he was looking for companionship, a warm body to keep him comfortable this night. She lowered her lashes. "I shall draw you a mug right away, Milord."

"You could draw me anything you like." He grinned, slipping easily into the banter that was as much a part of him as his skin.

The girl flashed her white teeth in a welcoming answer. She drew a mug of ale from the cask and carried it to the fire. Using her apron as a protective cloth, she picked up a poker from the fire and slipped it into the mug to warm the ale. The warm smell of barley and mead filled the room.

He glanced around, noticing the place seemed more Spartan than it had the day before. He looked closer at the fire and smiled, shaking his head. A table leg jaunted at a woebegone angle from the fireplace. The innkeeper was burning his furniture to keep his guests warm.

As the girl placed the mug of ale on the table in front of him, Conar winked, grinning at the girl's open invitation in her pretty face. He was about to speak when the kitchen door opened and the innkeeper's wife bustled toward her.

"Good morn, Your Grace," she greeted him, dipping her knees as she placed a platter of fried eggs, crisp bacon, rice with thick red gravy, puffy biscuits and sliced apples before him. "I have baked custard ready for you when you finish this, Highness."

"So, you found out who I am."

The lady blushed. "We found out this morn, Your Grace. We are sorely ashamed that we could not provide better for our Prince last eve." She twisted her apron in her lumpy hands. "We apologize to you, Your Grace."

"For what?" he said around a mouthful of succulent egg. He could well afford to be magnanimous on a full stomach.

"For not being able to make you comfortable, Your Grace," she said miserably.

"You don't owe me an apology, madam; but you do owe me a favor."

"Any favor at all, Milord!" The overweight woman seemed eager to please.

"Don't burn any more of your furniture." He smiled seductively at her and saw her blush. "Promise?"

The fat woman could barely answer. Her heart was pounding in her wide chest and she had to get away from those devastatingly blue eyes. She sent him a light curtsy and backed out of the room as he returned to his food. "You see to His Grace, girl!" she commanded as she disappeared through the kitchen door.

"More ale, Your Grace?" the serving wench inquired. No wonder the man was so handsome. He was the Prince Regent, no less. Conar McGregor, the man all the women of Serenia were after, was sitting before her and his smile told her he was pleased with her appearance.

"Please." Conar held out his mug and, as he did, her fingers grazed his. He saw her jump. He was used to that reaction from serving girls and it annoyed him. He looked away. "When did your master come by this food?"

"He ... he rode to Corinth."

"In this rain?" Corinth was a good ten miles away. "Did he now? That was most generous."

"We are generous people." Her eyes locked with his. "You have but to ask, Your Grace."

He stared at her for a moment and then nodded. He knew all too well what she was offering. "There is something you can do for me...." He needed to know the wench's name.

"Dorrie, Your Grace," the girl supplied breathlessly. "I will do anything for you."

"Would you prepare a hot bath for me?" His gaze lingered on her lush bosom, unknowingly putting more into his words than was intended.

Envisioning herself sharing that bath, the girl nodded vigorously. "I'll do it now, Milord!" She almost collided with Liza on the stairs.

"I take it we are staying again today?" Liza asked, frowning at his lecherous look as he watched the serving girl's rump while she climbed the stairs.

"I wouldn't be if it were not for you and 'Zelle," he answered, turning from Dorrie's pleasing rear to look into Liza's stormy gaze. Was that jealousy in those steady green eyes. He grinned. "If I were alone, I'd travel on, but you two can't be expected to venture out in this." He pointed to the window where streaming water distorted the panes.

"There's a lot of things you'd probably do if you were alone," Liza mumbled.

"True, but staying here wouldn't be one of them. I don't mind this weather. But you ladies would be highly uncomfortable out in this muck."

Liza bent her head as Gezelle sat beside her. She whispered to the girl that she knew it was his own comfort and not theirs he sought. When Gezelle giggled, Conar threw them a nasty glare.

"What's so gods-be-damned funny, Mam'selle?" he demanded of Gezelle.

"Nothing, Milord," Gezelle was quick to respond.

Having Liza smile sweetly only made him angry. He snorted and donned a much-put-upon face, then bent to the food before him.

"I'm having a bath drawn, Liza," he told her as he finished a strip of bacon. "You may use it if it suits you." He wiped his mouth with a starched white napkin.

Liza glanced up with suspicion. "You don't want it?"

"I want nothing that was offered to me, Mam'selle. I thought you might ward off a chill if you took a long, leisurely bath. If you don't want to...." He shrugged.

"I'll take it!" she said, happy he would not be sharing his bath with the tavern girl.

"As you wish." He stood, stretched, and then walked to the fire. He put out his hands to warm them. Speaking over his shoulder, his voice was dry. "I'm sure Dorrie will scrub your back for you."

"In a pig's eye, she will," Liza mumbled as she climbed the stairs.

Conar craned his neck and winked at Gezelle.

Gezelle smiled and bent to the plate of food that had been set before her. The sparring between the two of them would make this journey a fair treat.

## Chapter Eleven

The next night was far more comfortable than the first, for the innkeeper was diligent in his efforts to please his future King. Fresh linens, bought in Corinth, now graced the beds. Firewood, brought in from a covered cart, was stacked along the overhang between kitchen and common room. Roast pork with dumplings, apple sauce, baked acorn squash, pickled green beans, and glazed carrots had made a tasty meal that made all three travelers sleepy with fullness.

Beaming with pleasure as his guests made their way to their chambers, the innkeeper let out a sigh of relief as he settled beside his wife at the table where the Prince's dirty dishes still sat.

"Things turned out all right, eh, Meggie?" He grinned, stretching his arms over his head.

"Aye, he'll make us a good King, that one."

The innkeeper laid his head on his arms as his wife stood and began to knead the tight muscles in his neck. "I nearly did us in, Meggie," he sighed.

"He isn't mad. I think he's more amused than anything."

Her husband nodded. He thought back to the trip he had made before dawn in the pouring rain. Arriving in Corinth, he had described his visitor to a merchant and had nearly died from mortification upon learning his guest could be none other than the Prince Regent. He had paled with fear, but the merchant's old granny, who always kept a vigil by the fireplace near the front door of the shop, had cackled and bid him over.

"If the young one had wanted you to know who he was, he'd have told you, Harry Ruck. Don't you be letting on as if you know. Must have one of his light-'o-loves with him from the sound of it. Probably don't want his papa to know. I'll be telling you now, Harry Ruck, that if you be keeping his secret, he'll do right by you."

The old woman had laughed a toothless smile and slapped Harry on the thigh as he passed.

This morning, the rain still poured with a vengeance against the little tavern. The roads were a slick gleam of water. Cold wind blew with much less strength than the day before, but the temperature was even colder.

No visitors came to the tavern; no occasional traveler dared venture out in such weather. Not even a passing horseman could be seen through the rain-streaked windows. The world outside was like an alien landscape: uninhabited and inhospitable.

Conar spent a night filled with unpleasant memories as the rain beat against his window. The howling wind made eerie chills course down his spine. The darkness itself was ebony, not a trace of light in the sky. He felt as though he was locked inside a damp mausoleum. Sleep had eluded him for a long time, and when it came, it was filled with nightmarish visions that brought him wide awake, gasping for breath, his heart pounding against his ribcage. He sat by his window, absorbed with the driving rain until dawn. His mood was as gloomy as the weather as he sipped hot cider before the fire the next morning.

Liza sat beside him at the table, cheerfully greeting him with a warm smile. He all but ignored her as she waited for him to acknowledge her presence. She was accustomed to him not rising when she entered a room, not pulling out her chair for her, but at least he usually spoke a Good morn to her.

"Are you ill this morn?" she asked.

He didn't look at her. "No."

"Is there something wrong, then?"

He shrugged.

"You are too quiet, Milord. Something must be bothering you." She put a hand on his shoulder and he jerked as though her touch had burned him.

"Don't you dare touch me without my leave to do so, woman!"

Liza stared at him. "Have I done something to upset you, Milord?"

"You have...." he began in a troubled voice, but he could not seem to continue. His mouth worked, but no sound came out. He tried again and still could not speak. Coming to his feet in one movement, he was up the stairs before she could react.

"What did I do?" she whispered to the empty room.

He didn't come down the rest of the day. The innkeeper's wife took him both the noon and evening meals, leaving the trays outside his door, but they were still there, untouched, the next morning when Liza headed downstairs.

She glanced at his closed door and let out a ragged sigh. It was as though he had erected a steel barrier between the two of them. She felt alienated from him in a way that hurt deeply. Her footsteps on the stairs were heavy with confusion and frustration. She ate breakfast in silence, her face wooden. When she was through, she sat in the huge rocker beside the blazing fire and stared into the leaping flames.

Liza didn't look up as he finally came down the stairs. It was well after noontime. She sat staring into the fire, her legs wrapped in a heavy quilt to ward off the chill. She could feel him looking at her as he took a seat near the fireplace.

The ticking of the huge clock at the far end of the common room, the snapping of the fire in the hearth, and the keening of the wind among the eaves were the only sounds.

Conar sat hunched over his spread knees, his head bent, his hands clutched and dangling between his legs. His eyes, filled with the same inner pain that had been in them the day before, were glued to the floor. He had not slept well, his nightmares had blended too closely together to allow for rest.

He turned to Liza and opened his mouth to speak, but when she did not look at him, he lowered his head and drew his legs together in a position of withdrawal. He clasped his hands together and pressed them tightly between his knees.

Liza could feel his pain, his confusion. She sensed a great need within him to talk, but she could not force the conversation. She would not be the one to break the silence, so she waited for him to find the courage to speak.

At last, he slowly raised his head and looked at her silent profile. "I hear Gezelle is sick."

Liza nodded. "A cold. That's all."

"She will be all right, won't she?"

"She will."

He lowered his head. "We will stay until she is well enough to travel."

Still not looking at him, Liza answered, "You may leave if you wish, Milord. The rain has gone."

"I'll wait for you." His voice was almost a whisper.

"There's no need. I have decided to go on to my homeland instead of Boreas. We will burden you no longer."

He flinched at the thought, wanting to ask her again where home was, but her stony profile prohibited him. He thought he might never know from where the girl had come.

"You've not been a burden, Milady." His voice was a soft caress of embarrassment.

She didn't answer.

He pushed his hands lower between his knees and winced as the flesh on his left wrist pulled taut against his corduroy breeches. He held the wrist toward the lantern on the table. His flesh was red, puckered, and hurt worse than it had the day before.

"Does it bother you, Milord?"

He turned to see her watching him, concern in her green eyes. "I believe its worse." He stared at his wrist for a long time and then let out a wavering sigh. He let his hand fall to the table. "I believe everything is worse."

Her heart went out to him. She pushed the quilt from her legs and came to sit on the bench beside him. She took his hand, looking closely at the raw, swollen flesh.

"This needs attention. Why haven't you mentioned this before now?"

He shrugged and looked away, acutely ashamed of his own weakness. "It was of no importance. I had other things on my mind."

"More important things than your health? This could easily become infected." She pursed her lips with exasperation. "Nothing could have been more important than seeing to this wound."

"I have many secrets, Liza, secrets I have never told another living soul. Sometimes...." Taking a deep breath, he looked at her. "Sometimes I just need...."

"You can confide in me."

"Maybe you don't want to hear."

"Try me," she responded, instinctively knowing he hated to admit his failings. It seemed he was trying to make a decision--one perhaps he was not sure was wise.

"Sometimes the secrets with which I live hurt me deeply, Liza. They rend my soul; and when they hurt me, I unintentionally hurt those around me." He glanced at her with a look that seemed to ask her for understand.

Liza nodded. "I will see to your wound, Milord, and then we can talk."

He sat for nearly thirty minutes on the bench where she had left him. His face was turned toward the window. It had begun to rain again and lightning flashed outside the windowpanes, blurring the scenery and turning the glass to a bright flare of light. He didn't look at her when she returned. "You shouldn't have bothered. I don't deserve such kindness."

"There are those who would most certainly agree with you, Milord," she answered and knelt at his feet. She took his arm and began to spread the mixture of warm and freshly brewed herbs on his lacerated flesh. "At any rate, it is no bother," she answered, annoyed with his self-pity.

"I thank you anyway."

She could feel him watching her as she bent over his wound. He seemed to want to say more, but didn't. He waited patiently as she wound a clean strip of linen around his wrist and gently tied it, securing the loose ends under the knot of the bow. But, before she had finished, his free hand came up to touch her shining mane of raven black hair, and she glanced up. He was looking at her with such a deep, wounded expression; she placed her hand over his to mold it to her scalp. Her eyes narrowed with confusion.

"What is it that troubles you so, Milord?"

Tears shone brightly as he gazed at her and the hand in her hair tightened. His look was as hot as the crucible she used to steep her potion of herbs. Those wounded blue eyes moved over her face with a gentleness and need that sent the pulse leaping in her veins, brought heat to her face.

"Milord?" she whispered, "what is it?"

He took a long time in answering. He seemed loath to admit whatever it was that was causing him such intense pain. Finally he took a deep breath, screwing up his courage. "Are you still sure your destiny lies with me, little one?" He smoothed her hair with his hand.

"My entire being belongs with you."

He pushed the hair from her face and ran his fingers down her silken cheek, taking her chin firmly in hand. He forced up her head so she could not turn away. "Look at me, Liza."

Reluctantly, she did and found her knees growing weak as she gazed into his handsome face.

"If I were to ask you to come to my chamber this night, would you? Would you spend the eve with me?"

Liza's heart pounded in her ribcage, but she didn't hesitate. "If that is what you wish, Milord."

"It is what I want, sweet Liza." Then he shook his head. "Nay, it is what I need."

Her look was filled with hurt and she tried to pull away. "Then Dorrie will do as well as I."

"It is not Dorrie I need."

"And it is not me you want."

He smiled hopelessly. "I both want and need you, Liza, but tonight I need you more."

"I have never before slept with a man."

The smile that touched his face was sad, fleeting, and full of pain. "Then how can you be sure I should be the one to take that pride from you?" His hands threaded through her hair, anchoring her head. "Should you not wait for the man who can give you all, to offer such a precious gift?"

"I belong to you, Milord. What I have saved, I have saved for you and you alone. If you shall not have it, neither shall any other."

"Why me?" he asked, his eyes searching hers. "Why would you want me?" He half-smiled. "I'm an ill tempered bastard at the best of times and...."

"Perhaps it is because I know you, Milord," she said.

He shook his head. "No, you don't. You--"

"I know all there is to know of you," she interrupted. "For years I have watched you, been near you when you were unaware, listened to you speaking to your people, showing the real Conar McGregor to them instead of the Prince Regent in all his vain glory. I have followed you about the country and seen the good you do when you think no one is watching, the money you leave for the poor, and the farms you save from foreclosure. My heart has been warmed when you ride ten miles out of your way just to purchase a bolt of fabric for a young woman to have a fitting bridal gown when her parents could ill afford even food for their bellies. I have seen you lift children to your shoulders and play ring-a-daisy with them, scamper with them at the seashore, gift them with bags of candy and toys. I've seen you visiting the orphanages to bring food and clothing to those poor children and I once saw you visiting the lepers at Wyndsbridge. "

"Hell's bells woman, you make me sound like a saint," he said, shaking his head.

"Perhaps not a saint but a saintly man," she countered. "I have come to know you as the man--when you weren't watching, when you were unaware--and it is that man who won my heart long ago. It is to him I offer myself and all that I am."

"Even with my ill tempers?"

She shrugged. "Perhaps despite them?"

Conar cupped her face, his thumbs stroking the flare of her brows, and then gently pulled her toward him. He nestled her face against the soft material of his shirt, pressing her cheek to his chest.

He bent forward and rested his chin on her head, closing his eyes to everything around them. "I like that you see a different man than the one I perceive myself to be. It gives me hope that you think of me as a good man. I don't ever want to disappoint you. I don't ever want to hurt you, Liza," he whispered into the silk of her hair. "I can offer you nothing beyond the here and now; I can make no promises for tomorrow. What I have to offer may be only for this night. Think long and hard before you do this."

Her arms went around his waist and she pressed closer to him. "I will ask nothing more of you past this night, Milord."

* * * *

As rain pelted the windows with gale force, and Gezelle slept in her achy illness, Liza crept from her room to scratch at Conar's door. As he opened the portal to admit her, his naked chest rising and falling with the power of his arousal, she blended into his outstretched arms, and he gently closed the door behind her.

Conar took Liza's hands and placed a soft kiss in each palm. He could feel the thunder of her beating pulse against his tongue as he flicked the warm tip across her chilled flesh. His eyes never left hers, looking through his lashes to see the hunger on her face.

And the fear lurking there.

He knew he needed to proceed slowly, to ease her into the joys of womanly pleasure with as much gentleness as he could muster. With infinite care, he pulled the pins from her hair to send it cascading down her back in shimmering folds of ebony silk. Taking her face between his palms, he placed soft kisses on her forehead, her nose, closed each eye, and finally placed his lips to hers.

"Are you sure, little one?"

Liza nodded. "What I have to offer is for you alone, Milord."

He spread the fingers of his right hand through her hair to cup her head. His mouth claimed hers in a heady kiss that made them both senseless with longing. When at last he tore his mouth from hers, there was firm warning stamped on his unsmiling face.

"You will be mine this eve, Beloved. You will be mine and mine you will remain. If I take you now, I doubt I will ever willingly give you up to another man. If you can not accept that, you had best stop me here and now, for once I have branded your flesh with mine, there will be no turning back."

"And what of you, Milord?" She laid her hand along his cheek. "You give me no choice. I am to be yours and no other's? You belong to another already, but will deny me?"

Conar shook his head. "You know where my loyalty must lay, Liza. I am betrothed to that bitch in Oceania, yet I am greedy. I will have no other, but me, touch you."

Liza tried to pull away but his hand tightened in her hair.

"Do you understand what I am telling you, Liza?"

"And when this deed is done, Milord, when you have what you want from me, will you see me as you see the other women you have taken? Will you hold me in the same contempt as you do them?"

"Are you like those other women, Liza?"

"You know I am not, else you would not want to keep me only unto yourself. I am not here to take from you, Milord. I am here to give." Her voice was a mere whisper. "I want you. I care not a whit for the Prince Regent or his crown; I seek no bounty for my affections; I want no ability to boast at having slept with the warrior-knight. I want you … Conar. I want the man you are."

His hand tensed in her hair. "There has to be more to you than that, Liza-love." His old cynicism surfaced. "Conar, the man can give himself to you. The others: Prince Regent, future King, warrior-knight, what of them?"

"There is nothing those men can offer I don't already have. I have no need of title. I have no need of land or gold coins. There is no one for me to brag to that I have slept with the future sovereign of this land. There is no prestige in what I do for you or in what I give to you. It is between the two of us: you and I, and no one else. My needs are simple, Milord: I seek your love."

She took his hand and held it to her breast. She sighed as the warmth of his palm radiated through the fabric of her nightgown and his fingers molded around the softness of her breast.

"Feel my heart beating, Milord? Feel the woman beneath this flesh? She seeks you as her mate. She is asking you for nothing more."

"Are you sure?"

"As sure as I am the sun will rise come morning, Conar. What shall it be, Milord? Will you have Liza, the woman, or will you toss away what she is offering you because you fear she will betray you?"

For a long moment he stared at her, his breathing deep and full. Then, Conar took her hand and led her to the big cherry-wood bed dominating the small room. The coverlet was laid back to reveal crisp, fresh white sheets. He took a deep breath and pulled her in front of him, his fingers going to the laces at her throat. He pulled the knot loose, untying the silk ribbons with care. The gown's bodice shifted gently apart and he spread his hands over her shoulders. He pushed the gown over her shoulders, past her ribcage, slipped it over the curve of her hips until it lay in a silken blue pool at her feet.

His breath caught in his throat as his eyes moved slowly over the length of Liza's naked glory. The girl was a marvel of young womanhood: perfect, unflawed, smoothly muscled, and ivory-tinted.

He smiled.

"You are as beautiful as I had dreamed you would be, Milady."

Liza blushed. "Do I please you, Milord?" she asked timidly.

"You please me more than I can tell you, Liza."

Bending his head, he traced the tip of his tongue down the side of her neck and onto the soft flesh of her left shoulder. Very slowly, very gently, he drew her naked body against his own bare chest.

"You are more beautiful than any goddess in the heavens," he said, cradling her so tenderly she might well have been a delicate crystal vase.

As her nipples touched his flesh, Liza felt her knees wanting to give way. Growing warmth tumbled in waves through her lower body and she felt as though her flesh was on fire. She trembled, not so much from her shyness and awkwardness as from the heady sensations this man was causing her to feel. She was throbbing to his heartbeat; breathing to his own shallow intake of breath.

Conar spread his hands up and across her back, molding her to him. Her body seemed to be melting into his and he closed his eyes, willing their bodies into one inseparable entity. He could feel the entire length of her along his flesh and he was quivering with a passion so great he was aching from it.

"Oh, Liza," he mumbled against the top of her hair, "I am on fire with need for you."

"I am yours. "Do with me as you will, Milord."

Her words brought a groan of desire from his lips and he pushed her away just far enough so he could lower his head and slant his mouth across hers. His tongue prodded her lips gently open so he could delve inside and taste the sweetness of her mouth. Her immediate moan of pleasure was nearly his undoing.

Standing on tiptoes, straining against him as he kissed her, Liza could feel the rough warmth of his chest against her own flesh. Her nipples were erect with passion, tingling from the contact. She could feel the foreign hardness pressing along the lower part of her belly and she instinctively pressed against it. She heard the deep growl in his throat as his kiss deepened and he began to ravage her lips with his own.

Their kiss lasted a long time, neither wanting to break the contact. His tongue invaded her mouth, circled her tongue, flicked delicately along her lips. He nibbled on her lower lip and fleetingly caught her tongue as she shyly ventured to enter his mouth. Her little muffled squeal of protest made him smile around the kiss he was bestowing upon her willing mouth. He drew back and looked at her. "I didn't hurt you."

"No, but you did other things to me, Milord," she shot back.

"And I shall do more, my pretty!" He wagged his brows at her like a villain of the old tales.

Liza tossed her heavy tresses and her eyes blazed with challenge. "Will you, now, Milord?" She gave him a saucy grin. "Care to show me?"

Conar bent his knees and gripped her tightly around her waist, hefting her with no effort at all. He craned his neck and gazed up at her. "I shall have you begging me for release, Mam'selle!"

Liza's hands were on his shoulders as he held her aloft. She giggled. "Is that so?"

"Aye, it is."

She could feel the press of his manhood where she knew he wanted it to be and she gasped as he ground himself against her.

"Feel anything you like, Mam'selle?" he inquired, one tawny brow lifting in query.

Liza cocked her head to one side and pretended to think. "However would I, a tender virgin, know, good sir?"

Conar threw back his head and laughed, his chest rumbling with mirth. He swung her around and around, listening to her giggling bursts of protest. When he stopped, his arms tightened almost to the point of pain around her body.

"However, indeed, unless I show you, Mam'selle?" he returned.

Liza felt herself sliding down his body, could feel the roughness of his cord breeches as he raised his knee, bracing his foot on the bottom rung of the bedside chair and lowered her astride the steel muscles of his left thigh. Her mouth opened in a little round *o* of surprise.

"Aye." He chuckled, watching her expression. "And far more than just that, Milady." He grinned as her thigh muscles instinctively clamped around his own. He lowered his knee, breaking the intimate contact, and saw her lips form a deprived pout.

"I think you toy with me, Milord," she whispered.

"You think so?" he asked, pulling her to him again.

"Aye." She wiggled against him, wanting the pressure of that hardness between her thighs once more.

"All in good time," he told her, turning her around so her back was to his chest. He circled her in his arms and lowered his head to plant nipping kisses along her neck and shoulder. He could feel her body humming with pleasure and he breathed in the sweet aroma of lavender that was Liza's special scent. He threaded his fingers through hers and lifted her left arm above her head. His lips ran gently down her tingling flesh, his tongue circling the tender area inside her elbow. He trailed his fingers down her arm, drew his knuckles over the curve of her breast, and then pulled her to him as he locked her in his arms once more.

Liza squealed, feeling his manhood move along her rump. She tried to turn, but he wouldn't let her. He held her to him and slipped his tongue inside her ear.

"Milord!" she breathed and her body was on fire with a need she had only heard existed.

"Milady," he whispered and let his tongue work magic along the perimeter of her ear.

"Milord, please!" she groaned.

"Milady, not yet," he answered and moved his hips from side to side, letting her feel the tumescence of this shaft prodding her firm derriere.

"Oh, sweet Alel," she murmured and closed her eyes, panting.

"Nay. Sweet Conar." He chuckled. He spread his hand over her breast, molding her in his palm, reveling in the sound of her harsh breathing, her gasps as he stroked her. "Like that?"

"Aye," she whispered, her head falling back on his shoulder.

He fanned his thumb up and down on her left nipple as he hefted the sweet weight in his palm and then began to roll her left nipple between his fingertips.

"Oh!" she exclaimed and sagged against him, sure she would faint, but he held her up, molded her to him. "Please."

"Are you sure?"

Her breathing came shallow and quick. "Aye, I am gods-be-damned positive!"

Conar chuckled deep in his throat. Bending his knees, he placed a hand beneath her back, the other beneath her knees and lifted her high against him. Carrying her to his bed, he laid her on the silken coverlet and bent over her, his eyes smoldering with a passion he was finding harder and harder to control. The fine matting of blond hair in the center of his chest glistened with sweat.

"Aren't you warm, Milord?" she asked, moistening her lips with a nervous tongue.

His eyes followed the sweep of that pink flesh and lingered on the wetness left behind. He raised his eyes to her. "Woman, I am on fire."

"And I am ready, sweet Conar." Her face pinked with her own brazenness.

It was all he could do not to fall on her like a ravaging beast. When her tongue came out to lick at the fullness of her upper lip, he groaned with agony and his hands flew to the buttons of his breeches.

Liza followed those strong fingers as they tore at the pearl buttons, flinched as he shoved the breeches away from his lower body and stepped out of them, kicking them away with force. Her face burned as she took in the full, naked, male beauty that was Conar McGregor. She let her gaze follow every curve, every angle, every hollow, every rise and flow of his magnificent body. She caught a glimpse of a small scar here, a larger one there, but none of them distracted from his male perfection. If anything, the scars added a mystique and sexuality to his otherwise flawless physique.

She frowned prettily as he hesitated, hovering over her, one arm braced on the headboard as he gazed down at her with longing. She watched his smile become genuine, giving, loving, waiting.

"Do you want me, lass?" he whispered. "Me, the man. Not the Prince Regent?"

Liza answered his challenging smile with one of her own and lifted her arms to him.

He didn't touch her, only covered her body with his own, his elbows bracing him from coming into full contact with her as he joined her on the bed. He gently wedged his right knee between her thighs, easing her legs apart so he could insinuate his other leg between hers. Settling down, he touched her with his hard male length and rested gently atop her.

"Liza," he said, his voice tight with need.

"Aye, Beloved," she answered. Her left hand came up to cup his cheek.

"I can not wait, my lady."

Liza ran her thumb over his bottom lip. "And you are afraid you will hurt me?"

He could only nod, not trusting himself to speak for fear his voice would break like an eleven-year-old boy's and spoil the moment.

"I have always known it would hurt, Milord." Her arms went around his shoulders, pulling him to her. "Take me, Conar." She heard him groan. "Take me as you wish."

He wanted her first time to be memorable for her, for her to think back on it with pleasure and not with regret. He wanted to be gentle with her, to initiate her into womanhood with all the tenderness and respect that was her due. Stamping down the driving passion that was burning like a wildfire in his groin, he was trembling like a green youth as his hard cock pulsed against the entrance to her sweet sheath.

"Look at me, Milady," he said, holding her green gaze with him.

Liza smiled shyly into his hot gaze. She could feel a dot of slickness dripping down her nether lips and she blushed.

"He wants you more than he has ever wanted anything in his life," Conar whispered. He eased a hand down between them so he could take hold of his shaft. "He wants to worship you as the precious gift you are."

The weight of him upon her was so delicious, so heavenly blissful, she could have remained there for eternity with his warm cinnamon scent drifting under her nostrils, his handsome face etched in her mind's eye as he looked down at her--one errant golden wave dipping over his forehead.

"And she wants you, Milord," she told him. "More than anything in this life or any other."

Very gently he pressed the tip of his shaft against her moist folds, listening to his runaway heart thudding in his ear, feeling the blood rushing through his veins, the heat flooding his cock. He was keenly aware that he was breathing as hard as she was and when he insinuated the tip of him into her softness, he watched her eyelids flicker.

"Relax, Sweeting," he said in a low, soft voice. "Relax and let your man pleasure you."

Liza had to school her arms and legs to loosen. She had tensed as soon as she had felt him pushing at her entrance. Though it took some doing, she made her body melt into the mattress.

Slowly and with infinite care he pushed into her heated channel. She was so incredibly tight around his head, so lusciously hot and slick with her building juices. He went a bit deeper and felt the slight give of her maidenhead, saw her eyes widen as the minute pain registered, heard her suck in her breath, and then pushed fully inside her, breaking the fragile resistance and opening her for his deeper invasion.

"Conar," she whispered, relaxing beneath him, her hands stroking his neck. "Now I am yours."

He smiled tenderly at her. "For all time, Milady."

She instinctively wriggled under him, her shapely hips moving in a dance as old as time. A sparkle entered her green eyes and her smile was radiant as she began to experience the sweet pleasure having him inside her could bring. As he began to thrust--gently at first and then with a bit more force--she arched up to meet him.

"Put your legs around my hips," he instructed, sliding his hands beneath her tempting rump.

Liza didn't question him, just raised her legs, and hooked them around him, her breasts flattening against his hairy chest. "I could get very used to this," she said with a sigh.

"Wench, you haven't seen anything yet," he promised and increased his rhythm, the depth of his penetration.

What he thought was a frown creased her forehead for just a moment but then it smoothed out as dawning awareness settled in its place.

"I feel...." she said, drawing her bottom lip between her teeth. "I am...."

He smiled knowingly for he could feel the wetness of us increasing and her legs tightened around him. His movements sped up until he was pulling almost out of her then sinking deeper with each circuit.

"Conar...." she said, her breath coming in ragged little gasps. "I itch!"

"Then let's scratch it," he said and began pumping into her faster. He was as deep inside her as he could go and when that first ripple gripped the head of his cock and her eyes flared wide, her fingernails dug into his back, he lifted her ass up as high as he could to allow for his thrusts.

Unbelievable pleasure shot through Liza, like a new quarrel from a crossbow. Her nerve endings sang with the flickering little ripples that undulated inside her and seemed to be milking Conar. The sweetness, the unexpected glory of the feeling rocketing through her made her cry out. Her arms and legs clamped around him. She held onto him for dear life as the sensation continued on--trilling along her folds and enveloping her entire lower body with such intense feeling, such delight that she thought she was going to faint.

Conar held himself as still as he could with his cock pressed against her womb as the last of her pulsations echoed away and when they did, he spilled himself in her, allowing her to feel the spurting of his seed as it pressed at her very core.

"Oh, Conar!" she cried out and had it been possible, she would have forged their two bodies into one so closely was she holding him.

With his own sweet release, the most thrilling and pleasurable he'd ever known, he collapsed on top of her with his cheek pressed to her lush breast.

"You are mine," he whispered, his warm breath flowing over her heated flesh.

"For all time, Milord," she repeated his vow.

## Chapter Twelve

Liza awoke the next morning to a bright day filled with sunshine flooding through the casement window. Conar lay curled behind her, his arm draped possessively over her bare waist. She could feel the softness of his breath against her hair, the hard intrusion of one knee between her thighs. She could smell the warm and musky scent of cinnamon oil that he used as an aftershave lotion and the smell made her smile.

She tried to ease out from under the dead weight of his arm, but the slight movement must have startled him awake, for his hand tightened on her flesh and he mumbled against her neck as he shifted closer.

"Are you awake, Milord?" she whispered. Her smile widened as he mumbled again and placed his lips on the nape of her neck. A quiver ran down her naked spine as his tongue traced a light pattern on her flesh.

Conar had been awake for quite some time, content to just lie beside this beautiful woman, holding her to him. When he first opened his eyes, he had been surprised, disoriented, unsure of whom the woman beside him was. It was not an uncommon experience for the young Prince. He was nevertheless alarmed during that first full moment of wakefulness since he had sworn himself to celibacy only a few days earlier; but the wafting scent of lavender had drifted under his nostrils and an image of Liza, naked and glorious beneath him, flew across his mind.

His heart swelled with an emotion he did not recognize just as that part of him that had thoroughly enjoyed this lady the evening before swelled with the memory of her lovely body. His smile as he lay there was filled with rapt wonder.

"Milord?" Liza whispered again as his tongue swirled over her skin. "I must go now."

"Nay, you may not, Milady," he muttered as he drew his invading knee higher between her open thighs. "By royal decree, you can not leave this man's arms until he is sated."

"Milord!" Liza gasped and tried to wiggle away, but he wouldn't allow it, capturing her left breast within one hot palm.

"You are needed here," he said, his voice still groggy and hoarse from sleep. He bared his teeth and nipped her along the column of her neck, grinning as she jumped.

" 'Tis unseemly, Milord," she protested and tried to remove his hand from her breast.

Conar nestled even closer, raising his head and resting his chin on her shoulder. "I see no one watching us, Lady. Do you?"

She twisted her head to look at him. "The rain has stopped, Milord, and it is well past dawn. Gezelle will awake and find me gone. My bed has not been slept in."

"So?" he murmured, digging his chin into her shoulder and laughing as she scrunched up her shoulder in protest.

"Do you not wish to leave for Boreas this morn? And what will our good hosts think if we do not come down soon to break our fasts?"

"The Rucks can wait and so can Boreas. It will be there when we arrive." He ran his tongue along the ridge of her shoulder bone. "I have pressing business here."

Liza's stomach tightened with desire. "But you were in such a hurry yesterday," she said in a daze, as his hand began to knead the soft mound of her breast. "I think you would be glad for the good weather."

"The weather be damned." He yawned, pushed up on one elbow, and kissed the side of her face. "Besides, 'tis not my horse I wish to ride this morn, wench."

Feeling the tumescence of his shaft prodding her rump, Liza pushed against his arm, tried to pry his fingers from her breast. "Milord! In the daylight?"

"Daylight, moonlight, starlight, sunlight, firelight, what difference does it make, woman?" He withdrew his knee and allowed her to turn onto her back, although he still kept captive the soft mound of her flesh. "You light the fires of my passion whenever and wherever we are, Milady."

"But in the morning, Milord?"

Conar shrugged, his lips stretching into a leering grin. "Liza-love, it is most unseemly to arouse a man and then leave him aching with need."

Liza's eyes opened wide. "I have done nothing to arouse you!" she flung back at him and resumed her effort to free her breast from his light grip.

"You are lying naked in my bed, Lady. That is reason enough to arouse me." Withdrawing his hand, he moved with a liquid grace and settled on top of her, grinning in her startled face. "And I have an appetite not easily filled."

"So I have noticed. May I suggest having Dorrie bring you up something?"

"She has nothing to offer that I need to fill this appetite, Sweeting." He lowered his head and captured her lips.

\* \* \* \*

Watching Conar as he dressed, Liza admired the smooth curve of his lean flanks as he pulled on his breeches. The creamy tan cords settled with a snug fit over his hips and thighs and high-rounded rump. Stretching, she stared intently at him as he pulled the light blue silk shirt over his tousled blond hair, tugging it down his broad chest and tucking it into his breeches. Her knowing grin as he slid his wide leather belt through the thick loops of his waistband and then fastened the heavy brass buckle made him glance at her with a cocked brow.

"Am I entertaining you, Mam'selle?"

Liza nodded slowly. "Not as much as when you removed your clothing, Milord."

Conar chuckled. "Brazen hussy."

Liza remembered something she had wanted to ask him earlier. "Where did you come by those marks on your back?" she asked, thinking of the thin, almost transparent, crisscrossed lines all along his shoulders and waist. She had thought he must have been pitched from his horse into a bush of brambles. She wasn't at all prepared for his curt answer.

"Kaileel Tohre's belt," he answered calmly, glancing up as he drew together the laces of his shirt. He looked away again, searching for his missing boots.

"That priest who was at Norus? Why would he whip you?"

"Because I disobeyed him," he answered and then stooped down to retrieve a boot that was hiding beneath Liza's discarded gown.

"By what right did a priest have to whip you?" she asked, hating anyone who would hurt this beautiful man.

Conar came to sit on the bed beside her to pull on his boots. "I really don't want to talk about this, Liza. It was a long time ago when I was a small boy." He tugged on one shiny brown boot; his mouth set in a stubborn line she had come to recognize all too well.

Sensing she should change the subject, Liza brought up her knees and locked them together within the perimeter of her arms, resting her chin on top.

"You do have the most uncommonly perfect body, Milord."

Conar snapped his head around and stared at her. He laughed at her wistful expression and raised one golden brow. "And just how many naked men have you seen, my pretty?"

Liza shrugged. "A few."

"And where was this?" he asked as he drew on his other boot.

"About," she answered and grinned as he ruefully shook his head at her.

"You give away no secrets, do you, Mam'selle?"

"I have no secrets, Milord," she answered brightly, lifting her head to look him in the eye.

Conar guffawed, sending her a disbelieving look.

"Well," she corrected, drawing out her answer, "only a few."

"Such as where your home is." He stood.

Liza pursed her lips in a pretend pout. "Just why is that of such major import to you, Milord?"

He shrugged his wide shoulders into his soft leather jacket. "Because I am curious about you, Mam'selle."

"You know what they say about cats, don't you, my sweet Prince?"

Conar chuckled and headed for the door. "Be up with you, lady. We ride within the hour."

"What?" She threw him a disbelieving look.

"I changed my mind about the weather. 'Tis a fine day for riding my horse, too!" He grinned; shutting the door behind him as a pillow came flying across the room.

He skipped down the stairs two at a time, a wide grin of contentment on his handsome face. He felt alive and his heart was as light as the sweet rays of sunlight playing over the stair treads. He thrust his hands into the pockets of his breeches and whistled. It was, indeed, a very fine day for riding.

Gezelle looked up as her Overlord came down the stairs. She stood, curtsying as he joined her, swinging one long leg over the back of a chair and sliding down. She was amazed he would lower himself to sit at table with a mere servant.

"How do you feel this morn, 'Zelle?" he asked, grinning at the girl's bright red nose and watering eyes. "If you don't feel like traveling with us, you can stay and I'll send one of my Elite back for you in a coach."

Gezelle shook her head. "I'm well enough, Your Grace." She did not miss the self-satisfied look on her Prince's face any more than she had missed the unused bed in which her mistress should have passed the eve before. "Did you sleep well, Your Grace?"

"I slept very little," he answered, winking audaciously at her as he motioned for her to sit with him.

Blushing to the roots of her hair, Gezelle quickly settled opposite him, dipping her burning face so he could not see.

"Are you sure you feel well enough to travel?" When she nodded, he eyed her carefully. "You're really sure?"

She looked at him and could see true concern, not a hope that he and the lady might travel on alone. "I am well enough, Your Grace."

Conar nodded, picking up his fork as the serving wench placed a platter of pork chops before him. He ignored the girl even as she deliberately brushed her left breast against his arm as she straightened.

But Gezelle had not missed the action and turned a glare of disapproval to the tavern maid who still stood expectantly beside their Overlord. A protectiveness Gezelle meant for not only Prince Conar, but Lady Liza, as well, put steel in the former Norus servant's backbone.

"We'll not be needing anything, Dorrie," she hissed in an authoritative voice that surprised the Prince Regent. He glanced up at Gezelle's militant face.

Dorrie made no move to leave. Her frosty eyes glared at Gezelle with warning and she placed clenched fists on flaring and curvaceous hips. "Is that so? Who says?"

Conar lowered his head, his lips twitching with humor. "Thank you, Dorrie," he said, cutting a chunk of pork chop and spearing it with his fork. When the tavern wench still did not move, he looked up at her. "That will be all." He looked away again, dismissing her. As Dorrie stomped away, he did not miss Gezelle's hurmpf of finality. He had to take a hasty gulp of chilled apple cider to keep from laughing.

For a long moment, silence filled the common room. Conar ate his morning meal with all the gusto of a man whose carnal appetites cried out for energy-giving sustenance. When he became aware of Gezelle's worried face, he stopped eating. "Is something wrong, Mam'selle?"

Gezelle started in embarrassment and shame. "I shouldn't have given that girl orders, Your Grace."

"Why not? You're no longer a servant, 'Zelle. You have been given your freedom. You're a lady who now serves as companion to the Lady Liza." He laid down his fork and took up his napkin. "You are above that tart in social standing. It was well within your right to give her orders, and she had best heed those orders or I will know why." He wiped his mouth on his napkin and placed it beside his plate. He laid his hand over Gezelle's, feeling her flinch. "And I thank you for handling a situation I found most uncomfortable." He withdrew his touch. "I did not wish the wench's attention or her overture."

Gezelle's face turned redder still beneath his close scrutiny. "I knew you did not, Your Grace."

He stood and thrust his hand into the pocket of his breeches, digging out some gold coins. "I'll settle up with the innkeeper and see to having our mounts readied. Would you go see what's taking my lady so gods-be-damned long?"

Gezelle smiled at her Prince's unconscious possession of the lady. Her heart was light as she climbed the stairs to the upper rooms. They made such a fine pair, this god of sunshine, and this lady of the midnight hair. Sighing with dreamy regard to just how right these two beautiful people were for one another, Gezelle tapped lightly at the Prince Regent's door and smiled as Liza bid her enter.

* * * *

Conar looked in on the innkeeper's wife as she sat beside her cooking pot, peeling potatoes for the noon meal. He motioned for the rotund lady to stay seated.

"I wanted to compliment you, Madame Ruck, on the wonderful meals you have always prepared for us. If I stay much longer, they'd have to send a barrel maker's wagon to cart me home." He came to stand beside her then hunkered down, pilfering a chunk of potato from her large bowl.

"That's not good for you!" Meggie Ruck said automatically, swatting at the young man's hand. Her eyes widened as he looked at her with surprise. "Your Grace, I am...." she began, but he covered one rough, work-reddened hand with his own.

"You sounded just like my mama." He laughed and squeezed her fingers. "She wouldn't let me eat raw spuds, either."

"Her Majesty was a great lady."

His face darkened with memory. "Aye, Meggie, that she was." He patted her hand and laid two gold sovereigns on the table beside her. "That should cover our room and board." He added another sovereign. "And the furniture you were forced to burn."

Meggie stared at the coins. Three gold sovereigns were more than she and Harry would see in six month's time. She shook her head, scooping up the gold and extending them to her Overlord.

" 'Tis too much, Your Grace!" It wasn't mannerly to be sitting in the Prince Regent's presence and she tried to stand, but the young man put his hand on her shoulder to prevent her.

"I want to." Bending over, he placed a light kiss on her plump cheek, hugging her to him in a warm, compassionate embrace. "Thank you for making my stay so wonderful, Meggie."

Meggie Ruck could only stare as her Prince straightened, winking at her with that little-boy charm she had come to adore. His smile as he turned to leave would be forever stored in her memories.

"The Wind be always at your back, Meggie Ruck," he whispered.

Meggie sat frozen to her chair as she watched him leave. It took her a long time to be able to bring her hand, trembling as it was, to her cheek to touch the tingled flesh. He had kissed her, she thought with dazed wonder. Her Prince, her future King, had kissed her. She could still feel the feather-soft caress of those sensual lips, lips women were known to fight for, on her flesh.

"The Wind be always at your back," she said in a breathy whisper and felt a tear ease down her weathered cheek.

After paying the innkeeper for housing their horses, a tribute Harry Ruck had not wanted to accept, Conar whistled as he walked to the stables. He declined the stable boy's help in saddling Seayearner and set about the task himself, crooning to the great black beast as he slid the saddle over 'Yearner's broad back. He moved then to Liza's little gray mare and wasn't in the least surprised when the filly allowed him to saddle her with nothing more than a nuzzle of his cheek.

He could see the stable boy gawking at him with wonder. The boy no doubt thought his Prince had taken leave of his senses. Royalty did not saddle their own mounts when there were servants about to do it.

Conar grinned wickedly to himself. There were many things the old Conar wouldn't have done, he thought. With his mind on the lady in the tavern, he knew there were going to be a few things the new Conar might do that would make the world think him crazy. He didn't care. His world was right for the first time in his life and he would be damned if he would ever let it go dark and bleak again.

Gezelle was sitting on the stairs, her hands clenched tightly together between her knees. Her face was pale and pinched as she glanced up at him.

Conar's heart began to pound and he felt a wicked cold seep into the pit of his stomach. "What is it?"

Gezelle began to cry.

"Why in the hell are you crying?" He felt as though his world was grinding to a halt and he could feel the blood rushing to his ears.

"She's gone, Your Grace," Gezelle whispered. "Our lady's gone."

"What are you talking about?" Alarm filled his blue eyes as he glanced up the stairs, expecting to see Liza standing at the top. He took a step toward the stairs.

"She left, Your Grace." Gezelle's voice was filled with misery. Tears slid down her cheeks and she broke down in heaving sobs. She barely felt him push by her as he took the steps at a near-run. She could hear him calling the lady's name as he opened and shut every door above.

His shout echoed through the still tavern as he thundered down the stairs. He grabbed Gezelle's arms and drew her to stand.

"Where is she?" He shook the girl. "Where did she go?"

"She said to tell you ... to say...." Gezelle couldn't finish, for her throat was closing with tears.

He shook her again. The girl's head wobbled on her fragile shoulders and she grunted with pain, but Conar did not heed her soft whimper. "Tell me what?"

"To say goodbye for her."

"Goodbye?" Conar's voice lowered to a stunned whisper. Confusion, pain, even wounded pride filled his pale face.

"She left you a note, Your Grace." Gezelle dug into her dress and produced a white sheet of folded paper. She extended it, flinching as he jerked it out of her hand.

Conar glanced at the parchment, then, without reading it, crumpled it, and stuffed it in his pocket. "Did she say where she was going?" At Gezelle's shake of her head, he clenched his teeth to keep from bellowing. "Did she say where her home was?" When the girl shook her head again, he wanted to smash something.

"Damn it!" he yelled and spun around to face the four people who had gathered at the kitchen door, having all come at a run when his angry cries reached their ears. His anger swung from the innkeeper, to the serving wench, to the stable boy, and finally came to rest on the innkeeper's wife.

He opened his mouth to scream at the woman, but stopped before he could. He shook his head to clear away the anger, but the fury within him was boiling over. He doubled his hands into fists.

"She said nothing to us, Your Grace," the innkeeper answered for his people without being asked. "I did not hear her leave."

"We'll help you look for her, Your Grace," Meggie told him.

"Thank you, Madame Ruck," Conar said in as calm and pleasant voice as he could muster, "but I can travel faster on my own. Stay here, Mam'selle," he said over his shoulder to Gezelle.

"You're going after her?" Gezelle called.

Conar turned on her as he reached the door, his face ugly with rage. "What do you think?"

"I think you won't find her, Your Grace."

"Oh, I'll find her," he spat, yanking open the door. "I'll find her if I have to take this gods-be-damned kingdom apart stone by bloody stone!"

He slammed the door with a loud bang.

* * * *

Sometime toward dawn of the following day, Gezelle awoke to hard pounding on her door. When she opened the portal, she drew in a sharp breath as she took in the appearance of the man standing on the threshold.

Conar's eyes were haunted; his face was pallid with worry; his mouth was set in a hard grimace. Dark circles accentuated the dullness in his eyes, the tiredness of his face.

"How did you know I wouldn't find her?" His voice was hoarse as though he had been shouting the entire time he had been gone.

She took a moment before she could answer. The hurt look worried her and she didn't want to add to his misery. She was trying to decide how best to tell him her news.

He solved her dilemma.

Conar pushed past her and stalked into the room. "If you know something, Mam'selle, you'd best tell me now. I'm in no mood for equivocating."

She took a deep breath as she watched him sit impatiently on the edge of her bed. Letting out her nervousness along with her breath, she met his gaze.

"That last eve at Norus something strange happened, Your Grace. You sent me after the wine for the lady but when I brought it to her, she didn't want it. She let me have it." The girl ducked her head in embarrassment. When she looked up again, she could see he was struggling to control his rage and no doubt his desire to do her bodily harm.

"It, it made me real sleepy. I've never had wine before and I don't wish to sample its wonders ever again." She bit her lip as he growled with anger. "I remember someone coming to the door before I fell asleep. A man came. I think it was Sir Belvoir, the Master-at-Arms, but I was so sleepy I couldn't truly see him all that well. I heard him speaking, but I couldn't make out the words because he was talking so low. He seemed very upset and when the lady answered him, she was as mad as I've ever heard a lady get."

"What does any of this have to do with where Liza went?"

"If you'll be patient, Your Grace, I will tell you!" Gezelle shot back amazed she could speak in such a manner to her Overlord. Obviously he was, too, for he looked at her with an expression of surprise and admiration. At least she thought it could well be admiration and took heart that he hadn't thundered at her again.

"I heard her tell this man that she would take care of everything, for him not to worry. Then she said she would be sure to tell her mother of his kindness."

"Her mother?" Conar's eyes flared with surprise. "How would the man know her mother?" He thought back to the Master-at-Arms, at the way Belvoir looked with his black hair and green eyes. He remembered the black dagger stuck in the top of the knight's boot, a dagger similar to those Liza carried, and grimaced in speculation. "Could they be kin?"

"I truly don't know, Your Grace. All I do know is she told him to get word to the keep that she was on her way to Boreas with the Prince

Regent. She told him to be careful whose ears heard that message and then she closed the door and went to the fireplace."

"Then she must know Belvoir." His mind was working as he pondered the possibility of Belvoir and Liza being from the same place; but where the hell was that?

"I think she must know him, Your Grace. He seemed too concerned with the lady's welfare for him to be a stranger."

"Aye that he did." Conar ran a distracted hand through his tousled hair and stood, his hand still locked in the thick gold tresses. "What happened then?"

"The lady knelt by the fire, staring hard into the flames, and then she began to rub that black stone she wears around her neck."

"The rune stone."

"Aye."

He walked to the window and eased away the curtain with his knuckles. Squinting into the rosy glow of the morning sun, he combed his fingers through his hair and then let his hand drop. "Then what?"

"She spoke to the fire, Your Grace." When he glanced back at her with surprise, she nodded to assure him he had heard correctly. "She spoke the Old Language. It's the language my old granny used when she talked to the animals and such."

"A foreign language?"

"No, Your Grace. The language of the Great Lady."

"You speak the language of the Multitude?" When the girl shook her head in denial, he snarled, "Then how the hell do you know it was that particular language?"

"My granny taught me some of the protective words. Words to ward off ills and the like."

"And just how did she know this language?" He couldn't believe the girl was telling the truth. How did a servant come by such knowledge?

"My granny was a maid to one of the Daughters long before my mother was born. She was one of the Handmaidens of the Lady Moira Hesar before she left Virago."

Stunned disbelief hit him and he let go the curtain. "She was one of my mother's women?"

"Before she married her first husband, the gentleman who died. When your mother married your father, our King, my granny came from Virago to Serenia with the new Queen."

"If your granny knew the protective words she taught you, then she was no mere handmaiden, Mam'selle. Was she?"

"I don't know what her position was with the Queen. All I know is that when my granny got too old to work, she moved to the little cottage by the King's game preserve and then my mother came there to birth me when she was fourteen. I never knew who my father was, but I think he was a gentleman at the court because that is where my mother was born and where she held a job as a seamstress."

He could not have cared less about the girl's parentage. He was interested in knowing how Liza had come by her knowledge of the Multitude's language. Was she, too, a handmaiden to a Daughter? "What happened when she spoke to the fire?"

"The room became very, very cold, Your Grace. The fire in the hearth leapt and sputtered, but the room was like a freezing January day. I thought a window might be open, for a wind was whistling." Gezelle shook her head as though to deny what she was about to say. "Then I thought I saw things in the fire. Things that made little noises like cats purring. The lady was purring, too, except she was purring in that strange language."

"Cat things," he said in a flat, disbelieving voice.

"I know it sounds odd, and I know I was sleepy, but I swear I saw them, Your Grace."

"So she spoke to these cat things. What did she say to them?"

"She was chanting a protection spell. I don't know what the words mean, all I know is they have great power to ward off the beasties from the night. My granny used to sit before the fire on the eve of the Windless Night and chant them over and over."

Conar hung his head with exasperation. Would the girl never finish her tale? "What happened after she said the incantation?"

"She was angry, Your Grace, very angry. When she got up, that same man was waiting at the door for her and I heard him tell her he would take her to the place where her man was being kept."

"Her man?" Conar ground his teeth. "And what man was that?"

Gezelle flinched at his tone. "I don't know, Your Grace."

He returned his attention to the window. Had there been a man at Norus waiting for Liza? Who could he be? Could all of this have been planned, his meeting Liza?

"So he took her to meet this man?" Conar snarled.

"No, Milord. She told the man it wasn't necessary for him to go with her. She said her love would take her there." Gezelle saw his shoulders sag with defeat and felt a hurt go through her like nothing she had ever known. "She loves you, Your Grace."

"Aye, so she said," he said bitterly.

"I believe it with all my heart."

"I found no trace of her horse in the stable even though I had saddled it myself not five minutes before I came in to get her. There were no hoof prints leading away from the tavern and there should have been hoof prints in all the mud. The stable boy didn't leave until he heard all the commotion in the tavern. He neither saw nor heard that mare leave nor did he see anyone enter the stable." He leaned his head against the cool window glass. "How could that be?"

"What did her note say?"

He blinked. "Damn! I haven't read it!" He pulled the parchment from his leather jacket, smoothing the paper on his knee. He scanned the writing once, twice, three times then hissed, tossing the note on the bed. "She didn't say anything at all to you?"

"We were on the stairway, Your Grace. She was behind me and I heard her stop. I looked back at her and she was looking behind her, over her shoulder as though someone had called her name. I saw her trembling as with the ague. I thought something ailed her, but when I asked her what was wrong, she just shook her head.

"She looked down at me with the saddest expression I have ever seen and then she reached into her sleeve and drew out the note, telling me to bid you goodbye for her. I asked her where she was going. She just smiled, but that smile never reached her eyes, Your Grace. It was as though she was smiling with her lips, but her heart was breaking. I looked at the note, and I swear to you, Your Grace, by the holy name of Alel, when I looked up again, she was gone. She had vanished on the stairs."

Gezelle seemed to truly believe what she was telling him, but Conar found it hard to accept. He stared at her for a long time, seeing the worry in her eyes, feeling her own bewildered pain at Liza's sudden departure. A slow anger began to seethe in the blue depths of his eyes. Emotion after emotion grew until he looked away.

"Get yourself ready, Mam'selle." He pushed away from the window and strode heavily through the small room. Flinging open the door, he told her, "You and I are going to Boreas, with or without her. But I swear to the gods, Gezelle, if it takes the rest of my life, natural or otherwise, I will find that woman!"

Gezelle could hear his hissing words even as his booted heels thumped down the stairs.

"And I will make her rue the day she ever, ever played me for a fool!"

Gezelle glanced at the crumpled note lying atop her disheveled bed. She had never learned how to read and she was glad she couldn't. Whatever had been in that note had taken the heart out of Prince Conar McGregor.

* * * *

When Meggie Ruck changed the linens in the room where her two female guests had slept, she saw the note lying in the cold ashes of the fireplace. Picking it up, she read the missive, but the message made no sense to her. Wadding it up again, she tossed it into the fireplace.

"What did it say, Meggie?" Harry asked his wife that night as they prepared for bed.

"Didn't make no sense, Dearling. I thought it might have had a clue as to where the lady took herself off to. But all it said was: the journey's done."

"What journey?" Harry yawned.

"I don't have the faintest notion, Harry!" Meggie said with exasperation.

But as he rode ahead of Gezelle on the road to Boreas, Conar McGregor thought back to that message contained in the note and a fierce gleam came into his cold blue eyes. He had promised himself to Liza for the journey to Boreas.

"Well," he thought, rage filling his heart, "I didn't say the gods-be-damned journey was over!"

## Chapter Thirteen

"Your Grace?" Gezelle was trying desperately to keep up with Conar's long stride as he stomped through the main hall of Boreas Keep. Her shorter legs were pumping furiously beneath her light muslin gown as she tried to gain his attention.

"What?" he shouted, never breaking his stride.

"Your brother sent me to find you, Your Grace. The last search party you sent out has returned." She almost plowed into his broad back as he stopped suddenly, spinning around to glare at her.

He knew even before he asked that the searchers had come back as empty-handed as he had. "And?"

Gezelle bit her lip before answering. She hated to see him so hurt. "The men found no trace of her."

"How the hell can that be?" Blazing fury replaced the hope of a few moments earlier, etching deep lines in the sun crinkles at his temples. "I don't understand! How can she just disappear without a trace?"

It had been two months since Liza had left them at the Briar's Hold Inn. Conar had sent out mercenaries, soldiers, members of his own Elite, even men he had hired to cross borders into the neighboring countries, both friendly and unfriendly, to ask questions. None of the men had brought back even one clue as to the girl's whereabouts. What was more, not one had been able to gather any encouraging word concerning the girl's existence. It was as though Liza had never been.

"Did we dream her?" Conar asked Gezelle one night as he sat brooding in the keep's formal garden. "Was she some succubus, a NightWind who happened along to ensnare me, 'Zelle? If so, I would gladly sell my soul to the demons of the Abyss to have her back."

"Come inside, Your Grace," she pleaded with him. "It is too cold out here." Snow sifted through the branches overhead.

"Not as cold as my heart," he said miserably.

"We will keep looking, Your Majesty."

"I will find her, 'Zelle."

"I wish I could help. I have tried talking to some of the women here, but none of them admit to knowing any lady connected with the Daughterhood of the Multitude. Many of them have chastised me for speaking of the Multitude's existence."

"They'd better not 'cause you trouble," he said, a militant gleam crossing his features. "If the bitches so much as say one wise word to you, I'll have them banned from this court!"

And Gezelle knew he meant it. She smiled tenderly. "The ladies have been kind to me for the most part."

"They'd better be!"

She didn't dare tell him that there were a few she had caught looking at her as though they ached to say something they dared not. She wasn't sure if what the ladies wanted to say was good or bad or if it might pertain to the lady he was seeking. Gezelle only knew her Prince would pounce on those poor women like a hound on a rabbit if he suspected they knew something they weren't telling.

"You knew I had sent Rayle to Norus to find Belvoir, didn't you?" he asked.

"Aye, I had heard, Your Grace."

"Stop calling me that!" he thundered. He clenched his teeth and glared at her, striving to calm his raging temper. He sucked in a long breath, then exhaled. "If you must give me a title, 'Zelle, call me Milord." He saw her hesitate. "I command it, Mam'selle."

They had had this argument before. Gezelle shook her head. "It is disrespectful, Your...." She stopped at his warning growl. Her head dipped. "As you wish, Milord."

"That's better. I despise titles. By the gods, how I despise titles!" He sat on a bench beside a marble fountain and threw back his head. "I just don't understand any of this. I went looking for her at Norus that day, but she hadn't returned there. Both Belvoir and Galen were gone so I didn't get to question either of them. And when Rayle got to Norus, he found Belvoir gone again. This time on a leave of absence. That stupid brother of mine had given the man a leave of absence!" He glared at the ceiling as though he were glaring at Galen. "The bastard didn't even know where his man went." He looked at Gezelle. "And he didn't even know where Belvoir called home. Can you believe that?"

"Perhaps Sir Belvoir didn't wish for him to know, Milord." She hesitated only a moment before placing her hand on his shoulder. It was a mark of the growing friendship between them that she dared to do so. Her fingers caressed his tense shoulder beneath the fabric of his cambric shirt. "Someone will come forward eventually."

"The gods help anyone keeping knowledge of her from me!" His mouth twisted in a line of hurt. "I'll make them sorry they did."

Gezelle didn't doubt that for a moment. "Is there anything you wish for me to tell your brother, Milord?"

"Tell him...." He shook his head. If he didn't get out of this damned keep, he'd explode. "Never mind. There's not a gods-be-damned thing Legion can do!" He stormed out of the keep with his shoulders bunched in anger.

* * * *

Stomping through the Central Hall of Boreas Keep, Conar did not see the beauty that enraptured all those who viewed it. He did not notice the glory that was his birthright. The keep and the palace had become claustrophobic to him in the last two months. He spent more and more time outside, riding, searching, asking the same questions over and over and over again until he thought he would go insane. He would come back at night, late, exhausted, heartsick, but he would be up again at first light to start all over.

Taking the passageway that led from the Central Hall to the artisans' quarters and beyond that the drawbridge, his thoughts were not on the bustling activity surrounding him. He did not see servant and freeman stop in their work and nod to him. He saw nothing save the blazing red haze before him. He crossed from the artisan passageway to the rock-strewn path leading to the inner bailey and all but ignored two of his children who called to him as he passed.

Watching from the shaded overhang of the medical passageway, an older man paid close attention as Conar practically ran over the drawbridge and took the turn toward Lake Myria.

"In a foul mood again, eh?" the keep's physician asked the watcher.

"It would appear so, Cayn," the watcher sighed. "I'd better see to him."

Conar was walking rapidly through the thick trees that rimmed Lake Myria. He was wrestling with his fury, unable to bring it under control. He had become so irascible that his own father and brothers would not go near him. He snapped at anyone who dared annoy him.

His food was either too hot or too cold. His bed was too lumpy or too smooth. Not enough covers, too many. His clothes were either too limp or too full of starch. If his bath water was the right temperature, the towels were too scratchy. His boots could never be too shiny, or else they were so shiny they gave him a blaring headache.

Gezelle had been pleased when he had installed her in the tiny servant' room just off his own. It was a room reserved for his personal manservant, but since Conar had never wanted the services of such a gentleman, Gezelle took over the duties of the apartments where his lady-wife and her handmaidens would one day reside. She also took over the care of his bedchambers, saw to his clothing, his linens, and the cleaning of his office. Happy as she was with her new life, there were times when even she felt like pushing him over the balcony and into the thick brambles beside the sea gate.

Perhaps the only person other than Gezelle still willing to endure his outbursts, was his half-brother, Legion A'Lex.

Lord Legion--eight years older than Conar--was the eldest of King Gerren's bastard sons. Given the status of Vice-Commander of the Serenian Force, second only to Conar who was titular commander, Legion was a soldier first, a lover second, and a statesman third. His training at the hands of the Wind Warrior Society had honed his body into a prime example of young manhood. Weightlifting and wrestling competitions kept it that way.

With his dark brown wavy hair and startling blue eyes so like Conar's, Legion A'Lex never had trouble finding a female companion with whom to wile away the hours. His thick, dark lashes would sweep over the amber-fire of his flashing eyes and the lady would melt right into his bed. Twin dimples in his lean cheeks gave him just the right amount of boyish charm to soften even the hardest of maiden's hearts and loosen even the tightest clamped thighs. His tall frame--he was well over six feet--his heavily furred chest, wide and hard as flint, his long legs and thick hands, always caught the ladies' eye when he stripped down for competition in the soldier's compound each month.

Totally devoted to his father and his father's firstborn legal heir, Legion A'Lex had a strong attachment to Conar that went far beyond brotherly love and devotion. They were the best of friends and there was a bond between them that survived boyhood tantrums, fist fights, stolen girlfriends and lost competitions on horses, with weapons and in wrestling matches. There was naturally a rivalry between them and Conar tried to do everything his older brother could do. By the time he had reached his eighteenth birthday, there was precious little Legion could do that Conar couldn't.

Just as his love for Conar made him overly concerned and overly protective of his younger brother, Legion's anxiety over Conar's current foul temper and morbidity made him want to throttle the lad. In his wisdom, Legion felt Conar needed something only he, himself, could give him.

Putting aside his titles of lover and soldier, Legion A'Lex donned the mantle of scholarly statesman and fell into step behind his brother as Conar left the keep.

* * * *

Conar didn't look back; he didn't need to. He could hear Legion crashing through the foliage like a bull elephant. He grimaced, wondering why it was Legion could never leave him the hell alone. He angrily shoved a branch from his path, cursing at the world in general as a sliver of bark drove under his thumbnail. Sucking on his injured finger, he came into a clearing where a small pond fed from the waters of Lake Myria. He had often swum here when he was a boy and it was here that he came when he wanted to be alone.

Not that Legion was going to let him alone, he thought with malice. Legion had a way of interfering when he should keep his nose out of other people's business.

Conar didn't look up as Legion joined him. He continued to sit on his favorite rock, his head in his hand, staring at the ground. He was aware of Legion coming to sit beside him on the moss-covered ground, stretching his long legs, leaning back on his elbows, but he totally ignored the man, preferring the silence of the forest to conversation with unwanted company.

Legion glanced at his brother, shook his head, and lay on the ground, his head cupped in the palms of his hands. He started to hum.

For a long time neither spoke. Conar continued to pretend Legion wasn't there; Legion continued to hum.

It wasn't actually a tune Legion was humming. Legion A'Lex was tone-deaf, going about humming and singing off-key.

Conar could stand it no longer. He raised his head and snapped caustically at his brother. "Is there something you want, Legion?"

Legion shook his head ... and continued to hum.

"Did you come here for a reason?"

"Nope," Legion took the time to say before humming louder.

Conar turned his head from Legion's merry grin and stared into the forest, wishing with his entire being a were-tiger would hear that infernal humming and come to gobble up A'Lex. If it was bothering him, it had to be bothering every creature within earshot.

"Aren't you needed somewhere, Legion?"

"Nope." Legion began singing a song Conar knew all too well. And was murdering the little ditty.

"I don't need this, Legion!"

Legion gave his brother a lewd wink and wagged his bushy brows. "Oh, I think we are all fully aware of what you need!"

"The demons take you, A'Lex!" Conar shouted, coming to his feet in a lithe bound. Putting his hands on his hips, he glared at his older brother. "Leave, damn it!"

"And if I don't?" Legion began to whistle.

"I'll throw your ass in the pond." There was steel in his tone.

Legion snorted at the suggestion and resumed humming.

Conar blinked. "I've no great desire to fight you, Legion."

"I would think not, all things considered, but I think we shall see who throws who into yon pond." Legion unfolded his arms and braced himself. He wiggled his fingers at his brother. "Okay, come on. I don't have all day to put your snotty little butt in its place. Let's do it."

Conar risked a look at the pond. "Just go back to the keep and let me have some peace. I--"

"Let's do it!"

Conar knew that look in his older brother's eye. He'd seen that look too many times over the years. Not wanting to wind up in the pond, he feigned running to his left. When Legion started that way, Conar darted to the right. He'd gotten only a few feet before Legion tackled him from behind and sent him crashing to the mossy ground. He landed heavily, Legion's weight pressed solidly against his back.

"Get off!" Conar managed to gasp.

"No," Legion bent forward and purred in his ear. "Hey! Listen. You wanna feel something really interesting, Conar?"

Conar tensed, expecting a band of pain somewhere on his body. He wasn't prepared for his big brother's ultimate attack.

"Let's see if I remember how this goes," Legion said in a wondering tone. He thrust his tongue deep into Conar's ear, chuckling as the boy jumped, squirming desperately to get away.

"Shit!" Conar screeched, shuddering all over.

"And how 'bout this?" Legion crowed, jerking Conar to his feet, lifting him and tossing him like a bag of salt into the pond.

Legion chuckled as Conar's head broke the pond's surface. He heard Conar's gasp and knew the water must be like ice this time of year. He raised his head and grinned at Conar's wide-mouthed gape as the boy drew in quick gasps of air.

"Cold?" Legion inquired. When Conar didn't answer, Legion rubbed it in. "Who's in the pond, Conar?"

"The hell with you!" Conar sputtered, his teeth chattering.

"A little upset, are we?" Legion asked, clucking his tongue as though at an unruly child.

"Go to hell!"

"Not a happy soldier, huh?"

Glaring hotly at his brother, not an easy thing to do since he was freezing to death, Conar reached out his hand. "Help me out, Legion."

Legion's mouth dropped open. "Are you serious? You got yourself in; get yourself out!"

Conar mumbled and waded out of the pond, the water coming only up to his shriveled paps. He struggled up the slippery bank to flop on his stomach, coughing up some of the icy water he had accidentally ingested as he hit the surface. He shivered from head to toe.

Several minutes passed before Conar broke the silence. "You could have broken my arm, Legion." He bent his arm, testing it, wincing with the pain in his shoulder caused from the angle in which he'd landed in the pond.

"If that's what it would have taken."

Conar looked at his brother. "You've never hurt me before."

"I know." Legion turned his head also.

"Why did you feel the need to hurt me?"

Legion sighed. "Because," he said as though speaking to a not-too-bright child, "you haven't been the most pleasant of companions of late. You have managed to single-handedly make life most impossible to enjoy. If it hadn't been me, then someone less tender, and less inclined to play with you, would have taken your ass down."

"You call nearly drowning me being gentle, do you?"

"I pity this woman who has caught your attention."

Conar frowned with annoyance. "Just what the hell is that supposed to mean?"

"Have you forgotten your betrothal?"

Conar glared. "You know damned well I haven't. As if I could forget it!"

"Just because the wedding was postponed, doesn't mean you can go on with your dalliances. Papa made that clear the other night at table. Your marriage contract expressly forbids liaisons within six months of your marriage date."

Conar snorted. "I know what the gods-be-damned thing states."

"But you ignore it, don't you?"

"I'm not a damned eunuch and I'll be damned if I'll let Shaz and Medea and The Toad turn me into one!" His eyes were hard and unforgiving.

"And you know perfectly well there are ways of relieving yourself--"

"I won't do that!" Conar shouted.

"Will you let me finish? There are plenty of women at the keep more than willing to ease you, if that's what ails you. You don't have to engage in copulation to relieve sexual tension." Legion stared at his brother's angry profile. "Have you held to the bargain?"

Conar refused to answer.

"Conar, look at me." When his brother stared adamantly away, Legion lowered his voice to a plea. "Will you please look at me?"

Conar turned his head and fused his gaze with Legion's.

"Have you held to the bargain?"

"No."

Legion sighed. "I didn't think so. This woman you had me send men out to find, this woman you say was traveling with you, is she the reason you have not kept your end of the bargain?"

"I made no bargain."

"No, Papa and your mother made the bargain in your name."

"If you think to shame me with that useless piece of information, you can't."

"I wasn't trying to, Conar." He cleared his throat. "Is this woman special to you, little brother?"

"What do you mean?"

"You know precisely what I mean, Coni."

"I care for her, aye."

"Have you slept with her?"

"That's none of your business!"

"You told me and Papa that you were worried about this woman who just disappeared from the inn. You gave us the impression she was an indentured servant that you were bringing her here to Boreas along with Gezelle. But she isn't just a bondservant, is she?"

"I never told you she was a servant."

"You implied it." Legion let out a frustrated breath. "Who is this woman? And what is she to you?"

"A friend."

"A friend? Who do you think you're talking to? You have let this woman become an obsession and that's not like you, Conar. Any woman can--"

"I need her," Conar interrupted.

"You need a woman," Legion corrected.

"Damn it! I need this woman, Legion!" Conar shouted, turning his fierce gaze to his brother. His mouth was set in a hard line that brooked no argument.

"Why?"

"I just do."

"Why do you need this particular woman? What is she to you?"

"I told you. She's a...."

"A friend," Legion finished for him. "A man doesn't behave toward a mere friend like you're behaving over this woman. You eat and drink and breathe her. Don't you see that you have let her become all there is for you? No one else seems to matter." Legion touched his brother's shoulder. "I'll ask you again ... have you slept with her?"

"What if I have?"

"Damn it!" Legion spat with annoyance. "Have you slept with this woman?"

"Yes!" Conar shouted and looked out over the pond.

Legion shook his head and let a long, weary sigh. "That wasn't very smart, now, was it?"

"When is falling in love ever smart?"

Legion stared at Conar. "The gods help you. How could you have let that happen?"

Conar shrugged. "I didn't intend for it to." He turned his troubled gaze to his brother. "She was easy to love. For the first time in my life, the very first time, I met someone who loved me, a woman who loved me, not who I am or what I can give her. She asked for only a moment of my time, a few days of travel to the capitol. She made a promise that when that journey was done, she'd leave and never ask anything of me again." He looked away. "She kept her bargain. She left." His last two words were soft whispers of misery.

"And you can't accept that?"

"I can not."

Legion draped a protective arm around Conar. "And it hurts."

"Worse than you can imagine."

Legion squeezed his brother to him. "Like you, I've never known what it feels like to love, really love a woman, but I've always known one day I'd meet that special woman who turned my world upside down. With all the women you've been with, you should have realized it could happen. But you didn't, did you?"

Conar shook his head. "No woman has ever touched me like this woman, Legion. I don't mean just physically, although in that regard she was different from all the others, too. Making love to her was like riding on the wind. She touched me here, Legion," he said, placing his hand over his heart.

"You do know that if we ever find this woman, you won't be allowed to keep her with you. You would only have to give her up eventually. Best that it be now before it has gone too far and there is still time to turn back."

"If I ever find her again, Legion, I will not let her leave ever again. I can't and I won't."

"You won't be given the choice, Conar. They will take her from you in the end."

### Chapter Fourteen

The messenger came around noon on the eighth day after the incident at the pond.

Conar still stalked about the keep in a near-insane rage, but he kept mostly to himself. He ignored Legion, being civil to his brother only when in the presence of their father, for King Gerren detested turmoil of any nature within his keep.

Confining himself to the lower portions of the keep, daring anyone to either speak or look at him, Conar did not create the havoc of days before. He sulked, sitting by himself, glaring out the windows, turning a hostile eye to those incautious enough to venture too near; but he didn't start arguments, didn't voice opinions concerning the way he was being provided for. His frown and his narrowed eyes usually let those who encountered him know he was not in the mood for company.

Now a messenger waited in the kitchens with a note for the Prince Regent and no one wanted to carry it to him.

"Unh, unh! Not me!" vowed Rayle Loure as he sat eating his lunch. "I like my head right where it is." He glanced at his twin, Thom, who shook his head, as well.

"It may not be the prettiest head in the realm," Thom added, "but I like mine well enough." He ran his hand over a huge head devoid of hair. "Give it to Lord Legion. He's not afraid to take it to the Prince."

Making an ugly snort, the old cook swatted the tallest of the Elite Guard with her dishrag. "You call yourself a warrior? Some brave man you are, Rayle Loure." She turned her small black eyes to Rayle's twin. "And you," she snorted again, "you are a mealy-mouthed pussy cat, you are, Thom Loure!" She turned her angry gaze to the two men who also sat at the table with the Loure twins. "And just what are your excuses?"

Marsh Edan, second in command of the Elite Guard, filled his mouth with a biscuit and grinned. He had no intention of defending himself to the old hag. He turned to look at the man beside him and raised his brows in challenge.

"Give it to Lord Teal." Storm Jale, another Elite, ducked his head. "He hasn't got his ass in trouble with Coni lately. It'll do him good." He shoveled peas into his mouth and talked around the green gob. "It'll help keep the bugger humble."

"Lord Teal took the Prince's son, Wyn, hunting with him this morn," the cook snarled. "I don't see why you are so scared of the little brat. He's just a man!"

Storm coughed, glancing at the old woman with a look of disbelief on his handsome face. "He's the Prince Regent, Sadie. You tread easy around him these days or you're likely wind up doing duty in some godforsaken outpost on the Diabolusian frontier."

"That, I might add," Sadie scoffed, "would do you good, Storm Jale!" Her beady eyes assessed him. "You could stand to lose a few pounds."

"It's your cooking," Marsh said, defending his friend and cousin.

"It's him shoveling food into that pretty little mouth of his!" Sadie shot back. "Did it not occur to you men this message might be important?"

"And it might be the worst kind of news, too," Thom told her. "Why don't you take it to him, Sadie, if you aren't afraid?"

Sadie MacCorkingdale drew up her five feet tall, nearly as wide, frame and glared at him. "I would, but there ain't a soul in this damned keep that can do my work while I hunt down the little bugger!"

"But you aren't afraid of him, huh?" Rayle asked, winking at his brother.

"Not me, you overgrown oaf!" Sadie wiped her hands on her apron and folded her arms over her more-than-ample bosom. "You don't see me cowering behind this old cook's skirts so I don't get snapped at by the snotty young Prince!" She sniffed and swung her eyes to Marsh once more. "You're getting crumbs all over my table, Edan!"

Gezelle, who had been sitting quietly in the corner near the crackling fireplace, laid aside her sewing. She had been mending a shirt the Prince had ripped off; the third one that week. "I'll take it up to him," she said, reaching for the note. "Mayhap he won't bite off my head."

Handing the note to Gezelle, Sadie eyed the girl up and down. "He wouldn't dare, 'Zelle," she murmured, smiling a toothless grin at the former servant. "Who'd hurt a wee thing like you?"

"He would." Rayle grimaced. "You better not get too close to him, 'Zelle. Just hand it over and run like the devil was after your pretty little rump."

"Don't you be paying him no never mind!" Sadie ordered. She patted Gezelle's arm. "His Lordship wouldn't do you harm no matter what his mood!" Her beady black eyes squinted. "Least ways, he better not!"

Gezelle smiled. She liked the old lady. From the very first hour she was at Boreas Keep, Sadie MacCorkingdale had befriended her, taking her under a massive wing to show her about the keep and make her feel at home. It had been Sadie who let the other servants know Gezelle was no servant, but a trusted, valued friend of the Prince Regent. It had been Sadie who had held the young girl as she wept for the Prince's pain at losing the Lady Liza. And it was always Sadie who ran interference for Gezelle with those servants who would have caused the young girl a problem.

"You remind me of my darling Joannie, you do," Sadie had told her one day as she sat helping the old cook pare apples for a pie. "My girl what died."

The hard black eyes had softened and the pursed and wrinkled mouth had relaxed into what passed as a smile for Sadie MacCorkingdale. She had sighed and a tear slid down her weathered cheek. Putting up a rough, red and cracked hand, the old cook had angrily brushed away the offending sign of humanity.

"If things had been different," she had said in her rough, North Virago brogue, "my Joannie would have been a grand lady." Her cryptic remark was all Gezelle could get out of her.

"You better get that missive to His Grace," Marsh told Gezelle. "It might well be important."

Gazing at the rolled parchment, 'Zelle wished she could read. If it was bad news, she knew he'd more than likely snap at her for bringing it. Not that it mattered whether he did or not; the young Prince always apologized to her, if no one else, for his constant outbursts of bad temper. Nevertheless, her footsteps were slow as she started up the stairs to the sleeping chambers where she knew His Grace would be.

"How are you this lovely morn, 'Zelle?" King Gerren called to her from the library door.

Gezelle looked over the curving balustrade and curtsied to her sovereign. "I am well, Highness. How are you?"

King Gerren smiled warmly. "My days are always brighter when I chance upon your face." He laughed at the immediate blush that spread over the girl's delicate oval face. "What have you, pretty lady?"

"A note for His Grace," she said and a beam of sunlight lit her face as she smiled. "Would you like to take it up to him?"

"No!" Gerren said with mock horror, putting a hand over his heart. "Not I, Mam'selle! I prefer nothing, including that ill-tempered son of mine, to spoil my day!" He patted her hand on the balustrade, then continued on his way.

"It's going to ruin mine," Gezelle mumbled as she started her climb.

As had become her routine when ascending these stairs, 'Zelle gazed at the gallery of family portraits hanging on the walls. All the McGregor line from King Theils, the Elder, first Monarch of Serenia, to Prince Dyllon, King Gerren's youngest legal son and his lovely auburn-haired wife, were represented in portraits framed in rich, warm, ebony wood gilded with pure gold.

Conar's portrait, with the crystal circlet of Prince Regent shining atop his golden hair, was attached to Prince Galen's portrait by a thin golden chain, signifying the dual birth. Several such chains linked other portraits along the wall, for twins tended to run in the McGregor line.

Above the last four men of the Prince Regent's family--himself, Prince Galen, Princes Coron, and Dyllon--hung the portrait of their mother, Queen Moira of Virago. Her golden beauty with its sparkling hazel eyes always kindled sadness in Gezelle. The beautiful face that beamed down upon the viewer was gentle and warm. It never failed to make those viewing it smile. The lady had had that effect on most of those who knew her.

As she approached Conar's door, Gezelle heard a loud crash followed by a louder vulgarity that brought a blush of shame to the young girl's face. Pursing her lips, she timidly raised her hand and knocked lightly at the oak portal.

There was no answer, only a muffled, equally vitriolic curse from behind the door.

Taking a deep breath, she was about to knock again when the door was jerked open. Conar stood in the doorway, his shirt unbuttoned and hanging free of his breeches, his hair tousled, and his eyes glaring.

Seeing the girl standing at his door, Conar bit off the crude remark he had been about to make. Instead, he turned his back and stomped away, crossing to his armoire, the contents of which lay scattered about his floor. He kicked a large vase of flowers out of his way as he strode to the dark mahogany chest and rumbled inside. Knowing the girl wouldn't dare speak unless he did, he craned his neck and peered at her over his shoulder.

"Did you want something, 'Zelle?"

Tearing her gaze from the lovely vase that had been shattered with his vicious kick, Gezelle extended the parchment to him. "This came for you awhile ago, Milord."

Conar frowned. "Put it on the desk, then."

Gezelle bit her lip. The messenger had indicated that the message was important. "Begging your pardon, Milord, but I believe 'tis most urgent."

"It can wait," he snapped and resumed his ransack of the armoire with the total abandon of someone who does not have to straighten, iron or clean such things. Some clothes already lay in a tangled heap in the unlit hearth. Some lay discarded in a heap at the foot of his bed.

Gezelle sighed. Why did the man insist on ruining his clothing in such a manner? "Your Grace?" she said in exasperation as he ripped a shirt and threw it behind him, "the man said he needed an answer right away."

Conar spun around with an ugly grimace on his face. "And I said it could wait, Mam'selle! Don't belabor the point!" He saw her cringe against the door and snarled under his breath. He had his bastard brother, Galen, to thank for the girl being so easily unnerved. He lowered his voice. "What's in the gods-be-damned thing, anyway?" he sniffed, turning away again.

Gezelle had no way of knowing Conar was accustomed to having his mail perused by others. She was offended that he thought she had read his private mail, even if she could have done so. Her chin came up a fraction with indignation. "I would never presume to open your mail, Milord."

Sighing like a man much put upon and misunderstood, he raised his eyes to the heavens. With a sweet, mocking smile, he turned and spoke to her in a voice he reserved for his youngest children. "Well, then, sweet one, open it for me now and read it if it's all that important."

"I would rather not," she mumbled, her eyes downcast.

Not bothering to see the blush of embarrassment on her lovely face, he snapped before he thought. "I'm not asking you to read it, woman! I am ordering you to do so!"

"I can't, Milord," she said miserably.

"Mam'selle," he began, annoyed she would dare cause him further anger, "I have commanded you." He finally saw her face and it struck him like a blow to the gut that the girl probably couldn't read and was too embarrassed to tell him. Mentally kicking himself, he held out his hand. "Let me have it, 'Zelle."

Gezelle walked toward him, wary, her chin trembling. Not even his most charming smile, now bestowed upon her with mute apology, could still the wild beating of her heart nor dry the tears threatening to spill.

As he took the note from her, he lightly caught her hand in a gentle grip and wouldn't let go. He could feel her trembling. He bent his knees and craned his neck to look up into her downcast face. Enticing her with a dazzling grin, he made her look at him, making a mental note to see that someone began to teach the girl to read this very day.

Gezelle couldn't resist the impish grin. Her lips twitched with humor as he wagged his eyebrows, teasing her into a laugh she couldn't stop. She forgot all about her hurt.

"See," he told her, tugging on her hand, "I'm not such a great bad beastie, after all."

He tossed the parchment on the bed and then sat on the rumpled coverlet, patting the place beside him, indicating that he wanted her to sit. Since he still had a light grip on her hand, she had no choice but to join him, even though her knees were shaking and there was hesitation in her lovely green eyes.

"You do know you have nothing to fear at Boreas, don't you, 'Zelle?" he asked, stroking her hand between his own.

Gezelle nodded.

"And you do know that if anyone should offend you or harm you in any way, they would have me to answer to?" He could feel her shivering and he let go her hand, instinctively realizing she might think his intentions less than honorable. "No one in this keep, or any other that belongs to me, will force you to do anything you don't want to do. Not now; not ever. No man under my command would even dare suggest you do something you find wrong. And that includes me."

She knew he was trying to reassure her. She began to relax under the steady glow of his warm, engaging smile.

"There will come a day when some man will come to me and ask for your hand in marriage," he said as he stood and walked to the window. Looking back over his shoulder, he held her gaze. "If I don't find that man worthy of you, 'Zelle, he'll not have you. It's as simple as that." He turned to look outside. "I will see you happy, for I feel she would want me to see to it."

Gathering her courage, for his pain hurt her as deeply as though it was her own, she stood and joined him at the window. Hesitant at first, but overcome with her love for him, wanting to ease his torment and give him peace, she placed a trembling hand on his shoulder. He laid his cheek on her fingers and lightly rubbed the bristles of his unshaven face on their softness.

Conar sighed. He gently placed his lips along her knuckles and kissed the cool fingers. "Thank you for caring, 'Zelle."

"If there is anything I may do, Milord...."

"I wish to the gods there was," he said and raised his head to look out the window once more. "But there is nothing any one can do."

"If it is the gods' will, Milord," she told him, smoothing her hand over the tense muscles of his back, "she will return to you."

He nodded. "Do me a favor, Mam'selle. Have one of the guards saddle my steed. If I stay one more minute in this great pile of rocks, I shall go mad."

"The note?" she prompted, no longer afraid of his outburst.

"I shall read it," he warned in a soft voice.

After she had gone, he stood by the window, his shoulders bowed, his face buried in his forearm as he leaned against the casement.

Gezelle's touch had hurt him more than he could say. Out of all fairness to the girl, he couldn't send her away, not now that she had found a place well-suited to her, but he wished with all his heart he didn't have to see her, for her appearance bit deep into his battered soul. The two women bore such a strong, uncanny resemblance to one another--the black hair and green eyes, the delicate face, the slim and curving bodies were too similar, too familiar. The pain was too raw, as yet. The sight of Gezelle, so like his Liza, always served to remind him vividly of his loss.

Turning from the window, he snatched up his brown leather jacket. His gaze fell on the rolled parchment and he stared intently at it for a moment but then dismissed it from his mind.

As he left his chambers, he shouted at a hapless servant he chanced to pass on the stairs to make sure his room was cleaned.

"It's in a gods-be-damn mess!" he yelled as he skipped down the stone risers.

* * * *

Three days later, Conar came across the note Gezelle had brought to him. When he read it, bitter tears fell down his cheeks.

"Milord," it read, "please meet me today by the old crofter's hut on the road to Ivor Keep. I will be there until sunset. If you do not come, I will know you no longer want this woman for your love and I will leave you alone."

"*No*," Conar cried as he clutched the note to his chest. "Sweet Merciful Alel, no!" He bowed his head and gave in to soul-rending sobs.

When he had cried himself out, he went to the study, took a bottle of plum brandy, and brought it back to his room. Tilting the bottle, he drained it, and then smashed the delicate bottle against the fireplace.

He did not blame the messenger who had delivered the note nor Gezelle who had made sure he received it. He blamed no one but himself for missing the time and place of a meeting with Liza and perhaps giving her the impression he no longer wanted her.

Sinking deep into depression, abandoning his anger, he took to his bed with an arsenal of liquor and refused to leave his chambers.

Chapter Fifteen

"I have had all your shit I'm going to take, Conar!" Legion shouted at the top of his lungs. He threw open the drapes on the windows of his brother's room. "This foolishness will stop today! Get the hell out of that gods-be-damned bed. Now!"

Conar's eyes flew open as the harsh morning light flooded the room. Jerking up at the sound of his brother's bellow had been a major mistake.

Groaning, he grabbed his throbbing head and wiggled further beneath his covers. "Have pity, Legion. Shut the damn drapes. Can't you see I'm dying?"

Kicking several empty ale bottles out of his way, Legion stomped to the bed and screamed at the huddled mass under the covers. "Either get up or be dragged! Take your pick!"

Moaning in the after-throes of a violent drunk that had left puke splattered on his sheets, Conar scrunched deeper into his covers and pulled the pillow over his aching head to shut out both the noise and the light. Mumbling something about the fires of hell to his big brother, he also tried to shut out the agony throbbing in his head.

Legion put his foot on the bed and shook the mattress, gaining a muffled groan of pain from his brother. "Get up, damn it!"

Conar jammed the pillow harder over his head and mouthed a vulgarity that was meant to deter Legion from his attack.

It didn't work.

If anything, it made matters worse.

Snatching away the pillow, Legion grabbed a handful of Conar's golden hair and yanked up the young Prince's head, ignoring the sharp yelp of outraged pain.

"I said get up!" Legion yelled, releasing his hold on Conar's hair long enough to grab the young man's left arm with one hand as he flung the covers away with the other. With a mighty yank, he pulled his younger brother to a semi-erect position.

"Leave me the hell alone, A'Lex!" Conar barked, squinting up at Legion, trying to focus on the wavering face hovering over him. A sour belch bubbled out of his mouth and he grinned viciously as Legion turned his face away from the noxious smell.

"That does it!" Legion growled and leaned toward Conar, putting his hard shoulder to his brother's midsection and levering him up and out of the bed, onto his shoulder.

Conar's head swam unmercifully as he dangled over his brother's shoulder, his body limp, boneless in Legion's furious grasp. "God!" he groaned. "Put me down, Legion! I'm gonna be sick!"

Before Legion could react, he felt the rumble tearing up from his brother's throat; heard the god-awful sound of retching; felt the hot, thick liquid pour down his back and rump and legs.

A furious snarl of rage covered Legion A'Lex's face. "By all that's holy, Conar!" he screamed, "I'm gonna beat you black and blue for that!" He brought up his free hand and smacked his brother firmly on his upturned backside.

"Legion, don't!" Conar's voice was feeble and he was choking as his own puke bubbled down his nose. As Legion descended the stairs with him, the movement brought fresh nausea to his throat and as he opened his mouth to protest the treatment he was getting, more bile spewed out and dropped with a soft plop into the tops of Legion's boots. He was rewarded with another vicious swat at his backside. "Oh, god!" Conar managed to croak.

"The gods won't help you, you stupid fool!"

Everyone in the main hall looked up as Lord Legion A'Lex came down the stairs at a hard stomp. They ignored the groaning young Prince and looked to the mottled assortment of vomit that was left in the men's wake.

From his place by the library door, King Gerren smiled, nodding in satisfaction as his eldest son caught his eye. "I see you are taking care of the situation!" he called to Legion and then turned to the scribe who stood beside him. "Legion has had his fill of his baby brother's foolery, I see." He looked back at Legion as he neared the front door. "Don't hurt your little brother too badly, Legion!" He looked toward a young man. "Get the door for him, Tealson."

Lord Teal du Mer ran to the front door and jerked it open.

Legion nodded to du Mer in passing, and, never breaking his stride, headed out of the keep into the side courtyard; crossed under one canopied passageway and took another that led to the stables.

Booted feet on the wooden planks hit with hard thuds that made Conar's teeth click together and his head bounce.

Several guards and servants stopped what they were doing to watch in wonder as they realized what Lord Legion was about. They glanced at one another with worried frowns. Surely His Lordship didn't mean to do what it looked as though he was about to do. Some of the servants hurried away. Now was not the time to be a witness to Lord Legion's folly.

Stopping in front of the wide horse trough at the stable, Legion brought up his right hand that had been holding Conar's squirming legs, put it in the small of his brother's back and began to lean forward.

With a great deal of pain and effort, Conar craned his neck and realized where he was. He saw the water looming up at him. "Don't," he said weakly.

As Legion leaned further over the trough, Conar felt his body slipping off the hard shoulder and his eyes widened in stunned disbelief. "Don't you dare!" he screamed at the top of his aching lungs before he landed squarely in the center of the water trough.

Kneeling beside the trough, Legion caught Conar's head as it bobbed to the surface and pushed it back under, knocking away his brother's protesting hands as he held Conar's head under the water.

"Oh, no, you don't," Legion snarled as Conar tried to pry his brother's fingers away from their fierce grip in his flaxen hair. Legion tightened his hold and pushed the head lower in the trough.

Water flooded Conar's acrid mouth, filled his nose and ears, and threatened to rush down his throat. He fought Legion's strong grip, but he was too weak from far too much liquor and far too little food over the past two weeks. He began to see stars and thought he was going to lose consciousness, but then he felt a vicious tug on his hair and his head popped free of the water. "Damn your eyes, Legion!" he sputtered, dragging in long gasps of fresh air.

"Curse me, will you?" Legion thundered and pushed him back under.

Bubbles shot up from the water and Conar began to struggle in earnest, for water had sped down his throat. His hair was yanked up again and he came up coughing and gagging, water flowing from his nostrils. "You son-of-a-bitch," he said in a weak voice.

"Insult me?" Legion grated then shoved him under again and held him down. Conar clawed at his hands, digging furrows across Legion's knuckles, but the older man ignored the relatively minor pain. He was so incensed by Conar's behavior, he ignored the fact that Conar's struggling was less intense, the bubbles shooting to the surface, more intense. He kept his grip on Conar's hair until he felt a hand on his shoulder and looked up to see their father.

"Legion," Gerren said in a pleasant voice, "don't drown your little brother, now."

"I was only trying to get his attention," Legion answered, still holding Conar under.

"I think you have it." Gerren grinned.

"You think so?"

"Well," the King said, looking over into the trough, "it would appear you do, son." He saw that Conar had almost stopped struggling.

"You think he'll listen to us, now?"

"Aye," King Gerren told him, noticing his younger son had stopped struggling. "We don't want to kill him, now, do we?" He smiled at Legion and then continued his stroll into the stables.

Letting go of Conar's hair, Legion stepped away from the trough and crossed his muscular arms over his chest. Conar shot to the surface, leaned over the side of the trough, gasping, coughing and spewing water to try to clear his lungs.

As Conar continued to cough water out of his heaving body, Rayle Loure walked over to Legion and handed him a rolled parchment, whispering to him about its contents. Legion's face took on a gleam of vengeance and he nodded to Rayle. "I'll see to it," he said and glanced at Rayle's retreating back.

"You will be sorry you did that, A'Lex!" Conar managed to gasp, gaining Legion's attention.

"Is that so?" Legion tapped the rolled parchment against his lip.

"You'll pay for it," Conar spat as he stood in the trough, weaving, and his head spinning.

Legion's face split into a grin. Those closest to the trough backed away uneasily. "In what way, Your Grace?" Legion asked in a soft, challenging voice.

It took quite a bit of effort, but Conar managed to throw one leg over the edge of the trough, glaring furiously at his brother and the gaping crowd. He swung his angry eyes among those gathered.

"What the hell are you looking at?" he shouted at the servants. He swung the other leg out of the trough and sloshed water down the front of Legion's breeches.

Legion looked at the wet stain on his legs and got a good whiff of the vomit plastering the backs of his breeches, and he slowly turned to his little brother.

"I'll see you in hell for this, Legion!" Conar snarled. He spat a stream of water out of his lungs.

"Really?" Legion asked. "You'd better watch what you say to me, pup."

Conar wiped his chin with the back of his hand. "No man treats the Heir Apparent in this manner," he said in a haughty tone, looking down his nose at his eldest brother.

Legion drew back his fist and hit Conar in the mouth as hard as he could, a blow having enough force to topple the younger man and send him flat on his back.

"I knew it," Thom Loure, Rayle's brother, mumbled.

Conar landed with an audible thud, the wind knocked out of lungs already aching from lack of air. He gasped as his tailbone collided painfully with the ground and he gasped again as Legion came to straddle him.

"Get up!" Legion shouted, his fists clenched by his sides.

Conar recognized that look on Legion's face. He scanned the courtyard and knew those gathered knew the look, too. When Lord Legion A'Lex had the gleam of battle in his eye, it didn't matter who was on the receiving end of those meaty fists. That person was going to get hurt and get hurt badly. "Legion, I...." Conar began, stopping upon Legion's shout of outrage.

"You call yourself a man? Then get up and prove it, Heir Apparent to the Throne!" Legion taunted, his upper lip raised as though he smelled something not to his liking.

Conar's head pounded furiously and blood streamed out of his nose; his lip was swelling at an astonishing rate and he was sure one of his front teeth was loose. He put a shaky hand to his jaw and thanked whatever god was paying attention that his jaw hadn't been broken.

"You wanna be dragged up, Prince Conar?" Legion snarled down at him.

Coming to his feet, Conar sent a look of uncertainty at his brother. There was no longer anger and defiance in the blue gaze. There was hurt and wounded pride. He knew he couldn't take Legion. Not today and, he suspected, not ever. He had let his big mouth run away with him again and his face was going to pay for it.

Weaving in front of Legion, he put out his hand to stop the fight, but he could see the man wasn't ready for it to end. He saw the fist coming, straight for his left eye, but he didn't pull away, didn't duck. He took the hit hard in his face, felt the pain opening a gash on his cheekbone; saw stars; went to the ground once more, landing hard on his right side.

"Get up," Legion whispered. "Get up and fight like the man you like to think you are!"

"I'm sorry," Conar managed to say through the bulge that was his lip.

"I don't give a shit! You're gonna be sorrier still!"

Sighing, knowing he had more punishment in store for himself, he pushed up from the dirt and stood there looking at his brother. Blood caked his face, one eye was already swelling shut, and he could taste blood inside his mouth. He watched as Legion's face twisted with rage and he knew he was going to be hit again.

All the fight had been knocked out of him already. What was coming now was his final embarrassment. His final put down. Legion wanted him to know who was boss and it gods-be-damned sure wasn't the Heir Apparent!

He took the hit squarely on his nose and felt hot blood gush down his throat. The jab was powerful, so devastating, it propelled him sideways against the water trough, and he hit the hard wood side and slid once more to the ground, gasping in agony, for he felt a rib crack.

"Get the hell up and quit moaning, Conar!" Legion demanded. He kicked Conar's bare ankle with his booted foot. "I'm not through with you."

"Don't beat your little brother to death, Legion," the King called as he headed back to the keep. "That would be a hanging offense, son." He stopped and crossed his arms over his chest.

Nervous laughter rang out at King Gerren's comment.

Holding a hand to his side, Conar looked uneasily at Legion's stormy face. "Why don't I just stay down here?" he wheezed through his pain. "It would save you the trouble of knocking me down again." His ribs shot bursts of stabbing agony.

"Don't let these people gathered know you aren't man enough to take your punishment," Legion sneered. "If I have to tell you once more to get up, I won't be as gentle when I put your gods-be-damned ass down again!"

Hoisting himself painfully to his feet, holding his breath against the agony in his side, he stood up as straight as he could in front of Legion, prepared for the blows he thought were coming. He could see the others gaping at him. He could feel the pain in his side and still he wouldn't put up a hand to stop Legion. He waited for the blow that could conceivably push the broken rib straight through a lung.

Instead, Legion threw the rolled parchment at his feet. He looked down with a hope that was hastily quashed.

"It comes from King Shaz!" Legion told him. "He will be here with his wife and the wedding party this afternoon. You had better be on your best behavior when your betrothed comes through that gate. Do you hear me, Conar McGregor? If you aren't, I can guarantee you will regret it!"

Conar groaned. He didn't need The Toad today. His head spun crazily and he felt himself pitching forward and couldn't stop. The jolt as his knees hit the ground sent white-hot pain spearing through his side. Grimacing in agony, he reached for the trough, missed, his hand sliding down the side. "Oh, god!" he whimpered and a servant rushed over to him, but Legion's angry voice stopped the man dead in his tracks.

"Leave him be! Let the fool get up on his own!"

The servant looked to his King. When Gerren nodded, the man backed away, but his attention was on Conar's pain-twisted face and he was worried. "Prince Conar?" he whispered, darting a glance to Lord Legion's wrathful face. "Are you all right, Your Grace?" Just out of his line of vision, he saw Lord Legion take a step toward him and he backed away, fearful of incurring that man's ire. "Milord, he's hurt."

"Good!" Legion snarled. "I meant to hurt him!"

Conar groped for the edge of the trough and pulled himself up, hanging on with one hand while the other pressed tightly to his side. He had almost gained his feet when, with a gasp of shock, he doubled over, acute pain reflecting in his surprised eyes.

"Lord Legion, please!" the servant shouted. "His Grace is really hurt!"

Conar turned and saw Legion's face pucker in sudden concern. "Legion?" he questioned softly, weakly, and then he pitched forward into darkness.

* * * *

By the time Conar regained consciousness, the King of Oceania had sent word that he and his family were unable to visit after all, and would not be journeying to Boreas as planned.

Ordered to stay in bed, his ribs tightly bandaged, Conar was overjoyed at hearing the news. He breathed a sigh of relief that he would not have to entertain his future father-in-law or explain the mass of bruises that made eating difficult.

"Feel like a visitor?" his father called from the open doorway of his room.

"You gonna beat me, too?" Conar smiled.

"Do you need it?" Gerren asked as he took a chair by his son's bed. Craning his neck to get a better look at the cuts and bruises on his son's face, Gerren whistled. "By the gods, Coni, but you're a mess, son."

Conar's left eye was swollen shut; his right cheekbone cut open; his left cheekbone a deep purple; his lip had been torn and he had a long scratch across his chin where Legion's signet ring had cut a wavering gash. His nose had been broken and the flesh covering it had turned a most peculiar shade of green.

"If you see an inch on me that needs beating, let me know," Conar quipped.

"No," his father said slowly. "I think Legion did quite well on his own."

"I believe he managed to give me some other man's share, as well."

His father smiled. "How many times have you riled your brother over the years, Conar? Fifty? A Hundred? More?" At Conar's grin, Gerren went on. "And how many times have you come out on the bad end of things?" Arching a brow at his son, he laughed. "Then I think you should leave the man alone. I never bested any of my older brothers and I don't believe you'll ever best Legion."

Conar snorted. "I just might surprise him one day."

"Famous last words." Gerren sighed and leaned back in the chair. "Your big brother is a natural fighter. I've seen men challenge him, men twice his size, and I've seen those men carried off the field of honor on stretchers. There's not too many men who could beat him in a fair fight, I'm thinking." He laid his hand on his son's leg. "Besides, he's angry at himself for actually doing you harm. He didn't intend that, Conar. That rib could have punctured a lung." The King's face was grave as he looked at his child.

"He feels bad?" Conar gasped. "How the hell does he think I feel, Papa? I didn't deserve the beating."

"It wasn't a beating."

Conar cocked a golden brow at his King. "What would you call it?"

"A discussion. He discussed your recent behavior with you." He folded his hands together under his chin. "There is a certain morbidity to your nature at times that only violence seems to be able to deter, Conar. Merely speaking with you doesn't seem to have any effect. You need to have your nose rubbed in the dirt to gain your attention, and that was exactly what Legion did."

"Aye, the bastard got my attention, all right!"

"He thinks of you as a little boy still," his father reminded him.

"Well, let him think what he will. I am no child. He may just find that out one day!" He flung the covers from his legs. "As cold as it is, why the hell am I so warm?"

Gerren frowned. "I need to speak with you about this girl who is causing all these problems for you."

Conar tensed. "The missing bondservant?"

King Gerren pierced his son with a stern look. His once-blond hair was now totally white; his blue eyes beginning to fade to a watery shade of azure; his tall frame shrinking somewhat; his once-powerful physique shifting and settling in places; but his face could wither the most fearsome warrior. For all its masculine beauty as a lad, it still bore the unmistakable stamp of authority that now, in age, was a stern reminder of his position in the realm. He put the tip of one long finger into the deep cleft of his chin and fixed his son with an unwavering look of reprimand.

"This girl is not some bondservant, Conar. You would not have allowed a mere servant to cause all this trouble." He squinted. "Don't compound your offenses against your family with lies."

"I don't know that she isn't a bondservant, Papa," Conar defended.

"You don't know anything about her, do you?" his father shot back. When his son remained silent, Gerren pressed the issue. "Where is her home? Who are her people? Is she married? Engaged? Widowed? What exactly do you know about her?"

Conar flinched at the steady look his father gave him. "It doesn't matter now, Papa. It's been four months. She's gone; out of my life."

"But not out of your heart."

Conar tore his gaze from his father's stare. "It's over, Papa. There is nothing standing in the way of me marrying The Toad." He grimaced. Never had he meant to ever use that name for the bitch in his father's hearing.

"Both Shaz and his lady-wife are two of my closest friends, Conar. Medea was your mother's dearest friend. They were closer than sisters, for they were confirmed into the Multitude together. They shared a bond few women will ever know. It was your mother's fondest wish that Medea's firstborn daughter be your wife, and nothing, nothing, will stand in the way of that happening. I made a promise to your mother only a few days before that blessed lady died that I would see nothing stand in the way of that union."

"And nothing will." Conar looked away. "I'll honor my mother's wish, Papa."

"There is no doubt of that," King Gerren said sternly. "It is your lack of respect that needs work. You lack respect for Shaz and his lady-wife, as well as their daughter. If I ever hear that vicious nickname you have for the Princess Anya again, I will make you regret it!"

Conar turned to his father. "My marriage to her? I already regret it."

King Gerren stood. "Not nearly as much as I will make you regret ever having met this girl Liza if you continue with this foolishness!"

"Nothing anyone can do will ever make me regret having met her," he swore.

"You love this girl, don't you, Conar?" his father asked with astonishment. When his son did not reply, the King let out a hard breath. "Well, it is a love that will be terminated. Terminated today. This very instant!"

Conar locked gazes with his father. "And just how do you propose I do that, Papa? I can't turn my feelings on and off like a tap!"

His father placed his right hand on the tall headboard of his son's bed and leaned over him, forcing Conar to bend his neck to look up at his King.

"You will be King in my stead, one day. That is your birthright, Conar. A King must learn to control his emotions; to rule them lest they rule him. There will be times when showing a man, or a woman, how you truly feel, would be folly. You will have decisions to make that will involve putting yourself above emotion; detaching yourself from what you feel."

"I'm not sure I can do that."

"You will have to learn!" Gerren snapped. "You can not appear to be a weak and indecisive man, nor can you be a weak and indecisive King. The people would eat you alive!" King Gerren sat beside his son.

"I had many mistresses in my day, as you well know. I cared not a whit for any of them except one; one I cherished above all the others. I thought my heart would break when I had to give her hand in marriage to another. It was, by far, the hardest thing I have ever done in my life save burying your blessed mother." The King looked past his son to some inner memory.

"She had become my heart, this woman, Conar. I would have given her the world if we could have married, but it was not to be. She was in a class beneath me, not of royalty and therefore not material for the Queen who would sit beside me one day. When I married your mother, I gave up that woman. I had to. No man marries a Daughter of the Multitude and dares to sleep with another woman." A rueful smile touched his aged lips. "That would have been folly of the worst kind."

"But you loved my mother," Conar protested. "Did you love her less than this other woman?"

Gerren shook his head. "Oh, no. No. Once I had seen your mother, held her, there was no other for me. There was no other woman like your mother, son. She outshone the sun for me."

"And what became of this woman you discarded?"

King Gerren flinched. "You make it sound as though I considered her nothing more than a worn-out shoe, Conar! The lady was more than that to me, but I never saw her again after my marriage. She swore she would not bother me after I had spoken my vows to Moira and she did not."

Conar turned his head away, fearful his father would see the pain of Liza's similar words to him. "I will do nothing to shame you, Papa. You have my word of honor."

"I have never doubted that you would go through with the marriage, Conar. I only wish you to think before you say things that might get back to Princess Anya." He stood and gazed down at his son. "It is best you forget this girl, Liza. Nothing can come of it between you. I will not see you hurt with thoughts of what would never have been allowed."

\* \* \* \*

Teal du Mer was cute.

All the ladies who knew him said he was cute.

All the men who knew him said he was a bastard, but they said it in a nice, polite way. In truth, Teal was a bastard: the product of a wild affair between his nobleman father, Duke Cul du Mer, and a gypsy girl who had stolen more than the Duke's heart.

Teal bore the dusty complexion and dark, rum-colored eyes of his mother's people, the thick chestnut hair of his father, and the twin dimples that indented his rosy cheeks from his paternal grandfather. He also inherited the wild, sensual nature of his gypsy ancestor and their ability with vocal and instrumental techniques.

His one problem--among many, most people said--was his inability to lead an honest life. Everyone knew where that trait had come from. But all Teal had to do was flash his deep, wicked dimples, bat his rum-colored eyes, and grin his white-toothed tease, and no one could hold his lineage against him.

At the dining table where the noble class took their meals at Boreas Keep, Teal sat staring intently into his cup of hot ale. His thick chestnut brows were drawn together over his finely arched nose and a frown of horrible magnitude made his lips a thin, straight line.

"What makes you so intense, friend Teal?" Legion asked as he joined du Mer. Sitting on the edge of the long table, Legion took an apple from the centerpiece, tossed it into the air, bounced it off his biceps, caught it, and bit into the tart flesh. He waited patiently for Teal to answer. He took another bite and asked around a juicy gob of red flesh, "What's your problem, now?"

Teal continued to stare into his cup. "I wish you wouldn't automatically assume something is wrong with me every time you see me, A'Lex."

Legion grinned around another mouthful of apple. "Usually something is!" He chewed noisily.

Teal glared at him. "I'm a joke around here, aren't I?" The seventeen-year old frowned mightily. "Du Mer, the court jester, is that it?"

Legion nodded, grinning viciously. "So what did you do this time? Did the herdsmen catch you worrying the sheep again?"

Teal looked away, his mouth tight. For a long moment he didn't speak, but then turned to his friend and blurted, "Do you think I'm an honorable man, A'Lex?"

Legion held the apple to his lips, but didn't bite. A fierce look formed on his hard face. "Has someone impugned your honor, Teal?" It was perfectly all right if he or Conar did, but it was not all right for an outsider to do so. "Tell me who the bastard is, and I'll clip his tongue from the root!"

Teal shook his head in exasperation. "No, no, no, Legion! It's nothing like that. You know I make it a habit not to have trouble with anyone." At Legion's loud snort, Teal shot him a glower. "You know I detest trouble."

"Only when it suits your purpose and Conar and I aren't around for you to run to for help." Legion took a large chunk out of the apple. "Who didn't you insult today?"

"Are you calling me a coward? I can fight my own fights, A'Lex!"

Legion grinned around the large gob of apple and he wagged his brows.

"Well," Teal sniffed, "I think I'm honorable."

"Just like you thought you could fly when we were boys?" Legion chuckled. "I remember helping Cayn set a broken arm that day."

"Don't keep reminding me!" Teal snapped.

Legion shrugged and tossed the apple core into the fire. "So why are you so concerned about being honorable?"

"I went to the Tribunal today to make a request and they turned me down. They said it wasn't an honorable thing for me to have done." He took a long, angry swig of his ale and grimaced.

"What was it you requested?" Legion asked, swinging his booted leg against Teal's chair.

Teal tried to ignore the annoying thump of Legion's foot. "I wanted their permission to court this girl from the Green Toad Inn and they said I couldn't. They said I would be dishonoring my father's good name and memory by asking for the hand of a peasant." He sighed as though his heart was breaking.

Nearly choking on the last chunk of apple in his mouth, Legion stared wide-eyed at his friend. "You wanted to court a girl?"

Teal shot him a venomous glare. "Well, I didn't want to court an armadillo!" He sank gloomily into his chair. In actuality, he was immensely relieved the Tribunal had turned him down, but he didn't want to admit it to Legion.

Sensing how things stood with his friend, Legion schooled his face into a stern, fatherly, helpful line. "Shall I speak in your behalf, then?" He laid a commiserating hand on Teal's sagging shoulder. "I could tell them you are heartsick and want them to find you a bride posthaste." He nearly laughed as Teal's head snapped up in horror.

"I'll speak for you, Teal," Conar spoke from the doorway. He was pulling on his brown leather riding gloves as he spoke, but he didn't miss the look of annoyance on his older brother's face. "What ails you, now, Legion?" he snarled.

"Don't encourage him, Conar! He doesn't need you interfering in this. You know du Mer needs a rich wife with a dowry. He needs capitol for taking care of the du Mer lands. With Roget gone, Teal has been having a hard enough time seeing to things at Downsgate. He needs a wife who can give him status in the realm."

Conar put his hands on his hips and glared at his brother. "No matter that she will chain him hand and foot to her dowry? You would rather throw our friend to the she-wolves who lather outside in the courtyard? Ready to pounce on any young male stupid enough to fall for their coy smiles and phony sentiments? I would see him happy with a peasant girl than enslaved to a woman whose fists control his purse strings!" He slammed into a chair and stared at Legion. "I would see him happy, at least!"

"Unlike yourself?" Legion shot back.

"Aye! Unlike myself!" Conar snarled.

"You want to wish your own mistake on Teal, is that it?"

Snorting, Conar asked in a hard, clipped voice, "And just what mistake is that, Legion?"

"You still haven't given up the notion of finding that girl, have you? After all the talks Papa and I have had with you about this!" When Conar refused to rise to the bait, Legion shrugged. "It doesn't matter, little brother. No McGregor male has ever been allowed to take a peasant girl to wife. You will not be the first to break that tradition, I can promise you. Just as the Tribunal will see that Teal du Mer weds no girl beneath him!"

"I said nothing of marriage!" Conar shouted at his brother.

"Why are you getting so angry?" Legion asked in a calm, soft, reasonable voice that infuriated his younger brother even more. "You've thought of it or you wouldn't be so defensive."

"Why the hell don't you mind your own business, A'Lex? You have a hard enough time doing that!" He got up and stalked from the room, slamming the dining chamber door behind him.

Out in the main hall, Gezelle stepped forward and stopped him. "Milord," she whispered, tugging at his shirtsleeve to gain his attention. She was so excited, she was literally shivering. "A messenger came only a few moments ago." She grinned. "The lady waits for you by the swimming pond. She said you'd know where."

Conar grabbed her arm. "When?"

"Now, Milord." Gezelle squealed as he crushed her in a tight embrace against his hard chest.

Conar put a wet sloppy kiss on her lips, making the toes curl in her slippers. "Tell Sadie to break open a fresh keg of ale," he said as he put her back on the floor, oblivious to the stunned look of wonder on her red face, or the deep love in her green eyes. "Tell her I want Teal and Legion to get more than their fair share. I need no baby-sitters this eve!"

## Chapter Sixteen

He found her by the pond where he and Legion had fought. She was sitting on the same rock he had sat upon, her hand fanning the water beside her. She smiled when she saw him. Her face lit with tenderness and she slowly stood, not altogether sure of his reaction.

She was wearing a dove gray gown shot with silver thread and her long black hair was caught up in a glimmering silver snood. Jet earrings nestled in her earlobes and the black amulet rune hung between the soft cleavage at the gown's low neckline.

Conar stood for a moment, his hand on the low branch of a live oak, looking at her. His heart thumped wildly in his chest and he found breathing nearly impossible. One moment he was hungrily sweeping his gaze over her, the next he had her fastened tightly to his body, his mouth deftly plying hers with fevered kisses that sucked and drew on her lips with the heat of abstinence. He groaned as she opened her mouth beneath his assault and he plunged his tongue deeply inside. Cupping the back of her head with one hand, he forced her lips hard against his own; bruising; swelling; claiming the tender flesh. His slid his lips down her chin and throat to plant soft nips along the column of her neck and shoulders.

"I take it you are happy to see me, Milord?" she teased, her hands pushing gently against his chest.

Taking her left hand from his shirt front, he placed a light kiss in her palm then slowly moved her hand down his chest to the hard, demanding bulge in the front of his breeches; he molded her fingers around him. "What do you think, Mam'selle?"

Liza blushed furiously and tried to pull away her hand, but he pressed it harder against him and she could feel his manhood stir in anticipation. A giggle bubbled from her throat. "I would say you were very happy to see me, Milord!"

"Shall I show you just how happy this man is, Liza?" he asked as he rubbed her hand against the juncture of his thighs, dipping her fingers between his pant's leg.

She eased out of his grip. "Aye, Milord, for I have come a long, long way to make you happy," she whispered.

He put trembling hands to her shoulders and eased his fingers under the fabric of her gown, pushing it from her shoulders and over her arms until it lay gathered at her waist. The straps of her chemise followed the gown. A slight smile touched his full lips as he slid his attention to the creamy mounds of flesh that were revealed to him. Lowering his head, he trailed his tongue down her left arm and then across to the puckered jewel of one nipple as it grazed his cheek. Turning his head to her, he caught the coral tip between his teeth and began to nibble gently. His lips stretched into a wide grin as his lady writhed beneath his touch, her hands burying themselves in his thick golden hair.

Liza could feel the emotion building within the pit of her stomach and she pulled his head closer to her breasts. "I have missed you, Milord," she breathed against his tawny hair.

He went to his knees in front of her and gathered her to him, his face nuzzled in the soft valley between her breasts. "I thought never to see you again, Milady," he sighed. "I thought I had lost you forever. It has been so long."

She stroked the gleaming hair. "Five months and ten days, Milord. I tried, but I could not stay away."

He pulled his head from her chest and looked up. "Why, Liza? Why did you leave me?"

Her chin quivered. "Have we made a terrible, terrible mistake, my love? Were we wrong in what we did?"

He stood, took her mouth with his and the kiss was deeper and more breathtaking than anything either of them had ever known. Flicking his tongue across her full lower lip, he pulled back and looked at her. "If what we feel for one another is wrong, then the whole world is wrong!"

"I find I can not give you up, Milord." She hung her head.

He took her face in his hands and tenderly caressed her cheeks. "You will not have to, Milady. I would rather die in exile, an outcast, than give you up again."

He let go of her hand and crossed his arms to grasp the bottom of his shirt, tugging it fiercely from his breeches and over his head in one lithe movement. He watched her as she stepped hurriedly out of her gown and dainty underclothes. His hands jerked at his belt, ripping it from his breeches. His fingers tore through his buttons until he had them undone, then his boots and breeches followed.

She came to him as a soft blessing, falling slowly to her knees before him in offering. He turned her so her body lay upon the spongy bed of moss.

"I have longed to taste you since that first night," he said and before she knew what he was about, he slid down until his mouth was on the dark curls at the juncture of her thighs.

Liza buried her fingers in his thick blond hair and held his head as he placed a sweet kiss on her mound. Though she had no idea what he meant to do, she trusted him completely and when his fingers went to her folds and he gently spread them apart, she did nothing more than blush, tightening her fingers in his hair.

Conar ran his tongue along the creases just inside the outer folds and the taste of his lady was every bit as heady as any fine wine. She tasted of honey and warmth and silky juices that burst across his tongue. The texture of her skin was new to him for never had he done such a thing with a woman. Never had he expected to enjoy it as he was at that moment. He savored the feel, the scent of her, and the flavor of her body. He eased the hood of her clitoris back with his thumb and touched the tip of his tongue to it, swirling his flesh over hers, drawing it into his mouth to suckle the sensitive little nubbin.

Liza jumped, her hands gripping his head, her breath coming in little hitches of breath. Whatever he was doing to her was so thrilling, so exquisitely pleasurable, she felt every bone in her body had melted. He was lapping at some portion of her anatomy that sent wave after wave of shuddery enjoyment trekking through her body and bringing her the most intoxicating feeling she'd ever known.

He slipped one finger gently into her wet channel and when she groaned, lifting her hips for more, he inserted a second, tenderly twisting, thrusting shallowly at first then delving a bit deeper as her body stretched to accommodate him. With her eyes on his, he removed his fingers from her sheath and brought them to his mouth, licking away the juices that coated them.

"Conar," she said, a voice a husky trill of need.

With infinite care, he slid up her body to cover it with his own. Easing her thighs apart to house his length, he settled gently on her.

"I have waited so long," he sighed. "So very, very long." His body throbbed against hers.

She covered his lips with her fingertips and shook her head. Now was no time for words of love. Now was the time for lovemaking.

His hands held her head still so his mouth could plunder the sweetness of her lips. He moved against her, growling deep in his throat as her legs came up to clasp themselves around his hips.

"Liza," he breathed in, his heart thudding. "My Liza."

He had no need to guide himself to her, for the swell of his manhood found an unerring course to her secret warmth and slid home in one quick thrust.

Neither of them was prepared for the almost immediate release that shot through them to send them spiraling into space. The heady pleasure of their passion combined, traveled the same length of time and space, and burst simultaneously. He tore his mouth from hers, arched his head, and cried out his release, his body shuddering hard, and long, deeply within hers.

* * * *

A dove cooed in the distance as the late afternoon sun sank behind the trees, throwing scarlet prisms of light over the deep green of the pond's surface. Somewhere further away another dove answered her mate's mournful cry and the flutter of wings high overhead made the two drowsy lovers look up.

"Sated, Milady?" Conar asked the girl whose head lay on his shoulder, one of her hands caressing the patch of blond hair that rested between his breastbones.

Liza smiled, then yawned. "I think I shall never have my fill of you, Milord." She moved her attention to one hard pap and circled it with her finger. "Does that make me an uncommonly wicked bawd?"

"I would say, under the present circumstances, it makes you one with me, Milady." He squeezed her gently and laid his chin on her sleek hair. "I think I could love you every hour on the hour and never be sated."

"Just every hour, Milord?" she teased.

"How often would you like me to prove my love to you?" He planted a soft kiss on her hair.

"I was thinking along the lines of every ten minutes or so." She heard him snort and craned her head to look at him. "Too soon, Milord?"

"It takes time to...." Conar tried to think of a delicate way of phrasing his answer.

"Reload?" she furnished.

Conar chuckled. "I think that's an apt word." He puckered his lips and blew in her hair.

"Well?"

"Well, what?"

"Are you?" She bent her head to catch one of his paps between her pearly teeth. She smiled as she felt him suck in his breath.

"Am I what?" he whispered, his flesh shivering at the feeling she was causing as she flicked her tongue around his nipple.

Liza swirled her tongue around the erection of his pap and then grinned up at him. "Reloaded?"

Arching a brow, he laughed and proceeded to show her.

"How about you tasting me this time?" he asked.

Liza pushed him down until he lay flat on the grass. "Tell me what to do," she said and reached for him.

Conar drew in a sharp breath at the feel of her hand on his rigid cock. He didn't know if he was capable of speech for he was throbbing with desire, burning with lust.

"Like this?" she said and ran her thumb over the slit of his head, spreading the soft flesh apart.

Before he could answer, she leaned over him and dragged her tongue over the dewy moisture that had suddenly sprung to the tip of his cock. She tilted her head to one side.

"You taste salty, Milord."

He opened his mouth to speak but she took that moment to slide her lips down his entire length, enveloping him in her sweet mouth. He had to grab her head to keep her from going too far down.

"Easy, love," he said but he realized she had taken to suckling him like a tadpole to water. She was drawing on his flesh and slowly pulling her lips up him, pressing them down his rigid length, increasing the pressure of her tongue against the underside of his cock. It was his turn to bury his fingers in her long dark hair and hold her.

Liza spiraled her tongue over the head of his cock and flicked it across the slit. Some instinctual thing made her run her hands under his sac and cup him, squeezing lightly, kneading him with that hand while the other held him still for her mouth's assault.

"You don't need any instructions, wench," he said in a voice that came from deep in his chest. He was quivering beneath her touch, the hair standing up on his thighs. He knew if he didn't stop her, he'd lose control, and the last thing he wanted to do was come in her sweet mouth.

Liza gasped as he clamped his hands around her upper arms and turned, pushing her down to the ground. He was up and over her, his cock primed at her entrance. With one deft movement, he was in her and her legs were around him, their mouths fused, the taste of himself tangy on her precious lips.

Heat like an avalanche roared through Conar McGregor and he pistoned into his lady as though their very lives depended upon him taking her. Her fingernails were gouging into his flanks as he drove mindlessly into her. His hands were beneath her shoulders, molding her to him. His thrusts were hard and long and deep and when the climax came, his kiss turned brutal. He ravaged her mouth, slanting his head this way and that as his lips ground against hers, his body poured into hers.

With the last pulse came complete satiation and total submission of his soul into her keeping. Nothing--and no one--would ever sunder the love he had for this woman and the gods help he who tried!

* * * *

A rustling in the bushes brought Conar awake and alert. Instinctively, he glanced at the sleeping woman who lay curled against his side. As the noise broke through her slumber, Liza opened her eyes, but before she could question the sound, Conar placed a light hand over her mouth, cautioning her with his eyes to lie still. Easing his arm from under her shoulders, he came easily to his feet, his hand automatically reaching for the dagger that was his constant companion. Stabbing Liza's gown with the tip, he tossed it over his shoulder to her, his eyes never leaving the place from where the rustling came.

Finding his breeches in the darkness, he pulled them on over his nakedness and stood, listening intently as the stealthy sound came closer. A gleam of metal through a nearby bush immediately caught his attention. He moved with the speed of a jungle cat, striking out with his fist on the back of a pale hand as it came out of the shrubs.

"Ah, hell!" The two words were followed by a vitriolic curse.

"Du Mer?" a voice Conar knew all too well whispered with concern.

"Was that Teal that yelped?" another voice hissed.

With a heavy sigh, Conar threw his dagger into the soft ground and sat beside Liza. " 'Tis that gods-be-damned brother of mine and half the fools of the Elite," he mumbled and turned to glare at the man who came crawling through the bushes on his knees.

"By the good gods, I swear...." Teal came up short as he looked into Conar McGregor's scowling face. "Uh, oh," he mumbled.

"I'm gonna break your fool neck, du Mer!" Conar smiled sweetly through clenched teeth.

Legion plowed through the bushes, his sword held in front of him, a scowl of battle on his face. "Teal?" he shouted as though the man might well be on the other side of the world. "Are you in trouble? Are you attacked?" He skidded to a halt when he caught sight of Conar, spied the lady sitting with him. "You are in trouble, du Mer," he whispered.

"So are you!" Conar snapped.

"If I ever let you idiots talk me into going out in the middle of the night when I am barely sober, I swear I will...." The owner of the third voice ended on a loud belch as he stumbled into Legion's back. "Damn it, A'Lex! Get the hell out of my way! How can I save du Mer when you're blocking my gods-be-damned way?"

"Rayle," Legion softly warned as the man swung his huge head in Legion's direction. Legion nodded toward Conar.

A happy grin lit Rayle Loure's big face. "Hello, Commander. We've been searching for you!"

"I wasn't aware I was lost," Conar growled.

"We were worried when you didn't come back." Legion staggered to a nearby rock and plopped down, sticking his sword in the soft ground where it wavered back and forth. "No one seemed to know where you'd got off to."

Conar sent his brother a scathing look. "Did it ever occur to you that if I had wanted you to know where I was going, I'd have told you?"

Rayle Loure leaned against a tree and focused on Conar's face in the darkness. "It wasn't me that was worried about you, Commander." He hiccupped. " 'Tis you that should have been worrying about us, I reckon."

"And why is that, Rayle?" Conar inquired with a menacing snarl. "Could it be because the three of you wouldn't make a whole?"

"Well, maybe not at the present time, no," Teal answered.

"By the gods, but I have a splitting headache," Rayle said miserably and slid down the tree trunk he had been leaning against, plopping heavily on the moss-covered ground.

Legion leaned forward and peered at Liza. "Who are you?"

"And I think I may well puke," Rayle added, burying his huge head in his hands and slowly shaking it. His long red pigtail wobbled.

"I think she's Conar's lady, A'Lex!" Teal piped up cheerfully, his words slurring.

"If, of course, I don't pass out first," Rayle sighed, trying to still the rapidly dancing trees around him.

"Are you?" Legion asked Liza. "Are you the one all the fuss has been about?"

"Maybe I'll just lie down and die, instead." Rayle burped. He crashed fully to the ground with a thud and began to snore.

Liza couldn't help giggling, for the three men presented such a woebegone picture it was impossible to keep a straight face. "Your protectors, Milord?" she questioned with a raised brow.

With a snort of disgust, Conar stood and grabbed du Mer by the arm, jerking him to a half-standing position before propelling him backward into the pond, where he landed with a splash and a merry gurgle of mirth.

Before Rayle could react to Conar's foot jamming into his ribcage, he rolled into the water to join Teal. "What?" the big man murmured before sinking beneath the waves. A brief gurgle of bubbles shot upward.

Turning, Conar walked slowly toward Legion, who stood on wavering legs. Holding up a restraining hand, Legion tried to glower at his younger brother. He wasn't so sure his face obeyed the command. "I wouldn't if I were you."

"I'd leave off, Milord, else you may join your friends in the water." Liza smiled as Legion sat on the ground beside her.

"A word to the wise, eh, lady?" Legion smiled.

"I've seen you fight, Milord."

Liza looked at Conar.

He glanced over as Teal and Rayle dragged themselves out of the pond. "You are a sorry lot," he snarled.

"I find them adorable." Liza grinned.

"Don't encourage them, Liza." Conar kicked out with his foot as Rayle came to stand over him and shake his head to sprinkle Conar with icy drops of pond water. "Damn it, Loure!"

"Stop blustering and introduce us, Conar," Teal spoke up. "Where's your courtly manners, man?" He plopped down on the rock that seemed to be everyone's favorite seat.

"He has none," Legion snorted. "Never has."

Conar made a rude grunt. "The tall redhead is Rayle Loure. You remember him from the Hound and Stag."

"I don't remember meeting this lady," Rayle said. He stooped to pick up some twigs and set about making a fire.

"He's supposed to be my personal bodyguard." Conar snorted. "Sometimes I think it's the other way around. Actually, the man's not too bright."

Rayle waved his large fingers at her in greeting, scrunching up his shoulders. His big face became an elastic grin. "I'm older than all of these green boys!" he bragged. "You don't have to be bright when you're older." He puffed up his chest. "I've been an Elite longer than du Mer's been out of diaper rings. I've been married ten years. Ten years!" he repeated then lowered his voice. "And to the same woman, too." He seemed to need to clarify his marriage. "I am six feet eight inches tall and nine inches in--"

"That'll do, Rayle," Conar warned.

"See that ugly scar?" Teal chimed in, pointing to a long, jagged scar on Rayle's forehead no one could possibly see in the darkness. "Got that protecting Conar, he did. Might not be too smart up here." Teal pointed to his temple. "But he's got sense enough to protect Conar."

"You don't have to be too bright to protect Conar," Legion mumbled.

Hearing Rayle gag, Liza looked over to see the big man twist sideways and vomit in the grass. "I have a remedy for that." She got up and walked to where her mare was tethered and removed a vial from her saddlebags.

"Kindly let the fools suffer, Liza," Conar told her as he rejoined them at the fire. "They brought it upon themselves." He sat by the blazing flames.

"One sip is all you should need," she told Rayle as she handed him the vial. She sat and leaned back into the comfort of Conar's arms.

"Thank you, Sweeting," Rayle said, handing the vial to Teal. "If it were left to the Commander, we'd have surely died." He went back to fanning the fire into life.

"The night's not over yet, Loure," Conar warned.

"You have such an evil disposition, Conar," Legion quipped as he took the vial from Teal. "How do you stand him, Mam'selle?" He handed her the empty vial. "Women usually can't abide him for too long at the time."

"Be careful what you say to my woman, A'Lex," Conar told him, pulling Liza closer, resting his chin possessively on her gleaming hair.

Legion looked hard at his brother. The man was more than smitten with this girl; he was deeply in love. There was sure to be trouble whether Conar wanted it or not.

"There's no need in branding her, Conar," Legion said softly. "We have no intention of stealing her from you." He watched a look of defiance cross his little brother's face in the firelight.

"Just as long as you know to whom she belongs, there won't be any trouble." Conar's face was stern, untouched by the humor in Legion's.

"Stop baiting me, brat," Legion said, returning Conar's scowl. "If you glower at every man who stares at this lovely lady, you'll go blind."

Liza's lovely brow wrinkled with concern as she listened to the exchange. There was hostility flowing from Conar; resentment toward her from Legion.

"I will not be the cause of any strife between the two of you. If you can't stop taunting one another, I will leave." She said it quietly, reasonably, but she was not prepared for Conar's immediate reaction.

"The hell you will!" His arms tightened painfully around her in a steely, confining grip. "Your running days are over, Lady!"

A flicker of pain washed over Liza's pretty face and she opened her mouth to speak, but Lord Legion's voice cut through the tense atmosphere like a knife.

"Let go of her, Conar. You're hurting her." Legion's face was set with authority; his voice was hard and brooked no argument.

Conar shot a hateful glare to Legion before he turned Liza around to face him. "I am not going to let you leave me ever again. Is that clear?"

"Not for awhile--"

"Not ever again, Liza!" he shouted. Oblivious to the others staring at him, he locked his gaze with hers. "Swear it! Swear to me that you will never leave me again, Liza!" When she kept silent, he shook her. "I said, swear it!"

"Conar!" Legion's angry voice boomed. "Let the lady go! Can't you see you are hurting her?" He stood, hovering over the couple with rage on his handsome face.

"I can't, Milord," Liza whispered. "You know I can't swear such to you."

"Yes, you can!" Conar yelled, but she shook her head in denial.

"Let her go, Conar," Legion snapped. "Now!"

Cursing vilely under his breath, Conar bounded to his feet, dragging Liza with him, and shoved Legion out of his way. He turned a hard stare to Rayle, pushing Liza toward the tall guard. His teeth were tightly clenched as he spoke.

"Make sure she goes nowhere! On your miserable life, Loure, she had better be here when I get back!"

They watched in silence as he stalked off into the darkness, crashing into the bushes like an enraged animal. His outburst had stunned, and sobered, the men. He was flaunting his obsession before them and that was nothing like the Conar they knew.

Liza's face was wet with tears as she looked at the men. "You know I will never be permitted to stay with him once the marriage contract is signed. There was a time he knew that, as well, but I can see that time has passed."

"It's this gods-be-damned succession of postponements," Teal swore. "With each new postponement of his marriage, he gets worse."

"Mayhap if the marriage would be done with, His Grace would be in a better temper," Rayle ventured.

"The marriage has nothing to do with this," Legion acknowledged. He was looking at Liza.

"He was so miserable, Lord Legion. I thought I was doing the right thing in returning to him. I had heard of the postponements. I knew they were testing him, these people from Oceania. Their ill-care of his feelings is intolerable. I thought not to be the further cause of his sorrow. I have only managed to hurt him more by coming back." She buried her face in her hands, weeping bitterly. "I should have stayed away."

"Aye," Legion agreed, "you should have, Mam'selle."

Her head came up and she pleaded with him. "I love him, Lord Legion. I love him more than life itself! He is my heart."

"And can never belong to you, girl," Legion admonished. "You have caused him great pain and great trouble. Our people will not countenance a dalliance between their future King and some commoner. The monarchs of Oceania will see him put to a flogging post before they will allow him to commit adultery."

"How can it be adultery when even the marriage contracts have not been signed?" she asked.

"How do you know that?" Legion countered. "That is not common knowledge."

"I know everything there is to know about him, Lord Legion."

"Aye, you know more than you should." He took her arm. "I will not allow you to hurt him, lady. Not ever again."

"You have my word, sir. When the time comes, I will leave him and never return. I would do nothing to hurt him in the eyes of his people."

"Aye, I know that right well enough!" Legion spat.

"Legion," Teal warned.

Legion looked to his friend. "This foolishness can only cause Conar trouble, du Mer. Is that what you wish for your friend?"

Teal took Liza from Legion's hard grasp and pulled her against him. He could feel her sobs as she trembled against his chest. "Let him have his freedom until that freedom is snatched away."

"Snatched away?" Legion exploded. "Is that how you see his marriage?"

"Isn't that how you see it, Lord Legion?" Rayle asked. His face wore a kind expression. "It is how all of us see it. Are you different in your opinion of the bitch from Oceania?"

"This will only cause him more pain," Legion said stubbornly.

"He's a man full grown, Legion," Teal told his friend. "He is responsible for his own mistakes, if this be a mistake."

"You think it isn't?" Legion asked.

"I think he should be the one to make the choice. Not you."

Legion stared, looking from one man to the other. He could see they were both behind Conar's insanity and his shoulders slumped in defeat.

"All right," he murmured, his mouth pursed into a hard line. "I can see where your loyalties lie." He stepped forward and cupped Liza's chin in his strong fingers. "I love my brother more than anything in this world, and I would never see him hurt if I could prevent it. If you are what he wants, then you will be what he gets until the day he can no longer put off this hell-spawned wedding."

"As I stated, I love him as well, Lord Legion."

Legion could see the truth of what she said. "I know you think you do." He took his hand away and looked at Teal. "Keep this lady company while I see to him."

Teal nodded and glanced at Loure. Neither man was sure that this was the best thing for Conar, but neither would deny him the happiness he had long been denied. Neither were they sure it was the best thing for any of them, Liza included. Something dark and disquieting seemed to fill the night air like a warning and both men felt it to the marrow of their bones.

Legion found his brother sitting against a tall oak, one hand viciously stabbing the ground with his dagger. Conar glared at him as Legion hunkered down beside him. "I won't argue with you, Legion," he said testily.

"Then don't. I came to discuss with you a way we can keep Papa from finding out about Liza and having the flesh stripped from your backside."

"You would help me do that?" Conar's tone was incredulous, for he had feared opposition.

Legion shrugged. "Against my better judgment, aye, I will." He ran a hand though his prematurely graying hair. "But I swear, Conar, I don't see how you can keep this from blowing up in your face. What happens when King Shaz finds out? And he will. You aren't supposed to be consorting with a mistress for six months prior to the wedding."

"Does that vile man expect me to be a stone? He and that warrior-wife of his postpone the gods-be-damned wedding at their convenience, yet I am to remain celibate indefinitely?" He looked away from his brother. "I think that's a bit much to ask of any man."

Legion smiled. "Well, I do, too, but obviously they look at it differently. I can understand their concern for their daughter's health. I'm sure she has remained pure for you."

A rude snort shuttered from Conar. "Who the hell would bed the bitch?"

"True," Legion mused. "If she's as bad as Rayle says, I doubt anyone would try." He saw Conar glance at him. "Look at it this way. Burlap bags make suitable veils, too, little brother. If the bitch is a nag, put a feedbag over her ugly face."

Conar shook his head. "With my luck, she'll want to screw while every candle and chandelier in the room is lit."

"The better to see your magnificent body, sweet Prince," Legion whispered, nudging his little brother's leg with his own and wagging his dark brows.

"You can jest all you want, A'Lex," Conar snarled, "it isn't your body she'll be pawing!"

"Thank the gods!" Legion swore in a gush of relief that made his brother chuckle.

"I can always close my eyes, I guess." Conar laughed at his own expense. "Or I could use the burlap to drown her in Lake Myria."

"Now that's a thought," Legion said, pretending to think it over. "Maybe the bitch can't swim."

"She's probably got gills and fins. Most amphibians do," Conar said in disgust. "Only the gods know how truly bad the hag looks."

Legion smiled. "Maybe she'll surprise you and be as devoted to you as this Liza seems to be. Even if she's the ugliest hag in the Seven Kingdoms, kindness counts for something."

"As long as I have Liza, The Toad can be whatever she may be. It won't matter." He looked at his brother. "I won't give her up, Legion. Not now and not after the wedding. I'll tell The Toad that, as well."

"And risk being hitched to an Oceanian flogging post?" Legion shook his head. "That's folly, Conar."

"It doesn't matter! If pain is the only way I will be allowed to keep Liza, then pain I will endure." His face went hard with memory. "It's nothing new to me."

"Conar, just think before you act. That's all I ask."

"I have thought, big brother. I will not give up my one chance at love."

Legion turned his head away, hearing Liza's words in the back of his mind. Conar wouldn't be given the choice of whether or not to let Liza leave. The girl had meant what she had said. Once the wedding was sealed, Liza would leave, never to return. Legion didn't question how he knew that. It just seemed right to him.

"So where do we put your lady in the meantime?"

"I'll have to find a place in the village for her...."

Vehemently shaking his head, Legion discouraged that notion. "Servants' tongues wag. Soon everyone in the keep would know about her, including Papa. You can't put her in the village, and you sure as hell can't bring her into the keep. It has to be some place close so you can visit her and yet far enough away for Papa not to get wind of it."

"I don't know of such a place."

"But I do." Legion looked at his brother. "Ivor Keep."

"The old keep at Epstien?" Conar thought about it. Their father had given the keep to Legion as a present for his coming of age many years earlier. It was rarely used except as a place to spend the night when traveling to Oceania. Only a small skeleton crew manned the keep and the place was far enough from the capitol so those servants who did live there were not likely to make visits to Boreas.

"It's within a day's ride of Boreas."

"That was where Mama ran when she left Papa on their wedding night." A smile lit Conar's face. "I was conceived there."

A frown marred the humor on Legion's face. "You'd best make sure no child of Liza's is conceived there."

There was a hard note of challenge in Conar's voice. "What if there is?"

Legion fused his gaze with his brothers. "It would be unwise for a child of this lady's to be born. Such a child would be more than just a loved by-blow, Conar, and you know it. That child would be all."

"As the mother is all," Conar said softly.

"Aye, I can see that, Conar." Legion glanced toward the distant glow of the campfire, picturing Conar's lady sitting there. "But I would have you think long and hard on this. What if a child was born from this love and then a child was born from your marriage? You would be legally and honorably bound to make the second child your heir. What if no child came of your union with the Princess Anya? You still could not claim Liza's child as your heir. The crown would then go to Coron's firstborn because we both know Galen will never sire a babe."

There was pain in Legion's voice. "I know all too well how it feels to be illegitimate, little brother; to be the son of a man who can not do for you what he wants. When a royal offspring comes into this world and can not be claimed as anything but a moment's pleasure...it hurts. It hurts in a way you will never know."


Chapter Seventeen


Liza looked about the master's chambers at Ivor Keep and smiled. Lush furs were spread out on the cold stone floor and elaborate tapestries of naked wood nymphs being chased by randy satyrs lined the thick walls. A huge brass bed gleamed in the center of the room and was covered with a plush throw of pure white ermine, soft to the touch, sensuous to stroke. Sitting on the high mattress, she sank into a down-filled softness that made her eyes widen. The whole room was very masculine, not a single feminine frippery to soften the bold male look. The chamber even smelled masculine: the aroma of cinnamon and leather, tobacco and lime filled the air.

She glanced at the ceiling and giggled. A huge scene of frolicking wood nymphs played over the frescoed surface.

"I'll have the servants bring in different furnishings," Conar told her as he stretched out across the bed beside. She sat with her knees drawn up in the circle of her arms. " 'Zelle can help you decorate it to your tastes." He ran a finger down her leg and smiled as she squirmed.

"I rather like it this way. It has a certain decadent charm." She looked at the heavy velvet hangings tied around the four-posters. "This is a room for seduction, Milord."

"Aye that it has been." He grinned.

Liza cocked a brow.

"Not me, but Legion. And our father before him." Conar propped his head on his hand. "Have I told you about my mother's wedding night?" He wrapped his hand around her calf.

"No, but I would like to hear."

"I'm not sure you should."

"And why not?"

"You might get ideas."

"Oh, and I haven't already?" She grinned.

Conar laughed and tugged on her leg. "You have the most wicked eyes, lady."

Liza pursed his lips. " 'Tweren't my eyes that caught your attention, Milord."

"True."

"Your mother?" she prompted.

"Aye. She was from Virago. Her mother was a Serenian, but she married one of the royal heirs from that wild land. My mother was born in Virago and she was married there at the ripe old age of thirteen to a nobleman's son."

Liza's brows shot up. "Your mother had been married before?"

Conar nodded. "I don't know that much about him, for Mama never spoke of him. If Papa knows much, he hasn't told me. They say he was a traitor, this man, and he was hanged somewhere outside the town of Derry-Byrne. They wouldn't allow my mother to have his body for burial. Virago has the same laws as Serenia. A traitor may not be buried in his home soil; he must be cast into the sea." Conar's face darkened. "When I am King, that law will change."

"Were there children from that marriage?"

"No, no children. My mother was left alone. Within a week of his death, my grandmother died as well, and my mother was sent to live at Norus Keep with her maternal grandmother, my great-grandmother, Violette."

"She went to live in that horrid place?" Liza was shocked. "But why?"

Conar shrugged. "I don't know. It must not have been so bad back then."

"It is an evil place," Liza protested.

Conar looked away from her. "At any rate, my mother went to visit the dowager estate that is very near my father's game preserve in Colsaurus. Papa was there at the time with a few of his half-brothers, no doubt raiding the countryside for game as well as girls, and he happened to see this lovely lady riding by on a big white stallion. She had flowing gold hair to her hips and the most beautiful blue-green eyes he says he has ever seen. She frowned at him as she rode by, not realizing, I am told, that it was the Heir-Apparent to the throne of Serenia she was ignoring. Papa says his heart melted at the sight of her. He fell in love with her then and there."

"You McGregor males are ever taken to falling in love at first sight, aren't you?" she teased.

Conar looked up at her with steady eyes. "When we fall in love, Lady, it is forever."

Liza smiled. "What then?"

Conar was silent for a moment, but when he spoke again, his voice was soft and filled with wonder. "He followed her to Norus and when he tried to gain access to the keep, he was denied. Technically, the keep belongs to our family since it is on Serenian soil. But back then, Norus had been a wedding present to my maternal great-grandmother from her widowed grandmother and so her heirs had the right to say who could, and could not, enter the keep, whether he be King or not."

"How can that be? If the lands are held by your family?"

Conar smiled. "Norus sits on four acres of land that at one time was Viragonian soil. It was seceded to our family at the death of the Outlaw, Syn-Jern Sorn. But it was still held in the Hesar family up until my mother's marriage to my father."

"So Virago claimed it?"

"Aye. By right, my father, although he was King, could not enter without the King of Virago's permission and that wasn't likely to be given for they weren't on good terms at that time."

"But he did enter." Liza smiled at Conar's wink.

"He laid siege to the keep." Chuckling, he laid flat on the bed and crossed his hands under his blond head. "That siege lasted nearly twelve days."

"Sieges being a most uncommonly expensive enterprise," Liza commented.

"Indeed. But my father vows it was worth every gold coin he spent."

"What happened then?"

Conar looked at her. "My mother sneaked out of the keep late one night and made her way to the tent where my father slept. I am told they made love that very night and she agreed to marry him."

"He knew she was of royal blood?"

"He knew more about her than she about herself, he has often said." Conar smiled. "Less than a month later, they were wed at Boreas."

"And they lived happily ever after," Liza said dreamily and lay beside her lover.

"Not exactly."

"Oh?"

"Papa can be an obstinate cuss at times and on their wedding night he was less than mannerly in his way of handling the wedding feast. He paid more attention to his cronies than he did to my mother, and he winked one too many times at the servant girls for my mother's liking. As a result, she gave him an ultimatum. Either quit the banqueting hall and make haste to their rooms, or else she'd leave on her own. Papa had had too much to drink and it had gone to his head. He told her: I am Master here, woman; you are my property."

"Oh!"

"So, taking three servants with her, my mother left the keep and rode out of Boreas in the middle of the wedding reception and somehow wound up here at Ivor."

"Your father wasn't too happy, I bet."

Conar chuckled. "Not happy, at all, Mam'selle. He took chase and found her here, but she had barred the gates against him." He turned over on his stomach and laid an arm over his lady. "But McGregor men can be steadfast in their approach to their women. He climbed the damn east wall." Conar grinned, thinking of his father's escapade as a youth.

"You are joking?"

"He nearly broke his neck climbing the wall into this very chamber. When he swung his leg over the windowsill, he saw my mother lying in this bed, gazing at him with a tender smile."

"What did she say?"

"She said: What took you so gods-be-damned long, Gerry? The champagne is getting warm!"

Liza giggled. "She must have been a very wise lady."

"Indeed, she was. He opened his mouth to yell at her, demanding to know what she thought she was about, when she pulled back the covers and he could see she was naked beneath the great fur. He didn't ask her anything else that eve."

"She had wanted him all to herself."

He nodded, running his hand down her spine. "It would appear that was the case."

"So they spent their wedding night here in this bed?" she asked, snuggling against him.

"Aye, and they made the most of it." He nuzzled her head with his chin.

"How so, Milord?" She listened to the steady beat of his heart next to her cheek.

He moved over her, bringing his face to the nape of her neck to place a light kiss there. "They made me here that night."

* * * *

For four months Liza lived at Ivor Keep near Epstein. On occasion she would leave for days, even weeks; once nearly an entire month. Conar came to expect, if not accept, her sporadic departures, seeming to understand her need to go off to herself at times.

After the first few frantic episodes, he even stopped trying to find her, for he realized his attempts would be futile. If Liza did not wish to be found, she would not be.

He would rant and rave when she returned, but always they would end up in wild, twisting passion in the big brass bed, totally lost to what went on around them.

Including the constantly postponed wedding between Conar and the Princess Anya.

The friendship between Liza, Legion, Teal, and Rayle grew in leaps and bounds. Her expertise as a horsewoman, added to her aptitude with dagger and crossbow, had well-benefited them on occasion. Her constant good cheer and wit, her uncanny way with herbs and potions, did much to render her a saint in their eyes. But it was her great love for their friend and brother that made them care so deeply for her.

No woman would ever love Conar the way Liza did.

And if the wedding contract still lay in the Tribunal's vaults unsigned, then was that not proof the gods had smiled on Conar's love for the girl? Did it not mean this union had been predestined? Why in six months' time, had no one spoken out against the young Prince and his ladylove?

\* \* \* \*

"Highness!"

The warrior shook the Prince again, dodging the flailing arms and clawing fingers. "Highness, wake up! 'Tis the dream again. Wake now!"

Conar came bolt upright in the bed, his face pallid with terror, his body drenched in perspiration. He stared without recognition at the man who hovered over him, whose hands were tight on his forearms, gently shaking him. His breath came in great heaves as he tried to draw air into his collapsing lungs and his hands pulled at the flesh around his closing throat, desperately trying to open the closing passageway.

" 'Twas but the dream, Highness," his rescuer whispered. "Just the old dream."

Conar slowly closed his eyes and leaned into the reassuring arms of the man who now sat on the bed beside him, whose strong arms closed around him with gentleness, protecting, shutting out the demons that had ridden him.

"Don't leave me, Hern," he begged, burrowing his head against the massive chest.

"I'll be here for as long as you want me, son," the man said and raised a callused hand to wipe a sweat-drenched lock of fair hair from the young man's forehead. "Just you relax now. You ain't alone no more."

Conar could still hear the pounding of his own heart against his ribcage, could feel the blood roaring through his temples. He squeezed his lids shut even tighter and sank into the comfort of the arms.

"Is he all right?" Legion spoke from the doorway. He knew better than to come into Conar's room if Hern didn't want him there.

"He'll be right as rain, Lord Legion." The man turned. "Be back to bed with you, now."

Hesitating only a second or two, Legion knew he wasn't needed and closed the door behind him, motioning Teal back down the hall to his room. "Hern's with him."

Teal nodded. No one else would be allowed in the room, then.

As he closed the door to his own room, Legion sat on his bed and wondered for the hundredth time what terrible dreams ripped so badly at his younger brother. He stretched out and stared at the ceiling, wondering also why Hern could still the nightmares that had returned of late to plague Conar. Not since he was a young boy had his brother had such frightening dreams. Now, in the past two weeks, they had returned with a nightly vengeance that left Conar shaken and unresponsive for days afterward.

Only when he slept in Liza's arms did the dreams not come to terrorize him.

"What could have frightened you so, little brother, that you still keep the pain of it with you?" Legion asked the silent room. He could hear Hern's soft voice across the hall as he spoke to Conar. "And why can Hern soothe your spirit when I can not?"

* * * *

"Lie yourself down, Highness," Hern said gently and eased Conar out of his arms. "Rest yourself, now." He pulled the covers over Conar's naked chest, tucking them around the young Prince as if he were still a child.

"You won't leave me?" Conar asked.

"No, Highness. I'll not be leaving you." He smoothed Conar's hair away from his eyes. A light frown crossed the man's rugged face. "You need a haircut, you do."

Conar tried to smile, but his lips felt frozen and his mouth trembled. He looked away from the direct gaze that probed his own.

"When did the dreams come back, Highness?" Hern asked, his big hand turning over so he could run the backs of his scarred fingers down Conar's fevered cheek.

"Awhile ago."

"How long is awhile, son?"

He had never been able to lie to Hern. "Two weeks."

Sighing, the man put his hands in his lap and stared at the closed door. He wasn't sure he should say his piece, but his love for the young Prince outweighed any loyalty he had to his informants. "Even after you installed the lass at Ivor?"

Conar looked at the granite-carved profile of his friend. Nothing ever got past Hern and he wondered if anything ever would. "How long have you known?"

Hern laughed. "What you're really asking is if your Papa knows," he answered. He turned his fathomless gaze to Conar. "He doesn't. I've had no opportunity to tell him."

"How long have you known, Hern?" he repeated, relieved Hern hadn't told his father yet.

The man's gaze moved over Conar's damp face and what passed for a smile stretched the thin, hard lips. "From the very first night you brought her there."

"You've known all this time and haven't told Papa? Why not?"

Hern shrugged his massive shoulders. "I've been busy with this and that. The King's been busy with this and that. I'll get around to telling him when I think he can handle it."

Conar could only stare at the man. He had known this rugged soldier all his life. Sir Hern Arbra was the Master-at-Arms at Boreas Keep. He was also King Gerren's best friend and closest confidante. The two men had been suckled at the same breast as babes, Gerren's mother refusing such an onerous chore. Their loyalty to one another ran deeper than the waters of Lake Myria and the love they bore one another was legendary in the Seven Kingdoms. They had fought beside one another in battles too numerous to list; had shared wine and women and many a drunken song; had shared the same uncompromising love for Queen Moira: one man's bride; the other man's only love, unrequited as it had been. Hern bore the lady's sons the same affection; but Conar, he loved most of all.

A stalwart soldier in King Gerren's own Elite Guard before that good man had become King, Hern Arbra had taken a quarrel meant for the young Prince and had almost succumbed to the wound. Prince Gerren's own blood had been fed into Arbra's veins so the soldier might live, making them blood brothers in fact as well as in deed. What one felt, the other felt, so close was their attachment to one another after the blood-giving.

King Gerren liked to joke that it was royal blood flowing through Arbra's body that gave the man such a keen insight into Gerren's own mind. In truth, it was the common bonds of love, affection, devotion, and friendship that made it possible for Hern Arbra to know how his friend felt.

On the day Hern Arbra was knighted, Prince Gerren had wept bitterly. It was an honor he had wished to bestow upon his friend, but the duty had fallen to the young prince's father, the King. But it was Gerren's old silver spurs that graced Hern Arbra's black boots that day; a gift of love that had lasted their lifetimes.

Standing near seven feet in his stocking feet, Hern was a massive man weighing in at close to three hundred pounds. His wide chest, fully thatched with almost snow-white hair, stretched so far across it took a special tailor to make his uniforms. His boots were specially made, as well, and rivaled in size those worn by the Loure brothers, Rayle and Thom.

His thick crop of yellowish-blond hair was always combed straight back from his high, wide forehead and hung in a long queue down his back. His eagle-beak nose between those startlingly pale eyes gave his face the look of unmistakable authority that had shriveled many a young recruit on the training ground of the Wind Warrior Society where Arbra was Master-Trainer. His thin lips were straight with no noticeable curving in the pale pink flesh, and they rarely moved in anything but a grimace of anger.

When those lips did move, a voice that barked like the thunder of bull elephants on the run could shake the ground beneath a soldier's feet and make the poor young man soil his breeches in fear. And the heavens help any young soldier who did not heed Hern Arbra's angry words.

Conar, himself, had trained under Hern. Had taken his early training with crossbow and quarrel with the man when he had been hardly big enough to nock the fletch. Had learned to ride his first unwilling pony under the unforgiving eagle-eye of a man whose motto was: if you didn't break nothing when it tossed you, you can still ride! Had learned how to rub down a horse; how to curry the beast; how to saddle a steed who didn't want to be saddled; how to get the stuffing knocked out of you by a horse you didn't handle properly.

He had learned all those things and more from Hern Arbra by the time he was six years old.

He didn't see the man again until he was thirteen, but time had stood still for the Master-at-Arms. He looked no different than he had when Conar had been taken by Kaileel Tohre to the Wind Temple near Corinth. His hair was the same; his massive build was the same; his sharp eyes were the same. Conar realized Hern must have seen something in his eyes that no one had recognized, for Hern Arbra had become the young Prince's confidant, as well as, the boy's second father.

Looking now at the pale blue eyes regarding him, Hern could still see that something in the boy's face, something that had worried him that day six years earlier when the young Prince had come to find him on the training field.

"Do you remember me, Sir Hern?" the boy had asked, his gaze going past Hern's to a spot off in the distance.

"Aye, I know you still." Hern had crossed his arms and carefully watched the boy.

"If it pleases you, sir, I would like to be taught."

"Is that so?"

"Aye, sir." The blue eyes flickered. "I would like you to teach me all you know, Sir Hern."

"Do you now?" Hern asked him. "What makes you think you're able to learn what I can teach?"

The boy flinched, but he held his ground, his sight still locked on something only he seemed to be able to see. "I will do my very best, sir."

"And just what is it you wish to learn, boy?" Hern's voice was gruff.

The young Prince seemed to force himself to look up and in that young face was disquiet, a pain that went far beyond his young years. "Teach me how to be a man, Sir Hern." His voice turned husky with some inner agony. "I need to know I can be a man."

Hern remembered standing there on the training field under a broiling August sun that was turning his armor to a molten pit of discomfort and taking the boy's measure.

The lad had been thin, almost to the point of emaciation, pale, already beginning to turn a faint red from the merciless sun that beat down on his golden hair. Hern had always thought the boy's hair his most handsome feature, but on that long-ago day, the lad's golden locks were gone, the hair shorn so close to his scalp Hern could see flesh. The boy looked fragile, feminine, with his big blue eyes haunted by something that seemed to be eating at him like a ravaging beast. The little body trembled as the men about the field shouted at one another. The lad kept looking nervously about him as though he was afraid of being caught up by some beastie from the pit.

Hern had made a decision that he had never once regretted. He had reached out to put a hand on the boy's thin, slumped shoulder, not at all surprised when the lad jumped away. "A man always stands his ground, brat," Hern recalled saying. "He don't back away from nothing." He put his hand up again. The boy quivered, moved away from Hern for a split second before settling. "Or no one," Hern had finished and then laid his heavy, chain-mailed hand on the fragile shoulder. It was all Hern could do not to flinch, himself, as he felt the bones thorough the young lad's clothing.

The boy's chin came up a fraction. "Will you teach me, then, Sir Hern?"

Hern squeezed the thin shoulder in his huge hand. "Aye, brat. I'll teach you."

"I'll not let you down, Sir Hern."

What passed for a laugh rumbled out of the wide chest. "I know that, brat. If you do, I'll send your scrawny ass to the kitchens to bide your time peeling spuds for my next meal!"

Hern turned his back on the boy, dismissing him. He let the young Prince walk a few steps away before calling him back.

"Aye, sir?" Conar faltered, fear showing on his pale face.

"You'll get no special treatment just cause you was born on the right side of the sheets." He fixed his sharp gaze on the lad. "You'll be treated like any other raw recruit."

The boy nodded sagely. "I expect no special treatment, sir. I am not accustomed to it."

"That's good." Hern walked away. When he had looked around, he could have sworn there were tears in the boy's eyes, but he dismissed that. Princes did not cry.

It was later that night when Conar had moved his few allowed belongings into the barracks beyond the sporting and game fields that the bond between teacher and student cemented itself. Despite his vow to see the young Prince got no special treatment, Hern had, nonetheless, given the lad a room to himself; a room near his own.

The boy's terrified screams had awakened the others that night, but Hern had sent them back to their rooms, posting a guard at Conar's door so no one could enter. He had brought the boy out of the demon-ravaged nightmare that had threatened to suffocate him; his strong arms had held the boy close to his chest, whispering to him to calm him. His deep, bass voice had been as soothing as any nanny's; his callused fingers and fighting hands tender as they stroked the back of the sweat-dampened head.

" 'Twas only a dream, brat," Hern said, deep worry etched on his rugged face. "Dreams can't hurt you."

"They hurt me," the boy cried, tears streaming down his ashen cheeks as he clung to the big man. "They hurt me."

"But they're only dreams, son."

"Don't leave me, Sir Hern," the boy begged as though he had not heard. "Please don't leave me alone. They'll come back for me!"

"Nay, brat," Hern assured him. "The dreams be gone this eve. But I'll not leave you. I am right here."

Hern had made the boy lie down and tucked the covers over his painfully thin chest, shaking his head at the crisscrossed lines that marred the boy's shoulders, thinking them bramble scratches until he got a closer look. It was then he realized it had not been dreams that had hurt this child.

"Who whipped you like this?" he growled. "Who dared do such a thing to you, Coni?"

"Please don't tell Papa," Conar begged him.

"He should be told, brat," Hern snapped.

"Please, Sir Hern," the boy cried, clinging to the man in fear. "I could not bear him knowing what was done to me."

" 'Tis not your shame, brat. You have no--"

"Hern?"

Hern mentally shook himself from the past, coming back to the present with a jolt. "Aye?" he asked gruffly.

"Who told you about Liza?" Conar had to know. His whole life depended on it. He couldn't risk having his father find out about her.

Hern was aware he had said these same words before, long ago. "He'll not find out, Highness. You have no need to be worrying. If you don't want him to know of this, I won't be telling him. Your secret is safe with me. You have my word."

Conar relaxed. He trusted Hern Arbra more than any man alive. He had learned almost all he knew from the man: swordplay, fighting, wrestling, riding, archery, battle strategy. But most importantly, he had learned honor. Hern, and Hern alone, knew what caused the dreams, and he knew why Conar had never told another living soul.

"Does the lass know?" Hern asked, standing and leaning one huge forearm on the headboard of Conar's bed.

"I don't have them when I'm with her."

Hern nodded. "I would think not." He ran the backs of his fingers along the young man's high cheekbones. "Can you sleep now?"

"I think so." Conar knew Hern would settle in the chair by his bed and not leave until morning came to chase away any dreams left over from the night.

"Good eve to you, Highness," Hern said, settling his bulk into the overstuffed chair that sat beside the smoldering embers in the fireplace.

"Good eve." Conar turned over and couldn't help but smile. It had been "brat" until the day he had bested the old soldier at archery. Then it became "boy." On the day he had outdistanced Hern's mighty bay warhorse it had become "son." On the day Conar had thrown Hern Arbra to the ground in a well-timed flip during wrestling practice, it had become "Milord." When Hern was deeply affected by something, it became "Coni."

"And don't you be waking me no more tonight, Coni McGregor," he said as he drew a cloak around his shoulder. "Do you hear me, now?"

"Aye, Sir Hern," Conar whispered. "I hear you."

With his nightmares gone for the night, Conar thought of Liza. Her laughing, smiling, seductive face was the last thing he saw before drifting into a dreamless, easy sleep.

Chapter Eighteen

Morning brought with it a punishing rain that struck with hammering fists of hail and staggering winds. The sky had turned a dull gray, and thunder boomed across the courtyards like cannon shots. Lightning speared the grounds beyond the keep and lit the storm-laced day with eerie white flares of brightness. Howling in the eaves like an invading army on the loose, winds buffeted the arched windows of the study and shrieked down the chimney to attack the fires with invisible feet meant to stamp out the heat.

A shutter banged, and a hapless servant was sent to see to it in the strumming pelt of rain. Shingles flew from the roof, pinged against the window panes like gunshots, and set on edge the nerves of those who were forced to listen to the racket.

"You will not be riding out in this foul weather and that's final!" King Gerren shouted at his son and snapped shut the book he had been reading. "What the hell ails you anyway, Conar?" He took off his spectacles and fixed his son with a steely-eyed glint. "When I tell you no, I mean just that! Are you having trouble understanding my words, boy?"

Conar let out an angry hiss. "I can't abide these stone walls! They close in on a person." He flinched as a jagged snap of lightning hit outside in his mother's garden. The loud clap of thunder shook the panes in the window beside him.

"Come away from that gods-be-damned window before you're toasted like a meringue!" the King shouted. "Don't you have sense enough not to stand in front of a window when 'tis lightning, fool?"

Stepping away from the window, Conar plopped into a chair near the fire. "I'm not a child, Papa."

"Nor are you a gods-be-damned adult, either, it would seem!" his father qualified. "You can sit there the whole day and pout like a babe if you wish. You are not leaving in this weather!"

Barely able to contain himself any longer, Conar heaved himself out of the chair and stomped off, muttering dire predictions under his breath. His boot heels rang on the marble as he slammed out into the main hall.

"What ails him, Hern?" the King asked, turning his attention to the other man in the study.

Hern glanced up from his book on the Burning War and gave his King a blank stare. "I am not his keeper, Highness."

"Highness?" Gerren questioned. Was it that bad?

"Have you asked your son what ails him?"

Exasperated with the whole situation, for he and Conar had been going at their argument all morning, King Gerren met his friend's inquisitive stare with a frosty glare. "You know he wouldn't tell me a gods-be-damned thing; but you know more than you tell, now, don't you, Arbra?"

Hern looked down at his book. "If I did, I wouldn't tell." He licked his finger and turned a page.

"The demons take you and that wretched son of mine!" Gerren hissed and snatched up his own book, angrily turning to the place he had lost along with his patience.

Silence weighed heavily on the room even as thunder and lightning wrecked havoc outside the mullion windows. Blue-white flashes of light cast the frescoes on the ceiling into sharp relief and made the shadows of furniture and inhabitants swell along the whitewashed walls. Logs cracked in the fire, an occasional snap of pine knot exploding in cadence with the boom of thunder.

"Is he still seeing the girl at Ivor?" the King asked, his spectacles perched precariously on the tip of his nose as his head lowered and rose while he scanned the page.

"What girl might that be, Highness?" Hern inquired, marking his place with a wide thumb and giving his companion a steady look.

Gerren looked over the tops of his spectacles. "You do not have the monopoly on knowing things, my good friend." He smiled and returned to his book. "I, too, have spies at Ivor Keep."

"Isn't that nice?" Hern quipped and continued with his book.

\* \* \* \*

They were riding for their lives.

A cloud of sun-streaked dust followed close behind them as they made their way into a copse of trees, ducking under low-hanging branches and around thick live oak trunks, winding through the forest and beyond to the slithering stream that flowed behind the old stone abbey at Rommitrich Point. Water splashed up as the flying hooves sped over the cobblestones in the riverbed and dug into the soft silt at the water's edge as they crossed on into the old land that was the abbey's gardens.

Skirting the weed-grown formal gardens, they cut to a switchback trail and found the meandering stream again, urging their mounts into the water and deeper into a tributary leading off from the main stream. With their horses following the curves of the shallow rock-strewn riverbed, they managed to elude the angry mob of merchants who had caught them stealing goods from a street bizarre in Dullwitch.

Laughing and teasing one another, the group of thieves stopped at the ruined abbey and dismounted, hiding their horses deep inside the tumbled-down nave of the caved-in sanctuary. Keeping their mounts quiet with a hand to the heaving nostrils of the steeds, they listened intently as their pursuers galloped past, close enough to hear the straining horses as they snorted. No one breathed easy until no sound came from the roadway.

"Damn! That was close!"

"Too close for my liking!"

"And mine!"

"No more wagers. We damned near got caught this time!"

They gathered together the spoils of their raid that had nearly cost one of them his left hand and went to sit by the still-intact fountain in the middle of the old nave. Cold, fresh water flowed from an artesian well and fed the fountain with sweet, clear, icy water.

"Where's the wine, du Mer?" Conar dug into his saddlebag for the great hoop of cheese he had pilfered, holding it up to Liza.

"Well done, Milord!" She laughed.

"Have no fear, my sweet Prince." Teal smiled as he pulled five bottles of red wine from his own saddlebag. "Not a one broken, thank you just the same." He turned to look at Rayle, who was contemplating his left hand. "By the gods, Loure, that baker near lopped off your widget when you grabbed for that last loaf! I thought you were going to be nicknamed lefty for sure!" He bit the cork from a bottle and passed it to Rayle.

Rayle looked away from the ugly bruise on his wrist that was turning a most interesting shade of purple. "I thought so, too, du Mer. Luckily he hit me with the handle and not the blade of that slicer!" He took the bottle from Teal and passed it on to Legion. "Hurts like the very devil, it does."

"You should have been quicker, Loure!" Legion laughed. He held up a whole baked ham still dripping with juice. "Ain't she a beauty? Near to ten pounds, I would imagine!" He took the bottle and handed it to Conar.

"That's two pounds a piece for us, then." Liza laughed, taking the bottle of wine from Conar. "Thank you, Milord."

"And where is your loot, Mam'selle?" Conar asked before he took a second bottle from Legion and pulled a mighty swig of the red brew, and then wiped his lips on the back of his hand.

A secret smile spread over her features. Liza reached inside the voluminous folds of her cape. Soon apples, pears, pomegranates, oranges, apricots, bananas, figs, peaches, grapes, persimmons, tangerines, and even a small honeydew melon were stacked on the ground with the other booty. She beamed with pride as the men whistled. "I think I did well enough." She smirked at Legion's wink.

"Not altogether too bad," Legion confirmed. He leaned toward her and grinned. "But you didn't get those nectarines, did you? I saw that peddler giving you the eagle eye at his stall." Legion had dared her to swipe the rosy orbs from under the nose of the more than watchful old man, who had been eyeing them with high suspicion as they sauntered past the outdoor stalls.

"She may be good, but the lady ain't that good." Teal laughed. "She tried twice and the old man caught her both times."

Reaching inside her bodice, Liza pulled two rose-blushed nectarines from her gown. "But he didn't catch me the third time. 'Twas the charm, as they say." She handed the fruit to Legion. "I kept them warm for you, Milord Legion!"

A hardy laugh boomed out of Legion as he took the orbs and nuzzled their softness to his face. "Ah, my Sweeting! They have the smell of you on them still!"

"Enjoy it, brother," Conar snapped. " 'Tis the only smell and warmth of this lady you will ever know!"

A dark cloud moved over the ceiling less abbey, shutting out the light and turning the crisp autumn day colder. A sudden wind howled through the ruins like the moans of a dead man and the revelers shivered with the chill.

Liza looked to Legion's smiling face and felt a chill deeper than the one that had shut out the light. She shuddered.

"Cold, my love?" Conar asked and took off his cape to throw around her shoulders.

She turned to smile at him, but her face felt frozen with the cold. His dear face was beaming with his love for her and yet she felt as though he was far, far away. In her mind's eye, she saw him hot and sweating, alone and lonely in a vast expanse of sand and stone. She looked over at Legion, but when his gaze met hers, she thought she could see the same gleam of possessiveness well up in his eyes as was in Conar's.

"Liza?" Conar questioned, drawing her attention. "Are you all right?"

"Aye," she whispered, forcing a smile. "I am fine, my sweet Milord." She sat on the rim of the fountain.

Teal sat behind her, drawing up his knees and turning his back to Liza and Conar, who had stretched out on the other side.

Conar placed his head in Liza's lap.

"Why aren't you drinking, Loure?" Teal asked Rayle.

"I don't feel well," he said, cramming his big mouth full of ham. Grease dripped down his chin.

Liza chortled. "I can't imagine why."

Conar looked up. "Feed me, wench," he demanded in his most regal tone, turning his head to wink at Legion, who was still standing near the fountain.

"Listen to the pompous ass!" Legion smirked.

Liza held out her hand as Legion placed a bunch of grapes in her palm. As her lover gazed up at her with rapt attention, she plucked off the deep-purple grapes and popped them into his waiting mouth much as a mother bird would her fledgling. When the grapes were gone, she accepted a handful of figs from a snorting Legion and peeled the fruit. Her fingers oozed milky-white fluid down the palms.

Raising his hand, Conar pulled one of Liza's hands to his mouth and licked away the milk trickling between her first and second fingers. A fierce gleam of passion entered his face as his tongue traced the curve of her thumb and then sucked the digit deep into his mouth.

Teal peeked over his shoulder at them and made an ugly hiss. "Oh, would you look at this?"

Rayle glanced up and then back to his bread-slicing. "I'd rather not spoil my appetite, thank you."

With a bland look on his handsome face, Legion looked from his own food and made a disgusted sound. "Conar, have you no sense of honor, at all? If you are going to mentally love the lady in front of us, please do so less conspicuously." He ran a hand over the thick beard he had grown over the summer. "We aren't made of stone, you know."

Conar turned his head in Liza's lap and, with a cocky grin, he wagged his brows at his brother, opening his mouth for another fig. His tongue flicked out to lick Liza's hand and he laughed as Legion scowled.

"Well, that answered my question. You have no honor." Legion speared a slice of ham and poked it toward Teal.

"He's really shameless," Teal snorted. "The way he carries on is a disgrace to us all. It's quite immoral, you know. You'd think they were old married folk."

As soon as he said it, du Mer regretted his words. Everyone looked at him and he blushed a deep coral beneath his olive complexion. "I'm sorry," he said, unable to look Conar's way. "I am truly sorry I said that."

"Don't worry about it," Conar told him quietly. Hoisting himself up, he pulled Lisa to her feet beside him. Squeezing her hand, he took her with him into the shadows beyond the fountain.

"Legion? Shall we kill the little bastard now, or simply spear him?" Rayle snapped, throwing Teal a damning look.

"I said I was sorry!" du Mer defended. "It just slipped out."

Legion glared at him. "You never think before you open that big mouth, do you, du Mer!"

"I said I was sorry!" Teal snapped. "Stop belaboring the point, A'Lex!"

Legion snorted. He turned to Rayle. "Be sure you tally up what we've stolen so those people can be paid back."

"I always do," Rayle said quietly.

"If he didn't need the distraction, I would put a stop to these pranks," Legion stated. "Prince or no prince, it is an unseemly thing to steal from your people."

"At least Coni's enjoying himself," Teal mumbled. "These raids keep his mind off the Joining."

"Most of the merchants know by now who's doing the thieving," Rayle commented. "They aren't stupid."

"Most know one of us is a woman, too," Teal added.

"I should have stopped it," Legion sighed. "I could have. I should never have allowed it to go on for this long! I dread the day he'll be hurt by this, and hurt, he will be."

Teal stood, walked to his old friend, and draped an arm around Legion's slumped shoulder. "You have to let him make his own mistakes. He, alone, in the end, will have to be the one to pay for them. If he is to keep Liza, then he will; if he is destined to give her up, she will be taken from him." Teal squeezed Legion's shoulder. "You can't keep him from growing up, and you can't keep him from being hurt."

Rayle was gawking at Teal. His big mouth was crammed with bread and cheese, his hand raised with another slice of honeydew, ham juice running down his chin. "Since when have you commanded such wisdom, du Mer?" he mumbled around the gob of food.

"What wisdom?" Teal shrugged. "I merely repeated what my father said to me when my brother was sent away." His brown eyes went deep with remembered pain.

"Has there been any word of Roget?" Legion asked, knowing how Roget's leaving had hurt Teal.

Teal shook his head. "Not since our father died. I guess the Tribunal doesn't feel I need to know."

"What you don't know can't hurt Roget," Rayle murmured, his appetite finally gone. He laid down his food. Roget du Mer had been his best friend.

"He made dangerous mistakes," Legion said. "You don't go up against the Tribunal and win. Roget should have known that." He glanced at Teal's set and cold face.

"He was an honorable man. He did what he had to do!" Teal countered.

"Easy, Tealson," Rayle admonished. "Legion was only making a comment."

"He did what he had to do and he is paying for his mistake," Teal repeated. He looked at Legion. "Just as Conar will no doubt do."

"And what if he doesn't learn from his mistakes, Teal?" Legion snarled. "What if he refuses to stay with The Toad once the marriage is done? What if he tries to flaunt Liza in front of the Oceanian Empire, as is his intention? You know he will, if Liza doesn't make good on her promise to leave him. The way things stand between them now, I'm not sure she will be able to go. He is her very soul! She is his heart! What if Papa has to keep him in chains to keep him with that amphibious bitch? What kind of lesson will that be for Conar?"

"A hard one," Rayle assured them. "A very hard one, indeed."

## Chapter Nineteen

Conar leaned back against a gnarled tree trunk, his right leg stretched out in front of him, his left wrist resting on a bent left knee. A smile flickered across his handsome face as he gazed at the trio who sat playing cards by the wavering firelight. He had been thinking of the past, of the time at the beginning of his and Liza's relationship, and the world was mellow with him this chill fall night. A snort of laughter reached his ear and he tuned in to what was being said.

Teal du Mer was losing heavily to Liza. He was flashing a white-toothed challenge as he handed over his gold to her. The firelight turned his dark complexion to a warm caramel. "I fear you have won all my money, Liza-love," he said on a long, heavy sigh.

Legion, however, had face. "I know gods-be-damned well you are letting that guttersnipe win, du Mer!" He hissed at Teal's innocent look. "One of these days, I will find out how you do it!" he snapped, throwing down his cards and gathering up what was left of his own meager supply of gold coins to turn over to Liza.

"You sorely wound me, A'Lex!" Teal sniffed in his best petulant manner. "I do not have to cheat in order to lose. I fear it comes most naturally to me." Sighing again for emphasis, he stretched out on the ground, resting on his elbows and staring at the clear, crisp sky with its heavy dotting of brilliant stars. "I can see the Bear, Conar."

Legion folded his arms over his chest. "Well, I wish the beast would clamber down from the sky and gobble you up, du Mer! You are as innocent as your gods-be-damned gypsy blood!"

"Have a care, my friends," Conar called to them, "the girl will rob you blind, if you let her."

"I see you sulking over there, Milord," Liza told him, stacking her winnings in a neat column. "You're just in a fine pique because I won all your money first."

"I'm not sulking, little one." He yawned, stretching his arms behind his head, craning his neck to look into the tree above him where an owl hooted. "I just see no point in losing to you to keep you in a good mood." He lowered his head and looked across to her. "I can get you in a good mood by other, more challenging, means." He smiled widely at her as she puckered her lips and made a face at him.

"I do believe you have lost all control of her, Conar." Legion laughed. "See how the strumpet makes faces and mocks the royal heir? How she disrespects your royal person? 'Tis treason, you know."

" 'Tis sacrilege," Teal chimed in, dodging a card Liza flipped at him.

" 'Tis just her way of saying she loves him and is putting his royal ass in its place," Rayle added as he turned over in his blankets and propped his big head on an open palm.

"Aye, and 'tis grounds for having her smart rear smacked." Conar grinned.

"That is the royal punishment for making jest of your sovereign lord?" Teal asked in mock horror. "How positively dreadful a punishment, Your Grace."

"Try doling out such a punishment, Milord, and see what happens to your royal person!" Liza cooed to her lover.

"Oh, ho!" Rayle exclaimed. "She's flung down the gauntlet, good knight." He sat up and draped his blanket over his shoulders, huddling into its scratchy warmth. "I fear thee shall have to chastise thy most disobedient subject, Highness."

"Say it is not true, Your Grace," Teal muttered with a falsetto voice. "Say you have not lost all authority over this shrew."

Conar slapped his hand to his heart and looked mortally wounded. "I fear the bawd has sorely hurt my self-esteem. I have no control over this unruly subject and I fear I never shall." He winked at Liza. "What say you, disobedient subject, will you ever be broken to saddle?"

Liza tossed her long black hair over her shoulder and smiled. "Now that depends on who tries to do the saddling, Milord Conar!" she answered saucily.

Conar lost his smile. His face took on the granite look of a frown. He didn't like it when she made such remarks, innocent though they might be. He had to admit to himself what his friends already knew. Liza had become the closest thing to an addiction Conar had ever known. He was insanely jealous.

She affected him as no other woman had ever been able to before. When other men looked at her, he felt pride and intense possessiveness. When she looked at other men, as women are likely to do, no matter how innocent the look, he felt something evil stir in his very soul. Looking at her in the firelight, he realized with a jolt of understanding that their lives were now so interlocked, so finely attuned to one another, he would be hard-pressed to live without her.

"Quit frowning so, little brother!" Legion warned, not liking the look on Conar's face. "No man rides this lady but you."

Under normal circumstances, Legion would not have made such a vulgar remark to his brother, for he knew well how Conar felt concerning such jests within earshot of his precious Liza. But of late, the chill fall days and the silence from Oceania were wearing thin on everyone's nerves.

Conar glared at Legion. "If you can not speak in a way fitting for the lady's ear, you had best keep you mouth closed, A'Lex."

Legion returned the hard look, but wisely kept his remarks to himself. He looked at Liza and she smiled at him. "I tender my apology, lady," he said softly.

"None needed, Milord." She got up from her spread blanket before the fire and dusted off her velvet breeches.

Seeing Liza start to walk away, Conar looked up at her. "Where are you going?"

"For the love of the gods, Conar! The girl probably has to pee!" Teal laughed. "Why don't you go and hold her hand?"

"It's not her hand he wants to hold!" Rayle teased.

"You watch your mouth, too, Loure!" Conar hissed, sending Rayle a heated look.

"For the love of Alel, Conar. What's gotten into you tonight? Leave off!" Legion warned. "Liza knows we are only jesting. We share all the respect in the world for our lady. Your churlishness gets bothersome at times." There was a hint of steel in Legion's deep voice as he glared at his brother.

Conar turned his head from Legion's probing stare. What was wrong with him tonight? He felt a chill that could not be accounted for by the crisp weather. It was as though his soul was locked in the dreariest part of winter, bereft of warmth and companionship. He could almost feel the icy fingers of fate clawing down his spine and he shivered. His nerves felt on edge and his heart was heavy, although he knew not why. His thoughts went to Liza as he heard her scrambling among the bushes.

She has a way of never answering my questions, he thought. Liza was infamous for her secrets. Even after a full year of acquaintance, he still did not know either her surname or her homeland. She came and went when she pleased with no regard to how he felt or how he worried about her. She came back to him like the first rays of sunshine after a drenching storm, all soft and warm. And when she left him, his days became dark and chilled until she returned.

He tuned out his friend's low voices. He wiped all thought from his mind until his breathing was slow and deep, rhythmic. His concentration leapt to a bright point of light he could see behind his closed lids. Not even realizing he was utilizing a concept he had been taught as a very small child at the Abbey, he let himself drift into a light sleep.

She was there beside him in his slumber, curled lightly to his body like the other half of a matched bookend. He could smell her sweet scent of lavender, feel her hair tickling his nose. His arms closed around her, held her to him and he nuzzled her neck. Smiling in his sleep, he could feel her rump pressed against his manhood, inviting, offering, and needing. He wiggled closer to her and sighed. If nothing else in his lifetime matched his moments with Liza, he would nevertheless be content.

A stinging blow to his arm brought him instantly awake. He looked down in his lap and saw a small stick lying there. He looked up into three inquisitive faces staring at him from across the campfire. He didn't see Liza and her absence put him immediately on guard. He glowered at the three men. "What?" he growled, anger heavy in his tone.

"Is our companionship so dull that we put you to sleep, Milord?" Teal inquired.

Conar ground his teeth. "You might say that."

"He's such a bear when he doesn't get his beauty rest," Legion quipped.

"We wanted to know if you would like to stay here near Iomal for awhile longer or head to Corinth and maybe see your little brother, Coron." Rayle wiped his nose on the edge of his blanket.

"Where's Liza?" Conar wanted to know.

"Or we could go up to Ledo, although at this time of year the snows will have arrived," Teal reminded them.

"I asked you where Liza is." Conar stood.

"I give up!" Legion snapped, throwing his hands into the air. "Have you no thought beyond that woman?"

"Where is she?" He took a step toward the blackened trees.

"She hasn't left, if that's what you're worried about," Legion snarled, turning away from the anxious look on Conar's face.

"Then where the hell is she?" He didn't see the looks his friends turned to one another.

A soft rustling from behind them made all four men turn in unison, their hands going to the daggers strapped to their thighs.

When Liza's soft murmur of aggravation came from the moving bushes, the men relaxed their guard, three sets of eyes going to Conar's relieved face.

As she emerged from the forest, Liza glanced at the men hovering over the fire, staring at her. "What's wrong?"

"Where were you?" Conar asked, his voice tight.

"I went for a walk."

"In the dark?" Conar snapped. "Alone?"

"No," she quipped, putting her hands on her slim hips. "I had half the Elite Guard dancing attendance on me in the bushes!" She flashed a warning at him, for his jealousy always tended to infuriate her.

"If I find any man dancing attendance on you, Lady...."

Teal shot to his feet, intent on stopping the ugly scene he felt coming. He reached for Liza's hand and pulled her close to his side, never realizing his actions only made Conar madder. "I have a request, Your Grace." He turned a bright, eager face to his Overlord.

A momentary flare of red-hot rage flashed across Conar's face, but he stamped it down, hiding it behind a grimacing smirk. "Your requests usually cost me dearly, du Mer!" he snorted and turned away from the sight of Liza in Teal's arms.

"You cut me to the quick, you do!" Teal pretended to pout. "And me about to solve all your problems for you."

"Beware, Highness!" Rayle admonished. "When du Mer solves problems, he usually creates worse ones."

"I know that well enough." Conar fixed Teal with a glare. "What is it you plan to do this time, gypsy? Lend me some more money to flee the country before I am shackled to Shaz's Toad?"

Liza laid her head on Teal's shoulder. "I think he did that three months ago, Milord." She smiled as Teal placed a soft kiss on her brow. "Don't you remember?"

"How well I remember!" Conar snapped, his hands itching to tear Liza out of du Mer's arms.

"How was I to know the money was counterfeit?" Teal countered. "It looked real enough when I won it. How was I to know? I gave it all to you, didn't I, Conar?" He pierced his Overlord with a hard look. "Well, didn't I?" When Conar wouldn't answer, he turned to Legion. "Didn't I give your brother, my Prince and Rayle's sovereign, my friend, and yours, Liza, all the money I won that night?"

Legion grinned despite his worry over the look in his brother's eye. "You did give him the money."

"Aye, he did," Liza confirmed.

"He gave me the damn money all right, and when I went to use it to buy passage from Virago to Serenia, I was arrested quite promptly on the docks, as I seem to recall." Conar narrowed his eyes. "I did not like that gods-be-damned jail, du Mer."

"We got you out, didn't we?" Teal inquired.

"After I had spent four hours in that rat cage!" Conar could not suppress the shudder that went through him. Confining places didn't sit well with him any more than rodents did.

"No harm was done," Liza said softly.

"The only harm done was to his fierce McGregor pride." Legion scoffed.

"Fine!" Teal snapped, drawing away from Liza and sitting morosely on the ground. "Curse me if you will. Defile me. Make me an object of your jest. I just won't solve Conar's problem then."

"The best way you could solve my problem, du Mer, is to kidnap The Toad and wed her yourself to save me from her evil clutches."

Liza laughed. "How about that, Teal? Can you do that for His Lordship, your Prince?"

"Will you be serious?" Teal shouted, all his good humor erased.

"I am being serious," Conar assured him. "That would be the biggest help any of you could give me." He glanced at Legion. "Or you could marry the bitch."

"Hah!" Legion snorted. "Who do you think would look after Liza if I was shackled to some shrewish amphibian?"

Conar blanched. He had tried hard not to think of what would happen after the marriage. It had been put off so many times over the months that he had ceased to think of it seriously. Now with the wedding rapidly approaching still once more, and no word of another postponement from Oceania this time, he found he was reluctant to deal with the problem of what to do about Liza. Giving her up was out of the question; keeping her with him would be difficult at best. "I'll look to Liza," he mumbled.

Legion groaned. This wasn't going well. He glared at Teal. "What exactly is this plan of yours, du Mer?"

Clearing his throat, Teal bit his lip as Conar motioned for Liza to join him, reaching out his hand to pull her down beside him as he sat in front of the fire. Teal watched as the man nestled his lady in his arms and she turned an inquisitive face up to him.

"Well, Teal?" Conar said. "Let's hear your plan."

Du Mer looked to Legion for guidance and it became apparent to Conar that the two men had already discussed what Teal was about to say. That in itself did not bode well.

"Conar, you know well how much your brother and I love you, and you know there is not much we would not do for you."

Conar swung his look to Legion. "Aye, I know." He returned his attention to Teal, his eyes narrowed at du Mer's sudden nervousness. "Go on."

Teal had the look of doom stamped on his dark face as he continued. "And you know we both love Liza. Only a blind man would not see how it is between the two of you."

"I think what I feel for Liza is more than obvious," Conar agreed and looked down at Liza as she glanced up at him, smiling.

"We think you would marry her if you could. Are we wrong?" Legion asked.

Intently looking at Liza's sweet, upturned face, Conar agreed. "You're not wrong."

Liza stared at him, her heart trembling against his arms. "Truly?"

Placing the backs of his fingers along her cheek, he smiled at her. "Truly," he whispered and bent to place a light kiss on her lips.

"But since you can not marry Liza and that damnable contract prevents you from keeping a mistress under penalty of corporal punishment, we are offering you an alternate solution."

Conar frowned. He felt a cold hand grip his heart. "And that alternative being what, Teal?"

Seeing Teal had exhausted his courage, Legion cleared his throat and spoke. "That you allow one of us, either Teal or myself, to marry Liza."

Rayle had known what was coming, but he wasn't prepared for the sheer force of Conar's reaction. He groaned and pulled the blanket over his large head, screwing up his rubbery face.

"No!" Conar exploded. He abruptly pulled his arm from around Liza and stood. His entire body quaked. "Never! Is that your idea of helping me, A'Lex? Neither one of you has the right to make such a suggestion!"

"Then who does?" Legion asked, also coming to his feet. "Would you rather a stranger, someone we don't know, someone we might not trust, take her to wed?"

"No man will take this woman, but me!"

"Then will you have her locked away somewhere? Barren of husband or child? Caged in that vile nunnery? Or do you plan to hide her and visit her when The Toad isn't looking?" Legion's angry face was suffused with disgust. "Will you have Liza live like that?"

"What I do with her is my concern, not yours!"

"Then you had best make a decision concerning her, now, Conar, for the days grow short!" Legion yelled.

"Your days are growing shorter by the moment!" Conar warned his brother.

"Fool!" Legion snarled. "You have to deal with this, Conar! The problem won't go away because you wish it to!"

Conar turned from Legion's angry glare and stalked away, calling for Liza to join him.

She looked to her friends, wanting to say something, but Conar's shout stopped her and she hurried after him.

Teal blew out a long breath from his aching lungs, not even aware he had been holding it through the exchange between the brothers. "Well, I can see we didn't handle that well."

"What now, Legion?" Rayle asked, pulling the blanket from his head.

Legion's shoulders slumped. "I don't have any idea. He's not going to willingly give her up and if Papa finds out, or Shaz, there will be hell to pay."

"We'll pay, too," Teal said miserably.

"I wish you hadn't said that," Rayle moaned.

## Chapter Twenty

Liza nearly collided with Conar as he stopped in front of her. She gasped with shock as he spun around and grabbed her upper arms in his hard grip.

"They had no right, Liza!" he shouted. "No gods-be-damned right at all!" His back was to the moonlight so she couldn't see his face, but his voice was filled with a deep, quivering rage.

"They meant well, Milord," she assured him. "Now is not the time to be angry with them. They have your best interests at heart."

"My so-called friends would not be vying for the woman I love!" He let go of her and turned his back, but not before she caught a glimpse of his face in a stray beam of moonlight. His jaw was clenched tightly together, his lips a thin, straight line.

"Conar," she tried in a reasonable voice, "would you rather it be an enemy who takes me?"

She saw him stiffen, but he didn't answer. His back was like a brick wall to her.

"Listen to me, Beloved," she tried again. "You have responsibilities to your family; to your people. Your life will not include me when you marry. You have always known that."

Abruptly he turned and grabbed her arms. "You belong to me!"

He jerked her roughly to him, her body slamming into his with enough force to knock the wind from her. "I will never let you go, Liza. Never!"

His head swooped down and he slanted his punishing lips searingly across hers. It was as though he were trying to suck the very soul from her. His teeth ground into her lips, forcing them apart so his tongue could plunge deeply within her mouth. She moaned at the pressure, for she could taste blood on her lips. She wasn't sure if it was his or hers. A hot, wild streak of passion turned in her lower belly as his kiss deepened.

His arms went around her, pulling her even closer. She could feel the erratic beat of his heart beneath his silken shirt. He ground the lower portion of his body against hers, one leg forcing itself between her thighs.

Liza dragged her mouth from his and put up a restraining hand, but he ignored it. "Conar, don't."

He made a low animal growl deep in his throat and began to lower her to the ground. He did not hear her feeble protests of denial, ignored her weak hands on his chest. Every inch of him tingled at the thought of possessing her, of placing his own unique mark upon his woman. He ached to fall on her like a rutting beast, to mate with her in a frenzy of passion, to impregnate her with the very essence of him, to quell the hunger that ripped at his loins. His mouth found hers, silenced her pleas.

Liza was entrapped by his passion. She felt as though her body was engulfed in a furnace blazing with Conar's desire. Her head arched back and he found the sweet beat of her pulse at the base of her throat.

Hungrily flicking his hot tongue at the erotic indention at the base of her lovely neck, he heard her gasp of pleasure and his lips closed over the spot to suck and draw at the sensitive flesh.

"I need you, Liza," he begged, tears in his voice.

In answer, Liza arched her lower body up to his. She saw his head come up from her shoulder. A thick lock of long blond hair fell over his eyes and she reached a hand up to push it away. Moonlight fell over his face and she could see the sheen of tears.

"You know I am yours, Milord," she told him, answering the unspoken question. "I shall always be yours." Her voice caught in her throat.

Liza suddenly looked off into the forest as though she'd heard her name called. Her face paled.

"Look at me, Liza!" he demanded. "Liza. Look at me!"

"Oh, Conar," she mourned. "I hear...."

His eyes filled with a hardness she had never before seen, made even more effective by the tears now unheeded down his cheeks.

"By all that is holy, Liza," he swore, "you will always be mine. It is my voice you will heed!"

"Do you hear it?" she asked, listening intently for the softly sighed name wafting through the trees. "Don't you hear Them calling?"

It was the Wise Ones of the Multitude calling out to her. Theirs was a powerful voice and she was surprised Conar could not hear Them. He should have been able to. That he didn't concerned her.

"I hear *me* speaking to you," Conar snarled, his face screwed into a line of unforgivable pain. "I am here. Here with you. You need no other!"

Liza's lips trembled, her body shuddered beneath his, for the voice was closer now, more insistent. "Conar, I must--"

"No man will ever take you from me. I'd butcher any man foolish enough to try." His hands came from around her to bury themselves in the thickness of her long, jet-black hair. He held her face and locked his gaze with hers. "Do you hear me, Liza? You will listen to my voice and no other!"

She blocked out the calling; would not heed the summons. She gave herself up to this man's passion, to his need, to his hunger. "I hear you, my love," she whispered as his body began to claim hers.

Striving to block the call from her mind, Liza gave herself completely to him in a way she never had before. Tears obscured her vision as her hands ran all over him, her mouth and tongue lavished delight upon him. She became a virago of love, pressing kisses all over his body, touching him everywhere, presenting every orifice of hers for him to fill. She cupped his sac and flicked her tongue over that heavy area and suckled him so strongly he became as hard as iron but she would not allow him his release. Her fingers clutched at him, her fists milked him, her breasts rubbed against his turgid erection, bracketed it between them. She was like a wild woman who had been long denied the touch of her man and she ravished him there on the ground. She ravaged him with her body and her mouth and gave herself to him in ways they had not tried until then. She straddled his cock and rode him like a prized stallion then flipped over to have him thrust into her with savage, brutal prods that made her grunt. They rolled over and over with him atop her, her atop him, until the itch that began deep inside her began a roaring conflagration, setting fire to their bodies and enflaming them to such a degree they drew blood upon one another. She was a woman possessed and possessing and when it was over, when his lust was spent inside her and her arms cradled him as he slept, Liza lay awake, listening to the faint call that was her name, over and over again.

"Awhile longer," she whispered to the still night. "Only awhile longer."

"Liza," came the call, intense and prolonged on the night wind.

She lay with him in her arms, gazing down at the tousled blond hair. In sleep, he looked so vulnerable, so like a lost little boy. His long lashes fanned the blush of lovemaking still on his high cheekbones.

Now and again, he would smile, making her wonder what dreams made him do so. She stroked his bright hair and placed a feather-soft kiss on the top of his head.

"Forgive me, my love," she whispered. "Please, please forgive me."

* * * *

Teal and Legion sat staring into the campfire Rayle was stoking. The men had not spoken to one another for well over two hours, lost in their private thoughts. It was close to dawn, and Conar and Liza had not returned. The men had kept vigil all night and were tired and bleary-eyed, cold from the damp, chill fall air. They huddled closer to the fire, warming their hands, and listened to the eerie trill of a mourning dove.

"That damn bird's been at it all night," Teal snapped, hating the sound even more than usual. It was a spine-tingling cry that set his teeth on edge.

"Ignore it," Legion remarked. He hunched his shoulders inside his great cape and blew on his cupped hands. "By the gods, but it's cold."

"I've been thinking," Rayle told them. "I think we should leave them alone. The wedding is in a few weeks, and if no postponement comes, they'll want all the time they have can together."

Teal stood and stretched. "I think that would be wise. He's angry with us as it is. Our presence may only serve to further irritate him."

"You just don't like discord, du Mer," Legion snapped.

"True, but I think Conar would like this time alone with Liza."

"Maybe so," Legion concurred. "He's hurting so bad. I can feel it."

"Liza's with him. She knows how to handle him," Teal remarked. "This is nothing new for her."

"My heart aches for him," Legion admitted. "I see nothing but pain, and more pain, ahead for him."

Rayle stood and gazed off into the distant, his soldier's ear cocked for a sound he had heard as the men talked. The mourning dove had stopped its infernal trill, a sign something had disturbed the bird's songfest. His hand came up to still the conversation and when he knew the others were heeding his warning, he stooped and drew his sword from the scabbard by his bedroll. "Rider coming."

Legion and Teal took up their own weapons. Out in the middle of nowhere, as they were, precaution kept one alive. The threat of some blackguard holding the heir to the throne of Serenia hostage for ransom was not something Conar's friends took lightly. Despite their playing around with Conar and Liza, the three men took their responsibilities to their Overlord seriously.

As one, the men moved out of the clearing and through the thick foliage leading to the roadway, careful to make as little noise as possible. Crouching low beneath the branches, they blended in with the silent, still-dark forest and made their way to the strip of roadway beyond.

The sound of hooves on the pre-dawn air was easily heard now, the rider not bothering to silence his steed's snorting and jingling harness.

Coming onto the road, the three men waited for the rider to approach.

Rayle grimaced, then let out a sigh. "I think it's my brother," he said, relief in his voice.

"What's he doing out here?" Teal inquired.

"Ho, there!" Thom Loure called as he spied the men. "Been looking for you!"

"What are you doing out of bed so early, Thommy?" Rayle snapped as his brother drew near.

"Wasn't by choice!" came the merry reply. He reined in his huge palfrey and came down from the saddle with a heavy thud of big feet. "Good morn."

Thom Loure was only a few minutes younger than Rayle, looked exactly like him except for one minor difference. His hair--or what there was of it, for he kept most of it shaved--was jet black where Rayle's was flaming red. One long pigtail hung down from a three-inch-wide section of hair from brow to base of skull. The rest of his skull was blue-black with stubble. Both men had a wicked sense of humor, a disposition that remained hidden by their scowling faces, and comical expressions that made children love them dearly. Rayle doted on Thom, and Thom idolized Rayle.

"Why were you looking for us?" Legion asked.

The smile left Thom's congenial face. "Things are in a mighty uproar, Commander. The King sent me to bring back his son. Is he with you?"

"Aye, he is." Legion turned to Teal. "You'd better go get him."

"Me?" Teal gasped. "Why me?"

"Just go, damn it!" Legion snarled.

Teal glanced at Thom. "Is there some hurry?" He sensed he wasn't going to like Thom's answer.

Thom glanced at his twin. "The wedding party has arrived and they want to move up the wedding."

Legion cursed beneath his breath and turned his back on the men so they could not see the look on his face.

"Is *she* there, too, this time?" Teal asked, now more hesitant than ever to go after Conar. As far as Teal knew, the Princess Anya had not, as yet, stepped foot inside Serenia. Not once during all the times the marriage had been postponed for first one reason and then another. If she was here now, that was trouble.

"Aye," Thom said, causing Teal to groan.

"Did you see her?" Rayle asked.

"I saw this little woman in a veil hobble up the steps to the keep."

"You saw her," Rayle mumbled. "Then it is this time," he said to no one in particular.

There was a moment's silence as the men digested this news before Legion turned on Teal and snapped at him. "Go fetch him, now, du Mer!"

"Is our lady with him?" Thom asked his brother.

"Aye," Rayle said and put an arm around his twin, "and this ain't gonna be a pleasant journey home."

Legion watched Teal disappearing through the trees. His heart was filling with a hot pain. He knew there was going to be trouble and also knew he would be the one expected to handle it. "How soon is the wedding going to be moved up?" he asked Thom.

"This weekend," Thom answered, making Legion flinch.

"That's only three days away!" Rayle muttered. "How do they expect him there by then?"

"They knew where you were," Thom told him.

"How?" There was disbelief in Rayle's voice.

"I don't know. They just did."

Legion tuned out Rayle and Thom's conversation and wondered at the new feeling creeping into him, something alien he had never before experienced. He poked at it as one would an aching tooth, worrying the pain, marveling at it. He shook his head. Was it relief he was feeling? Relief that it would soon be over and done with.

Turning away from the twins, he crossed near the picket line where their horses were and thought he saw movement in the trees, but when he stopped and looked closer, there was nothing there. He listened hard, but nothing moved. Sighing at his own nerves, he hunched before the fire and stared into the flames.

He now realized what he had felt was more than relief that the marriage was about to take place. He also felt guilty. He was experiencing an unnerving happiness that made him giddy. He was too afraid to examine that feeling closely for he feared it had everything in the world to do with Liza's upcoming availability.

He began to steel himself for the battle of wills between himself and his brother that he knew was coming.

\* \* \* \*

He turned over in his sleep and reached out for Liza. When his hand encountered only empty space, he opened his eyes and looked beside him. He raised his head and peered around, softly calling her name, but there was no answer. He heard footsteps coming through the trees and laid down his head, waiting for her to return. He listened as leaves crunched and bushes were pushed aside. Frowning, he realized the footsteps were too heavy for a woman's and he sat up again, listening more intently.

At Teal's summons, he ground his teeth together and stood, dragging on his breeches.

"Conar?" Teal called and nearly jumped out of his skin as Conar answered.

"I'm here, du Mer," Conar snapped. He had emerged out of the forest like a specter.

"Your father sent Thom Loure after you," Teal blurted, wanting to get this over with.

Conar was beginning to feel a cold dark finger of dread tracing its way down his spine through his shirt. "Why?"

"You won't like it."

Rapidly losing what little patience he had, Conar squinted at his friend. "Get on with it! What does Papa want?" The cold finger had slipped down to claw at his spine.

Taking a deep breath, Teal answered in a rush. "They are here. They've brought The Toad this time, Conar, and are demanding the wedding be moved up." He took one look at the horror stamped on his friend's face and had to look away.

"Moved up to when?" Conar asked quietly, wondering what was taking Liza so long.

"I think Thom said this weekend."

Conar stared at him with a sudden understanding that made his face turn white. "Liza," he whispered.

"You can't take her back with us," Teal protested, gathering courage from Conar's quietness. "Maybe Thom can take her to Ivor."

"Is she with the others?" he asked, his heart hammering painfully.

Teal stared at him. "Isn't she with you?"

The wound down his spine gaped open and Conar wanted to groan with the agony of it. Breaking into a run, he skirted the clearing where they had camped, rushing past the three men who looked up in alarm at his flight. He heard Legion call to him, but he was incapable of answering. His total concentration was on the picket line where their horses had been tethered just outside the clearing.

He knew even before he got there what he would find, but still his throat constricted as he lurched to a stop. Reaching out for a nearby tree to keep from falling in his headlong rush, his eyes swept the horses. There had been five last evening.

Now, there were four.

His breath was ragged as he gasped in air and a trembling hand went up to push the hair from his eyes.

"Liza?" he asked so softly he could barely hear himself. He could feel the wound along his spine dripping away his life's blood. He shook his head to clear it of the agony throbbing there, but the pain only intensified. He stared straight ahead at the empty place beside Seayearner where her mare had been tied. Her saddle and bridle were gone as well.

She was gone.

Somehow with her witch's sight, she had seen this coming last evening. She had asked him had he heard Them calling to her. He had not heard the voices but he had felt the strangeness in the air that had accompanied it.

Who? He thought. Who had called to her? Who had made her leave him? He feared it was the Multitude, and a cold horror flooded his body as his father's words came back to him: "No man marries a Daughter of the Multitude and sleeps with another woman."

Had They taken Liza from him? Was The Toad more than she appeared? Was she like his mother, a Daughter of the sect?

Liza could not stay. She had tried to tell him as much. She had known that, if she stayed, he would have tried to prevent her from leaving him. She had given him no choice. She had taken the decision out of his hands.

Or had she?

Who was responsible for Liza bringing his world to a grinding halt?

Not since his mother died had he felt this kind of pain. He had put his tears aside then, as he had put his childhood aside, but now hot tears of sorrow slowly ran down his flushed cheeks to scald him. His hand trembled as he reached to brush away the treacherous signs of weakness. He gazed in confusion at the wetness that clung to his fingertips, staring at it for a long time before he let his hand fall to his side, and he gave way to the tears.

Then he raised his hand again and stared with surprised eyes to see a thin braid circling his wrist. He touched the gleaming black strands with the tip of one finger and knew she had tied the lock of her hair around his wrist while he slept.

Before she left him.

"Liza?" he questioned softly.

*"To remember me by, Milord,"* flitted through his mind.

His proud shoulders sagged as his entire body shook from the effort to hold back the wrenching sobs. He tried desperately to stop from whimpering with the pain, but his tears grasped him with unsheathed claws, tearing at his vital organs, eating away at him with a vengeance.

With his fists tightly clenched, he sank to his knees on the cold ground and his head fell forward to his chest. Unstoppable tears burst from him and a piteous moan came from his very depths. Wrapping his arms around himself, he began to rock back and forth with the rhythm of his pain, gripping himself so tightly the flesh along his ribcage began to bruise, but the agony of losing Liza cut too deep for him to feel physical discomfort.

"Liza," he whimpered to the silent morning.

Deep in his soul, he knew he'd never see her again. She had taken his heart as she fled. The thought of never being with her was more than he could bear.

Life without Liza would be a living hell.

Legion and the other men entered the picket area behind him. The wretchedness of his sobbing tore at their hearts, brought tears to their own eyes.

Legion bent to put his arms around Conar. "She's gone?"

Conar turned fierce eyes on his brother, daring Legion to touch him. One look at the hard and cold face was enough to make Legion back away.

Conar didn't hear them leave. His head was bent, his heart breaking. He felt such intense hurt within him, could barely breath for it. "Oh, Alel, why?" he asked his god. "Why?"

He felt so alone. He was alone. He would forever be alone, now. There was nothing left, no future to cling to. In her arms, the world had been held at bay. Nothing could hurt him as long as he had her. Now, that peace, so fleeting in his life, like his innocence, his trust, and his future, was gone. Life would forever be filled with memories he would never let die.

"What did I ever do to deserve what You've done to me, Alel? Have I been so wicked You must punish me?" He turned his head to one side in anguish and the tears flowed down his cheek. "What did I do?"

He felt broken; shattered beyond repair, the pieces of his heart bleeding and torn. Shaking his head to clear it of confusion, he looked around, trying to find the reason, any reason, any explanation, for it all, but only the soft soughing of the wind and the miserable sound of a mourning dove answered his silent questions.

He listened, thinking the mourning dove's cry the loneliest sound he had ever heard. It, like him, called for its mate.

"Gone," it seemed to say. "Ever gone."

A cold blast of frigid air came hurtling down from the high peaks of Mount Serenia and the trees swayed with the force. Branches rustled overhead, dropping leaves about him. His golden hair blew about his face, the cold wind freezing the tears on his cheeks, chilling him to the very marrow of his bones.

"I have nothing," he whispered to the mourning dove. "Nothing at all."

And the knowledge cut him deeply.

In despair, he arched back his head and an unearthly animal cry of torment burst from his throat.

Legion's head snapped up at the sound. It was an eerie sound, long, and echoing as it hovered on the morning breeze. There was defeat in the cry, soul-wrenching agony, abandonment; it had been a sound meant to be silent. Never heard. Never felt.

"Should you go to him?" Teal asked. With his gypsy instinct, he could feel Conar's great pain.

Legion couldn't answer. He didn't know how to answer. He wanted to go to his brother. Felt that he should, but he couldn't move. Conar's cry had paralyzed him. The sound, shattering the morning silence, had come from the very pit of his brother's bleak soul and it had deeply hurt Legion. There was nothing he, nor the other men, could do for Conar McGregor.

What hundreds of his enemies had tried to accomplish had easily been done to Conar by the carelessness of one small hand. Nothing had ever before brought the man to his knees. Not punishments when he was growing up, nor disappointments as a man. He had always seemed to be able to withstand all the loss and pain, hurt and disillusionment thrown at him over the years.

But this had been too much to ask.

Legion swiped angrily at his tears. "She knew this would happen," he said, his face blazing with resentment. He ground his teeth together. "I knew this would happen."

"She won't be back, will she?" Thom asked his twin.

Rayle shook his head and blanched as another heart-rending cry came from the forest. "I think not."

"The gods help him," Teal whispered. Another pitiful cry rent the air and Teal turned on Legion. "For the love of Alel, do something, A'Lex!"

The fall air had turned as cold as the darkest winter night, and a wind now shifted among the trees; chilling, freezing; killing. Snow wasn't long in coming, for the smell of it was in the air. Legion went to his brother, carrying a blanket and a flagon of hot mulled wine from Thom's saddlebags.

Conar sat beside the horses, his knees tightly drawn up and clasped within the perimeter of his arms. He was shivering badly, his lips blue, his cheeks a bright red, but he didn't seem to notice the cold. He didn't look up at Legion or acknowledge in any way that his brother had joined him. He stared straight ahead to the empty space beside Seayearner.

Legion placed the blanket around Conar's shoulders and sat the flagon of wine beside him on the ground. Hunkering down, he put his hand on the tousled blond hair and stroked back a heavy, wind-dampened lock that had fallen across Conar's forehead.

"Do you want me to stay with you?"

Conar heard him. He didn't answer, but he had heard. He couldn't seem to do anything but stare at the horses.

Legion stood, his face tight with emotion. Looking at the defeated slump of his brother's shoulders, he felt a great pain enter his heart.

"I love you, Conar," he whispered, then abruptly turned, and headed back to the fire.

Conar's lips trembled and a single tear crept down his right cheek. He turned his head and watched his brother walk away. He wanted to thank him. He wanted to tell him he returned that love, but it took too much effort. He was too tired. Too heartsick. Too devoid of feeling, now. He was numb to the core of his being. All the fight had been drained from him and it had left him hollow. There was such a vast emptiness inside his chest where his heart had been, he felt used up, discarded.

His head sagged to his knees as fresh sobs shook his body.

"How is he?" Rayle asked.

"Is he all right?" Teal wanted to know.

"No," Legion snapped, "he isn't all right. There isn't anything any of us can do to help right now."

"Should we keep watch over him?" Teal asked.

"Surely you don't think he'd do harm to himself!" Thom gasped.

Legion leveled a steady gaze at the man. "He tried once before," he said quietly.

Rayle shook his head in protest. "But he was young then. What was he, twelve? Thirteen?" He glanced at Thom. "It was why he was sent home from the temple. He nearly died."

"I didn't know," Thom mumbled, lowering his head. Surely the Prince wouldn't do such a thing now.

"We don't know what to expect. You never truly know what he's thinking." Teal pulled his cape closer. "I've seen him down, but never like this. Not when he came home from the Temple or when his mama died."

"It galls me to spy on him," Rayle remarked.

"You didn't see the look in his eyes," Legion reminded him.

"How did he try to do hurt to himself as a boy?" Thom asked.

"He cut his wrists. You have to look closely to see the scars. Healer Cayn carefully stitched the wounds."

"But why?"

"No one knows, Thommy. He has never talked to anyone about his reasons."

"Except maybe Hern," Teal corrected.

"I wish Hern was here now. He'd know how to handle him," Legion sighed.

"Do you think we ride for Serenia tomorrow?" Thom asked.

"No," came a firm voice from the trees.

The men looked up to see Conar standing behind them. His mouth was a thin, straight line and his hands were clenched into fists by his side. There was hardness and brittleness in his voice, a foreign firmness to the set of his jaw that brooked no argument. He turned his fierce gaze on his brother.

"We ride for Serenia within the hour, A'Lex," Conar snapped. "I have a surprise for the Princess Anya Wynth!" He headed back toward the picket line.

"I like not the gleam in his eye, Legion," Teal remarked as Conar strode away, his head erect, his spine straight.

Standing up slowly, Legion ran a weary hand through his graying hair. "You'd best get used to it, du Mer. Something tells me it's going to be there for a long time!"

Chapter Twenty One

"Damn you," Conar snarled, jerking cruelly on Seayearner's cinch, making the animal sidestep in surprise. He cursed his horse, hitting it with the flat of his hand on the high flanks. "And damn you, too, you black piece of shit!" he spat as he took a firm grasp of the pommel and swung himself into the saddle. He put spurs to his horse, something he had never done before to any animal.

The steed shied, arching high into the air in stunned protest. But as its heavy hooves struck the ground, Conar urged it forward. The horse dug deep into the frost-laden grass and shot toward the roadway at a fast gallop. Seayearner cleared a small clump of bushes in one smooth leap before thundering down the dirt pathway.

As the wind rushed past, blowing his hair wildly about his head, Conar knew in his heart he held no blame against Liza. She had fulfilled her bargain to him ten times over. She had loved him, and loved him well; giving him all of her, holding nothing back. And she had kept her promise to leave him when the time came; and leave him, she had. She had never once denied her going. It had always been there between them. He had just never taken her seriously.

No, the blame did not lie with Liza.

"Damn you, Anya Wynth, to the deepest crag in the Abyss," he ground out between tightly clenched teeth.

The blame lay squarely on the deformed shoulders of the bitch crouched at Boreas Keep, ready to slurp him under her wretched body and devour what was left of his life. He could feel the wet, slick, hideous feel of her hands on his flesh and he shuddered. He would be at the bitch's mercy unless he put her in her vile place as soon as he reached the keep. And he intended to do just that. He would not let her paw at him, slither over him, and trailing slime in her wake. He would make her pay, and pay dearly, for the loss of the woman he loved.

In his mind, he could see Liza, smiling, laughing, and teasing him. The thought of her in the arms of another man, laughing, smiling, teasing, drove him nearly insane with a jealous rage. It made him want to scream.

It was almost an hour before he slowed his pace enough for the others to catch up. Seayearner could not keep up the pace Conar demanded, and horse and rider had fought for the bit. Seayearner had won in the end, doing nothing to improve his master's mood.

As the others joined him, the young Prince didn't speak in greeting or acknowledge them in any way. Legion was close on his right side; Teal on his left. The twins rode slightly behind, and to the flanks of du Mer and A'Lex.

"Are you planning on riding all night?" Legion inquired, turning his head to gaze at his brother.

Conar's stony profile let the man know he was in no mood for idle chitchat. His frosty stare was colder than the air around them as he glared at the road. He moved out ahead of Legion and Teal, for the track was just wide enough to accommodate one horse at the time as they came to the bend in the roadway.

With no warning, and coming with blinding speed, Thom was knocked unconscious from a sharp blow to his head. A wickedly aimed caltrop opened a long gash along the back of the man's skull. Thom tilted sideways off his big roan stallion and toppled to the ground in a heap.

Rayle opened his dark eyes wide, and gasped, his hands going to his throat where a quarrel buried itself in his windpipe. The Elite Captain gurgled and a stream of bright crimson bubbled from his lips. He pitched to the ground beneath the hooves of his own steed. Rayle Loure was dead in a pool of his own blood.

"Take the bastard alive!" one of the murderers shouted as they rode down from the high dunes bordering the roadway. "They want the Prince alive!"

Conar's head snapped around at the shout and he saw two of his men down. He glanced up at the eight men who were skidding down the dunes, sand tumbling away from the flying hooves of their massive mounts. In a flash, he was able to make out three men carrying crossbows already drawn; two others brandished maces. The other three waved heavy broadswords as they drew down on the Prince and his men.

"Conar!" Legion shouted, spinning his horse around. "Ride out!" He leaned forward over his horse and started back toward the place where Thom and Rayle Loure lay on the ground.

Teal jerked on his horse's reins, forcing it up the sandy incline. The horse lost its footing in the soft grass along the base of the smaller dune as the gypsy fought to get his steed out of A'Lex's way.

"Guard his back, du Mer!" Legion yelled as he shot past Teal and his floundering horse.

Du Mer kicked his stallion in the ribs and blocked the roadway between his Prince and the eight men bent on taking him. He looked back at Conar once, saw the wild gleam of battle in the young man's face, and groaned.

"Get out of my way, Teal!" the young Prince shouted as he urged his horse toward du Mer.

"Get out of here!" Teal yelled, his attention on Conar. "Get out of here!"

The men attacking them were desert nomads from one of the Hasdu tribes. Their flowing white garments and turbans claimed them as such. Their weapons gleamed in the mid-morning sunlight, and their thick-bodied horses had been bred for speed and endurance. As fighters, the Hasdu were a formidable force.

"Teal, watch out!" Conar screamed.

The nomad had his weapon looped to his left wrist and his arm came up, the mace snapping forward on its tarnished link of chain. Teal took the blow high on his right arm, yelping with the agony. Conar saw him tumbling backwards from his horse, but there was nothing he could do.

"You son-of-a-bitch!" Conar yelled. With a savage snarl, he yanked his sword from the scabbard slung over his back and bent low in the saddle, kicking Seayearner forward with his heels. He rode down on the first man, drawing back his arm and, with a mighty sweep of his weapon, lopped the head from his foe's body. The backward swing of the heavy sword took a mortal bite out of the mace-wielder before the man could leap off his horse and out of Conar's way.

Legion was having difficulty getting his sword free of the chest of the man he had just impaled so he didn't see the blow coming that knocked him off his horse. He hit the ground hard enough to crack his teeth together and he spat a mouthful of blood as he rolled to his feet.

"Don't kill the Prince!" someone shouted above the din of horses' hooves. "Wound him if you have to, but take him alive!"

"Legion, watch yourself!" Conar shouted as he galloped toward his brother.

Throwing his leg over his steed's neck, Conar slid to the ground beside Legion and pulled his brother's sword free of the dying man who had at last tumbled from his horse. He tossed it to Legion.

Placing himself at Conar's back, Legion brought up the blade in time to deflect a blow headed for his chest. He lunged forward under the attacker's arm and his blade buried into the man's midsection.

"Better odds wouldn't you say?" Legion quipped, dancing away from one of the three surviving attackers.

"Aye," Conar had time to answer before one of the men came at him with enough force to knock him to the ground. His attacker stabbed downward toward his shoulder with the curved blade of a scimitar. Conar managed to roll away in time, and the man's gleaming steel dug a furrow into the sand only inches from Conar's left cheek. Lashing out with his foot, the young Prince kicked the man in the groin and sent his opponent doubling over in pain.

"I've never liked nomads," Conar snarled as he brought up his own blade to skewer the man like a shish kebab.

"Conar, be careful!" Legion snarled as the Prince stumbled against him.

Legion's adversary had no real proficiency with his blade, his expertise lay with the crossbow he had had to abandon at such close quarters, but he more than made up in sheer determination what he lacked in skill.

Conar, however, had a more formidable foe. The broadsword he wielded with a heavy hand connected hard with Conar's parries and each one of the robber's hits landed squarely on Conar's sword. The Prince felt the shock of them all the way down his lighter weapon.

The nomad smiled. There were great craters in the man's oily, sweaty face above his beard, and his hair, now loose since his turban had been knocked off, was lank with grease. A stench like spoiled meat rolled off his heavy body and made Conar's eyes water as he came close enough for the young Prince to get a good whiff.

"I'll take you alive, Pretty One," the nomad whispered as he circled Conar. His black gaze swept over Conar, lingered on the young man's crotch before coming back to lock with the pale blue eyes. "But you'll regret it."

Conar was being slowly backed up to a stand of gnarled trees that lined the roadway. He knew he couldn't last long with his back to the shrubs, but he couldn't get around the man facing him. Every sidestep he took, the heavy-set man followed, edging Conar ever back toward the trees.

"Getting tired, pretty boy?" the nomad asked. He feigned a thrust at Conar and laughed as the young man stumbled, his ankle twisting in the loose sand. "I'll let you rest. After I nick you a time or two, I'll let you lie down and rest." A smile of victory eased over the nomad's bearded face. "For awhile, anyway!"

Lack of sleep and the emotions that had drained him were playing a heavy toll on Conar's defense capabilities. His anger was slowly dwindling with his supply of energy and adrenaline. He stumbled again, his blade catching his opponent's down the cutting edge as the man sprang forward. He felt the man's sour breath on his cheek as they came face to face.

"I'm going to take you, pretty boy," the nomad whispered. "As you took my Master's woman!"

Conar's forehead crinkled with confusion. What woman was the nomad bastard speaking of? He'd taken no Hasdu tribes-woman. Had never even seen one to his knowledge, unless...

Liza's ethereal beauty flashing across his mind and Conar stumbled once more, nearly falling as he unknowingly spoke her name aloud.

"Call your whore if you like." The nomad laughed. "See what good it does you, McGregor." He lunged forward with lightning-quick speed, his blade flashing in the early morning sunlight.

Conar tried to push away from his opponent only to come up hard against the twisted trunk of a scrub pine. Shock flitted across his face and he tried to twist away from the nomad's arcing blade as it loomed toward him. He miscalculated and the sharp blade ripped along his thigh, scratching a furrow in his flesh. He felt the pain all the way to his toes.

The nomad grinned. "By the Prophetess, I missed." The nomad chuckled, and danced away as Conar lashed out at him. The attacker brought up his blade. "Do not worry, McGregor. My Master, himself, wishes to relieve you of that offending growth between your infidel legs!"

Conar groaned, the pain stinging and burning. He threw himself to the right, violently twisting away from the man's blade pushing toward his crotch. His left knee struck the nomad's wrist and the blade flipped up, jagged forward, and pierced the tender flesh of Conar's side, opening a wide, deep gash just under his left ribcage.

"Fool!" the nomad hissed. He backed away, his eyes stunned by the damage his blade had caused.

Conar stumbled forward, landing heavily on his right hand as he lost his balance and fell to the sand. He pushed himself up and dug his toes into the ground to get away from the man behind him. Grabbing his left side, he winced in pain, feeling the warm gush of blood flooding over and down his breeches. He was badly wounded and knew it. He was bleeding profusely from his thigh and his rib. He gained his feet, turned, and began to stumble backwards, away from the advancing man. He met the nomad's unwavering stare and something inside him seemed to give way.

His sword arm throbbed from the blows he had countered and his head swam from the loss of blood. He glanced toward Legion, saw his brother triumphing over his own opponent. Saw Teal struggling to get up and Conar said a quick prayer of thanksgiving. Caught sight of Thom as that man tried desperately to remain standing on wavering legs. Both Thom and Teal were alive, he thought with relief. That was good.

He looked into the face of the nomad and thought he saw death emblazoned on that dark countenance. He swung his head toward Legion, saw his brother rushing forward, knew Legion would kill the man who was about to kill him. He flinched as he stumbled again, pain flooding his entire being. His breath was low and shallow, agony to draw into his aching lungs. His head hurt miserably. His heart beat so fast he thought it would burst.

"Stop struggling, McGregor," the nomad said as he put out his hand to grab Conar. "You are bleeding badly."

"Let go," Conar hissed, pulling away. Then the earth tilted beneath him and he fainted, whispering the one name he thought of as a talisman to ward off evil...."Liza."

## Chapter Twenty Two

Bright shafts of sunlight stabbed into the room, sending agony through his eyes and jarring his brain into a million pieces of fragmented pain. He tried to turn his head from the sunlight, but his neck wouldn't obey. Hot sweat dripped down his temples and into his hair. He could smell his own fetid body odor and it made him ill. His throat was so dry that, when he tried to speak, only a whisper came out. Footsteps echoed on the plank flooring and a face swam into his vision. Squinting, he tried to make out who it was, but the effort was too great. Something wet was laid across his forehead and he tried to force himself awake, but he drifted back into a hot, troubled sleep.

"Legion?" Storm Jale, one of Conar's Elite Guard called softly as Legion laid the cool rag on Conar's forehead, "how is he, Sir?" Jale entered the room dressed in full battle gear, his sweaty face red from the weight and cumbersome heat of his leather armor.

"Badly hurt, but he'll live," Legion told the man, but there was grave doubt in his voice. "We're watching him closely."

"The King sent eight of us to guard him. We've reports other nomads have been seen nearby. Another four Elite will come to take Rayle's body home later today." Storm's face twisted with pain. Rayle had been a good friend. "His wife gave birth to their third son just yesterday morn."

Legion flinched. "I didn't need to hear that." He took the rag, wet it again in the basin of cold water beside the bed, and laid the cloth on his brother's fevered brow. "How's du Mer?"

Storm shook his head. "Mad as hell because Thom won't let him come in here. I hear you had quite a time with Teal."

"We had to tie the little bastard to his bed. Thom was in no mood for his foolishness and rather enjoyed trussing up du Mer like a feast goose. Being whacked on that big pate of his did nothing for the man's good humor. He had a rather nasty headache and couldn't remember who he was for awhile there." Legion wet the rag again and wrung it out. He glanced up as Storm took the rag out of his hands.

"Rest yourself, awhile, Commander. I'll do this." Storm gently placed the wet cloth on the young Prince's brow. "Has he awakened yet?"

Legion ran his hands over his tired face and spoke through his fingers as he rubbed his mouth. "I don't think so. He mumbles and his eyes open every now and then, but I don't think he's aware of what's going on. It's been four days and that gods-be-damned fever is no better. We talk to him, bathe him in iced water, dribble broth down his throat." He put down his hands and slumped into the chair by his brother's bed. "But he hasn't responded to anything."

"He will," Storm said with confidence.

"Does his father know how badly he's been hurt?" Legion asked and saw Storm shrug his broad shoulders.

"When you sent word there had been trouble, His Highness was mad as hell. He thought you guys had been up to no good. When the second messenger arrived with the news of Rayle's death and His Grace's injuries," Storm said, glancing at Legion, "I'll wager he knew the trouble had been fierce enough to warrant protection for the Prince. He took precautions by sending us."

"I'd like to know just who it was that wanted Conar so badly," Legion answered, leaning back his head. "The man who wounded him so gravely had orders to bring him in alive."

"Did you get to question the bastard?" Storm asked, frowning.

"We questioned him, all right. He died screaming, but we got no answers."

"He was a Hasdu, wasn't he?"

"Aye, but there's so many different offshoot tribes, we'd be hard-pressed to find the right one." He let out a tired breath. "Besides, they might have been hired by someone else."

"I doubt they'll try again, Commander," Storm assured him. "No harm will come to him now."

"I hope you're right, Storm," Legion sighed, his words slurring as he began to fall asleep. "I pray you're right."

* * * *

Down the hall from Conar's room, Thom Loure swatted Teal's hand away from the doorknob. "Get your ass back in that bed, du Mer!"

"I want to see him, Thommy," Teal protested and tried for the knob again, only to find himself picked up bodily and handed to another Elite.

"Keep this jackass in his room!" Thom bellowed and fixed Teal with a steady, menacing glower. "You'll do yourself more harm. That gods-be-damned shoulder is broken, du Mer!" Thom put a hand up to his head. "And you're making me hurt again, fool!"

Grimacing with pain, for his shoulder had banged hard into the Elite's broad chest as Thom had plucked him off the floor and swung him into the other man's arms, Teal felt his knees grow weak and his head swim unmercifully with the pain.

"I'm worried about him, Thommy," Teal gasped as the Elite laid him as gently as he could on his bed. "I'm no invalid."

"He has men with him. They'll come tell you if anything changes." Thom's face softened as he saw Teal wince from trying to relax. "Will you be all right?"

"Go to him," Teal motioned with his good arm, his throat closing with emotion. "Don't waste your time with me. I'll be fine."

"As soon as there's any change, I'll send for you."

"I know."

Thom walked out of the room, nodding to the guard who stood outside du Mer's door. "Call me if the gypsy needs anything. I'll be in with His Grace."

Outside Conar's room, two guards snapped to attention as Thom strode forward. One of the men reached for the doorknob, pulling the portal open with quiet ease. "Captain," he said as Thom nodded at him, "you have our deepest regrets, Sir."

Despite his loss, his weariness, and his own aches and bruises, not to mention the headache from hell that pounded inside his giant skull, Thom Loure couldn't help but smile at the man's mistake. He laid a big hand on the fellow's muscled shoulder. "I'm Thom. It was the Captain who ... who...." He couldn't seem to say the words.

"Captain Rayle Loure is no longer with us," the Elite answered, tears building. "His brother, Captain Thompson Loure, is our leader now." The man held Thom's astonished gaze. "We will serve you as we served your brother, Cap'n."

"Surely there is another from among the Elite who deserves this honor!" Thom protested.

"There is none we would honor as we do you, Sir," the other guard spoke. "Lieutenants Edan and Jale nominated you, Captain, and the vote was unanimous. The Prince will have to confirm the vote, but we all know what he'll say."

Thom's heart pounded and he couldn't find the words for these men. He managed to nod, hunching forward, his forehead wrinkled. He walked through the doorway before he could unman himself in front of the men.

Legion glanced up as Thom entered and he smiled. "Captain Thompson Loure," he said softly. "I rather like the sound of it, Thommy."

Thom could only shake his head. "I don't deserve it," he mumbled and nodded at Storm. "I am honored you have such confidence in me, Jale." His attention went to Conar and he was struck anew by the pallor of his friend's face, despite the red flush over his high cheekbones. A sickly yellow tint had chased away the summer's tan and the bright blond hair was dull with oil and sweat as it lay brushed back from the Prince's forehead. "No change?"

Legion shook his head. "How's Teal?" He couldn't hide the yawn.

"Better than you. Go get some sleep, Commander. I'll watch him."

Again Legion shook his head. "I can sleep in the chair as well as any bed."

Storm met Thom's gaze and smiled. "If you'll give me a chance to get out of this leather-work, I'll bring you men some supper."

"Take your time, Storm, I'm not all that hungry," Thom said. "Get something to eat yourself, first." He sat on the foot of the Prince's bed. "His Grace isn't going anywhere and neither am I." He laid a big hand on Conar's cheek. "I'm here for you, Highness," he whispered, "in my brother's place."

"Bring up some broth when you come back, Storm," Legion said. "We'll need to feed him again soon."

"You don't worry about that!" Thom snapped. "Just go to sleep."

Legion looked at Thom. In the fading light from the window, Thom reminded him painfully of his twin and it was like looking at Rayle's stern visage that never brooked argument. "Aye, Captain."

Thom settled his broad back against the bed's tall foot board and watched Conar's ragged breathing. The young Prince lay naked with only a thin sheet covering his hips and legs. He had tossed so violently in the throes of the raging fever that gripped him, A'Lex had ordered him tied to the four posts. His wrists and ankles were held down with padded silk rags as he lay spread-eagle on sheets that were changed every three to four hours as they became soiled with sweat and fluids from Conar's wounds.

Sometime toward dawn, Conar's breathing grew more ragged and strained. His flesh had become so hot that it burned the hands that touched him. The wound in his thigh had puffed up to the size of a large man's fist and was a scarlet red against the paleness of his flesh.

The Healer who had come from Iomal stood over the young Prince once again, and shook his head. He had cleaned and stitched the wound in Conar's side and the long cut on his upper thigh, near the groin. But there was an infection that not even the most powerful of the Healer's herbs seemed able to destroy.

The older man's hands were on the puffiness, shifting the fluid-filled flesh, probing it for signs of hardening masses. He craned his neck to look at Legion. "I will have to open this wound again, Lord Legion. It must drain."

Legion nodded. "Tell us what you need."

"I have the instruments with me, but I need a small brazier with fresh coals to sterilize them."

Storm left the room in search of a small brazier. Thom, who stood at the foot of the bed, his lanky arms folded across his chest, waited to be told what he could do.

Glancing back at the tall man, the Healer asked, "He may be unconscious, but when the wound is opened, he will feel it. Despite these bonds, he will need to be held so he will not injure himself as I scrape the wound clean."

Thom winced. The physician's words made his flesh crawl. As red and puffy as Conar's thigh was, having an instrument gouged into the tender flesh was bound to rebel with excruciating tenderness. "Is there no other way?"

"Not if you want His Grace to live."

"Healer Mayaeux knows what he's about, Thom," Legion said quietly.

Storm returned with a small, black, wrought-iron brazier and lay in on the stone hearth before the blazing fire.

"I'll have to pour scrubroot juice into the wound," the Healer remarked. "It has to be cleansed thoroughly."

Legion caught Thom's eye. Neither man would like to suffer the Healer's potion on an open wound.

The Healer ordered Thom, Storm, Marsh, and one of the other Elite Guards to hold the Prince's arms and legs steady. Legion he placed opposite him, and gave Conar's brother a warning.

"You must hold his hips and chest to the bed, Lord Legion. If he bucks and my instrument slips, it could geld him. He must be kept as still as possible."

"I understand," Legion said grimly.

When the incision was made, a putrid smell of dead tissue and festering infection pulsed from Conar's thigh in a stream as thick as a man's finger. Pressing gently around the puffiness to rid the wound of the thin yellowish-red fluid, the Healer watched the noxious stream run down Conar's leg and soak the towels that had been laid beneath him. Nearly a cup of vile poison oozed from the wound. When he was sure all the ichor was squeezed from the wound, he used his scalpel to enlarge the incision.

"Hold him still, men," the Healer told them.

He reached into his medicine pouch and removed an instrument that had the shape of a small flattened spoon. After holding it for a moment in the red-hot coals of the brazier, he removed it and poured brandy over the metal. The instrument hissed.

Legion settled his knees on the bed, his hands on his brother's still body. With one hand on Conar's breastbone, the other just above the thicker patch of pubic hair, he pressed down firmly and glanced up at the Healer. "Try not to hurt him too badly."

The Healer did not reply. His eyes were on the oozing hole in Conar's thigh. He took a deep breath, parted the wound with the fingers of his right hand, and slipped the hot, sterilized instrument into the wound.

If Legion had not been holding him down, Conar would have soared upward from the bed. As it was, even with four men rushing to grab his arms and legs and Legion pressing him to the bed, he came off the mattress in a surge of agonized screaming. His spine stiffened, his neck arched back on the pillow and his eyelids flew wide open. The screaming went on until the Healer was satisfied the wound was clean.

"Hand me the astringent!" he yelled at Thom and the big man jumped to pass the small goblet of scrubroot juice to the Healer. Not even bothering to take time to breathe, the Healer poured the fiery concoction on the gaping wound and was rewarded by an inhuman bellow of agony.

Conar's body went limp, and he was unconscious once more.

"Are you all right, sir?" Thom asked the Healer.

"I hurt him," the Healer mumbled. "I hurt my Prince." His lips were trembling. "I had to do it. I had to. There was no other way. I had to do it."

"We know that," Legion assured him. A groan from his brother made him turn toward Conar. Legion put his hand on his brother's brow and eased aside a lock of lank hair. "Rest easy, little brother."

"It's going to be a long night," the Healer prophesied.

\* \* \* \*

Dawn broke the next morning and with it came a light frosting of snow. Frost rimmed the window out of which Legion gazed at the calm countryside. He spied a lone wolf loping across the meadow and smiled. Other than what was happening inside Conar's room, the world was going about its business as usual. He heard his brother moan and turned from the window.

"He's worse," Thom said, his hand on the sweat-drenched blond head. "Why is that?"

The Healer sighed, his tired shoulders sagging beneath the weight of his burden. "I fear he's giving up the will to live."

"Don't say that!" Teal shouted from the doorway and all eyes turned to him.

"Get back to bed, du Mer!" Thom snapped and started toward the gypsy. He stilled as Teal held up a dagger in his trembling left hand.

"I'll slit you wide open if you try to keep me out of this room, Loure!"

Legion put out a hand to Teal. "Join us, old friend," he said and felt better as Teal wobbled forward and grasped A'Lex's hand in his own.

All twelve of the Elite from Boreas gathered in the room. Storm and Marsh Edan sat quietly on the floor at the foot of the bed. The man who had been guarding Teal entered shortly after the gypsy, embarrassment on his lean face at having been duped into going after fresh cider for the invalid who now sat cross-legged beside bed. He started to apologize to Thom, but the big man waved away his words.

"The little bugger was determined, Roy," Thom growled.

Three other guards stood at the fireplace, two flanked the door, one stood in the doorway, and two sat on a long chest in the corner. They were all quiet and subdued.

Easing open the door to the room, the new innkeeper of the Hound Stag Tavern, where Conar had been brought, placed hot mugs of spicy brewed tea on the table for the men. If not for the young innkeeper's cart, Thom would have had no way to bring Conar and Teal the five miles to the tavern. Without the young man's help, Conar would, without a doubt, have died on the roadway near Iomal.

"Do you think he knows where he is?" Thom asked, breaking the silence, as the innkeeper left.

Legion glanced at him. "What difference does it make?"

Thom looked away. "Rayle said this is where he met her."

Legion sighed, closing his eyes. "I had forgotten." He glanced at his brother's still face.

"And you think this is where he wants it to end?" Teal asked Thom.

"He's getting no better," Thom explained.

Legion watched the shallow rise of his brother's chest. He walked to the bed and knelt, taking Conar's limp hand in his own. "Is that what you're doing, little brother?" He put his face close to Conar's. "If it is, you are being selfish!" His voice rose. "There are people here who love you."

"And need you," Teal added.

"People, who would be hurt by your leaving," Thom joined in.

"Men who need your guidance," Storm stated.

"Who need your friendship," Marsh put in as he came to stand beside Storm, resting a hand on his cousin's broad shoulder.

"Your father misses you," the Healer chimed in. "There are a lot of folk who care about you."

"Think of your children, Your Grace," one of the Elite suggested.

"If you leave us, Commander," another Elite said, "there will be no decent King to sit on our throne."

"Think of all the people you would hurt if you left, Conar!" Legion challenged.

"What about Aunt Dyreil?" Teal asked. "What about Gezelle? Hern? Your brothers?"

"Liza!" Conar screamed and the men jumped. They were stunned as his head whipped about on the pillow and he began to struggle violently.

"Conar!" Legion shouted, watching the breathing grow more shallow with each breath. "Don't do this! Do you hear me?" He fumbled to untie the silk binding that held the limp wrist to the bedpost. "Get this gods-be-damned cording off him!" he shouted at Thom, who hastened to untie Conar's right wrist.

Climbing onto the bed, Legion took his brother's body in his arms and brought him against his own chest. "Don't do this to me, Conar!"

"Don't hold him up like that, Lord Legion!" the Healer warned, pulling at Legion's arms. "You're putting strain on his wound!"

Legion looked at the Healer's worried face. "He's my brother. I love him," Legion cried, tears falling down his cheeks. He gently laid Conar back on the bed.

"Then tell him, Lord Legion," one of the Elite said. "Make him understand."

Legion leaned over Conar's still form and took his brother's face in his hands. "I love you, little brother. I love you more than anything in this life; more than I will ever love anything else." He placed his lips to the silent lips of his brother. "I love you, Conar."

Then the room went deathly still, for Conar McGregor had ceased to breathe....

"Coni!" Legion cried. He swung his leg over his brother's inert body. "Don't you die on me! Do you hear me? Don't you *dare* die on me!"

"Milord Legion," the Healer said quietly. "Let him go. He is in the arms of the Gatherer now and She will...."

"No!" Legion shouted. He clenched his fists, lifted them over his head, and hit his brother in the center of his chest.

"By the gods!" Storm whispered and looked away, his face pale.

Teal and Rayle did nothing as Legion hit Conar again and again. The two men were like statues as they stood watching the scene playing out before them.

Legion bent over, placed his lips to Conar's, and blew breath into his brother's mouth. Once. Twice. Three times. Pushing back to his haunches, he stared at Conar's chest and, when there was no movement, he bent forward again and placed an ear to the young man's chest.

No one took a breath. Every eye was locked on the two men on the bed. When Legion straightened up and they took in the look on his grieving face, every eye closed.

"Conar!" Legion sobbed as he drew his brother's limp body into his arms. He shifted Conar against him, the young man's arms hanging behind him. Crouched on his knees, rocking back and forth, Legion pressed his tearful cheek against Conar's and began to keen.

"Milords, please," the Healer insisted, looking to Teal and Rayle for help. "This is wrong. The Prince has succumbed to his wounds. We must prepare him for...."

"Get out!" Legion screamed, turning an enraged glower to the Healer. "Get the hell out of my brother's room, you quack! My brother is not dead!" He swung his wild stare to Rayle. "Get him out of this room, Loure!"

Rayle took three steps forward and grasped the Healer's arm. Without saying a word, he ushered the man from the room then closed and bolted the door. He folded his arms across his massive chest and leaned against the barred portal, his tearful gaze lowered to the floor.

Teal hobbled to a chair. Storm helped du Mer sit, then placed a comforting hand on the gypsy's shoulder, tightening his grip for a moment.

The other Elite warriors found reason not to look at Legion as he continued to rock his brother. Now and again the sound of Legion whispering to the man in his arms would make one of the Elite glance up, but none seemed to be able to look long upon the scene.

"Don't leave me," Legion sobbed. He kept one strong arm around Conar's back and lifted the other--hand trembling--to caress his brother's still face. He pushed back the hair from Conar's forehead and bent to place his lips on the cool flesh. "Stay with me, little brother. I need you." He kissed Conar's lips, whispering against them. "No one loves me as you do, Coni. Don't leave me." His voice broke. "Please don't leave me!"

Teal put a hand to his face and shielded his eyes. His shoulders quaked. He was oblivious to Storm's gentle pressure on his shoulder.

"*Coni!*" Legion screamed.

Everyone in the room jumped. Every gaze locked on A'Lex.

"Give him back to me!" Legion raged, glaring at the ceiling. "Do you hear me, Alel? You give my brother back to me!"

"He's losing it," Rayle said to no one in particular. "We should put a stop to this."

No one moved.

"*Give him back to me!*"

Teal flinched at the volume of Legion's demand, for the words were like thunder booms. He looked up at Storm, but Storm shook his head.

"Give him back to me," Legion whimpered, his voice cracking with emotion. He stretched out on the bed, pulling Conar into his embrace and buried his face against Conar's neck.

"Don't take him away from me," was Legion's final, pitiful plea.

But Conar McGregor lay still in his brother's arm, his flesh beginning to cool.

Chapter Twenty Three

"Go back, Conar," the Gatherer commanded, Her voice shattering into a multitude of swirling lavender light.

"Let me stay. I am at peace here in the light." He turned his head, following the bright rose light that beckoned him onward.

"Your time has not yet come; your destiny not yet met." The Gatherer was more insistent, Her voice soft, yet firm.

"There is nothing left for me in my world. I have no one." He moved toward the shaft of light. He could see someone standing there, blending into the light from the deeper darkness surrounding the beam.

"You have more than you know, Conar. You have all there can be." The voice was sterner. It denied resistance.

"You took from me what was once mine. You gave and You took away." He could almost see the figure, now, as it stood with open arms, pleading for him to come.

"What you had was not yours to keep forever. It was a gift, Conar. A lesson and nothing more. It let you see beyond your own limitations into the world of what could be. You have yet to meet that which you will cherish most."

"Let me stay. I am tired. I need rest."

His footsteps moved ever closer to the bright, welcoming, peaceful light. He could see that the figure waiting for him was a woman, and he could feel her love flowing to him as she beckoned. The ground beneath his feet shook as the voice boomed fire and ice at him.

"You will find rest once you have fulfilled the Prophesy, Prince of the Wind. Until then, your soul is not your own! Go back. Go back and meet your destiny, Conar McGregor. Go back, now!"

He could see her clearly now as she waited for him in the beam of light, bright, welcoming, loving. She had her arms out wide to him as she bid him hurry to her side.

His footsteps quickened and he put out his own arms to embrace her. He could see her golden hair glowing around her head, smell the sweet scent of lilac wafting toward him on a summer's breeze. Her pale peach gown swirled about her slender body and he smiled, remembering well that gown from his childhood. He spoke her wonderful name and heard her gentle, welcoming laughter.

"Do not tempt him, woman!" the voice thundered through the darkness and echoed over Conar. The beam of light wavered, shifted, flickered, and began to fade.

"No!" he shouted, straining to follow the fading shaft of light into that which he had almost entered. "Don't leave me!" he cried to the woman who had dropped her arms in sad denial. "Don't leave me again!" He wanted the peace his soul had known in the shadows of the light. He wanted the comfort of those precious arms around him. "Take me with you this time! Please take me with you!"

He ran forward, almost put a foot into the rapidly shrinking light, but he stumbled, fell, and as he did, he put out his hand and briefly touched the bright beam. It ran down his arm, lit his face with a rapturous glow. His smile was as bright as the light, his eyes glowing. He pushed hurriedly to his feet and stepped into the wavering light, reaching out.

With a suddenness that brought him to his knees in agony, the light fled, not even an after-image left to see. He buried his face in his hands and wept bitterly, whimpering in misery and loneliness. "No," he whispered. He raised his head. "Please come back for me, Mama, please!"

Then he was soaring backwards through time and space. The fever was leaving him in waves he could feel. He could feel his head clearing of the ache and blackness inside. His stomach heaved, but he knew he would live and that knowledge hurt him.

He had been thinking of Liza before the light came and now, she, too, was gone.

He moved in his tortuous sleep and tried to call out. He could feel lips on his own, blowing breath into his mouth, making him breathe, and he wanted to pull away his head, to deny the life-giving air being forced into his lungs. His body jerked, for he thought he had heard Liza's sweet voice--or was it his Mother's?--speaking to him in quiet whispers of love.

He groaned. Illusion held so much more peace than the reality hovering over him, for reality inflated hard breathes into his shrunken lungs and pummeled with iron fists against his chest. He strained to get back to the shadows, to find the light once more, but he could feel his body surging upward through the dark into an unnatural light that hurt his eyes and made his soul ache with hopelessness. He tried with all his might to deny them the right to bring him back to the world of the damned, but his lashes parted and he looked into the beaming face of his eldest brother.

"Thank the gods, Conar," Legion swore. "You are going to be fine, now. You're going to be just fine."

Conar wanted to cry. He searched his brother's face, saw the great relief, and love residing there and he wanted to cry.

He had been brought back against his will and he felt deceived once again.

\* \* \* \*

Two weeks after Conar's brush with the Gatherer, Legion found his brother in the stable of the Hound and Stag. Conar was staring intently up at the loft. His face was set and hard. He didn't even acknowledge Legion's greeting.

Tousling his hair to rid it of the fine coating of snow that had covered him on his way to the stable, Legion sighed and walked past Conar to his horse's stall to lead out the animal. "They say it may snow again before we reach the keep." Legion lifted his horse's saddle from a low stool and slung it across the animal's back. "Are you sure you're able to travel?"

"I'll be fine," Conar assured him. "I'll damn sure get no better here." His gaze left the loft and strayed to a corner of the stable where a pitchfork was stuck in a mound of hay. His voice was clipped and as cold as the air outside. "Is du Mer going with us?"

"Aye. The little bastard is chomping at the bit to get home." Legion patted his steed's velvety brown nose as the stallion craned back its neck to nudge his shoulder. He watched his brother's stony profile as Conar walked to the pitchfork and withdrew it from the hay mound. "Papa sent word this morn. The wedding party is concerned for you. I think the Princess was worried about you."

Conar frowned and drove the pitchfork as hard as he could into the hay. "Let her worry. She'll get used to disappointment. I'm in no haste, and in no condition, to hurry home."

"If you can't ride...."

Conar speared his brother with a haughty glower. "I'm fine."

Legion shook his head and handed his steed to an Elite who had come in after the beast. "I wish you would reconsider and ride in the coach with Teal." He saw his brother start to explode with anger and he held up his hand. "I said I wouldn't argue with you over this and I won't. You're a grown man, but you've been in bed nearly three weeks, Conar. If I see you weakening, I will have them put your ass in the coach anyway."

"I am not a child," Conar grumbled. "Don't treat me as one."

"Don't act like a child and you won't be treated as one," Legion snapped back. He sat on the lower rung of the ladder that led up to the loft. "Papa also sent word of Rayle's widow. She thanks you for the money you sent to her and she says she wishes you Godspeed."

The squeaking of the ladder as Legion shifted startled Conar and he turned. His hope swiftly fled. "Rayle was a good man." Loss crept into the hard voice. "If his wife is willing, I will have her and her children declared members of my personal household. Her family will lack for nothing."

Legion had not missed the look of expectation that had crossed his brother's face as he looked up to the loft. His heart ached for the disappointment that he knew Conar felt. "She isn't going to return this time, Conar," he said softly. "If she were going to, it would have been while you were so gravely ill."

"She was here." Conar put his hand over the braid of Liza's hair circling his wrist and longingly caressed the silky strands. "I could feel her."

"I wish you wouldn't hold out hope that she'll come back like she did before. If you think she will, you're only deceiving yourself, little brother."

"She won't be back!" Conar snapped and reached for Seayearner's saddle. "I know that, A'Lex!"

Realizing his brother's intent, Legion snarled, "Don't even think about it!"

"I can saddle my own nag!" Conar growled, but he was pushed none too gently out of the way as Legion swung the brown leather saddle from the low partition and draped it over the steed's broad back.

"You can get the hell out of my way, too," Legion told him.

Conar glared at his brother, but kept his mouth shut. His thigh ached like the very devil and he wasn't even sure he could have lifted the saddle. His gaze went once more to the loft and he felt another pain, this one, deep in his heart.

Legion ground his teeth as he saw where his brother's attention had gone. He pulled tight the cinch and walked the steed to where his brother stood, leaning against a stall.

"I wasn't joking, Conar. If I see you not feeling well, I will have you put in the coach with du Mer."

"Try it. I give the orders here, A'Lex, not you. You are my servant, not the other way around!"

Legion blinked. Servant? Him? Conar had never said such a thing before. "I am not your servant," he said quietly.

"No matter what you call yourself, it is my will that will be done. It is best you started to remember who the Crown Prince in this family is!" He walked his horse into the stable yard, Legion following close on his heels.

Something hard had entered Conar's voice and for a moment Legion had actually feared the lad. Conar had never taken seriously his title of Prince Regent unless he was in a foul mood and wanted to annoy someone or get his way when he knew he shouldn't. The disdainful look on his face, the look of unmistakable authority was something new. Watching his brother swing into Seayearner's saddle, he grimaced at the pain that flashed momentarily over Conar's face. Instinctively he put up a restraining hand, but Conar gripped his hand in a steel-like clinch.

"I don't need a mother hen, A'Lex. Leave off!" He pushed away his brother's hand, and although his face twisted with pain as he straightened in the saddle, he held Legion's gaze.

"I am worried about you."

"I said to leave off, Legion. I meant it."

"I can't help worrying."

"Then worry about the woman I'll be wedding come next week. She'll need all the worry and pity she can get!"

Conar clucked his tongue and sent his horse into the snow-laden countryside.

"Damn it, Conar!" Legion shouted, running after him. "Get your ass back here!" He turned to his own horse and was about to mount when Thom's hand fell on his shoulder.

"Let him go, Commander," the big man said and pointed to the two horses that had fallen in behind Conar's. Marsh Edan and Storm Jale rode only a few yards behind the black destrier. "They'll watch him."

"There were four of us on the road with him a few weeks ago, Thom. Remember what happened then?" Legion shook off the big paw. He put his foot in the stirrup and pulled himself up. "I want his ass with us!"

Thom smiled and nodded to the group of eight riders who were even then turning their mounts to the roadway.

"They'll have to ride a helluva lot faster than that to catch my brother and that hell-steed of his!" Legion fumed.

"He'll not ride fast for long with his thigh the way it is," Thom told him and crossed his arms over his wide chest. "He's hurting whether he lets on or not."

Legion snorted. "I know." Glancing up, he saw du Mer hobbling out of the kitchen door, supported by the young innkeeper. His face turned red with suppressed fury. "What the hell happened to you now, du Mer?"

Teal had the good sense to lower his head, but when he glanced up at Legion's scowling face, he couldn't stop the sheepish grin that touched his firm lips. "Tripped on the stairs and twisted my ankle."

Legion mumbled something vulgar and then pinned Teal with a steely-eyed glower. "Get in the gods-be-damned coach, du Mer. I don't want to see your half-breed face for the rest of the gods-be-damned day!"

"What did he mean about you worrying about the Princess?" Teal, ignoring the slur, asked as he hobbled toward the coach. "Does he doubt he will be good to the lady?"

"I think he means to punish her for being the reason his Liza left," Thom put in.

"Her love made her leave," Teal corrected.

"Love?" Legion exploded. "She took his heart and crushed it, leaving him alone in his grief. I fancy I'll not ever want a woman to love me so tenderly!"

* * * *

When Legion and Thom rode away, the coach rolling along behind them, from the straw-strewn loft came a hitching sigh. A trembling hand brushed at the drops of moisture clinging to pale cheeks. "No, Milord," the watcher whispered. "He will never be alone. The Princess will be with him from now on."

Chapter Twenty Four

As hard as it had rained that spring day when Conar, Liza, and Gezelle had first stepped foot in the tavern at Briar's Hold, it snowed the cold autumn afternoon that Conar and his men arrived there. During the last two miles before reaching the snug haven, the heavens had opened to send blinding, stinging, driving white cascades of snow to cover the ground and freeze both traveler and animal alike. Close to a complete whiteout, the landscape, sky, and distance before the men were an unrelieved glare of brightness.

It was with a sigh of relief that they saw the half-covered signpost advertising the inn, a twisted bramble bush, and a single scarlet rose on a jet-black background.

Entering the cheerful warmth of the little tavern, the men smiled with pleasure. The sweet aroma of baking apples, cinnamon and hot spiced wine filled the air.

"Your Grace!" Meggie Ruck cried out as she caught sight of her visitor. Sinking into a deep curtsy before her Prince, she raised her head to smile, but his flushed face and pain-filled eyes brought her immediately to her feet. "Are you not well, Highness?" she asked with concern.

Conar stood beside the front door, wavering on his feet, his left hand gripping the upright beam that supported the little alcove leading into the tavern. His right arm was around a tall, bearded man who had a deep scowl on his handsome face. "Don't feel real good, Meg."

Legion didn't know the woman, but he had heard many times of her generosity and her loyalty where his brother was concerned. He dusted the snow from his hat, beating the wide-brimmed felt on his knee. "He pulled loose some stitches in his thigh, Madame Ruck. Could you sew them closed for him?"

Meggie only glanced at the tall man before turning her complete attention to Conar. She winced at the silent pleas for help on the young Prince's pale face. "Get my boy up the stairs, Sir. I'll fetch my sewing basket and some potions." She reached out a hand to her Prince and laid her work-reddened fingers on his cheek. "We'll have you right as rain, Highness," she said, and answered the small smile of gratitude before turning to bellow for the tavern wench who stood gawking at the group of men who had entered. "Dorrie! See to the Prince Regent's men!"

"Thank you, Meggie," Conar managed to gasp before pitching sideways into his brother's arms.

\* \* \* \*

When he awoke, Meggie Ruck was hovering over him. He tried to smile, but his thigh was throbbing with pain and he felt warm trickles of blood easing down between his legs.

"You fair did yourself harm," Meggie told him as she surveyed his fever-shot face.

"How've you been, my Meggie?" he asked and held out his hand to her.

"Better, it seems, than my Overlord," she snapped before taking his hand and pressing it to her weathered cheek. She looked up at Legion. "You'll need to help me, Sir."

"Just tell me what to do," Legion told her as he sat on the bed next to Conar.

"You'll need to be holding the flesh together as I stitch. My old hands ain't as agile as they once were, but I can still weave a fancy enough stitch." Meggie laid Conar's hand beside him on the bed and told his brother to lay aside the leather jacket Conar was wearing.

When he did as he was bid, Legion let out a quickly in-drawn breath in a long sigh of disgust; Meggie grimaced, turning an accusing eye to her Overlord.

The whole left side of Conar's shirt was soaked with dried blood that had turned a dark, ugly brown.

"Conar, by all that's holy, look what you've done!" Legion let out a raging breath as he glared at his brother's calm face. "You knew you'd opened this wound! You knew it!"

"We weren't far from the inn--"

"I ought to beat you black and blue!"

"Wait until he heals and then do it, Sir," Meggie snapped. She plucked at Conar's shirt and jerked back her hand as the young Prince gasped and flinched away from her touch.

"The gods-be-damned, Conar!" Legion exploded. "The shirt's stuck to you, fool!"

"I know," Conar replied calmly. "Don't you think I can feel it?"

"It's got to come off," Legion said.

"I know that, too."

"And it's going to hurt like the devil when it does!" Legion growled.

"Tell me something I don't know."

"Do you know you're a bloody jackass?" Legion inquired.

"I said to tell me something I don't--"

"Just shut the hell up!"

Meggie straightened from her crouched position over Conar and went to the door, calling for Dorrie to bring up another basin of hot water. She tromped back to the bed and nodded to the basin already prepared for the sewing. "We'll use that hot warm to wet his shirt and loosen the blood. You pour and I'll ease off the shirt. And you be careful of what you do to him, you hear?"

"The men are all settled, Legion," Thom said as he entered the room. "Teal was hurting a bit, himself, so I gave him laudanum and made him go to bed." He glanced at Conar, grimacing as he viewed the bloody shirt.

Meggie's eyes flew to Legion. "You're Lord Legion A'Lex?" she asked with astonishment.

"Aye." He grinned at her. "Unfortunately I have that dubious distinction."

"You have my sympathy then. Will you unbutton his breeches, now, Lord Legion?"

"It's just Legion."

"Then Legion it is," Meggie mumbled. "Get them breeches undone, I told you!"

Legion winked at his brother. Meggie Ruck was every bit the woman Conar had said she was. As he undid the ivory buttons on Conar's breeches, he smiled. He would lay odds he was the only man to ever unbutton Conar McGregor's pants.

"Is there anything I can do?" Thom asked, wincing as Conar did when the band of his breeches caught on a clot of dried blood and stuck, pulling the tender flesh around the wound on his side.

"You can keep your big hands to yourself," Meggie said, eyeing the massive paws. "This takes precision and delicacy."

"And a heart of steel," Conar added.

"Who has a heart of steel?" Meggie inquired. Her gaze went to the soft nest of blond curls revealed in the opened V of Conar's breeches and then leapt away, her face red, and her thoughts like those of any woman who had seen that blond thatch. "You pour the water now, Lord Legion."

Warm water flowed over his side and hip and under him. It was not a particularly pleasant feeling and it made his bladder lurch. He kept his attention focused on Meggie's intense face as she put her hands on his shirt.

"It may hurt you some, Your Grace," she told him.

Conar shrugged. "What doesn't, Meggie?"

Legion glanced up at Thom. "Take that water from the girl, Thommy."

Thom grabbed the basin of water from a diminutive tavern wench whose bold scrutiny ran down him from bald pate to muddy boots with unconcealed interest. He grinned at her and turned away, his brow crinkling with delight as Legion winked at him.

As Meggie gently pulled on the shirt, Conar sucked in his breath. The fabric was stuck fast to the tender, hot flesh and he ground his teeth to keep from crying out. He pursed his lips tightly shut as sweat popped out on his forehead and upper lip. Meggie was gently working the material loose as Legion poured the too warm water over him and it was an intense agony that nearly made him faint.

"I want you to go riding again tomorrow, you stupid little shit!" Legion snapped as he caught sight of Conar's pain-dampened face and trembling lips.

"Don't you be calling my bonny boy no names!" Meggie snarled as she eased the material away from the gaping part of the wound.

Conar's brows shot upward and he grinned mischievously at Legion as if to say: She put you in your place!

"He's incorrigible, Meggie," Legion fumed. "Look at the little bastard smirking at me!"

"He has every right to smirk at a fool baiting him when he can't do nothing else but smirk!" Meggie defended her Prince. She grasped the shirt and jerked it away from the half-inch spot left attached to Conar's skin.

"Damn!" Conar gasped, digging his hands into the mattress to keep from passing out.

"Like I said--go riding again real soon!" Legion grunted.

Meggie sighed as she looked at the puckered, gaping hole that had formed along the old stitches. The flesh around the wound looked red and puffy and an ooze of watery blood dripped down the young Prince's side.

"You there, big fellow!" Meggie called to Thom who had turned green in the last minute of her work. "Hand me the little bowl of brandy with the needle and thread in it."

Thom handed her the bowl with shaking hands. He met the fat woman's raised eyebrow with a sheepish grin. "I ... I'm...."

"An overgrown child," Meggie sniffed and dipped her hand into the brandy to pull out the needle and thread. "Some Elite you are. Hold the flesh tightly together, Lord Legion."

The needle stuck into his flesh. Conar gasped with agony. The pain was even more intense than he could have imagined. Thankful he had been partially unconscious for the first two sewings, he was intensely sorry he wasn't for this one. The sutures on his ribs didn't hurt nearly as much as the ones Meggie was putting in his thigh. With every poke he cringed and had to bite his lip to keep from moaning aloud. At one point, the needle drove home and he felt a slight stream of urine dribble from his manhood. He couldn't stand any more without comment.

"Damn it, Meggie! Are you trying to sew me to my breeches?"

Meggie didn't bat an eye, didn't even glance up at him. Her full attention was on the last three stitches she had to make. Her voice was as dry as aged parchment as she spoke. "I thought I would. I've heard tell you have a hard time keeping them on, Milord."

Conar blinked and his face turned red. He heard Legion sputter, heard Thom answer, and blushed harder. "Meggie, I...." he began, but felt the needle drag as the thread caught on a knot. He gasped and shuddered, then sank into merciful oblivion.

"Pull them britches of his off while he's out, Lord Legion," Meggie ordered. She turned her face to the wall. "And then cover him." Her lips twitched. "This is one woman who don't need to be seeing him in all his glory, for I'm sure the sight would stay with me a goodly time."

Legion hastened to do as he was told.

* * * *

Several hours later Conar opened his eyes to bright candlelight and Meggie Ruck's nodding head as she sat slumped in the chair beside him. Her mop-cap was slightly askew on her graying head and her snores would have roused even the dead. He saw her shift her enormous bulk and then jerk up her head, sputtering and licking her lips. When she came fully awake and focused on him, he smiled at her.

"Are you awake, then?" she asked and stood, wincing as she unfolded her stiff body from the uncomfortable chair. She reached out a hand to put it on his forehead. Pleased with his cool flesh, she stroked a stray lock of blond hair from his eyes. "Do you need anything, Your Grace?"

With an effort, he reached up his own hand to take hers. He brought the chapped, rough flesh to his dry lips and planted a soft kiss in her callused palm. "Only your love, Sweet Meggie," he whispered, for his throat was as dry as his lips.

"She's a married woman, little brother," Legion called from the deeper shadows of the room where he had sat for most of the night, unable to sleep for Meggie Ruck's snoring and unable to dethrone the staunch woman from her bedside vigil.

Conar grinned wanly at the woman's blushing face. "Alas, I am all too aware of that fact." He kissed her palm again and then nuzzled it close to his cheek, flinching as a shooting pain coursed through his side.

"I will get you something for the pain, Highness," she said, unable to bear his hurt.

Conar shook his head. "No need, Meggie," he answered, willing the pain to go away. "Just sit here beside me, sweet lady."

Legion stood and stretched, coming to stand over Conar. "Let her get you something. It's snowed a good six inches since we've been here and it doesn't look like we'll be traveling any time soon. I've sent word to Papa. You need to rest and let those stitches mend."

Conar kept Meggie's hand in his, holding the rough fingers to his cheek. "I don't take drugs for pain, Legion. You know that."

"You won't leave this bed until I am sure those stitches are healed this time," Legion snapped. "You'd better make use of the time to rest. It's only a sleeping potion she's offering."

Conar turned his head so the light was out of his eyes, dragging Meggie's hand with him as she chose to sit on the bed near him. "I can sleep well enough without help, thank you."

Legion met Meggie's worried frown with one of his own and something silent passed between them. The lady nodded and eased her hand from Conar's.

"I need to have more wood sent up, Milord," she told her Prince.

"Legion can see to it," Conar said petulantly. "Don't leave."

"I'll be back before you know it." She astonished herself as she planted a light kiss on his brow. She placed her fingertips over his lids. "You close those pretty blue eyes and rest until I get myself back." She nodded at Legion and left.

"Don't you have a bed to go to, Legion?" Conar asked without looking at his brother's smiling face.

"Aye." Legion was amused by Meggie Ruck's ability to make his brother mind her. Idly he wondered if he could hire Meggie as a nanny for the ill-tempered little brat.

Conar glared at him. "Then make use of it. Quit hovering over me." He nuzzled down into the comfort of his plump pillow, dismissing his brother.

Legion stood there for a moment, then shrugged. He knew a dismissal when he had been given one. "Sleep well, then," he advised, and shut the door behind him with more force than was necessary.

Conar took as deep a breath as his stitches would allow. He knew where he was. He had known from the moment he had awakened. His heart had told him what his foggy mind had forgotten.

It was this very room, this very bed, where he had made Liza his woman. He could almost smell the scent of lavender still permeating the room and it hurt him more than he cared to admit.

His hand strayed to the pillow beside his own and a muscle worked in his jaw. He could see her lying beside him, could feel the warmth of her body close to his own and wanted to scream with the injustice of it. That was why he hadn't wanted Meggie to leave. He had needed a feminine presence to help banish the pain that was invading his heart.

He jerked his head to the door as it opened, ready to do fierce battle with whomever had dared to intrude on his misery, but Meggie Ruck's cheerful face peered at him from a tilted mop-cap and he couldn't help but smile.

"I've brought you some broth and you will drink it down," she said without preamble. She came to sit beside him.

"Promise me something, Meggie."

"I make no promises until you have had this broth. You need to build up your strength." Her tone told him she wouldn't take no for an answer.

He eyed the cup and let out a helpless sigh. He was putty in the woman's hands. "I'll drink the gods-be-damned broth if you make me a promise." He tried to sit up, but his breath caught on a ragged gasp and he stilled.

"You young men are all alike," she hissed and put one huge arm under his shoulders to lift his head with as little effort as if he were a babe. "You all think you are made of steel instead of flesh and blood." She brought the cup to his lips. "And it takes a woman to let you know otherwise!" She frowned down at him as he looked up at her. "Drink the broth, lad!" she commanded and emphatically nodded, her mop-cap coming perilously close to tumbling off her head.

He was given no choice whether to drink the brew. She was holding it to his lips and the liquid was running into his mouth. It had a wonderful, beef-flavored taste that seemed to make his dry and scratchy throat feel better. He drained the cup and only winced a little as Meggie laid his head back down on the cool pillow.

"Now. What's this you want me to promise?" Meggie asked, tugging his covers over his naked chest and tucking them under his arms.

"I want you to...." He stopped, frowning. His tongue had suddenly gone numb and he knew instantly what the lady had done. Slowly he raised his gaze to her triumphant face and was angry with her. Once more he had been betrayed by a woman. Once more he had no say in his own life because of a woman. "Who's bright idea was this?"

"Now, don't you be getting your feathers all ruffled! It was mine and your brother's. Nobody is doing you a hurt, especially not your Meggie. You need your rest and I aim to see you get it!" She took his hand and brought it to her lips. "I'd never do naught to bring you hurt, sweet Prince."

"I told you I didn't want any drugs!"

"And I told you to get some rest! Now. Yourself to sleep!"

His head was beginning to get fuzzy and heavy. It was all he could do to focus on her face. "The promise?" he managed to get out.

Meggie sighed. "All right. What promise is that?"

"Go to bed, lady."

Meggie drew herself up. "I will not!"

He wedged open his eyelids and tried to glare at her. "I have asked you to go to bed, Madame Ruck." His words were beginning to slur, his tongue expand in his mouth. "I now command you to do so." His glare attempted to change into a regal scowl. "Else I'll have you fined for not obeying a royal order."

Her spine stiffened and she meant to do battle, then and there, but his sweet face seemed to fill her very soul and she knew he meant what he said. She ducked her head and the mop-cap slid down over her quivering nose. Angrily she pushed it to the back of her head. "The hell you will!" she ground out and stomped furiously to the door, her heavy footsteps rattling the panes in the window. His slurred words brought her head around.

"Thank you, Dearling," he whispered and then burrowed into the pillow.

"You're welcome, my bonny boy," she whispered as she heard his almost immediate light snore.

* * * *

Sitting in front of the crackling fireplace in the common room, Teal and Thom drank hot mugs of steaming ale Harry Ruck had supplied. The wind howled around the eaves and sent blasts of snow crashing against the windows. Legion came down and joined them.

"You look like I feel," Teal mumbled as he sipped his ale.

"That bad, eh?" He laughed. "I just can't seem to sleep," Legion said as he sat at their table and plowed his thick fingers through his graying hair. He glanced up as Dorrie placed a mug of ale before him. He watched her swaying hips as she walked away and winked as she turned at the kitchen door to send him an inviting look from beneath her long lashes.

"Yours for the taking," Thom joked.

"Anyone's for the taking," Storm quipped from his place near the front door where he and Marsh and three other Elite sat playing cards.

Legion sat back in his chair and sipped the ale. "Maybe I can sleep, after all."

## Chapter Twenty Five

"This is Maud, Your Grace." Meggie introduced the middle-aged lady to her Prince. "She'll be sitting with you while I'm about my chores."

Conar glanced up in puzzlement at the red-haired matron. The lady smiled warmly at him, dipping her knees in a quick curtsy before coming to sit beside him in the chair. She opened the sewing pouch she carried and pulled out knitting needles and yarn. He looked back at Meggie who stood in the doorway, her massive arms folded over her equally massive bosom.

"Maud is my best friend. She offered to take my place. Get her to tell you about her grandmother's invention." Meggie turned to go, but Conar's confused voice stopped her.

"Meggie?...."

"And get her to tell you about the time her piglet got stuck in the privy and nearly scared her old man to death. That's a riot, it is!"

Before Conar could ask just why Meggie thought he needed a baby-sitter, the red-haired lady had begun her tale. He turned his startled gaze to her.

"It was when me granny saw a need for a new type of churn. She...."

\* \* \* \*

Conar woke the next morning and looked at a white-haired old lady with only one tooth in her head. Her lips grinned, and she sat in the chair beside him and reached for his hand.

"I'm Sybie, Your Grace," she sloshed through her almost toothless mouth. "Meggie says to tell you about my grandsons and the bear."

He gawked at the old woman, then turned confused eyes about the room as the lady began to speak, spitting flecks of spittle as she did, her cackling laugh filling the room. Where the hell was Meggie and what the hell was going on?

Despite his calling and protestations, no one came to see him until later that afternoon. The old woman lay snoozing in the chair, her white hair falling over her wrinkled forehead, her rubbery lips looking much like a snorting horse. When he looked up to see yet another strange woman peeking around the door to his room, he exploded. "Where is Meggie Ruck?"

The new lady, younger by far than the other two, shyly walked into the room. Once her body had cleared the doorway, it would have been obvious to the most near-sighted that the lady was far gone with child. She waddled close to the bed and shook Sybie, who came awake with a splutter of half-phrases.

"Time to go home, Granny," the young woman said. "The carriage is here."

Sybie let the woman help her to her feet. She turned a bright smile to Conar, winked at him. "You're a bonny boy, you are," she told him then trundled out of the room on sliding feet.

"My name is Suzie, Your Grace," the younger woman said as she settled in the vacated chair. "Perhaps you know my cousin, Roy Matheny? He's one of your Elite. He...."

\* \* \* \*

For nine days Conar did not see Meggie Ruck, nor Legion, nor Thom, nor Teal, nor Storm, nor Marsh, nor any of his Elite. Despite his angry retorts, especially about urinating in front of these strange women, he was reminded sternly that they each had a husband, father, son, grandson, brother, or nephew who had managed well enough with their care. What they might see, they told him, had been seen before.

What he encountered was a succession of strange women, each different from the next in appearance and temperament and age, but alike in the same perfect way. They were each kind, considerate and loving, apparently without a duplicative bone in their bodies. It became obvious to him after the third day what Meggie and Legion, no doubt, were doing.

"Good morn, Milord," still another woman spoke as she dipped him a clumsy curtsy. "I'm Greta." Her merry blue eyes twinkled and she switched her long, thick blond braid from one shoulder to the next. "I'm Sybie's great-granddaughter. She says you wanted to hear about the windmill falling down last year?"

Throwing his hands into the air, Conar scrunched down in the bed and smiled evilly at the girl as she began her tale. By far, she was the prettiest of the lot, her voice sweet and melodic, but he really didn't care. Enough was enough.

"Mam'selle," he interrupted her humorous tale of a wildly careening windmill, "just where is Meggie?"

"Why, in the kitchen, Milord." She smiled. "Do you need her?"

His grin grew even more evil. "Aye, sweet girl. Would you get the lady for me?"

Greta stood and dipped him another clumsy curtsy. "Right away, Milord!" She beamed, eager to do his command.

Conar locked his fingers together in his lap and began to twiddle his thumbs. He couldn't wait to get Meggie in the room.

He waited for what seemed like an hour before he heard heavy footsteps on the stairs. His grin went hard, his eyes hot with combat. As the door opened, he was about to singe Meggie Ruck with a tongue on fire with fury, but he blinked.

Standing in the doorway was a woman twice--if that was possible--as big as Sadie, the cook at Boreas. Her huge, round face was red with the exertion from her climb up the stairs and her quadruple chins wagged as she chortled, her gargantuan bosom heaving up and down as she laughed. "Meg says to tell you she's busy just now, Your Grace. My name is Tandie. I'll sit with you since Greta had to leave."

She wobbled her massive bulk to the chair, frowned down at it, no doubt realizing she couldn't squeeze her huge frame into the thing, shrugged and then sat on the bed beside him, dipping the mattress nearly to the floor.

Conar was so astounded, he couldn't make but a squeak of protest as he rolled toward her, bumping his hip into her big thigh. He could only gawk as she brought up one giant, swollen paw to push hair off his forehead.

"Such pretty hair you have, Your Grace." She fingered the golden lock between her pudgy fingers. "My Mort had hair like that when he was a babe." She laughed and the entire bed trembled. "You should see him now. Not a single shaft on his pate!" Her laugh was like the cawing of a buzzard. "Let me tell you about when he...."

\* \* \* \*

"Meggie!"

There was no answer.

"*Meggie Ruck!*" he bellowed at the top of his lungs. His sharp gaze pierced the pleasant face of the elderly lady sitting in the chair by him, grinning. "Meggggie!"

"What's that you're saying, Your Grace?" the nearly deaf woman inquired.

"Meggggieeeee!"

"You'll have to speak up, Your Grace," the old woman said, pointing to her ear. "I don't hear so well no more."

"*Meggieeeeeeee!*"

The door opened. "What is it, Milord?" some chit of a girl asked.

"Get me Meggie Ruck!"

The young girl bobbed him a quick curtsy then quietly closed the door. It was a good ten minutes before Meggie threw open the door and stood frowning at her patient.

"What are you yelling about?" Meggie asked.

Conar glared at her as she shooed the other women from the room. His lips were a thin line of fury. When she shut the door, folded her arms and stood at the foot of his bed glaring back at him, daring him to start anything with her, he opened his mouth, then clamped his lips shut.

"So! What was so all important you had to drag me from my baking?" she prompted, tapping one foot. "There are other folks in this world besides you, you know!"

He sighed, letting out his anger with his breath. His shoulders slumped in defeat. "I've had enough, Meggie," he whimpered.

"And have you now?"

"I understand."

Meggie glowered at him for a moment and then came to plop down in the chair where dozens of women had sat in a nine-day period. "And just what is it you think you understand?"

Conar sighed. "Every woman has a different personality. They are caring, even of strangers, and cheerful and they can make you laugh." He pursed his lips. "Even when you don't feel like it and don't want to." He shrugged. "And some of them won't be bullied even if the man doing the bullying is their Overlord."

"You figured that one out all by yourself, did you?"

He shook his head and smiled at her, but Meggie's face was devoid of good humor or encouragement. "I think the ladies helped me see that."

Meggie nodded. "And so now, you think you know all there is to know about women on the good side of a disposition, eh?"

"I didn't say that."

"It's good that you didn't, because every women is different, Your Grace. There ain't no two of us alike nowhere in the world." She sniffed disdainfully. "No more than there are any two men alike."

He sighed again. "I can see that, Meggie."

"Good that you do," she snorted and stood. "I got baking to do." She started to walk away but he caught her hand, wincing only a little as he did. She glared down at him.

"Sit with me awhile?"

"I can't. I've got work to do!"

"You'd make a fine Master-at-Arms, Meggie Ruck." He grinned.

After squeezing his fingers for a second, she snatched away her hand and made a humpfing noise as she waddled out his door.

Conar lifted himself in the bed, crossing his hands behind his head and smiled. Meggie was a dear, sweet woman, and she had meant well. He knew she loved him and he returned that love. It was a special bond he had never before had with a woman. She treated him, not as a Prince or future King, but almost as though he was one of her sons. His grin grew wider. Much as his own mother would have treated him.

The door squeaked open and he glanced at it, still smiling. "Did you decide to sit with me after all, Lady?"

His smile disappeared.

"Hello, Your Grace," the girl said. "My name is Henrietta."

\* \* \* \*

"We'll be leaving at first light," Conar told his brother as they sat eating their evening meal of fried chicken and creamed peas in the common room. "If I stay here much longer, I'll be as wide as Meggie Ruck."

"I heard that!" Meggie yelled from the kitchen.

Conar spooned a mouthful of mashed potatoes into his mouth and grinned, his lips pursed tight around the buttery gob as he chewed.

"I know well what you mean," Teal spoke up. "I've gained ten pounds since we've been here." He pushed back his plate and rubbed his aching shoulder. "I figure that's about a pound every other day."

Thom snorted. "You've eaten more than a pound of food a day, du Mer!" He shoveled a large amount of peas into his huge mouth and spoke around the mushed-up mess, making the others look away with disgust. "You've eaten that in bread alone!"

"You feel up to traveling, then?" Legion asked as he wiped his mouth on his napkin. "No pain?"

"A twinge, nothing more." Conar glanced at him, then pulled up his shirt. Since it wasn't tucked in his breeches, but hanging free, he brought it all the way up to his neck. "See? Want me to shuck my breeches, too, so you can have a look at my…"

"No!" Legion examined the wound he could see. It had healed nicely. There was no chance it would come undone again. "It looks all right to me." He leaned back in the chair until the front legs were off the floor. "But if you look the least bit ragged, I will have your horse taken away from you for your own good."

Conar fixed him with a stony stare. "Aye, and if I slap your fat ass in the dungeon at Boreas, it will be for your own good!"

Legion shrugged. "As if you could." He stretched his arms over his head. "Or would."

"I might fool you one day, A'Lex," Conar snapped and stood, tossing his napkin on the table.

"You going up to bed?" Legion asked. "Want Meggie to send up some tea?" His eyes twinkled.

Conar leaned over his brother, putting his nose to Legion's. "I've had more than my share of nightly cups of tea from Meggie's slumber garden!" He straightened and turned his head to gaze at Teal. "Remind me to never drink anything given to me by my brother or any of his co-conspirators."

"Want Meggie to sit with you?" Legion chuckled.

Conar glared. "I intend to sleep tonight without the accompaniment of your hovering, Meggie's cover-tugging, Thom and Teal's looking-in and Meggie's friends' bedtime stories! My door will be bolted, gentlemen." He raised his voice. "And Lady!"

"I got better things to do than nursemaid you tonight, lad," Meggie snapped back at him from the confines of her baking domain.

"Suit yourself," Legion assured him. "Just so long as you're up at first light." He arched back his head as Conar went past him to the stairs. "Sleep well, little brother!"

"Command suits you." Teal laughed, watching as Conar stomped up to the bedchamber, and mumbling dire consequences if anyone dared disturbed him.

"I rather like to think so." Legion grinned.

* * * *

Conar closed the door to his room and started to bolt it, but his sixth sense nudged him and he slowly turned, his spine tingling as he felt another presence in the room. If it had been one of Meggie's women friends, they wouldn't have been waiting for him in the dark. He knew it wasn't one of his own men or Harry Ruck, for each of them was in the common room.

His hand went down to his thigh and he grimaced, realizing his dagger was in the drawer by his bed. He felt the hair prickle on his arms. He was about to shout when someone moved out of the darkness of the room and his vision adjusted to the small amount of light cast from the simmering logs in the fire grate, focusing on the silhouette of a woman outlined against the far wall.

For one heart-stopping moment, his hopes rose, his heart slammed against his ribcage, but the woman's words brought him crashing back to earth with a thud.

"I came up to see if there was anything you might need, Milord."

Conar's hope turned instantly to anger as he recognized the tavern wench, Dorrie, and her husky voice. He didn't bother answering, but lit a candle, cupping the flame in his hand as he carried the light to his beside table.

Her pretty cornflower blue eyes roamed down his lean shape and she boldly met his look as he turned his attention to her. Her tongue licked at her smiling lips. "If there is anything you might need, Your Grace."

Anger turned to jaded appraisal of the woman offering herself so blatantly. He knew she had been tumbled by every man there, including his own brother.

"Some of the other ladies have no doubt taken good care of your, uh…needs," she said, hesitating, "but I can take far better care of you than any of them."

"Is that so?"

"Well," she drawled, coming closer, close enough to lay her hand on his hard chest. "I know Greta is a handful for most men, as is Jannie, but I taught them all they know." She let her hand roam over him.

Conar's brows came together. "Greta isn't married."

Dorrie laughed and her laugh was tinkling. "You don't have to be married to know how to care for a man, Milord."

Conar's upper lip curled in disgust. "And Jannie?" He had truly liked the little Chrystallusian girl who had sung songs of her homeland to him.

Dorrie shrugged. "She's married to that sailor man from down Ciona way, but she never grows lonely." She winked. "If you know what I mean."

Conar had no way of knowing if the girl was lying, making up tales to belittle the other women. As her other hand came up to smooth over his chest, he sent her a fiery look she thoroughly misunderstood.

"I could make you feel much better than any of those women did."

The blue eyes flicked over her and finally settled on her grinning lips. "I have no wish to insult you, Mam'selle, but I never swim in dirty water."

Dorrie's head came up and she pursed her lips in mock hurt. "No one likes to be insulted, Milord, but I would venture to say you should not go swimming any time soon."

"Meaning?"

The girl's smile widened and she removed her hands from his chest to place them on the top of her blouse. Drawing the white cotton fabric over her slim shoulders until her naked breasts were gleaming in the soft candlelight, she held his fierce gaze.

"There is no reason you can not be eased by gentle means, is there, Milord?"

Conar folded his arms over his chest and stood staring at her. Despite having grown fond of Meggie's friends, and though he now looked differently at them, he was more familiar with women like Dorrie Burkhart, and her kind sickened him.

He didn't move, didn't speak, as the girl stepped out of her skirt and blouse and faced him, her nude body inviting him to touch her.

He let his gaze wander down the perfection of his temptress and grudgingly admired the curves and mounds that had given his men such pleasure. There was no denying the girl was an armful. She was pretty, young, her body taut and shapely. He looked in her face and saw the very fires of hell blazing there.

Encouraged by his silence, Dorrie put her arms around his neck and pressed herself to him.

Conar grabbed her arms and put her away from him. His pupils flared into pinpoints of dislike that she read as passion.

"You want me, Mam'selle?" he snarled.

She gasped. His touch set her mouth to watering and her loins to fire. Here was the Prince Regent, the future King of Serenia, holding her near him. It didn't matter that his eyes were unkind and cold; his touch was hard and hurting on her soft arms; his lips drawn back with some emotion she couldn't fathom. Her tongue flicked out to wet her full lips. "Aye, Milord, I want you as I have wanted no other man."

The smile that slowly settled on his lips was malevolent and evil. "Any way you can get me?"

She looked up at him from under her lashes and her own smile was triumphant. She had him, she thought. "Any way at all, Milord."

He released her arms, put his heavy hands on her shoulders, and pushed. His gaze followed her as she sank to the floor at his feet, then locked with hers as she tilted up her head. A long silence swept around them as she looked at him, her lips puckered into a coy smile.

Her hands came up to the buttons of his breeches and she put one hand at the juncture of his thighs to softly stroke the bulge. She smiled in victory as she felt him stir. "Shall I ease you, then, Milord?" she asked in a breathless tone.

He stared down at her, his face hard with scorn, and then buried his hands in her thick, red-gold hair. "Aye, Mam'selle. Take all you want."

Her fingers undid the buttons of his breeches and pushed aside the fabric to free his manhood. She smiled. His size had not been over-exaggerated, she thought with lust. "I shall, Milord," she whispered.

He pushed her head against him and raised his head to stare into the distance. He stood very still as her lips moved over and around him, sucking, drawing, nibbling.

Though his body reacted to the expert attention it was receiving, Conar felt ashamed. His manhood throbbed, aching for a release from weeks of abstinence, but he was as detached from what was being done to him as he was to the howling wind outside his window. The pleasure Dorrie's lips brought to him also brought disgust. He felt dirty, embarrassed that he took any measure of comfort from what she was doing.

His hands tensed in her hair for a moment and then his lids flickered a fraction as his release came with surging speed. He looked at her bent head as she licked the seed from his shriveling flesh and he smiled. It was a smile full of hate and revenge.

And he thought he just might have found a way for Anya Wynth to earn her keep in Boreas.

## Chapter Twenty Six

A trumpet sounded on the battlements of Boreas Keep. The royal pennant of the McGregor family snapped in the stiff breeze as a guardsman attached Conar's own personal standard to the hoist to run it up alongside King Gerren's, a signal the Prince was home. As the last echo died from the trumpet, the drawbridge began to lower on well-oiled hinges, for it was late in the evening and the keep had been secured for the night. The stamp of hooves rang out over the hard-packed snow and the jingle of harnesses and coach wheels broke the midnight silence.

High on the crenellated walls, King Gerren stood huddled in his great cape, his hair blowing about his head. He was chilled to the marrow of his bones, but was here to watch as his sons and their guards rode through the flare of torch-light and onto the massive drawbridge. He was there to assure himself Legion had spoken true: Conar was well and able to ride.

He had worried about his child, not only from the seriousness of the wound, but from the moroseness it was said Conar was steeped in. Something vital was wrong with his boy, and the King, like any father, was concerned.

Although both Legion and Conar thought him ignorant of the situation with the girl, Liza, King Gerren had known all along. At first he had been angry. Nay, more than angry. He had been incensed that his firstborn heir would flaunt honor and custom as he had. But when the marriage postponements heaped upon one another, Gerren had changed his mind; altered his opinion of Conar's right to know some happiness. He had his doubts, as his son did, about what Shaz's daughter looked like. If she was as bad as Rayle had suggested, then Conar would spend the rest of his life regretting what his mother and father had done to him by allying him with the Wynth family.

Over the past year, the King's spies had warned him that the love affair had grown far beyond the ordinary. He, himself, could see the marked difference in the way Conar had both treated, and looked at, the women at court when the girl was in his life.

And the way Conar reacted when she left him.

Truth be told, he thought having the girl at Conar's side--though against Tribunal law--might be better than having his son alienating the entire kingdom, for word had reached the King that his son was ill-tempered to the point of outright insolence. His irrational demands and seething irascibility made his earlier outbursts before the girl had returned seem tame. Everywhere along the trail from the tavern where he had recuperated to the city of Boreas, whispers concerning the young Prince's mood and disposition were the talk of the common man. And woman.

Watching the defeated slant of Conar's shoulders, King Gerren wondered for the millionth time if he had been more fool than loving parent in letting the thing go on without hindrance. He had not expected this much trouble with Conar when the boy was forced to give up his mistress. He had thought his son would lose interest in the girl, as he had all the others over the years. His spies had disagreed with him, telling him Prince Conar was truly, irrevocably, in love with Liza.

Gerren sighed, pulled his cape tighter around him. He saw his son glance up at him and he raised his gloved hand in greeting, but Conar did not return the signal of welcome. Sighing again, Gerren knew that did not bode well.

Mentally preparing himself for the clash of wills he knew would ruin the new day come morning, the King headed wearily to the outside stairs.

Glancing up at the pennants twisting in the chill November night, he looked long and hard at his son's personal flag, a flying white dove on an azure background: The sign of the firstborn male heir. One day, Conar's would fly there alone, side by side with the standard of the Princess Anya of Oceania.

The thought, however, did not bring as much happiness to the King as it once would have.

* * * *

Hern threw his riding gloves across the table where they skidded to a stop in front of the young man sitting hunched over the cook's table in the kitchen. He growled a greeting at the old woman, then hooked a long leg over the back of the only other chair at the small oaken table. Leaning back precariously on the chair's rear legs, he folded his arms over his massive chest and pinned the young man with a sharp gaze.

"Do you want hot tea, Hern Arbra?" Sadie asked, eyeing the two men sitting at her table. When the Master-at-Arms didn't answer, Sadie made herself scarce.

Conar dropped his spoon into the oatmeal he was trying to force down and returned Hern's stare. "May I help you?" he asked, sarcastically.

Hern snorted and continued his silent regard. His scrutiny swept over the Prince with insulting appraisal. He twisted his neck and scanned Conar's legs and back before straightening and resuming his intent gaze.

Lowering his head, looking at his own body, Conar evaluated himself and then returned his look to Hern. "Have I grown an extra set of arms or am I that handsome you can't keep your eyes off me?"

"You ain't that handsome to me, boy!" Hern growled. He pursed his lips beneath the bush of his grayish-white mustache and made a clicking sound with his tongue. "You look rather sissyish to me."

Hern's display of rudeness and his intended insults didn't fool Conar. He knew exactly where Hern was leading him. He'd been there before.

He lifted one tawny brow. "And you want me to prove otherwise."

Hern moved forward and the chair's legs returned to the floor. He bent his head and looked Conar up and down. "Heard tell you was sick for awhile. Heard you nearly died. Got yourself a wicked wound." Hern sniffed. "Probably wasn't paying attention as you're wont to do!" He put his elbows on the table and hitched himself closer to Conar. "Maybe you should just keep yourself calm-like for awhile longer. Stay indoors out of the cold." He nodded at the bowl of oatmeal. "Eat soft foods and such. Maybe drink some sugar-milk."

"I'm fit enough," Conar ground out from between clenched teeth.

"Is that so?" Hern fixed him with a steady glower.

"Aye, it's so."

"Think you're a warrior, do you? Able to fight with the big dogs?" Hern smirked. "Don't look that way to me!"

"I'm as fit as ever, Hern."

"Prove it."

"When?"

"Ten minutes."

"Where?"

"The training field." Hern stood and snatched his riding gloves from the table.

"I'll be there." Conar took up his spoon and started to eat again, ignoring Hern.

Hern flicked a glance over the oatmeal. "Baby's food." He turned his back and started to walk away. "Ten minutes, brat!"

Conar nodded, his mouth jammed full of oatmeal to keep himself from snarling.

"And don't make me come get you," said Hern, leaving his parting shot as he stomped out the side door.

"Are you up to that?" Legion asked as he strolled into the kitchen from the hallway.

Conar had to swallow hard to rid himself of the sticky goo in his mouth. He shrugged as Legion occupied the chair Hern had vacated.

"He's determined to make sure I'm fit. If I'm not, he'll be the first to know." He pushed away his oatmeal bowl, his appetite gone.

"No, little brother," Legion reminded him, "you will."

\* \* \* \*

Conar took the stairs to his chambers very slowly and very painfully. He ached all the way from his head to his toenails and back again. He had more than a few bruises on him that weren't there earlier in the morning. His head ached, his back throbbed, his knee cramped and his nose was still sticky from dried blood in his left nostril.

He slammed his door with his booted foot, wincing as his pulled knee muscle screamed in protest. He caught the startled look of some Lady-in-Waiting he did not recognize as he hissed a particularly vulgar obscenity when the door bounced back open from the force of his kick. She dropped into a deep, respectful curtsy, her elegant neck bent, her pretty round face red with embarrassment at his unseemly language, but he chose to ignore her, not to apologize for his vulgarity. He slammed the door in her surprised face.

One of The Toad's toadies, he thought viciously and kicked the door just for the hell of it. He groaned in agony as the shock of the kick ripped through his knee. "Go tell your Mistress Princess Bitchlet what an ill-tempered ogre she will soon be shackled to!" he shouted at the top of his lungs. He heard a sharp gasp outside his door and it brought a wicked grin of pleasure to his full lips. "Take that to Her Gracelessness!" He chuckled as he moved away from the door.

Flinching, he jerked off his clothing, and then plopped down on the silken coverlet. Lying naked on his back, his hands behind his head, he glared at the ceiling.

There wasn't a muscle in his body that didn't hurt. Hern had seen to that. Being tossed over the man's hard shoulder too many times to count, landing on his backside so often his tailbone was numb--the only part of him that didn't hurt--Conar had decided he wasn't in the best of shape, after all. He hadn't needed Hern to bellow his confirming opinion in front of thirty raw recruits. It was bad enough to be put down when there was no audience; but to be put down with an audience was hell on one's ego.

"Sissyish!" Hern had proclaimed before striding away.

Angrily, he flung out a hand and gripped the amber silk coverlet in frustration as he mouthed the insult that had been hurled at him. His dark thoughts filled the room, giving the air a decided chill. As if things hadn't started out bad enough this morning, he had been forced to endure Hern's planned humiliation later when a sidesaddle had arrived with a note that said: Compliments of the Warrior Knights of the WindWarrior Society.

On top of that, one of the servants had told him, as Conar hobbled up the steps into the keep, that King Shaz was looking for him.

Not of a mind to meet with his future father-in-law, Conar had hobbled down the steps and went around to the back of the keep, scurrying inside like a scalded dog lest Shaz or one of his minions see him.

Disgusted with his cowardice, he clenched his teeth to keep from bellowing.

All that after the heartbreak he had discovered earlier that day.

He had ridden out before dawn, not having had more than two hours sleep, and returned to Ivor Keep in the hope of finding Liza. He had ridden back in a near insane rage, pushing his steed to its limits, when no trace of his lady could be found at the old keep.

Her clothing, her toiletries, her portrait--one he had had commissioned the summer before--were gone. He stood a long time, gazing at the empty place where the portrait had hung, angrier than he had ever been. Not only was she gone, he had no visible, tangible proof that she had ever been there.

Slamming against the cook's chair, his mood as black as her old cooking pot, Conar had returned to the keep in a worse mood than when he had left. In silence, Sadie had sat a hot bowl of oatmeal, his boyhood favorite, in front of him and he began to eat, not really wanting the lumpy mess, but eating it for lack of anything else rational to do. "And then Hern had to come along," he said aloud, "and beat the crap outta me!"

Now, glaring at the ceiling, he was almost as angry at Hern as he was with his situation. When a discreet knock sounded at his door, he didn't bother to answer. He was in no mood to be bothered. Even less in the mood for company. After the second knock, the door quietly opened and he lifted his head to see who would dare intrude without permission. Snorting as he recognized his visitor, he laid his head back down.

"Have you no care for my privacy, Mam'selle?"

Gezelle firmly shut the door behind her, studiously avoiding looking at his nakedness. "I thought you might like someone to talk with, Your Grace."

"Gezelle!" he warned.

"Milord," she corrected. "Do you wish me to go?"

He shrugged, not answering her.

Advancing into the room, Gezelle stood before the blazing fire and warmed her hands. "Has she gone for good this time?" she asked softly, not looking back at him.

"Why would you ask that?" he snapped and then flipped over to lie on his stomach.

She smiled at the fire. "I think you're mad at the whole world today and there is only one person capable of causing such intense anger in you." She added a log to the fire. "Did you enjoy playing with Hern today?"

Conar snorted, his disgusted breath sounding loud in the room.

"Want a back rub?"

"If you want to."

Gezelle smiled as she walked to the bed. He would never condescend to ask her to rub his aching back; would never deign to let anyone know he was hurting. That was the nature of the man.

"I think I have a few spare moments," she replied. Her gaze swept over the smooth perfection of his back, avoided the faint crisscrossed lines along his shoulders and buttocks, and settled on the bright gold of his hair. "Did she say anything to you before she left?"

"Nothing of consequence," he replied, refusing to think of Liza's last words to him telling of her love.

Gezelle sat beside him, nudging him further over in the center of the big bed. She had long since lost any fear she had of him. She placed his needs before her own. Putting one small hand on his shoulder, she felt the hard-bunched ridges in the muscles.

"You are as tight as a drum head, Milord."

"Rub hard, then. You know how I like it."

Gezelle nodded. She knelt on the bed, straddling Conar's back and sat on his firm, lean flanks. With infinite care, she began to knead the tight flesh along his shoulders.

"Would it have helped if she had said goodbye?" she asked as he sighed with the pleasure she hoped her hands were having on his aching muscles.

"No, because she knew I would have done everything in my power to stop her." He let out a small groan as her fingers found a spot that hurt worse than the others.

Her fingers moved into the thick gold of his hair, massaging the scalp with tight little circles. Working her way down the column of his neck, she leaned forward, putting pressure on the area where neck and shoulder met. She looked closely at the white lines over his shoulders and frowned. "Milord?"

"Um?"

"What caused these marks?" She had often wondered, but had never asked.

He was almost asleep, her fingers working magic on his tired and sore body. "What marks?" he mumbled and then realized what she was referring to. "They aren't important."

"They must have hurt you," she said and traced one wavering line from his shoulder blade to his hip. "What did this to you?"

"I've known hurts much worse, Mam'selle," he countered, wanting to avoid the subject.

"And endured them, as well, haven't you, Milord?"

He stared at the far wall. "That I have."

Gezelle looked at his profile and felt her heart aching for him as her body often did. "She knew the only way you would ever be free of her would be for her to leave without you being able to stop her."

He let out a harsh breath. "Aye, and she was right in sneaking away, I suppose?"

"In her way it was the best thing to do. She has given you your freedom."

Conar twisted, almost unseating her. He reached up and gripped her shoulders. "But I'm not free of her, sweet one. I will never, ever be free of her, nor do I wish to be."

"You must forget her, Milord." Gezelle saw him flinch. "Or at least try to do so."

He moved again, bringing Gezelle on the bed beside him. He pushed himself up and pressed her into the soft mattress, looking down at her with hurt.

"She is with me everywhere I go." Taking one of her hands, he slammed it against his chest, over his heart. "She will be here with me for the rest of my miserable life!"

Gezelle brought up her free hand to caress the hot flesh on his cheek. "Be thankful for what you shared with her and get on with your life."

"I need her, Gezelle."

"It was not your destiny to--" His warning hiss stopped her.

"Don't say that! Don't you dare say anything to me of destinies! I will hear no more talk of my gods-be-damned destiny! I am sick to death of it! From now on, I make my own destiny, Mam'selle, and the gods help any man or woman who thinks to stop me!"

With gritted teeth, he pulled her beneath him and his mouth slammed down over hers in a punishing kiss that stunned them both.

Conar had never once looked with anything close to passion at Gezelle and the girl was shaken to her very core. Never once in all the times she had come to his room and massaged him had he ever taken advantage of her or the situation. Her trust in him was explicit. He had always been the perfect gentleman.

"Gezelle, help me, please!" he begged, his lower body grinding against hers, his mouth trailing hot kisses down the column of her throat. "Please, I need...."

Although his touch thrilled her, it alarmed her as well. She had never known a man's body and his was one she'd often dreamed about. He was breathing against her hair, his lips touching the soft wisps that grew along her temple. She knew what he needed. Knew what he wanted. She was not ignorant of the ways of men and women. His hand was sliding down her thigh and she felt a heat in her loins that both surprised her and made her weak with a need she could not name.

"Milord?" she questioned, knowing he was not even aware of who lay beneath him. He didn't want her for herself; he was trying to take his frustrations out on the nearest female body and hers happened to be available.

But Gezelle knew an intense longing for this man deep in her soul, and even though terror filled her mind, passion filled her body with a quickening she found breathtaking.

"I need ... I want ... please, Gezelle," he said with tight emotion, his hands insistent on her shoulders and then her breasts.

As his hand moved inside her bodice and his thumb stroked her erect nipple, Gezelle sucked in her breath and nearly passed out from the hunger building within her.

"I need you, Gezelle," he whispered. He moved his hand to her chest and pulled away the top of her gown to free her breast. His mouth closed around one rosebud peak and Gezelle moaned deep in her throat.

She knew this young man had never had to beg for sexual pleasures, but she could hear a warning in his pleas for release. Instinct cautioned her he would take her with--or without--her consent, if she tried to deny him. She could feel his power surging through his taut body and she knew he was well beyond controlling his lust.

"Aye, my sweet Milord," she whispered, lifting up her arms to his shoulders. She heard him groan in relief as she embraced him.

Conar's mouth slid up her throat, across her chin and slanted across her lips. His tongue invaded her mouth and sent white-hot sparks of arousal coursing through her. She whispered his name against his mouth, needing her longing fulfilled. Her hands went to his hair, pulling, gripping, and pressing his mouth harder to hers. She drew on his conquering tongue, heard him growl deep in his throat and then softly clenched her teeth around him. The immediate shudder that ran through his body thrilled her, and she let him go, watching with fascination as he pulled back his head to stare down at her.

"I love you, Conar McGregor," she whispered. "With all my heart."

He was beyond hearing. The blood pounding in his temples drowned out her words. There was a soft feminine body beneath him with a warm scent, so like Liza's, her unbound black tresses, so like Liza's, her seductive green eyes, so like Liza's, spurred him to a height he had not reached in a long time.

Nudging her thighs apart with his knees, he pulled up her skirts and settled between her legs, his shaft seeking the spot that would allow him some measure of peace. He brought his hands down to her firm rump and positioned her against him, prodding her with the steel tip of his manhood. He felt her arch against him and he hastily shifted himself to thrust. With one quick stab, he impaled himself upon her, heedless of her cry of pain, mindless of the slight obstruction her maidenhead offered. He drove home with a lunge that made her scream with pain as he went deeper still, driving relentlessly into her with frenzied thrusts that made the bed's headboard strike the wall.

Gezelle's release came at the exact moment his did and she clung to him, stunned by what she had experienced. Other women had told her the sexual act was pleasant, but this was beyond pleasure. This was ecstasy! She stared up at him and was amazed they were both still alive. Their bodies were slick with perspiration, wet with the heat of passion. His cinnamon-scented flesh was intoxicating despite the sweat from his exercise with Hern, and now this. She inhaled deeply the smell of him and knew she would forever remember the exact aroma of their lovemaking.

Conar shuddered against her one final time and then rolled off, flopping to his back, one arm flung over his eyes. She could feel the bed shaking beneath them and knew he was crying. Rising above him, she gathered him in her arms and cradled his head against her breast. She could feel his hot tears of frustration against her flesh through the fabric of her gown and she held him tighter, crooning softly to him as though he were a lost child. She stroked his damp hair and placed a soft kiss on the heat of his forehead.

Conar held on to her, burying his face against her bosom. His arms were around her as though he would never let her leave him. Only a moment after his climax had come to give him ease, he had realized the woman beneath him had been pure, untouched, and he had soiled her for the rest of her life. The knowledge tore at him like a ravaging beast.

"I am sorry, Gezelle," he wept, his throat closing with tears. "So sorry." His shoulders shook with his misery.

"Hush, now, my sweet Milord," she whispered. "I offered you the use of my body. You shall always have that right."

He shook his head in denial, pulling back to look at her. He tried to speak, but she placed her fingers across his lips.

"We will speak no more of it. Sleep now. I will stay with you. You will not be alone." She moved her fingertips to his hair and nestled his head against her once more.

Her body throbbed where he had taken her and she could feel the oozing flow of her blood mixed with his juices easing down her thighs. She was ashamed, terribly ashamed, for at the moment his seed had entered her body, she had felt the joy she knew Liza felt each time this golden man had taken her. It was a joy mixed with guilt, for Gezelle had loved him for a very long time.

She felt her own tears coursing down her cheeks and she bit her lip to still the sob of self-pity she was feeling. She pulled him closer and knew in her heart she would never know the love from him she craved so much.

His breathing became less ragged and eventually he fell asleep in her protective arms, his arm around her waist, and his thighs between her own.

* * * *

When Legion came to find his brother, he found the two of them lying on the bed. He hurriedly went into the room and shut the door behind him. To his knowledge Conar had never taken a woman into his own bed within the keep and never in his wildest dreams would Legion have thought Gezelle and his brother lovers. Seeing the girl looking at him with fear, he quickly shook his head, held up his hand to forestall any hysteria on her part.

"Is he all right?" Legion asked.

Nodding, Gezelle looked away from the Vice-Commander. She gently shook Conar, easing herself from under his arm, straightening her skirt about her legs where it had ridden up with the intrusion of Conar's naked thigh. When the Prince opened his eyes, she answered his inquiring look with one of caution. "Your brother is here, Milord."

Conar raised his head from Gezelle's shoulder and frowned. "I should have had you lock the gods-be-damned door, 'Zelle."

"Gezelle?" Legion asked, not looking at the girl as she stood and adjusted her clothing, "would you leave us please?"

"What do you want, Legion?" Conar growled, embarrassed for the small girl.

"I wasn't spying on you, Conar," Legion snapped. "Papa sent me to find you. The Oceanian King and Queen have requested your presence at the midday meal." He waited until Gezelle had curtsied to them and closed the door behind her before he turned his angry glare to his younger brother. "There are those who would not understand the scene I happened upon, Conar." Legion retrieved Conar's shirt and flung it at him. "That was a particularly stupid thing to do! What the hell were you thinking, or am I flattering your intelligence?"

Deftly catching the blue silk, Conar jerked the material over his tousled hair. "I don't give a damn what you think, A'Lex! What I do before being bound hand and foot to Shaz's frog is none of your concern." Conar plucked at the shirt laces, tangling them, cursing as his fingers jerked at the offending strings.

Legion had to bite his tongue to keep from shouting. "Have you no care for that young girl's reputation within this keep? I have heard no tales of her immorality. I would not have thought her a loose woman, but...."

"She isn't!" Conar shouted. He spun around and pierced Legion with a stony glint. "I made a stupid mistake, that's all. I, and I alone, am responsible. And I had gods-be-damned well better not hear one thing about this from anyone's mouth. Do I make myself clear?"

Legion tore his gaze from Conar's guilt-ridden face and looked at the tumbled sheets. He winced as he saw the bright splash of red on the coverlet. Hurrying forward, he snatched the silk from the bed and wadded it up, then stomped to the fireplace and stuffed the telltale evidence into the flames. Angrily shoving the material into the grate with the fire poker, he snarled over his shoulder. "For the love of Alel, Conar! How could you have done this? The girl was a ... she was a...." He turned his head and fixed his brother with a malevolent look. "If Liza had known this would happen, she would have never left Gezelle in your care."

Scowling, tasting the guilt Legion had intended for him to feel, Conar tucked his shirt into his cream-colored leather breeches and sat on the bed to pull on his boots. He couldn't meet his brother's eyes.

"It won't happen again."

"It damned well better not!"

Conar lifted his head and sent his brother a hateful frown. "Don't tell me what to do."

"Someone has to. You seem incapable of doing what is right on your own." He watched Conar come to his feet, his hands bunched into fists at his sides. "You take exception to that?"

It takes a strong man to back down when he knows he's in the wrong, and although it galled him to do so, Conar did. He ignored the jibe and dug his hands into his pockets.

"I told you it won't happen again. I sign the papers today and that will be the end of it."

"And what if the whore from the tavern was diseased?"

Wondering how Legion knew of what had transpired in Conar's room the night before they left the Briar's Hold, Conar couldn't meet his brother's eyes. "I didn't sleep with her." At Legion's snort of disbelief, he glanced up. "I didn't. That's the truth of it."

Legion nodded, his body relaxing. Conar never lied. "Will you come down for the meal?"

"Do I have a choice?"

"Not unless you want Papa up here looking for you."

"Have you seen her yet?"

Legion knew who his brother meant. "I passed her on the stairs. I spoke to her and she answered. Her voice is rather raspy beneath that silver veil."

"Does she limp?" All the fight had gone out of him. He had hoped it wasn't true that The Toad was actually here this time.

Legion laid a hand on his brother's shoulder. "Aye, but it isn't a bad limp."

"But a limp just the same."

"I heard Hern telling Sadie the girl has a way with animals. She was out in the kennels with Tuck's hunting dogs when Belle had her litter. She got down on the ground with the Kennel Keeper and helped him deliver the pups. Tuck's wife gave her one as a wedding present." Legion smiled. "She took the pup up to her room."

Conar glanced at his brother's smiling face. "Stupid female. I don't want dogs in the keep."

"It proves she has a gentle nature."

Conar made a rude sound. "Let Papa know I'm on my way." He reached for the bottle of brandy on his bedside table.

"You go down there drunk and Papa will have your balls, Conar," Legion warned and tried to take the bottle, but his younger brother snatched it from his reach.

Throwing Legion a look of pure venom, Conar tilted the bottle and brought it to his lips, taking a long draft, grimacing as the warm fire licked at his nearly empty stomach, colliding with the undigested oatmeal to make him suddenly queasy.

"I'm warning you, little brother. If you do anything to embarrass Papa, he'll geld you, himself."

Conar smiled. "I don't think I will, but you never know."

Legion sighed, not really sure of the glint in his brother's eyes. "Give me your word you won't do anything to upset Papa today." He folded his arms over his chest.

Conar's smile widened, a wicked grin that deepened the dimple in his right cheek. He placed his hand over his heart. "I give you my word as Prince Regent and Lord High Commander of the Serenian Forces that I will do nothing to embarrass our father today."

Legion probed Conar's face for a moment and then threw up his hands. "You'd better not, that's all I can say!" He stalked to the door and left, his head shaking at his brother's stupidity.

"I promise I won't do anything to embarrass Papa, today," Conar repeated, bringing the bottle to his lips once more. He took a large sip of the brandy, shrugged, and then drained the entire bottle, wiping the back of his hand across his mouth. He grinned. "But I didn't say anything about tomorrow."

### Chapter Twenty Seven

King Gerren looked up as his son came down the spiral staircase. There was a lethal frown on Conar's handsome face that quickly turned to a false smile of greeting as he caught sight of his father waiting.

Gerren sighed. By the gods, but the boy was going to be difficult, the King thought. He watched his son cross the main hall toward him and was struck anew at just how much Conar looked like his mother. Conar had Moira's hair and her coloring; his eyes, although blue like his father's, were tilted just as his mother's had been. Mother and son had the same sensual smile that could melt even the coldest heart. As the King gazed at his most beloved child, he saw the false smile turn to genuine affection as Conar reached out to take his father's hand in greeting.

"Are you well?" Gerren asked, looking his son up and down. He had gone to Conar's room during the night only to find the boy fast asleep. He had covered Conar's bare chest with the coverlet, placed a light kiss on the smooth forehead, and stood watching his child sleep as he had done many times before. He had wanted to assure himself Conar was all right.

"I feel fine, Papa, no thanks to Hern." He turned his head to listen to the sweet sound of music coming from the drawing room. "Tell me that's The Toad..." He stopped, warned by the sudden scowl on his father's face. "The Princess Anya," he corrected, "who plays so beautifully." His voice was slightly thick, but only someone who knew him well could tell that Conar was just a little more than tipsy. Unfortunately for him, his father knew him all too well.

Glowering, Gerren took hold of Conar's upper arm, yanking the young man around to face him. "By the gods, I told your brother to see to it that you did not come down to this hall in an unacceptable manner!" He looked about him to see if anyone was near. Lowering his voice, he shook Conar's arm. "I will not have you offending Shaz and his lady-wife. Do you understand me, Conar?" He gave his son another hard shake. Looking down at the boy's clothes, he at least approved of them. His voice was cold and clipped as he commanded, "Get your ass back up those stairs and stay there until you are in a fit condition to appear!"

Conar drew himself up, sticking out his chin. He had always prided himself on being able to hold his liquor. "I am sober enough for the likes of The Toa..."

"You are drunk!" his father hissed. "I won't tell you again to get up those stairs, Conar; I will have you carried up them!"

"Ah, so there you are, Gerren!" a deep voice called from the drawing room door. "And this must be our Conar!"

King Shaz of Oceanian strode forward and held out his hand to Conar. The young Prince would have gone down on one knee in honor to the King, but Shaz spoke up. "No, no, son! You are family. A son does not go to his knee to his father in Oceania."

"But he crawls on his belly to his father in Serenia," Conar mumbled and was rewarded with a swift kick to his shin that made him yelp and turn hurt and surprised eyes to his father.

"My son likes to make little jokes." Gerren laughed, slapping Conar so hard on his back, the young man lurched forward, coughing.

"Such is the way with my boys, too," Shaz agreed. "I've resorted to a few kicks in my time, Gerry."

King Shaz Wynth was a tall man, well over six feet. A thick mane of salt and pepper hair that had once been as black as midnight glistened over his high forehead. Wiry and straight, the full head of hair was his most striking asset. His dark brown eyes glittered with good humor and his full lips seemed ready to smile at a moment's notice. That they did was obvious in the crinkles near his mouth. Thick, shaggy brows and a thin, straight nose hovered over a thick black mustache that gave the man an air both of authority and sensuality.

His build was excellent for a man pushing the last few years of his fifth decade. There were no bulges or sags, only well-muscled arms and belly that attested to a daily regimen of fitness adhered to all his life. His white teeth were straight and evenly spaced and there were laugh lines around his eyes that said much for the man's overall disposition. His handshake was firm and welcoming as he gripped Conar wrist.

"At long last I get to meet my Anya's betrothed. I had feared this day would never come," Shaz joked.

"I had hoped not," Conar answered, biting his tongue as he realized what he had said. He heard his father growl a warning, and corrected himself. "What I meant to say was I had hoped to meet you sooner."

Shaz draped a strong arm around Conar's shoulder and hugged the young Prince. "Ah, well, the vagaries of Fate, eh? But now we are here, the papers will be signed today"--he leaned toward Conar--"at last, and the wedding will be tomorrow night. I can hardly wait!"

There was a gleam in the man's eye Conar couldn't understand. His mind was becoming foggier by the minute and he had to reassess his opinion of just how well he could hold his liquor. The man's face was beginning to blur out of focus.

"It's a shame you have been kept so busy running things around here, Conar. We would have loved to have had you come to visit with us." Shaz smiled.

Conar glanced at his father's set face and realized his parent had lied about his son's constant refusals to make the trek to Oceania. An inherently honest man, Gerren must have been offended by having to lie for his son. Conar's guilt rode him like a vicious trainer. He looked at his father in apology.

"I have been busy," Conar said quietly.

"Well," Shaz said, patting Conar's back, "I know you regret not having met Anya."

Conar could only nod. He regretted ever having to meet the man's daughter, he thought with despair.

As he removed his arm from around Conar's tense shoulder, a slow smile spread over King Shaz's face. The look he gave Conar said it all. With a jolt, Conar realized the man was laughing at him. "You'll have a lifetime to get to know one another, though, won't you, son?" He grinned. "What's a few carefree days of bachelorhood with your friends, huh?" He laid a strong hand on Conar's shoulder and squeezed. "I can remember my youth. Gallivanting all about the countryside; getting into mischief"--he lowered his booming, deep voice--"meeting girls!"

Conar nearly groaned. The man knew precisely why he hadn't come to Oceania to meet his future bride. Just how much Shaz did know worried Conar. With the King's next words, all doubt about the extent of his knowledge was removed.

"I understand you had some problems with a runaway bondservant? A girl named Liza?" Shaz shook his head. "Heard you had to travel far and wide to bring her back. You must tell me how you handled that situation. I have just such a girl who runs away from time to time. She is a continuous source of irritation to me." Shaz chuckled with mirth as he held Conar's stunned look. There was a look of challenge on the older man's face. "How did you settle the situation, Conar?" Shaz lost his smile. "Or is it settled?"

Conar's father feared what his son might inadvertently say. "Conar's bachelor days are over, Shaz. There is nothing standing in the way of his marriage to your daughter, is there, Conar? That old problem with the girl who gave him so much trouble is over." The King shot a look of pure malice at his son. "Isn't it, Conar?"

Conar lowered his head. Liza's loss still had the power to hurt him deeply. Hearing his father put finality to it only made the pain run deeper. "Aye, Papa." He glanced up at Shaz's unsmiling face and saw something lurking there. Was it contempt? Understanding? Spite? Conar couldn't tell. The man was watching him closely and Conar managed a weak smile. "I will have no more trouble from the girl, Papa."

He wasn't relieved when King Shaz gave a snort in answer to his reply. "One never knows, though, does one, eh?"

"Your lady-wife does play so beautifully," King Gerren said, trying to change the awkward subject. He had an idea Shaz was aware of Conar's indiscretion. "Conar, shall we go in and listen to Medea for awhile?" He put his arm tightly around Conar's shoulder and jerked the young man toward the drawing room.

Upon entering the room, Conar almost tripped over his own feet as he caught sight of the woman seated at the harpsichord, and unknown servant girl standing beside her, turning the pages of her music. The lady was in profile to him, but the long, loose hair that hung to her waist in thick waves was as jet black as a starless night. There was slimness and curvaceous shape to her that belied the years Conar knew to be hers, and for one heart-stopping moment, he had seen someone else seated at the instrument and his heart had thudded painfully in his chest.

The servant girl turned to look at him. Her lashes lowered and she mumbled something to her mistress.

At the moment the lady turned to face him and her velvet eyes bored straight into his, the breath caught in Conar's throat and he felt his mouth drop open at the sight of the Queen of Oceania.

Although there was not that much physical resemblance between Queen Medea Wynth and Liza, the emerald eyes were identically shaped and tilted. Long, thick black lashes slipped over the forest green orbs and a taunting smile, so uncannily like that of Liza's, stretched the full, sensual lips. When the lady spoke, her voice was soft, a sultry breathlessness of melodic tone. "Is this our new son, Shaz?"

"Aye, my love. This is Anya's husband. What think you of him, Medea?" The King came to stand beside his wife, placing a loving hand on her pale shoulder.

Conar managed to shake the image of Liza from his mind and walk on shaky legs to the lady. Going to one knee before her, taking her proffered hand in his to plant a light kiss on her upturned wrist, he looked up at the Queen and a deep frown marred the smooth flesh of his forehead.

Withdrawing her hand from Conar's, the Queen put it on the young man's forehead and smoothed the frown with her fingertips.

"He would be heartbreakingly handsome if he did not frown so!" she teased and glanced up at her servant, who smiled in answer.

"Your pardon, Majesty!" Conar stammered, his face pale with the realization he was not acting as he should. "I was taken aback by your looks."

Medea laughed and her voice was a crystal tinkling of silver bells. "What a compliment, Conar! I have had my looks cause quite a few things in men, but never can I remember them ever causing a frown!"

Conar's face turned red with humiliation. "I meant no offense, Majesty. I meant to say ... that is, I...." His tongue wouldn't obey.

"Be quiet before you make things worse!" his father hissed. "Get up!"

"Leave him be, Gerren!" Medea scolded. "I was only teasing him." She caressed the flesh of his cheek. "Can you smile for me, Sweeting? I would like to see what all the women find so devastatingly appealing!"

His face deepened in color and he blinked. A genuine smile lit his face at her teasing. "I would imagine men always smile when in your presence, Majesty."

"But some young men frown!" she shot back and giggled.

"I'll not do so again," he promised, bringing her fingers to his lips.

"He looks somewhat like his portrait, doesn't he, Liza?" the Queen asked the servant girl.

Conar's head snapped up and he stared at the girl on the other side of the harpsichord. He was relieved to see she bore no resemblance at all to his lady.

"Aye, Highness, he does somewhat," she agreed in a smoky voice.

"Liza is the girl I was telling you about, Conar; the one who runs away on occasion." Shaz chuckled. "She has a beau in Serenia, don't you, Liza-love?"

"I did, Highness. But not anymore." She looked steadily at Conar until he looked away.

"A year ago an artist visited from your brother's keep in Eurus. Anya commissioned a portrait done of you." Medea turned her head slightly to one side. "But I must say the portrait did not do you justice. You are far more handsome." She stood, looking down at his upturned face. "He did not capture the sensuality in those beautiful eyes. Did he, Liza?"

"No, Highness. Not at all."

"You flatter me, Majesty," Conar said with bewilderment. There were undercurrents shifting between the two women he could only guess at. If Queen Medea knew, as her husband obviously did, of his involvement with his own Liza, then perhaps these two women were deliberately baiting him.

The thought didn't set well with him.

"I would like it if you called me 'Mother.' After all, I will be one to you shortly. I must see to our daughter, gentlemen. She is like all new brides and is more nervous than I would have imagined."

"Will she be joining us for the midday meal?" Conar asked.

The Queen smiled, her eyes twinkling. "You are anxious to see her, aren't you, Conar?"

King Gerren cleared his throat and Conar glanced sideways at him. There was a stern look on the older man's face. "Conar has been most anxious to meet his bride." Gerren smiled.

Conar looked away from his father. Aye, Papa, he thought, about as anxious as I am to have a tooth pulled.

Medea laughed. "I am afraid you shall have to wait until your wedding eve, Conar. Our customs prohibit you from seeing her face from the sunset of the day before her wedding until the ceremony has been sanctioned by a holy man. It is a pity you haven't come to Oceania to visit over the years. You and our daughter would have had time to adjust to one another."

Conar winced. Time to adjust? Adjust to what? His mind filled with horrible images of a hideously slick and corpulent bulk clinging tightly to his arm as he was forced to go walking in the gardens of Serenia with The Toad.

"You must take better care of yourself, Conar," the Queen cautioned. "You look rather green."

He stared at her and saw the same laughing humor he had seen on her husband's face. One quick look at the servant and he saw the laughter lurking in hers as well.

Well, he thought viciously, his forced smile hard on his lips, they all had reason to be happy. They were getting rid of the amphibious bitch!

"I'll be fine," he grated through his tight smile.

"Oh, I know you will, dear," Medea told him, patting his cheek as she walked gracefully away. "Come, Liza."

The young Prince stared after the Queen and her servant. Not only because the lady moved with a sexual grace that made men look after her, but because the servant girl limped behind her, rolling from side to side in a slight, listing gait. He turned to Shaz.

"An accident when she was a babe. She fell beneath the wheels of my wife's coach and her foot was crushed. We took her in to live with us mainly because Medea was so distressed the thing had happened. But there was the added incentive of a father not wanting the burden of a crippled child. More fool, he, for Liza is a delight to all who know her."

"I am sure she is," Conar thought and wondered if something similar had not happened to their own daughter to cause her limp.

"Enough morbidity," Shaz proclaimed. He pointed to the harpsichord. "You play, don't you, Coni?"

"Aye and quite well. Do play something for us, son," Gerren encouraged.

Conar didn't really want to, but one look at his father's stern visage and he seated himself at the harpsichord and ran his fingers over the keys. He was quite adept at the instrument and the song he began to play was executed with style and grace. His long fingers moved over the keys much as they would have a woman's beautiful body. "Does your daughter play as well as her mother?" he asked to fill the silence more than to actually know whether The Toad played.

"Anya?" Shaz gasped. "No! The girl has two left hands!"

Conar's fingers tripped over the keys, making a mistake that caused him to wince.

Two left hands, he thought in horror. That might even be true. How many other spare parts did the haglet have? The image of a frog with scores of arms waving in the air flitted through his mind and he banged down hard on a chord, hissing at his flub.

"Pray, play something that does not require mistakes, Conar," Gerren suggested, much put out with his son. He wanted to show Conar in a favorable light and the brat did know how to play.

Softly caressing the keys, running his hands up and down the keyboard, Conar lost himself in the haunting and eerie beauty of an ancient folk song he had learned two summers before. His fingers arched gracefully over the keys and he closed his eyes to the sweet, sad melody, humming it to himself.

Gerren wholeheartedly wished he had kept his mouth shut when he asked his son the name of the beautiful piece.

Conar glanced up at his father and held the inquisitive gaze of the older man. "Shall I sing it for you, Papa?"

"Aye!" Gerren agreed. The boy had a good voice, as well. Not as good as the du Mer boy, but a helluva sight better than Legion! "Sing for us!"

"The name of the song is 'The Prince's Lost Lady.' In a clear, deep voice, he began to sing:

*"Where are you going, my lady, my love? Where are you going this day?*

*Said she to him, 'It shall not take long; For I go but a very short way.'*

*And how long will you be, my lady, my love, how long will you be gone this day?*

*Said she, 'I'll be gone a very long while; And will not be back this way.';*

*Will she ever return, my lady, my love?" he begged of her mother one night;*

*Said she, 'I fear my daughter is dead; And will never return to our sight.'*

*He mourned for the lady, his lady, his love; He wept for her night and day;*

*Said he, 'I will go to meet my love; For I believe I have found the way.'*

*He took to his bed in the fading light; Turned his eyes to the sky above;*

*Said he, 'I seek what I know I shall find; I go to be with my love.'*

*They laid him down in the green, green grass. On the hills overlooking the town.*

*And on his grave they carved these lines: The Prince's Lost Lady Is Found."*

Silence filled the room as the last note sounded. Conar sat over the keyboard, lost in thought. His voice had wavered on the last line and he was valiantly trying to recover his composure.

"That was a very lovely song, Conar," Shaz said quietly, placing his hand on Conar's slumped shoulder. "Very beautifully sung. I have heard it many, many times before, but never have I heard it sung with such emotion."

"Thank you, Majesty," Conar answered and was surprised at the reassuring squeeze the King gave him before removing his hand. He looked up into those warm brown eyes and saw, what?--Pity?--Remorse? Surely not.

"Will your son, Legion, be joining us, Gerren?" Shaz asked. "I have heard he is quite a warrior. I would like to meet him."

"He'd be honored to meet you, Shaz." Gerren beamed.

"And Conar?" Shaz turned to his son-in-law as Conar stood. "I hear you have a good friend here, also. Is it du Mer?"

"Aye, Majesty," Conar agreed. "He lives with me most of the time. His father was Duke Cul du Mer of Downsgate." He frowned in concern. "Why do you ask?" He hoped Teal hadn't already gotten into any trouble with Shaz's entourage.

Shaz chuckled. "I have heard he's a very good card player and I thought we could all sit down to a game or two this afternoon after the meal. Would he join us, do you think?"

"He'll turn cartwheels to do so, Majesty." Conar grinned. "He feels put out when someone important comes to visit and we don't invite him to join in."

"Why wouldn't you invite him?"

"Teal isn't known for his diplomacy, Shaz," Gerren answered for his son. "He's a lovable young cur, but he has this impossible bad habit of not thinking before he speaks. I don't include him all that often because you never know what he'll come up with next. He was a constant embarrassment to Cul. Teal's mother was a gypsy dancer and I fear he has her love of getting into mischief."

"So I have been told!" Shaz grinned. "My boy, Chand, shares that same trait with the du Mer lad. The boy is forever getting into things my elder boy has to get him out of. He's taken more knocks from Grice than I can count and yet he still insists on doing things his way, right or wrong!"

"Sound familiar, Conar?" Gerren teased. "I've loaned Conar more money from our treasury to pay off du Mer's gambling debts than I have spent on anything else in the kingdom!"

"Papa!" Conar warned, laughing at the horrible exaggeration.

" 'Tis true!" Gerren laughed and slapped Shaz on the back. "Money that Conar has yet to pay back, at that!"

As the three men headed for the dining hall, Conar stopped to pick up a parchment that had rolled off the hall table. Replacing the scroll, he felt a nudge along his sixth sense and glanced up to the balcony that ran above the dining hall archway. He froze.

Standing perfectly motionless at the top of the stairs was a heavily veiled figure, her entire figure obscured by the billowing silk of her gown and silver net veil. Her hands gripped the balcony rail, her head slightly tilted to the side, and he knew her eyes were entirely on him.

He squinted, staring up at her for a moment, his face still and calm, expressionless. The only sign of his agitation was the constantly flexing fingers by his side. He knew who he was looking at, knew it was his betrothed, and felt a great hate well up inside him. It was because of her he had lost his Liza, the love of his life. His stare went cold and hard as steel, and his mouth filled with a bitter acid as he ground his teeth so tightly together a muscle in his jaw jumped and locked.

It took every ounce of his manners to slightly bow his head to the woman. She hadn't moved, hadn't acknowledged in any way that he was staring up at her.

It took every ounce of control he had not to openly curse her as she turned away from the balcony, her back to him. A cold, icy fury flashed through his heart as he watched her bulky figure limp away, passing out of his fine of vision.

## Chapter Twenty Eight

Legion and Teal arrived together, greeting King Shaz with a wariness that soon turned to pleasure as they got to know him. Teal was on his best behavior, after a warning by both Conar and Legion, to think before he spoke. He smiled a great deal, showing his deep dimples, and answered questions put to him with a simple yes or no.

One man had come late to the meal, apologizing for his lack of manners, and had taken a seat next to du Mer. He greeted the King of Oceania with exquisite politeness, and had turned to his own King in recognition of the invitation to eat with King Gerren and his visitor.

"I am honored you invited me, Highness." The man smiled. He adjusted the sleeve of his robe and dusted away a fleck of lint. "I have been anxious to meet His Highness, King Shaz. The other priests will envy me my good fortune."

"Since it will be you who performs the ceremony, it is your right to be here," Gerren said. His eyes flicked to his son, but the young man was staring intently at his plate, his hands in his lap, his head bowed.

"I understand you did not bring a priest from your homeland with you, King Shaz," the priest commented. "Are you willing for the wedding to be done in the name of our god, Alel?"

"We will adhere to your son's beliefs, Gerren. Our daughter is willing to forego a blessing by our clergy. Your religion's dogma is not that far removed from our own."

"Your daughter has been consecrated to the precepts of your goddess, Iluvia, has she not?" When Shaz nodded, the priest held up his hands, palms facing to the ceiling. "Well, then it is no problem. In our pantheon, the goddess is one of Alel's many wives. According to custom, whoever is dedicated to one of His, is dedicated to Him."

"I am sure the King knows that," Conar snapped, his head still averted from the priest.

"I am sure he does, too, young Prince," the priest said soothingly. "I meant no offense to our guest. I am pleased you remember the precepts of our religion still, considering it has been a long while since you stepped foot inside our Temple." The priest smiled as Conar tensed, willing the young man to look up at him, but Conar adamantly kept his head down.

A thick shock of white-blond hair covered the priest's forehead and fell to his shoulders in long black beaded braids. Icy pale blue eyes narrowed with the intensity of his gaze upon Conar and the thin, almost transparent lashes dipped with a slow, insulting speed.

One thin pale hand stroked his chin where a long, pointed bush of beard hung. He pulled at the goatee and tapped his index fingernail on the bristly hair. The nails were long, too long, and sharply pointed, lacquered with gold, and tipped with vermilion. His hawk-like, skeletal nose dominated the thin face and his slit nostrils seem to flare in anger with each breath he took.

Heavy folds of skin draped down from his neck to his collarbone and the flesh over his chest and upper arms was mottled with white discoloration, for he had been badly burned at some point in his life.

With his hooded eyes never leaving Conar's face, the priest watched as the young man laughed at something the visiting King said. The priest's tongue came out and flicked at the left corner of his mouth, revealing yellow-stained teeth.

From his position at the opposite side of the table, Legion studied the priest. A strong dislike, combined with a natural fear of the priesthood, made Legion wary in all his dealings with this particular priest. Unfortunately due to the man's elevated rank within the priesthood, the cleric was allowed free access to all social gatherings within the keep. Thankfully, he rarely attended unless Conar was there, as well.

Legion often caught the priest staring at his young brother with the same loathing he was exhibiting now. His uncanny surveillance of Conar, his eerie way of never wavering his attention when Conar was present at the table, unnerved Legion. It was almost like watching a snake mesmerizing its prey before lunging for the kill. Even when the priest was asked a direct question, he never took his eyes from Conar, who made it a point not to look in the man's direction if he could prevent himself from doing so.

Legion had suspected for a long time there was something between the two men, but even though he had asked Conar on several occasions why he appeared so ill at ease in the man's presence, Conar consistently refused to say why.

Kaileel Tohre knew Conar's bastard brother was studying him. It didn't matter. He continued to watch Conar. Nothing could have prevented him from doing so. His close scrutiny of the young Prince seated down the table was the only thing of importance to him. Knowing his unwavering inspection made the young man nervous immensely pleased Kaileel Tohre. Every movement, every word, every facial expression, every breath Conar took, he carefully examined. If Conar raised his hand to sweep back a heavy fall of blond hair, Kaileel followed his hand until it was down again. If Conar got up from the table to get something from the sideboard, the hawk-like eyes would make every step with him, missing nothing the young man did.

Tohre grinned, for he caught the flicker of blue eyes--nervous, uneasy, and fearful--slip his way and then hastily lower. He sat back in his chair, pressing his fingers together under his chin as he studied his former pupil. It delighted Kaileel Tohre to see the young Prince so jittery. He always was when in Tohre's presence. This eve, Conar was more unnerved than ever, most likely due to his impending marriage; but his fidgeting and his deliberate snubbing of Tohre were signs the young man's neurotic tendencies were close to the surface.

And that pleased Tohre even better.

Teal du Mer, who was seated beside the priest and not at all happy with the position, asked Conar a question and the Prince turned in Teal's direction. There was a smile on his face and he was about to answer when his attention was caught by a movement of Kaileel's hand and his eyes involuntarily strayed to the man's cadaverous face.

It was as though a bucket of icy water had been thrown on him. Conar's smile vanished, his body tensed. He held Tohre's hateful stare, unable to break the gaze locked with his own. A look of pain passed quickly over his suddenly still face. Something strange shadowed Conar's eyes as the priest sat forward and began playing idly with the candle flame in front of him, a sinister grin on his thin mouth.

Kaileel moved his gaze away, but not before everyone had seen the malicious smile that spread over the priest's face as Conar lowered his head and stared at his lap.

Conar could only shake his head at Teal's repeated question, no doubt repeated to break the silence that had settled over the table. Kaileel Tohre's direct gaze had stunned him, and he found his body shaking uncontrollably. He swallowed and willed his heart to stop the erratic beat it had started at the precise moment his gaze had met Tohre's. He flinched as the steward moved beside him and offered fresh wine. Glancing up at the steward, he nodded.

Tohre smiled as Conar's wine was poured.

Conar could feel Tohre looking at him again. He always felt Tohre's stare every time he was near the priest, but tonight he was feeling it more keenly than ever. He glanced at his half-eaten food and his stomach heaved. There was no way he could eat now. He had only sipped at his wine during the meal, his head still a little numb from the morning's unwise consumption. He had not been allowed wine with his midday meal and he knew his father was watching him closely for this one. When the servant placed the goblet before him, he glanced at his father with pleading and was surprised when the King nodded his reluctant permission. He hastily reached for the goblet and drained the pale pink liquid.

"Is the wine to your taste, Your Grace?" Tohre inquired. When the prince did not answer, the high priest leaned back in the chair and cocked his head to one side.

Conar wiped his mouth with his napkin, his attention on King Shaz's rambling tale of horse trades. He listened for a moment and then his attention wandered. He looked at Legion and smiled as his brother winked at him. He took a deep breath and tried to regain his focus on what Shaz was saying, but found he could not concentrate. He looked to the head of the table where his father sat.

"I have often thought women should not be allowed entry into the horse sales. If Medea and Anya had not come, I'd have been one hundred gold pieces richer!" Shaz laughed.

Gerren nodded in complete agreement with his friend. He asked, "Does Anya ride as well as her mother, Shaz?"

"Considering Medea taught her, I would say so, yes."

Conar could hear the words the men said, but they made no sense to him. His ears were beginning to ring with an odd, high-pitched trill that was most unpleasant. A strange, queasy feeling had invaded his belly and he could barely swallow the spit in his mouth. He shook his head, felt a slight throbbing under his right eye, and shook his head again to clear his ears of the ringing that had now grown louder, drowning out Shaz's laughter.

"Are you not well, Highness?" Tohre called to him.

Conar could not stop himself from turning to the priest. Looking directly into those dark blue eyes always made Conar ill, but the sickness boiling in his gut was beyond anything he had ever felt. He shifted his gaze to Teal, then Legion, then Shaz and finally his father. None of them appeared to have heard Tohre speak to him, question his health. They were speaking, their mouths moving, but Conar couldn't hear their words. The ringing was a clanging agony inside his head and he put his hands over his ears to blot out the pain.

"Do you wish to leave us, sweet Prince?" Kaileel inquired and his smile was evil as Conar's head jerked toward him.

Kaileel Tohre was the only man Conar McGregor had ever truly hated. Or feared. He had more than his share of reasons to hate Tohre; even more reason to fear him. He avoided the man as he would any deadly animal. When near the priest Conar knew a terror so intense it was like suffocating.

His hatred for the man was like an unquenchable thirst: never satisfied. Not only because the priest was the Abbot of the Order where Conar had began his training as a boy in the Wind Warrior Society, but also because the man was second highest in position of importance in the Brotherhood of the Domination, the malignant sect that Conar had vowed to destroy.

Tohre was the Cardinal of Ordination, a man to be greatly feared, for he was in charge of the sacrifices and sinister ceremonies upon which the Domination thrived. Yet the hatred Conar bore the man went far deeper than Conar's own sense of morality concerning the practice of human sacrifice and murder. It went far deeper than his breaking away from the Temple before being ordained as a priest into the Wind Warrior Society where Tohre had been his sponsor.

"You look uncomfortable, my Prince," Kaileel whispered, and Conar heard the caress of the man's voice inside his head. "Perhaps you should go to your bed and let the wine soothe you."

King Gerren glanced at his son's sweat-slick face and could have thrashed the boy then and there. Had his son been able to snitch more wine while he had not been looking? He frowned, keeping a close watch on his son.

Conar's mind was cotton-numb and he could taste a strange metallic tang on his tongue. He swallowed and bile rose with lightning speed to gag him. He jerked up his napkin and quickly covered his mouth.

"Would you like to be excused, Conar?" his father snarled.

Conar didn't hear his father. He was trying hard to swallow the bitter vetch in his throat. The banging gongs were an agony that ripped at his skull and set his entire body to trembling.

"Your father is speaking to you," Tohre purred.

Conar turned his head, glanced at Tohre's leering face, and thought he would pass out. His breathing was coming in quick, painful, ragged gasps and his vision was blurring a bright shade of red. His hatred went farther than his own personal animosity toward Kaileel Tohre, Conar thought with dismay. Only he and Tohre knew why. His thoughts went back to a time, long ago, best forgotten, when he had felt similar to the way he was feeling now. He had tasted this same acrid flavor in his mouth and his forehead wrinkled as he tried to remember exactly when and where he had experienced it. Tohre had been responsible for whatever he had undergone then and, with a lurch of his soul, he knew he was responsible now. He locked his gaze with Tohre's.

"*It is good to remember the past, little Prince,*" Kaileel cooed though his lips never moved. "*It is the wise man who never forgets.*"

The king stood. "Conar! Are you listening to me?"

Conar shook his head, unaware his father was striding down the table toward him. His attention was on Tohre, his mind somehow linked to the bastards. It was Kaileel who was making him so ill; it was Kaileel now and it had been Kaileel then. Kaileel, who had always been his waking nightmare; Kaileel, his worst fear. Kaileel, who had turned his normal life into an evil horror that had nearly driven him insane and who had been the cause of him trying to take his own life. Kaileel, who had laughed at his weaknesses and played on them, turning a little boy's fears into something even more terrible. It had been Kaileel, then a Proctor in the Wind Warrior Society, who had been Conar's patron, his mentor, and ultimately his....

"Conar!" King Gerren's voice was loud and booming, chasing away the banging gongs inside Conar's head as he gripped his son's shoulder in a cruel grasp. He shook Conar hard. "Damn it, boy! Where is your mind that you do not pay attention when I speak to you?"

Conar gasped, jerked back from his memories. Confusion and dismay filled his young face and he involuntarily returned his eyes to Tohre, looking at the man with fear.

"Conar, I am speaking to you!" His father shook him again, very hard.

It was all he could do to look away from Kaileel Tohre's smirking face. He looked up at his father. "What was it you asked me, Papa?"

"Do you wish to remain at my table?" Gerren asked through clenched teeth. "Or do you wish to be excused?"

"No," Conar said, shaking his head, only to make the nausea worse. "I would like to stay, Papa." He found he couldn't swallow past the constriction in his throat.

He knew what was causing it. He knew Kaileel Tohre knew, as well. He took up his freshly filled wineglass and brought it to his dry lips. The wine tasted so odd, but he drained the glass, glancing up at his father's set face.

King Gerren took the glass from his son's trembling fingers and purposefully set it down on the table with a snap.

"That will be all for you this eve," Gerren snarled and spun on his heels to go back to his chair, fixing the wine steward with a level beam of command.

Shaz realized something was bothering the boy, but he had no right to intervene. Instead, he decided to draw everyone's attention away from the scene.

"I had hoped my sons would be attending the wedding but matters of the crown have kept them at home, although three of my daughters came with us. Our fourth girl, Laura, she is eight years younger than Anya Elizabeth, stayed at home. She's still nursing a broken ankle. Helen, Francis, and Ann wouldn't have missed their sister's wedding for anything." He smiled. "Helen Louise gazes up at Conar's portrait and sighs like a moonstruck ninny. I fear she has a schoolgirl's crush on you, son."

"Women find Conar most appealing, don't they, Your Grace?" Kaileel laughed. "He has that same affect on many a man, as well."

Conar slowly looked at his tormentor without speaking. His temples throbbed with a vicious headache and he felt as though cotton lined his mouth. The odd metallic taste made him lick his dry lips and he saw Kaileel glance at them with a sneer. The look Kaileel gave him brought the nausea surging up Conar's throat and he gagged.

"Legion!" Gerren called, "get your gods-be-damned brother to bed!"

"Aye, Your Grace," Legion said, taking Conar by the arm. "Up you go, little brother."

Conar tried to stand and found he couldn't. He looked up at Legion who shook his head. He tried again, clutched at the table to keep from falling, and only managed to pull the tablecloth nearly off the side. He felt Legion's arms going around him.

His head no longer ached; it spun with a viciousness that made him grab hold of Legion to keep from passing out. He blinked, shook his head to clear it, gagged again at the nausea, and then swung his gaze to Legion's amused face. "I didn't drink that much," he whispered, "truly I didn't."

"Just put your arm around my neck," Legion whispered, draping Conar's arm over his shoulder.

"Truly I didn't, Legion," Conar repeated. "The wine must have been...."

Legion caught his brother as he began to topple forward and swung him over his shoulder as he had so often done of late. Nervous laughter followed him up the stairs as he carried an unconscious Conar to his bed.

Teal ran ahead of him to open Conar's door and turn back the covers. He shook his head as Legion dropped his brother on the bed and then began to unlace Conar's shirt.

"Your Papa isn't too happy."

"I don't blame him." Legion tugged Conar's shirt up and out of his breeches so his brother could rest better. "Get his boots for me, Teal."

Standing with his hands on his hips as Teal took off Conar's boots and socks, Legion couldn't help but laugh at the picture of innocence his brother made.

The long tawny lashes were closed and a stray lock of hair had fallen across his forehead to dip low over his right eye. He smiled as Conar turned in his sleep, drew up his knees, and gripped his pillow beneath his head.

"He looks like a child when he sleeps," Teal remarked.

"Aye that he does." Legion tugged the coverlet over his brother's legs. "Sleep well, brat," he said softly and motioned Teal ahead of him out of the room.

The footsteps of the two men had barely died away before the door to Conar's room opened slowly and shadows drifted silently into the room. A keening wind howled, flared the fire in the grate, and shifted the drapes along the windows. Stealthily, the shadows emerged on Conar's bed, two at the head, and two at the foot, on each side of the big wood four-poster.

Once more the door opened, closed, and the barrel bolt was thrown, locking out those who might come to interfere.

A dark shadow glided across the thickly carpeted floor and came to stand beside Conar's sleeping form. As the shadow moved over him, the young Prince moaned in his sleep and stirred, caught in the throes of a reoccurring nightmare.

"Turn over," a hissing voice commanded and the young Prince whimpered, shifting automatically to his back, one hand flung out on the bed, the fingers twitching.

A thin hand threw the coverlet off Conar's legs. The figure nodded and the two shadows at the top of the bed reached out cold, impersonal hands and drew the young man to a sitting position, removing his silk shirt with ease. Conar's head sagged to his chest as they held him erect and then fell back as they lowered him to the mattress.

Leaning over the bed, one of the shadows ran a calm hand over the hard muscles of the Prince's chest, caressing the firm, manly breasts that rose and fell in agitation at the touch. The shadow's left hand came down and unrelenting fingers closed around one taut pap, pinching, digging sharp nails into the dark coral-colored flesh, causing pain Conar could feel even in his drug-induced sleep.

"A taste, sweet child, of the pain to come," the voice murmured. The hand smoothed over the firm belly with its ridges of steel-like muscle and stroked the thick hair that nested above the waistband of the Prince's cords.

Conar groaned, his head whipping back and forth as though denying what was happening.

"Lie still!" the demanding voice spoke, a strong hand digging into the smooth muscles of Conar's belly, the long nails gripping the firm flesh in a taloned clasp.

Conar immediately stilled, his body going rigid, and his lungs gasping air through lips parted with terror.

As the long-nailed fingers unbuckled his belt and slid it from the loops, Conar let out a moan of protest, his lids flickering. The pale hands moved to the buttons of his breeches, unbuttoning the first three pearl studs, and the unconscious man began to whimper deep in his throat, his lips trembling.

Gleaming hawk-like eyes stared at the naked man lying before him, and two thin lips stretched wide in anticipation.

"Hold him."

Conar had no will of his own. He was perfectly aware of what was happening to him. He always knew while he was in the grip of his nightmare. It was when he awoke that he did not remember, that a veil was cast over his memories. Only the feel of cold, hard, and unrelenting hands on his flesh would stay with him when he woke screaming, sweat coursing over his body in stinking waves.

He was as unable to do anything about the impaling evil atop him as he was to force his eyelids open to view the horror that rode him. He stilled as he was told to, but his soul twisted in agony as he felt the hands roaming his shrinking flesh.

He felt tears falling down his cheeks and he turned his mind from what he was feeling, calling out to the love he had lost, to save him.

## Chapter Twenty Nine

Hern softly closed Conar's door and leaned against the portal. It was nearing dawn and he had been with the young Prince for most of the night.

His own room was just across the hall from Conar's, between Teal's and Legion's. He had moved into the keep not long after Conar had completed his training with the WindWarriors as a lad of seventeen and he had stayed on at Conar's request even as the young Prince reached his coming of age. It made it much easier when the young man awoke with his chilling cries and fevered nightmares if Hern was close by.

"Is he awake?" King Gerren asked as he came down the hall toward Hern.

Hern glanced up, pulled from his memories of a night filled with holding the boy, crooning to him, telling him he had only been dreaming the horror that had engulfed him. He shook his head. "He's sleeping."

The King's chambers were on the floor above Conar's where dozens of Kings had slept for hundreds of years. From the comfort of those vast rooms that took up an entire floor, Gerren could not hear the nightly screams of terror that tore at his son. His knowledge of those nightmares that plagued his child came from Hern Arbra.

Not that the King knew the root of the trouble that brought such vile dreams to his son. Hern did not seem to know either. The tired look about the Master-at-Arms this morning brought immediate alarm to King Gerren and alerted him that the nightmare had ridden his son once more. "Was it bad?"

"Worse than usual, Gerren," Hern answered and ran a weary hand over his face. "I think he'll not be feeling so well this morn." He turned to the window at the far end of the hall and squinted at the glow from the rising sun. "He must have had more than his share of the brew last eve, for he puked all over the floor."

"He seems to be doing quite a bit of that of late," King Gerren snorted.

"Will you be going in to sit with him?" Hern needed sleep, and although the dreams seemed to disappear whenever he hurried to comfort Conar, he still did not like leaving the boy alone.

"Aye. Go rest, my friend." Gerren slapped Hern's back and sent him off. He turned toward Conar's door and frowned.

His son needed a lecture on the moderate use of alcohol.

* * * *

"Oh, god!" Conar moaned. His head was twice as bad as it had been the day before and ringing with the gongs of millions of iron bells. His stomach heaved as he tried to lift his gigantic head from the pillow, but that brought another quiet invocation to the gods from his swollen lips. Bringing an unsteady hand to his face, he ran it over his aching eyes that seemed to be glued together.

"I've gone blind," he mumbled, unable to get them open.

It was just as well, he reasoned, for if he had been able to see, he knew the faintest light in his room would blind him if it didn't kill him first.

His mouth that had felt cotton-encased the night before, now had grown a full coat of moldy slime, as well. Even his teeth felt covered with fur. He ran his tongue over them and wished with all his heart he hadn't, for the motion brought along with it a sour belch and the awareness of nostrils burning with the residue of vomitus.

Once more he tried to lift his head, but the banging gongs turned to piercing shrieks of scraping metal and he gave up with another quiet plea to whatever god wasn't pissed at him, and who might take pity on a dying man. Clutching the bed covers on which he was sprawled, his naked hips covered only by a draping of sheet, he tried valiantly to still the rocking, heaving bed.

"You'll live," a voice thundered out of the depths the room, making him grab his ears.

In actuality, his father had spoken softly, but the laughter that followed was hardy and loud. It brought tears of agony to Conar.

"Papa, have pity on me," he gasped.

Gerren got up from his chair and poured a tumbler of fresh water for his son, then walked to Conar's bed. "Pity is reserved for fools and handicapped folk, Conar." Gerren chuckled. "Which are you?"

"Both," his son moaned. "I deserve twice the pity." He managed to wedge one eye open and look at his father, who was holding a tumbler. "What's that?" Conar asked suspiciously.

"Water," Gerren said and laughed as Conar grimaced. "I want you to drink it. Your lady-wife has sent some elixir to cure you of this hangover, but you need to get something in your belly first." He put his free hand gently under his son's neck and lifted the tousled blond head. "Come on, now. Drink." He grinned in wonder at the awful agony stamped on Conar's face as he tried to sip the water. It ran down his chin and over his chest, running through the golden chest hairs to pool in the indention of the boy's navel.

Conar gasped, feeling the water running over him like the run off from a snow-laden mountain. "I'm dying here, Papa, and you're trying to drown me!" he croaked as his father laid his head down. He turned his face into the pillow as his mouth flooded with the god-awful taste. He kept his fingers closed on his nostrils.

King Gerren laughed as he set the glass on Conar's bedside table. "No matter how old you get, Conar, there is still some of the little boy left in you."

"If I've been poisoned, you'll not be laughing so, Papa."

"I doubt you've been poisoned, Conar."

Easing his fingers from his nose, Conar sniffed. He couldn't taste anything. He dared to swallow. No, nothing. There was no aftertaste at all.

"How did you come by such a wicked gash on your belly?" his father asked, pulling the sheet lower to examine the thin, wavering line.

"What gash?" Conar cautiously raised his head, but the room still wanted to skid away from him. He laid his head down to keep the ceiling from twisting to the left.

"There's an ugly-looking streak across your belly, below the navel." Gerren bent closer to look at the wound and then tugged down the sheet to see similar scratches and bruises on his son's thighs and hips. "Did you get these while you and Hern were fooling around yestermorn?" The scratches looked fresh and raw.

"I don't know." Conar looked up. The ceiling remained where it was.

The cotton inside his mouth seemed to have been folded and put away, the slime gone, the fuzz shaved off his teeth. He ran his tongue over them and felt only the slick, clean enamel. The shrieking metal and clanging gongs were now only tiny tinkling brass bells that sounded rather pleasant. The nausea was gone, the spinning head stilled, the ache non-existent.

"What was in that stuff The Toad sent me?"

Gerren winced. "Don't call her that, Conar! I have warned you about that before! What if you slip up and call her that in her presence, or the gods forbid, her parents'?"

Conar shrugged. It didn't matter to him one way or the other if she heard or what the bitch felt. As for her parents, he guessed they knew how he felt about marrying their deformed tadpole. He hoisted himself up and pushed his pillows more comfortably behind him. He opened his mouth to say something, but thought better of it.

Gerren sighed, clenching his jaw in frustration. He sat on his son's bed and pierced him with a stern look. "You really annoy the hell out of me sometimes, Conar. What is it you were going to say?"

Conar hesitated, not sure if he should ask. He took a deep breath. "Have you seen her without her veil?"

"No. No one has."

Conar turned his face, but his father took his chin and forced the unhappy face around.

"This should have been settled long ago. You should have gone to Oceania instead of sending Rayle; the gods rest his soul. That way you would know what's in store for you this eve."

"Oh, I know, all right," Conar said bitterly.

"No, you don't." There was deep concern in the King's eyes, for he knew what troubled his son. He caressed Conar's cheek. "You only think you know what lies behind that veil."

"And you will still have me chained to her, sight unseen, knowing how terrified of her I am?" The disbelief in Conar's voice was an accusation in itself.

"Conar, we have been through all this many, many, times before. Whose fault is it that you have never seen her? You have had ample time to do so. To have sent someone else to do your dirty work was cowardly."

"If I had gone, do you really think they would have let me see her? If they had, they might well have lost their chance at getting rid of the girl."

"You know that wouldn't have mattered."

"Papa...."

"Conar, you are perfectly aware that this marriage was arranged even as Medea carried the girl in her belly. It was your mother's wish, Conar. I will see that wish fulfilled, for I promised her!" He stood and walked to the window. "There is nothing left to discuss. Nothing will change what must be."

"I'm afraid, Papa." Conar's tone was defeated, lost. It hurt his father to hear such a tone.

"Of what, son?" Gerren returned to the chair beside Conar's bed and sat. "What frightens you so? The way she might look?"

"Aye!" Conar ground out. He bounded off the bed in a lithe spring of his long legs, surprised that he felt no aftereffects of his drunk.

"I have spoken to her, Conar. She has a soft, throaty voice and a sense of humor." He chuckled. "One of the Tucker's dogs had pups a few days ago and Anya went with Hern to see them. She found one she thought adorable and asked Mistress Tucker if she could have the pup. You know the Tuckers; they have more in that kennel than anyone else in the kingdom. They were glad to find a good home for the dog. Anya took the pup to her room and I see her carrying that little brown ball of fuzz around with her all over this keep." He chuckled again. "She named it Brown Stuff, for it seems that was the first thing the pup did on her floor!"

"Stupid name for a dog," Conar mumbled as he stalked to his armoire. "I don't like dogs in the keep."

Gerren shook his head. "I have never understood why, either." He shrugged. "At any rate, it shows what kind of sense of humor she has that she named the dog as she did."

"Or how stupid she is," Conar mumbled, remembering that Legion had told him about the pup once before.

"And she was concerned for your health after your run-in with those kidnapers. She fretted, even had to take to her bed for almost the entire time you were ill. Her mother wouldn't let anyone in the room. Does that sound like she has no care for you?"

"It sounds like she's spoiled to me. If she thinks she's going to be waited on hand and foot in my keep, she'd best think again! I'll have no self-centered females in my home!"

"Conar, keep an open mind about the girl. Did you know she even asked her father to see that Rayle's widow receive a death portion from their treasury, for she was concerned for his children's welfare? Does that sound like some ogress?"

Conar's heavy scowl lifted. "Why did she do that?" he asked as he pulled a pair of breeches from his armoire.

"I suppose it was because Rayle gave his life in your defense. She seems to be a caring girl in that way. She spoke to one of our servants who had a bad cold and she gave the man a potion to help clear his lungs and nose. Her thoughtfulness has extended to many members of this household since she's been here." He watched as his son pulled on his burgundy breeches.

"But she must be as ugly as a salamander if even her parent's can't abide looking at her. Her parents are handsome people. Why the hell did their eldest daughter have to be so gods-be-damned ugly?"

"I have often heard that beauty is in the eye of the beholder. Perhaps this lady has qualities that will endear her to you. There may be more to this woman than just a face, Conar. She is willing to be your wife. Can you not meet her half way? Do you think your marriage is the first one not based on true love?"

"I had a true--" Conar stopped, looking at his father's shocked, cautioning face. He flopped down on his settee and thrust his long legs out in front of him.

"What is bothering you so?" Gerren snarled.

"What of my physical needs, Papa? I am a man. I'm no monk. If I can't have a mistress to satisfy...." He held up his hand at his father's angry snort. "If I can't have a mistress, and I find this woman so detestable that I can't bring myself to mate with her, to even mount her, what then? What do I do then, Papa? You want heirs to this throne. Our people need heirs to this throne. I don't know of but one way to get heirs to this throne!" He pulled in his legs and stood, pacing the floor like a caged animal, his long fingers plowing through his thick mane of golden hair. He stopped and looked around at his father.

"And there are circumstances involved here for why I'm bothered!" He started counting his reasons on his right hand with the index finger of his left. "I can't live the rest of my life in celibacy; that's not natural. I can't screw her. I can't screw anybody else. I have hot blood running through my veins. I have needs!" He put down his hand. "I have known the pleasures that beautiful women can give my body. If memories of that are all I'll have after this gods-be-damned hateful joining, then you had best have me castrated before the wedding!" His lower lip thrust out in a pout.

His father smiled. "Before you even know what she looks like for sure? Isn't that rather drastic, Conar?"

Conar glared. "Well, after the wedding night, then!"

A discreet knock at the door saved Conar from the bitter remark he had been about to make.

"Come!" Conar shouted, missing his father's pained expression at the loud command.

The servant girl who had turned the pages for her Queen at the harpsichord the day before entered the room and dipped into a low curtsy before the King. "His Majesty, King Shaz, asked me to find you, Highness. He has gone to the registry and asks that you join him there." She shifted her gaze to Conar and saw the look of despair ravaging his handsome face. Her face seemed to glow at his misery.

"I suppose Shaz wants to go over the contracts one more time. By Alel, but the man is thorough!" Gerren frowned.

"He wants to make gods-be-damned sure there is no way I can get out of this accursed marriage," Conar growled, turning away before he could see the look of reprimand on his father's face.

"But he's fair, Conar," his father said. "The addendum concerning your children surprised me, but you have to admit, Shaz and Medea have been very accommodating allowing you to maintain contact with your children. That, in itself, is highly irregular, as you well know." He shook his head. "Highly irregular, indeed. I was very surprised they agreed to your suggestion."

Conar smiled, thanking Liza for giving him the idea to have the Tribunal lawyers add that particular phrase into the Joining papers.

"Well, I'm off to haggle some more," the king sighed. He smiled at the servant. "You are looking quite lovely today, Liza."

"Thank you, Highness," the girl replied, then dipped another low curtsy. She made to follow him, but Conar's strident voice stopped her. "Stay where you are, Mam'selle, and close the door."

She hesitated, her hand on the knob, but then eased the door shut and turned to face him, her hands demurely folded before her. "Aye, Your

Grace?" Her eyes flicked over his naked chest then settled somewhere over his head.

Conar could see the dislike in the way she looked at him, in the way she seemed to be looking down her nose at him. He folded his arms across his chest and regarded her. "You don't like me very much do you?"

She shrugged. "It is not my place to either like or dislike you, Highness."

One tawny brow cocked. "But you don't, do you?"

She looked him in the eye and lifted her chin. "No, Highness, I do not."

Conar blinked. The girl kept eye contact with him, not in the least afraid of his reaction to her answer. He turned his head to one side. "And why is that, Mam'selle?"

A tight, smirking smile formed on her pretty lips. "I don't think you'd cared to hear my reasons, Your Grace."

"Oh, but I would!" he answered, leaning against the footboard. "Please, tell me."

"If you wish," she said as though eager to do so. "You are a conceited man, Highness. You are vain, self-centered, unconcerned for other people's feelings, obnoxious to the point of being uncouth."

Conar's brow rose even higher.

"You are an uncivilized bore, so pumped up with your own sense of self-worth you are unable to see the value of those around you. Your manners are deplorable and your language at times is vulgar and inappropriate."

His other tawny eyebrow shot up.

Conar glared at her, his mouth tight with a building fury that brought color to his cheek "Are you finished?"

"Not quite." She took a step toward him. "And you are a snob."

He looked at her face, pretty, but filled with the unholy light of total dislike. Her jaw was clenched, her hands tightly clutched and she stood her ground as though she wished he would try to attack her. "And you're a bitch," he said sweetly.

The girl dared to smile at him. "And you, Highness, are a bastard."

He blinked. How dare the woman say such a thing? He wanted nothing more than to slap the smirk off her lovely face, but he didn't. He unfolded his arms and pointed at the door, not even trusting himself to speak to her again.

Her smile flared with triumph at having had the last word. She turned to go.

But he could not leave it at that. "And just what is your mistress like?" he shouted.

She spun around and fixed him with a level stare. It was as though she had been waiting for him to ask. She pounced on his question.

"The Princess Anya is a lovely, caring, intelligent woman. She puts others before herself and is careful of what she says so other people's feelings are never hurt by some careless word. She is filled with compassion and she helps anyone who needs her help without regard to any reward for doing so." Her nose rose. "She is a lady who deserves a gentlemen as her husband."

"And you'd rather she married someone else."

"There is one who would gladly have her hand in marriage. He has told me as much."

"Really? And who is this marvel of manhood?" He chuckled.

"Lord Saur, Prince Grice's best friend. He would gladly exchange places with you!"

Conar's mouth dropped open. "Lord Saur?" His lips closed, twitched. "Brelan Saur?" he managed to ask.

"Aye."

Conar broke into a fit of laughter, bending double with the effort. He had to sit on his settee to keep from going to his knees in merriment.

The girl stiffened her spine. "He's a better man than you!" she spat.

He waved his hand at her, motioning her away, laughing so hard he had to hold his side.

"You will pay dearly for having said all the horrible things about my lady," she warned. "I would love to be there this eve when you remove her veil. We will see who has the last laugh then!"

Conar stared at the girl's retreating back as she slammed the door behind her. He sobered, her parting shot taking the laughter from his soul.

Gezelle passed the servant in the hall and was startled by the fury on the girl's face. She looked at Conar's door. Going to the portal, she raised her hand and lightly tapped.

"Go away!" Conar shouted. "You've insulted me enough!"

" 'Tis me, Milord," Gezelle said through the oaken panel.

"Then get the hell in here."

Gezelle came in, saw him leaning against the mantelpiece, staring into the blazing fire, his forehead resting on his arm. She eased the door closed and threw the bolt. Taking a deep breath she walked to stand beside him. "How may I help you, Milord?"

For a long moment he didn't speak. When at last he raised his head and looked at her, his face was filled with shame. His lips twisted and he snapped them shut, pressing them tightly together. How could he voice that all the things the other girl had accused him of were true? How did you tell a friend that you were aware you were a fool and an uncaring bastard?

"Is it the Lady Liza?" Gezelle asked, her face hopeful. "Have you heard from her?"

Conar shook his head, pain instantly filling his heart.

"What is it, Milord?" she asked and put her hand on his back, rubbing the broad expanse of flesh.

He was obviously trying to maintain his composure. There were tears hovering behind his thick lashes. "Would you do me an enormous favor, Mam'selle?" he asked, looking at his bare feet.

"I would do anything for you. You know that."

Taking his arm from the mantle, his body seemed to sag beneath the weight of his depression. He turned so that he faced her completely, uncertainty stamped on his troubled features. He lifted his head and looked at her. Inhaling a deep breath, he held it for a moment then let it out slowly. In a voice so soft she barely heard him, he made his request. "Will you hold me, 'Zelle? Just for a little while? Nothing more; just that."

She wanted nothing more than to protect this man, to keep his pain at bay. Neither spoke, but there in the late morning sun, nothing needed to be said. She opened her arms.

When his arms tightened around her, she pressed her body against his. "Do you need me, Milord?" She felt tears on her neck and wanted to cry.

"Aye, Sweeting. I need you. I need you more than I ever have before." His voice broke. "Take the hurt away, 'Zelle. Please just take the hurt away for a little while."

"I will always be here for you, Milord," she whispered. "All you ever need to do is ask." She gazed down at his bent head.

He lifted his face and fused his eyes with hers. He brought his hands up to her cheeks and slowly drew her lips to his, lightly caressing the full flesh with his own. "I am grateful, little one," he said against her mouth. "I am truly grateful."

"Did that girl say something to hurt you?" she asked, her face filling with a murderous light. "The one who just left?"

"She did no more than remind me of how great my sins have become." A single tear eased down his cheek. "I know what it is that I do, 'Zelle, but, the gods help me, I can't seem to stop." He lowered his head.

"You have done nothing wrong and anyone who says you have is lying!" She pressed his face close to her breast. "And I shall tell them so!"

"You are a good friend," he whispered, his throat closing.

"And you are not alone."

\* \* \* \*

Gezelle sat on the edge of his bed after he had gone to the Temple to get ready for the night's wedding. Tears streamed down her cheeks, for she knew this time he had needed her, had wanted her body beneath his, had wanted what she could give him.

"Oh, Alel," she cried and sank to her knees, her heart aching. She bowed her head and didn't try to stop the uncontrollable sobs that tore through her.

She didn't hear the door open through her cries.

"Gezelle?" a soft voice called to her.

Glancing up, Gezelle's eyes widened.

Princess Anya stood framed in the doorway.

Gezelle rocked back on her heels and was about to stand when the lady lifted the silvery gauze from her face.

As she looked upon the face of the Princess, Gezelle's eyes rolled back in her head and she slid to the floor in a faint.

## Chapter Thirty

As Conar left the main hall of the keep, one of the cook's helpers came forward and bowed to him. It was obvious the man wanted to say something and Conar welcomed any distraction from the Temple. He smiled at the middle-aged man, a signal that he would stop and talk.

"Look, Highness!" the man said with a wide grin. He held out his bony hand to his Prince.

Conar looked down and saw nothing. "What is it I'm supposed to see, Herbie?"

"My hand, Your Grace!" The man laughed. "Look at my hand!"

Conar dropped his gaze to the man's proffered hand, but still did not see anything to warrant his attention. "I see nothing," he said, confused.

"Exactly!" the man cried with glee. "There ain't nothing there to see!"

Thinking the man had delved one time too many into the cook's wine cellar, Conar patted him on the back. "That's nice, Herbie." He turned to leave and was stopped by the man's giggle.

"Don't you remember my warts, Your Grace?"

Conar turned around and squinted, sudden memory breaking through to him. "Aye," he said and took the man's hand and looked closely. The thin, slender hand with its bulging veins and dark brown liver spots had been covered with huge warts.

They were gone.

Conar looked into the man's beaming face. "How did you get rid of them?"

" 'Twas your lady, Highness. The young princess. She saw my hands and she said she had something to help." He rubbed the back of his left hand, a faraway look of adoration in his rheumy eyes. "They used to pain me sometimes, but your lady-wife gave me a cream and in a few days the warts was gone."

"The Toad got rid of your warts?" he asked. Weren't toads supposed to give warts, not take them away?

"And she cured the cook's rash. Remember that rash Sadie used to get on her neck and shoulders? And she gave the dairy girl a potion to help her monthlies. Then she saw Master John Boggs limping--you know how cold weather makes his old bones ache--and she told him about some root that would help. And you know how old Rufe had that sore that wouldn't heal? Well, she healed it with the same potion! She even went out with one of her serving girls and got the root, herself."

"Why would she--"

"Mistress Donna don't have her aches and pains in her joints no more after your lady gave her some potion or other to take every morning." The man smiled lovingly at Conar. "She's a good woman, your lady-wife, Highness."

Conar managed to smile as the cook's helper left him standing in the main hall. He watched the old man sidle away, his stooped shoulders hunched forward as he went about his business.

"Why the hell would she go to all that trouble?" Conar asked and felt someone watching him.

He turned to see the lady in question standing just inside the library door. On her shoulder was a little brown blob of wriggling fur whose pink tongue was licking at the edge of her veil. One slender hand was stroking the puppy's back as she gently bounced it up and down on her shoulder.

He stared at her, not moving, not greeting her in any way. This was the closest he had ever been to her, but he sure as hell didn't feel like speaking to the bitch. Not now. If truth be told, not ever.

"Lady," he grated out in a harsh greeting.

When she stepped back through the door and silently closed the portal, shutting him out, he fumed inwardly at her lack of manners until he realized with a pang that his had been no better.

"I don't need this crap today," he murmured as he spun around. Angrily slamming the front portal shut behind him, he thrust his hands deep into the pockets of his cords and stalked across the courtyard toward the Temple.

His mind numb with anger, Conar plodded wearily under the high wooden canopy leading to the Temple's portico. As he passed the Tribunal's Main Complex, he looked up at the black marble entranceway and his blood ran cold.

There was something about the place that had always unsettled him. Although he had never once had reason to be admitted inside the Hall of Laws, he always felt a dark fear whenever he passed the place. Today was no different, for he felt a great unease grip him as he neared the entranceway. He glanced to the rear of the center courtyard where the scaffolding and whipping post stood. Conar shivered.

He had seen men die there in the Punishment Yard, hung from the scaffolding until they strangled. The wooden structures never failed to make him ill, for it was a barbaric practice he detested. Capital punishment was carried out in Serenia with great determination by the Tribunal.

Few men had ever entered the main facilities of the Tribunal Hall beyond the Hall of Laws where courts were held. Those who did were never the same when allowed out, for torture was part of their physical penalty within the Punishment Cells of the Tribunal.

Those who were chained to the whipping post were later transported to either the prison colony at Guilder's Cay or shipped to Labyrinth Prison where the worst elements were incarcerated.

None of the three options--hanging, whipping, or transportation to a penal colony--was easy. All of them entailed humiliating abuse and physical torment that might well be considered inhuman and unjust.

Conar looked away from the tall black doors with their shiny marble columns of bronze plate and the crest of the god-Clere--the Lawgiver. For some reason, the Tribunal Hall caused him more unease than usual.

"Papa!" a young voice called to him as he neared the first step up to the Temple and he turned and smiled.

"Where've you been, Wyn?" He laughed and caught the young boy who flew at him, picking him up. "I haven't seen you since I got home." He set down the boy and tousled his bright blond hair.

"I went with Healer Cayn to help Master Tucker with the birth of one of Lord Teal's mares. They let me help, Papa!" The boy's freckled face shone as he looked up at his father. "Today's the day you wed, isn't it, Papa?"

"Aye," Conar said with a frown, his good humor at seeing his five-year-old son vanishing. "Tonight is the Joining." He sat on the bottom step and patted the stone beside him. "What have you been up to lately?"

Wyn plopped down beside his father and turned so he could look at Conar. "I met your wife, Papa," he said eagerly as he threaded his fingers through his father's.

"You did?" Conar couldn't have cared less. He looked over the courtyard to his left where a servant raked the leaves from a huge cottonwood.

"She sent for me!" His small chest puffed up, and when his father turned, surprised, the boy giggled. "You did know that, didn't you, Papa?"

"What did she want?" Conar asked, his tone filling with suspicion.

Wyn's young face split into a grin. "She wanted to meet all your children!"

"Why?" His suspicion turned to fury.

"Papa!" Wyn cried with exasperation. "Because she's going to be your wife, Papa, and she wanted to see your children." He scooted on the ground at his father's feet and wedged himself between Conar's legs, his small hands gripping his father's waist. "You know what she did?" His face was eager, excited.

"I'm afraid to ask," Conar mumbled under his breath, as he stroked his son's upper arms.

"She gathered all of us together in the garden and told us all about herself. We sat on the ground around her and listened. She has such a pretty voice, Papa."

No doubt the only pretty thing about her, Conar thought wickedly. "What did she say?"

"Oh, you know! Where she was born, who her Mama and Papa are. That sort of thing." The little boy made a wry face as if to say that was of no importance. "She has four sisters and two brothers!" His nose wrinkled. "As if I need any more uncles!"

Conar chuckled. "I guess you don't, huh?" He sighed. "What else did she say?"

His little voice took on an air of excitement. "She told us all kinds of stories about her homeland. All about dragons that can fly and wizards that can make themselves disappear right from under your nose. She taught us songs and jokes and riddles and she told us she would teach any of us who didn't know how to read." Wyn drew himself up and patted his thin chest. "She appointed me her helper because I'm the oldest and you already taught me how to read. Well, sorta, anyway."

The boy got up and sat on his father's knee, hooking his arm around Conar's neck and leaning his forehead against his father's. "And you know what else she did, Papa?"

Conar shook his head. "What?" He was staring at his son as Wyn continued on with the marvelous things the lady had done and said to his children. He was amazed. This boy was very shy, easily frightened, preferring to spend his time in the stables, transferring his love to the animals, rather than take a chance on humans and their fickle natures.

"She said that if we ever needed anything, we were to come to her because we were your children and now we were hers, too!" Wyn smiled. "Isn't she a grand lady, Papa?"

Conar hugged the boy and then eased him off his lap, standing up to stare at the palace doorway. "Have you seen her face, Wyn?"

The boy shook his head. "She wears a pretty veil, Papa. Tia asked her why she wears it and she said because she could see other people and they couldn't see her."

"A good reason."

Wyn frowned. "I asked if that was so she could judge people and not have them judge her."

Conar glanced at his son. As a bastard son of the Prince Regent, Wyn had fought many times with boys who had insulted his parentage to his face. He had become quite adept at hiding his own little feelings except around those he loved.

"And what did she say to that?"

Wyn looked up at his father. "She said sometimes people judge you wrongly before they even meet you. She said the veil hides many things from prying eyes, but it hides tears especially well."

Conar felt as though he had been sucker-punched in his gut. "But what if what is beneath the veil is a face others find too horrible to look upon, Wyn?" he asked, searching the boys blue eyes that were a mirror image of his own.

Wyn shrugged. "What difference does that make, Papa?" he asked with the perfect innocence of childhood. "Isn't it what's in a person's heart that matters, not what they look like?"

Conar flinched. He had heard much about the lady who was to become his wife that night. From his father. From the cook's helper. Now from his son. If what they were telling him was true, she would make a worthy wife.

Or a formidable enemy.

He touched his son's cheek. "I have to go to the Temple, now. I'll see you tomorrow."

"I'll see you at the wedding!" Wyn laughed.

"Oh, you will, will you?" Conar asked, one tawny brow lifted in challenge. "How so?"

"The lady told Mistress Emmie Lou that all of us could watch the wedding if we took naps this afternoon; and we stayed in the balcony of the Temple and didn't make any sound during the Joining. We all made a pact to be good so we can see you marry her, Papa."

"Wyn?" a voice called and both father and son turned to see Mistress Emmie Lou beckoning the boy. The children's nanny waved at Conar and crooked her finger at Wyn. "Time to go in, now, Wynland!"

"Well, then, you see that your brothers and sisters behave," he said, slapping his son's rump.

"I love you, Papa!" the boy called as he ran off, turning around once to wave goodbye.

"I love you, too!" Conar yelled.

For a long moment Conar stood staring after his running child. The woman was obviously trying to endear herself to his children and he couldn't help but wonder why she had gone to so much trouble over her husband' bastard offspring.

"What kind of game are you playing, Toad?" he asked and was startled by a gentle hand on his shoulder. He turned and frowned. "What?" he asked, although he knew gods-be-damned well the answer.

"It is time, Highness," a brown-robed acolyte from the Temple informed him. "You must come in, now, too."

Conar let out an angry snort of breath and fell in beside the acolyte.

"Tonight will be some night, won't it, Your Grace?" the man asked politely as he and Conar started up the Temple steps.

"Aye," came the bitter reply. "Some night!"

## Chapter Thirty One

The bathing chamber deep within the bowels of the Temple was a delight to the senses. Lush green plants cascaded from the high vaulted ceiling where soaring redwood beams framed panels of pale green crystal skylights. Massive copper pots, hung from the buttresses over and to the sides of the freeform pool, were suspended from thin copper wires, braided for strength with tempered steel. It gave the illusion that the flowing plants within the pots were suspended in midair. Their burdens of leafy green plants, some with tiny yellow or white flowers, hung all the way to the floor in some places while others trailed down the walls and into a far section of the pool to hide the fieldstone wall beyond.

Tall vines of honeysuckle, wisteria, sweet shrub and clinging rose climbed almost invisible trellises and clung to black, gold-veined marble columns that held a canopy of vines in place over a wooden swing. An espaliered wall of thickly-grown ornamental pear formed a perfect backdrop for the nude statue of the goddess, Serena, for whom the country was named.

The bathing pool itself was set in the center of a dark red brick floor, its water heated by a natural underground hot spring. The edges of the pool had been capped with a shiny, pale pink marble that sparkled in the glow of hundreds of candles burning in tiny clear votive cups about the chamber.

Mists of steam rose in lazy waves above the water's surface and drifted over the rim to lap at the brick flooring. A pleasant smell of flowers and vines filled the air and seemed to weave their magic fragrances with the vapor floating above the pool like so many lush perfumes.

There was stillness to the place; tranquility, a calm, soothing effect that everyone who visited there seemed to luxuriate in. It was a warm place, humid with the vapors of steam and oxygen given off by the plants, and yet it was cool and welcoming, a cocoon of serenity where the troubles of the outside world did not exist.

Everything within the chamber glistened with a soft green glow cast from the ceiling. The sloshing of the bubbling waters was the only intrusion into the peace and harmony offered by the bathing chamber and it helped to enhance the notion that there was nothing left on earth that was of any consequence.

Conar stepped into the knee-high water and waded out a little ways until the lapping waves were mid-thigh. He felt a sigh of pleasure come from him as the bubbling hot water broke over his thighs and wrapped their calm around him.

"Is the water too hot for you, Your Grace?" James Brigman, one of the Temple deacons, asked his Prince.

Conar shook his head and gingerly lowered himself into the pool, gasping as the hot water touched the tip of his manhood. With a slight grimace, he lowered himself all the way, sitting on the black sand bottom, emitting a soft laugh as the sand wedged itself between the cleft of his naked rump.

"Any warmer, Jamie, and I'd be of no use to my bride this night," he quipped.

An uncivilized thought crossed his mind, but he shrugged it away. Boiling his genitals to keep from having to service The Toad wouldn't stop the wedding and he was pretty gods-be-damned sure he wouldn't enjoy the process. He chuckled as a vivid image of his manhood being boiled in a pot flashed across his mind's eye.

"I'm glad you find this amusing!" a snarl erupted from behind Conar.

Arching back his head, Conar squinted up at his older brother. Legion was staring at him with hostility. The man looked massive in his white silk robe.

"May I help you with your robe, Lord Legion?" James asked.

Conar had to tightly press his lips together as Legion noticed the deacon staring unabashed at his rather legendary manhood.

"See anything you like?" Legion snarled.

James looked upward to Legion's angry face and shrugged. "Nothing of consequence, Lord A'Lex."

Conar snorted and then laughed as Legion stomped into the pool and flopped beside him, making the water lap hungrily at Conar's chin.

"Damn your eyes, Conar!" Legion growled as he felt his own manhood shriveling from the heat. "Are you trying to maim us?"

Conar didn't answer, but the wicked grin on his face said it all. He tuned out Legion's grumpy comments as the larger man tried to get comfortable in the raging heat and concentrated on the bubbling warmth that lulled him.

Legion stopped grumbling and glanced at Conar's serene face. He snapped his mouth shut with an audible click.

"Afraid you might shrink, A'Lex?" Conar joked, glancing down at Legion's lap.

"Shithead," Legion said under his breath as he wiggled in the water, grimacing at the feel of the sand oozing under his genitals.

Legion had never been allowed in the bathing chamber before but Conar had requested his presence today. Spreading out his arms on each side of him, Legion hooked them on the pool's rim and looked about, awed by the place's beauty. He hoped he could forget about his shaft turning a most peculiar shade of red as it bobbed about in the water.

"You don't have to go to the steaming chamber with me if you don't want to," Conar told him.

Legion glared at his brother. "I've steeled myself to bake alongside you."

"You don't have to." Conar let his toes rise to the surface then wiggled them. "Galen's here."

"I know," came the terse reply. "Seen his ugly face."

Conar grinned. "He bears a striking resemblance to your Prince, A'Lex."

Legion snorted. "As much resemblance between the two of you as between a viper and an earthworm!"

Conar's brows rose. "I hope that remark was meant to be a compliment, not a judgment."

"Take it any way you feel fit," Legion retorted, out of sorts and not really knowing why.

"I won't have the bastard insulting you or your mother. If you prefer not to be in his company, I will understand."

Legion rolled his eyes to the heavens. "Oh, for the love of Alel, Conar! You know gods-be-damned well you want me there to protect you from the vile little prick!"

Conar shook his head. "I do well enough with Galen on my own."

Legion turned. "You let the fop get away with murder. Besides"--he shrugged--"I suppose I could slit his gullet for you if you're inclined that way. Wouldn't mind doing so."

"I'll get back to you on that," Conar said with a laugh in his tone.

Legion glared. "You do realize I am making a supreme sacrifice on your behalf by even being in this hot cauldron, don't you?" Legion took a lot of cold showers.

Conar smiled. "I am well aware of your loyalty to the crown, Legion."

"Just as long as you are."

They stayed another ten minutes, until Jamie Brigman came to tell them it was time to head to the steaming chamber, and from there, to the masseur.

Legion glanced up as Conar stood in the water. His eyes went to the juncture of his brother's thighs and he stared unabashed at Conar's manhood. "It's still there, little brother." He cocked his head to one side. "Has it always been that small or did this boiling water make it shrink?"

Conar looked woefully down at himself and shook his head. "I believe it did shrink somewhat. But it has this tendency to expand sometimes."

"Not much expansion possible with a little pecker like that." Legion grinned.

Conar stepped up the wide pink marble steps and wrapped one of the fleece towels around his waist. But before he had the end of the towel folded into itself, he felt the nudge of someone watching him and turned to the entranceway. His gaze met Kaileel Tohre's and he couldn't stop the violent tremor that ran through his limbs. Instinctively he stepped closer to his older brother.

Tohre stood there for a moment and then his mouth stretched into a thin, wicked line. He nodded at Conar, completely ignoring A'Lex, and then disappeared down the hallway leading to the sacristy.

Legion tucked his own towel around his waist. "Why does that bastard stare at you like that, Conar?"

A shadow of memory crossed Conar's mind, a shadow of certainty, and he looked down at the streaks on his thighs. He glanced once more to the entranceway. The suspicion of how he had come by the wicked marks on his belly, thighs, and legs made him clench his teeth in fury. "Who put me to bed last eve?"

Legion halted drying his chest and glanced up. "I did. Why?"

"Where was Tohre?"

"Still at the table." Legion tossed his robe over his shoulder. "He was gone when I got back to the meal, though. Like he always is when you're not there."

"Where did he go?"

"How the hell should I know? Why does he bother you?"

"I hate him," Conar answered, turning away. "I have reason to hate the bastard."

"Well, I gathered that much, brat."

He would have continued the conversation, but the closed, set look on Conar's face made him hesitate. It had always been that way when the subject of Tohre was brought to Conar's attention.

Not wanting to upset his brother further, Legion draped a heavy arm over his Conar's shoulder. "Well, now that you've boiled that little prick, let's go bake it for awhile!"

\* \* \* \*

Prince Coron McGregor, third in line to the crown of Serenia, was a handsome young man only two hours short of being exactly one year younger than Conar and Galen. He was the scholar in the family. Coron would rather turn in with a good book than sit a horse or pull a bowstring. His knowledge of swordplay was limited to the volumes of books on the subject he devoured with relish.

Seventeen-year old Prince Dyllon McGregor had a smile that was impish and wicked and challenging, all at the same time, and he had a few select, choice friends to whom he vowed allegiance. As intelligent as his brother, if not as scholarly, Dyllon weighed carefully a problem, looked at it from as many angles as were visible, and even from views that were not, and calculated the problem's affect on his life. There were no half measures with Dyllon. It was either all or nothing.

When the young men saw their older brothers coming, their faces lit up and they abandoned a third man with whom they had been carrying on an uneasy conversation. Jockeying for a better bear hug on Conar, the young men pushed each other out of the way.

"Move, Dyllon!" Coron snapped and shoved his younger brother against Legion A'Lex.

"Make me," Dyllon hissed and shoved his brother back.

"My god, how you've grown, brat!" Legion remarked as he looked into Dyllon's eyes. It wasn't that long ago when he had to tilt down his head to look at the boy. Now they were at the same eye level. "How do you find boots to fit you?"

Dyllon punched Legion's arm. "That's not all of me that's oversized!"

Coron snorted, rolling his eyes. "No, his ego is, too."

"Go to hell, Coron." Dyllon smiled sweetly.

"Been there," was the terse reply. "You forget I used to bunk with you."

"I'm happy the two of you were able to come," Conar said as he tousled Coron's short hair. "How long will you stay?"

"Coron will stay until the end of the year, but I'm having the same old problem with that Necromanian jackass. The man's a veritable pest!" Dyllon feigned a punch at Conar's midsection. Hitting Legion was one thing. Actually hitting his idolized older brother, Conar, was considered inappropriate.

Coron snorted and draped an arm over Legion's shoulder. "Dyllon wouldn't have all that trouble with King Shalu if he didn't go raiding in Necroman all the time. You know Dyllon ... any excuse to fight. I have no such troubles with Chale and Ionary or Virago."

"Ionary and Chale don't have Princes who take exception to being raided," Dyllon sniffed.

"That's because I never go raiding there!"

"Isn't your wife an Ionarian, Coron?" Legion countered.

Coron blushed. "I went raiding once," he mumbled.

"Aye, and Chase Montyne came looking for you, too," Conar teased, referring to the golden-haired aristocratic Prince of Ionary.

"I married her, didn't I?" Coron grinned. "It tied our two families together. Chase couldn't bitch about me abducting his baby sister when it was she who engineered the entire thing!"

"Aye, and who was it that made her want to engineer her abduction, Coron?" Dyllon barked.

Coron grinned. "I admit I coerced her a bit."

"Aye and that's why both of you boys had to marry far too early," Legion quipped. "It was either that or lose your danglies."

"Leave off, Legion. They're McGregors." Conar chuckled. "We always go after what we want."

"Like the woman you've been running with of late?" a tired, bored voice broke into the conversation. "Against the Tribunal's orders, I might add."

Conar slowly turned and the look he gave the man who sat beside the steaming chamber door would have cowered any other man. But Galen McGregor was immune to dirty looks and he had no fear of reprisal from his twin. His pale blue eyes glared with confidence that Conar would do nothing in front of their brothers.

"Not that it is any of your business, but the Tribunal hasn't given me any orders, Galen," Conar stated.

"Not yet, anyway, but once this Joining is done, you touch any other woman, ever again, and the Tribunal will have your precious hide."

"I wouldn't let that concern you, Galen," Dyllon said, his voice crackling with challenge. "Conar knows where his obligations lie."

Galen smiled and the frost in his words was telling. "What happened to the lady you were hiding for Conar, A'Lex? Is she still at Ivor?"

"I don't know what you're talking about," Legion growled. "There's no woman at Ivor."

"Maybe not now, but she was there, wasn't she? Conar thought no one knew he had a mistress at the keep." He swung his gaze to his twin. "You are being watched whether you are aware of it or not. Do one wrong thing, and the Tribunal will flay the hide from your back, Conar."

"Why don't you leave Conar alone, Galen," Coron asked, trying to bring peace as he usually did. "This isn't any time to mention his past affairs. Those are over and done with."

Galen threw back his head and chuckled. "You don't know about her, do you, Cory?" He spread his hands. "This was a woman Conar worshipped. I have a feeling big brother intends to keep on with the beauteous Liza despite his marriage vows. If he does, she will suffer alongside him when the whip descends."

"Shut up!" Conar snarled. "Liza's done nothing wrong here. Accuse her and it will be the last thing you say this side of hell!"

"See?" Galen asked his two younger brothers. "See how he protests? The woman he had A'Lex hide for him at Ivor has caused him to lose what little sense he had."

"If you don't shut up, I swear to the gods I'll--" Conar started forward, but Legion grabbed his arm.

"I say whatever I feel like saying. You don't scare me, Conar." Galen glanced at Legion. "Let him go, A'Lex. Let him start something. The Tribunal will drag him to the Joining in chains."

"Are you tired of living, Galen?" Conar asked in a pleasant voice. "If you are, I can easily accommodate your death wish. Say one more word and, wedding or not, I will call your ass out."

Galen's smile faded. If there was one thing he was certain of, it was Conar's ability with a sword. Even though Galen had been taught swordplay and hand-to-hand combat, he was nowhere near Conar in ability and he knew it. While Galen had sat in the schoolrooms of the

Wind Temple, Conar had been on the battlefield learning his warrior ways at the hands of Hern Arbra.

If there was anything else Galen was sure of in this world, it was Conar McGregor's willingness to kill. It galled him to back down from the challenge in Conar's eye, but he did, for he knew that look well.

Conar waited patiently for Galen to make a move. When he didn't, he turned his back on his twin, ignoring him. "Will you two join me and Legion in the steaming chamber?" he asked his younger brothers.

Galen had not wanted to enter the steaming chamber, but his failure to be invited stung badly. He was as much a part of this family as Dyllon and Coron were, even more of a part than Legion. He wanted to hurt Conar, to humiliate him, and the only way he knew how was to strike directly once more at the exposed nerve that was Conar's heart.

"I have my men out looking for Liza, by the way." Galen smirked. "I have told them to be very careful of her, for I fully intend to make the lady my mistress." He started to get up off the bench, but instead, he found himself plastered tightly to the wall behind him, his throat caught in a deadly grip as Conar bent over him, his nose only a fraction of an inch from Galen's.

"I'd slit her throat before I'd ever let you put your filthy hands on her!" Conar shouted, spittle flying into Galen's white face. "If I thought you could find her where I haven't been able to, I'd hunt you down and make sure you never touched her, or anyone else, ever again!" He shoved Galen away, wiping his hand down his robe as though the contact with Galen's flesh had soiled him, shaking off the restraining hand Legion had on his arm. "Get out of my sight before I kill you, Galen!"

Galen put a hand to his throat and rubbed the ache caused by Conar's sword hand. His heart was pounding, fury having risen in his throat like bitter acid. All caution had fled and his ego blinded him to normal restraint. He opened his mouth to speak, but he was so furious, words wouldn't come out.

"You want to say something, Galen?" Conar taunted. "Go ahead, you little bastard. I just might let you live long enough to regret it."

Standing slowly and facing his brother, Galen spoke so low only Conar could hear him. "There will come a day, Conar, and I promise you it will, when you will be forced to go to your knees before me. You will beg me to let you die and I will not. You will beg for mercy and I will see you get none. You will have to live with the punishment that has been reserved for you."

"You're a bigger fool than I thought if you really believe that shit, Galen," Conar said and turned his back, motioning his brothers to precede him into the steaming chamber. Before he closed the door, he locked his gaze with Galen's and smiled. "You are a fool."

Closing the door behind him, Conar bolted the inside lock, shutting out his twin.

* * * *

"Never let your enemy know how you truly feel about him, Galen," a voice chided.

Turning around, Galen shook his head. "I can't help it, Master. The bastard infuriates me."

"Hate him all you will, dear boy," Kaileel Tohre said. "Your brother will pay dearly for his disregard of your feelings." He put his hand on Galen's cheek. "Very soon now, your brother will know the full extent of the Domination's wrath and rue the day he ever defied us!"

## Chapter Thirty Two

"Are you ready?" Legion's voice was quiet as he spoke to his brother.

Conar stood beside the arched window in the Temple's Registry where he had just signed the final papers linking him to Princess Anya. He had already dressed for the wedding ritual, had sat perfectly still and silent through the lectures and warnings, disciplines and information bestowed upon him by the Brothers of the Wind, and now all that was left was his appearance in the Temple's Chancel. He leaned his head against the cool panes of glass and closed his eyes.

"It's nearly time, Conar. They'll be coming for you," Legion warned as he laid a hand on his brother's shoulder.

Conar inhaled deep and long and let out a nervous, wavering breath. He felt sick to his stomach again and his head ached with a throbbing, blinding pain behind his right eye. He was sweating and shivering at the same time and his palms were itching, his fingers trembling.

He had been watching the snow outside as his father and father-in-law-to-be had signed their names, witnessing the papers he had already signed in their presence. His mind had been on the gently falling crystals as they covered the Garden of Solace outside the Registry window and he had totally detached himself from what was going on about him. Legion's voice had broken the spell under which he had placed himself.

"Conar?" Legion gently prodded.

He shook his head. "I don't want to do this, Legion," he said quietly, his voice filled with emotion. "I truly don't want to do this."

Legion had nothing to offer his brother. He could speak no words of encouragement that wouldn't sound false and hollow. All he had was his great love for his brother and that was something Legion A'Lex gave unconditionally.

"I know, little brother, but Papa isn't going to allow you out of the contract."

It deeply hurt Legion to see the flinch that broke his brother's icy calm when the Wedding Gong sounded for Conar's father to enter the Chancel.

The gong sounded again, signaling King Shaz's entrance into the Temple.

Conar looked at Legion, hesitating only a second as Legion held out his arms. He went into those strong arms much as a child would have and gripped his brother to him, laying his cheek on Legion's broad shoulder. "I am so afraid," he whispered.

Legion's grip tightened. "I know you are, brat."

"Don't let me shame myself before them, Legion. Please don't let me do that."

Legion's throat closed against the raw pain in Conar's trembling voice. "I have no fear of that happening."

"I do," was the shaky reply.

Conar withdrew from his brother's arms and took Legion's head in his hands, staring intently into his brother's eyes. "Promise me something."

"Anything." There was no hesitation on Legion's part.

"Promise me you won't stop looking for Liza." He saw his brother wince. "Find her and bring her to me, Legion."

Legion felt a knife go through his soul. He shook his head. "Conar, I can't--"

"Find her for me. When you do...." Tears began to form. "... I will betroth her to you."

Legion's face went perfectly still. He couldn't believe what he was hearing. "You don't mean that!"

Conar turned, his breath hitching in his throat. What he was about to say would be the hardest thing he had ever said in his life. "I will see her wed to no other man, but you, Legion." He felt a part of him dying, shriveling away. "I will have no other man touch her but you." He turned and found Legion staring at him. "With you as her husband, I will not be tempted to stray from that bitch I am being forced to wed. I would not dishonor you in that way."

"Conar...." Legion's face was filled with concern.

"If she is still available, if she married another, someone I didn't hold in high regard, I would go after her, Legion. I would move heaven and hell to have her again. But if she belonged to you, I would keep my distance. I would never try to take her from you and I would never make her break her wedding vows."

Legion shook his head in denial. "Conar, I care for her. You are not being fair to ask this of me." He shook his head again. "I think I may well be in love with her myself."

A sad smile settled on Conar's lips. "I've known that all along, Legion."

For a long time, Legion held his brother's gaze. There was no guile in Conar's blue stare. There was only love and a terrible, terrible pain. A pain Legion could not soothe.

Twice more the gongs called out, calling for the mother of the bride and the surrogate mother who would stand beside Conar. Conar broke the silence between Legion and himself.

"Say something, brother. Give me an answer."

"Are you sure this is what you want?"

"I am sure."

Legion put out his hand and the two men grasped each other's wrists. One heart was breaking; the other's heart already broken. Legion's words were soft and spoken with tired resolve. "Then I will gladly accept her to wife if she will have me."

Conar smiled, sadly. "If we can find her."

"Aye, if we can find her. But if we do, I'll damn sure never let her leave us again."

For one brief moment, Conar hesitated. He wanted to take back what he had said. Wanted to deny any claim Legion might make to the woman they both loved, but he knew in his heart that if Liza ever should return, unattached, to Boreas or to Ivor, he would, himself, never let her go.

He loved this brother more than all the others and his promises to Legion were inviolate. With Legion as Liza's husband, he knew he would not be tempted to stray. He also knew Legion would probably kill him if he should try. "Liza will be yours one day," he said, knowing in his heart it was true. "I feel it, Legion."

The gong broke over them like a death knell and Conar blanched white. "It's time."

A'Lex couldn't speak as his brother turned, squared his shoulders, and began the walk that would end his happiness forever. Following Conar to the Chancel, Legion couldn't help but admire the graceful male animal that was Conar McGregor.

His long legs were encased in russet breeches of soft leather. They molded his legs and rump as though he had been poured into them. Soft boots of dark brown kid made only a whisper of sound as Conar walked across the highly polished marble floor. His tunic was a pale yellow silk, opened to his waist and belted with a cincture of intricately twined gold links. Around the hem of the tunic, stitched in bright copper thread, was the runic lettering symbolizing the Four Ways To Happiness.

The writings spelled out the four things Conar would need to be a good husband to his wife: Fidelity, Prosperity, Good Health, and Wisdom. Circling each of the long, billowing sleeves was the writing of the Two Ways of Immortality: Fertility and Fecundity. The silken, crystal bead-tipped laces of his shirt had been left untied and hung down, their ends swaying gently against his chest as he moved.

Around each of his wrists were heavy gold bands that kept his cuffs in place. One hammered band was engraved with the name of his father, the other with his mother's maiden name. A single thin loop of finely-wrought gold rested in his left earlobe and, around his neck, partly hidden by the tunic, was the medal of the Wind Warrior Society. His golden hair was banded with the crystal circlet of the Prince Regent.

The gong sounded again, a warning, signaling Conar enter the Chancel or have guards come get him. Legion squeezed his brother's shoulder. "The Wind be at your back, little brother," he said, a catch in his voice.

Conar didn't answer. He nodded and reached up his right hand to cover Legion's. His attention was on his father as King Gerren began his walk from the Chancel to the Altar where High Priest Kaileel Tohre waited.

Conar took a deep breath, let it out slowly. "The gods help me," he whispered and then he walked into the Temple.

\* \* \* \*

Legion had to make himself stand still. He wanted desperately to run, to hide. He didn't want to be a witness to his brother's unhappiness. His heart ached and tears threatened to come. He braced his feet wide apart and clutched his hands behind his back. He bit his lip to keep from shouting at Conar to come back, to leave, and to forsake this travesty.

He knew he wouldn't.

He knew he couldn't.

Teal was in the fourth section of wedding guests and he felt his face twisting with emotion as he caught sight of Conar's. There was such blatant misery on that handsome young face, such agony; it was a wonder the man could even walk. Teal had never seen Conar looking so unsure of himself, so terribly defeated, so vulnerable.

The gods protect you, my friend, Teal thought. The gods protect you.

Gezelle stood just inside the Sacristy doorway. Behind her, the servant girl, Liza, was attending to the Princess Anya's wedding train. She could hear the soft words of encouragement from the Princess' mother, the stern advice from her father. She winced as the Princess laughed nervously.

"Oh, my sweet Milord," Gezelle said as she saw Conar step to the altar. "I am so sorry. So very, very sorry."

From his place in the first tier of seats, Galen folded his arms over his chest and leaned back in the chair. How awful you look, big brother, he thought. You look as though these are your final hours on earth! He exchanged a smile with Kaileel Tohre.

Coron and Dyllon exchanged looks, as well, over the heads of their lady-wives. Both men frowned. It was only too obvious to them that Conar was on the verge of collapse and that it wouldn't take much to push him right over the edge. Never had they seen their big brother so nervous and rigid.

Hern snorted, his anger filling the last row of seats as though they were empty of the valued warriors and servants who had been asked to attend. He shot a hateful look to Healer Cayn and saw the man shrug.

"There is nothing you can do, Arbra," Cayn warned.

"Don't be so gods-be-damned sure!" Hern spat. He thrust his chin toward Conar. "Just look at that face, Cayn! Look what they're doing to the brat! I don't like it. I don't like it one bit. It ain't necessary!" His wizened countenance hardened. "It could have been avoided."

Storm, Thom, and Marsh sat nervously on the edges of their chairs beneath the balcony where Conar's children were sitting as quietly as any children ever had.

Marsh let out a harsh sigh. "I don't like the way he looks."

"Aye, he looks terrible," Storm exclaimed.

"You would, too," Thom snarled, "if you were marrying a frog!"

Kaileel Tohre smiled. How miserable the boy looks, he thought with glee. Handsome as he was in the wedding shirt that had been worn by generations of McGregor men, Conar looked pale beneath the tanned planes of his face. The trembling hand Conar put to his right eye signaled a bad headache and there was a pinched look to his face that said he was no doubt nauseous, too.

Tohre looked to a servant in the back row and nodded slightly. Adding just the right amount of tenerse to the boy's morning ale had brought on the pallor the nervousness he was exhibiting. Another sip when the wine was given to him during the ceremony would push him further under the drug's strong influence and make him feel the anger he was beginning to feel even more.

King Gerren closely watched his son as they walked to face each other at the altar. He could see paleness that shouldn't be there. There was a glazed look about the boy that meant Conar was having another of his bad headaches and that did not bode well for the night festivities. The nervous way Conar licked his full lips told his father that Conar was on the very edge of turning tail and running. Conar's blue eyes skidded toward the exits, skipped back to his father, and then away again.

No, you don't, Gerren thought, willing his son to look at him. Don't even think about it, Conar. Nothing would stop the Joining from taking place, Gerren vowed silently. Conar had a duty and honor to the royal house of Oceania, not to mention an obligation to his own royal parentage. If it came down it, Conar would be forced to go through the wedding at sword point.

Conar kept his gaze straight ahead, ignoring the men and women of the nobility who had come from as far away as Chrystallus to be witnesses to his mating with Princess Anya of Oceania. He could feel the blood pounding in his ears and, with it, the godawful pressure on his skull the headache was causing. The vision in his right eye was blurring, doubling objects as he tried to concentrate. He looked from one doorway to another, trying to focus properly, but his wavering sight made him ill, so he settled his gaze on his father's face. He was deeply afraid that if he looked up at Kaileel Tohre he would bolt and run like a wounded stag.

Other than the slight trembling in his hands, he prayed he gave no other outward sign of the agitation that flowed through him like molten lava. He willed himself to stand still, not to fidget, and to pay attention to what was going on around him, although his brain had seemed to shut down the moment he walked into this vile place.

As the Wedding Gong was struck for the seventh time, signaling the procession of the bride's and groom's mothers to the altar, Kaileel could not stop the giggle of malice that came as Conar cringed.

Conar heard the snicker, but he didn't look at the priest. He glanced to the doorway beyond his father where his father's only sister, the Empress Dyreil of Chrystallus, was being escorted into the Temple by Coron. So nervous and detached from his surroundings, he had not even seen his two younger brothers get up to offer themselves as escorts to Queen Medea and their aunt.

Since his own mother was dead, his aunt would be surrogate mother to him for the Joining. Conar managed a weak smile for her as Coron walked her forward and then took her hand from his forearm and placed it on the forearm of their father.

Behind him, Conar could hear the soft rustling of silk and knew Dyllon would be escorting the Queen of Oceania to her place at the altar. As she moved past him, Conar was struck anew by the woman's loveliness. When she looked his way, he cringed at the pain that lovely face caused him.

Since his aunt had only arrived in the middle of the afternoon while Conar was going through the lengthy processes in the Temple, Conar had not spoken to her. In fact, he had not spoken with her for over six years, and even though he was her favorite nephew, she was not privy to his reluctance, nor had she been advised of his reasons for that reluctance, to marry the Princess Anya.

Looking at him now, her troubled blue gaze shifted over his nervous face and she pursed her lips tightly together.

So that was the way of it, Dyreil mused. The boy isn't happy about this. No doubt there was either another girl or there was something wrong with the one he was being forced to marry. She looked up to her brother and saw him frown at her with warning. Tossing her long blond hair over her shoulder, the lady dug her sharp nails into her brother's arm, letting him know just what she thought of this situation. She felt him flinch and knew a moment of supreme satisfaction.

"Damn it, Dy," he gasped. "That hurt!"

"Tough!"

Dyllon and Coron looked at one another and smiled. They recognized that look on their aunt's face. She might be only four feet and seven inches in height, weigh only eighty pounds, and possess a face that looked as though she had not a mean bone in her body. But Dyreil McGregor Shimota was a force to be reckoned with when she was mad. And at the moment, she looked more than mad. She looked fit to be tied.

Gerren felt his sister's nails gouging into his flesh again and looked at her with alarm. She sent him a merciless smile full of pure venom and he groaned. By the gods but the bitch was going to skewer him, yet. He flinched as the nails dug deeper.

Teal saw that look pass between brother and sister and grinned. Conar had a champion in the Empress Dyreil, and his father would be severely chastised for what her beloved Conar was being forced to endure. To keep from laughing as the King shifted nervously from one foot to another, Teal stared ahead of him to the altar stone.

Queen Medea touched one graceful hand to her shining black hair and saw Conar look her way. He caught her watching him and hastily turned, but not before she had seen the sheer terror ravaging his handsome face. You poor boy, she thought. The young man did not know what was coming. Had no idea what it was that he must endure. Her heart went out to him and she looked away from the hopelessness on that face.

When the clatter of silver bells rang out over the Temple, Medea heard the groan that had come from her son-in-law's lips.

Gerren saw Conar stiffen as the bells chimed. He looked into his son's face and was not encouraged by what he saw there. There was hot resentment registering and, beneath the long lashes, his father caught the fleeting flash of panic.

Conar's lips were pressed tightly together in a thin, white line. He clenched his teeth so hard a muscle began to jump in his taut cheek. His hands had fisted at the exact moment the silver bells rang out and the knuckles were beginning to turn white from the pressure.

There was rigidity to his posture that had not been there a moment before. His back was ramrod straight, his shoulders squared, his chin raised, but the color had drained from his face. He didn't seem to notice how terrible his appearance was to the rest of the wedding party standing with him between the four-foot-high altar rail of carved ebony wood and the black hematite altar.

King Gerren cleared his throat and gained his son's immediate attention. There was no word for the degree of stubbornness stamped on Conar's face and Gerren had a real fear that the defiance glowing in Conar's eyes would flare into total rebellion.

"Behave, son," he whispered and saw a muscle in his son's cheek throb.

"Get it over with," Legion mumbled from his place in the Chancel. He could only see Conar's back from where he was standing, but he didn't need to see his brother's face to know how tense the man was.

Tohre fixed his Prince with a sweet smile of revenge, his thin lips slowly moving back over yellowed, fang-like teeth. "It is now the designated Hour of Joining," Tohre called, watching Conar's face. He raised his hands above his head, spread them wide, and turned his palms outward to those assembled.

The guests rose and stood silently.

"Who comes to seek the blessing of Alel on this ritual?" Kaileel Tohre looked more than pleased with the crowd's unwavering attention.

King Gerren took a deep breath and stepped directly in front of the altar. He bowed slightly to Tohre. "I, King Gerren McGregor of Serenia, have come to seek the Great God's blessing."

Kaileel looked down at his King from his place behind the altar. "And why have you come, King Gerren McGregor of Serenia?" He could barely wait to hear the words.

"I have come to ask the Blessing of Joining for my eldest son, Conar Aleksandro McGregor, Prince Regent of Serenia." Gerren glanced at Conar as his son exhaled a long, hard rush of breath.

"Has this man a mother to ask for the Blessing of Mating for her son?"

Empress Dyreil hesitated for only a fraction of a second before going to stand in front of the altar, curtsying to the god Clere. Her bearing and her own unique brand of honor would not let her interfere with what was being done so cruelly to her beloved nephew, for she had been taught since early childhood where her duties to the McGregor men, and later, her husband, lay.

"I, Empress Dyreil Shimota of Chrystallus, have come as surrogate mother to ask the Great God's blessing on my son, Conar's, mating," she said, her eyes boring into Tohre's with extreme dislike.

"And can you, Empress Dyreil Shimota of Chrystallus, vouch for your son that he is worthy to take unto him a bride for this Joining?"

"I can," she said, her gaze on the High Priest.

Kaileel sneered. "Then take your place beside your son."

Dyreil took her place behind Conar.

Tohre brought his pale blue stare to his King. "And can you, King Gerren of Serenia, vouch for your son that he is free to Join, unencumbered by a previous marriage?"

"I can."

"Then I declare him fit for Joining. Go to your son, King Gerren."

Gerren walked to Conar's side. He could almost smell the fear rolling off Conar. He could hear the ragged, shallow breaths of nervous anticipation his child was making as he stood beside his father. He saw the fingers of the young man's right hand twitching.

It was not a good sign.

Conar glanced up at the High Priest, holding the fierce gaze directed toward him, and kept himself from wincing as Tohre's loud words rang through the Temple.

"Since I have tested this man and found him worthy of Joining, and since he is free to take unto himself a bride, I now declare the Joining may begin!" His voice turned lethal. "Let the bride come to her groom!"

Crystal bells tinkled and Conar tensed, his spine ramrod straight. It was time! In only a few moments, the woman he would be chained to for the rest of his wretched life would walk down the ermine pathway and wreck his life forever.

He heard the "oohs" and "aahs" of the assembled guests. Heard his aunt's sharp intake of breath. Heard his father's low whistle of either shock or admiration--he couldn't tell which--and thought he just might let fly with part, if not all, of the ale he had downed before going to the Temple this afternoon.

He jumped as his father nudged him with a not-so-gentle elbow and he looked up. When he did, he found himself staring straight into the intent face of Queen Medea.

There was no smile on her lovely face now. A mysterious light lit up her green eyes, eyes so like his beloved Liza's; and with a jolt, he realized the woman pitied him. It was written on that lovely face and he felt like groaning. He looked away and found himself staring into Kaileel's smug face.

That was no better. The only other option he had was to look down the pathway to his left.

He took a deep breath and slowly turned his head, mustering up all the courage he could find to look at the woman who was now only a few feet away from him.

No one was looking at Conar's face. They were looking at his bride. No one saw the look of shock on his face when he beheld his bride.

He blinked, blinked again, and let his vision travel slowly from the top of her veiled head to the sparkle of jeweled slippers on her feet and back up again.

He heard Dyllon's voice clearly from his place in the first row of seats, "My god, Coron! Look at her!"

Although the woman's face was hidden beneath the thick silver net, the rest of her in her wedding gown was in plain sight. Her ample curves in the truly priceless gown were lush and soft, her waist so tiny Conar knew he could span it with his hands. Her legs were long, and although she limped slightly beside her father as he escorted her to the altar, her feet did not appear to be misshapen in any way.

Her slender arms were bare except for the tiny puff of silver lace sleeves on her shoulders. Her neck was swan-like, arched and slim, her shoulders smooth, and creamy-looking. The bosom that thrust from the gown's low scalloped neckline had ample cleavage with which to garner a man's attention. There was no trace of her hair showing, but her coloring was warm and honey-tinted like her mother's.

His father had been right, Conar agreed begrudgingly. She was trim and she carried herself well despite the faint limp. Even if she was hideously deformed beneath the safety of that gods-be-damned veil, the rest of her wouldn't be so bad to mount. He snorted and felt his father's hand on his shoulder, squeezing none too gently.

King Shaz reached the altar rail, stepped up the three steps, held out his hand for his daughter to join him, and then escorted her the few feet forward to her husband. The King's beatific smile was glorious to behold.

Seeing that smile and the faint exchange of looks between the King and Queen of Oceania, Conar couldn't help but groan beneath his breath. As well he might grin like a jackanapes, Conar thought viciously. The King was getting rid of the bitchlet! Conar looked back at the girl, now only two feet away from him.

Her wedding dress had been a gift to her from the people of her homeland. Lovingly sewn by over a hundred ladies from all over the country, the gown had traveled from town to town with as many as three hundred pairs of hands fashioning the adornments, lace, netting, undergarments, and slippers. The worth of the gown left no doubt in anyone's mind why the dress had made its journey with dozens of guards in attendance.

Conar had to admit the gown, if not the woman wearing it, took his breath away.

Kaileel swung his gaze from Conar's stunned face to the woman who had joined them. Being the kind of man he was, he was oblivious to the curvaceous form beneath the priceless gown, but his greed valued it with close scrutiny and he was impressed.

"Who has come to the Joining this night?" Tohre asked.

"I, King Shaz Wynth of Oceania, have come to ask the Great God's blessing."

"And why have you come, King Shaz of Oceania?"

"To bring this man's bride, the Princess Anya Elizabeth Wynth, Firstborn Daughter of Oceania, for her Joining."

"And has this woman a mother to ask for the blessing of mating?"

Queen Medea didn't glance at Kaileel Tohre. Her gaze was intent on Conar. "I, Queen Medea Brell Wynth of Oceania, have come to ask the Great God's blessing on my daughter's Joining."

"And can you vouch for your daughter's purity?"

Medea smiled at Conar. "I give my word of honor as this woman's mother, and as her Sovereign Queen, that this man is her first." Her face shadowed as she watched Conar's face twist into a line of bitter scorn.

"Then I declare her worthy as this man's bride."

Conar glanced away from Medea's worried face. Did the woman think he was going to fall into a screaming fit at any minute? Why was it necessary to stare at him in that way? Where the hell did she think he could go? Where the hell did she think he would be allowed to go?

"And do you, King Shaz of Oceania, vouch for your daughter that she is not, nor has she ever been, betrothed to another?"

"I do." Shaz reached for his wife's hand as he joined her opposite Conar and his father and aunt. "Since birth, she has been betrothed to Prince Conar and no other."

"Then I declare this woman worthy of her new husband's loyalty."

Conar wondered if any man had ever kissed the lips behind that veil to tempt her to adultery. With a revolting surge of his belly, he wondered if she even had lips to kiss.

"And who has come to seek a mate for the Joining?" Kaileel's hawk-like stare went to Conar.

Only the slightest hesitation showed on Conar's part. He stepped forward with grim determination and deliberately looked into the hateful face that glared at his own.

"I, Conar Aleksandro McGregor, Prince Regent of Serenia, have come to seek a mate for the Joining."

King Shaz could see the fury brimming in the young man's icy eyes as he glared at the High Priest.

"Who comes to be joined with this man?" Kaileel had to strain to hear the grating whisper of sound that came from behind the thick veil.

"I, Princess Anya Elizabeth Wynth, Firstborn Daughter of Oceania, have come to be united with this man."

Kaileel looked to Conar. "Do you accept this woman, Prince Conar?"

Conar couldn't look at Kaileel's smug face, couldn't stand looking at Medea's pitying one or Shaz's suddenly angry visage. Nor did he want to look at the girl, so he kept his head down. His voice was totally devoid of inflection as he spoke. "I accept her."

Kaileel was disappointed. He thought Conar had more spunk. He had fully expected the boy to balk. He decided to press the issue.

"Of your own free will?"

King Gerren glowered at the priest. That was not part of the wording of the wedding ritual.

Conar's gut was twisting so painfully, his head throbbing so terribly he didn't realize Kaileel Tohre was prolonging his misery. "Aye," he said, barely able to breathe. "Of my own free will."

Again Kaileel was denied his pleasure and twisted the knife deeper. "Without coercion?"

"Aye, without coercion."

Kaileel's face narrowed with hatred. "Do you swear this is by your own choice and that you are not being forced into this Joining?"

"Tohre!" Gerren hissed, but was ignored.

Conar looked at Kaileel Tohre. With sudden understanding, he knew what the man was about. That knowledge cut through him like the knife

Kaileel had used on him as a boy. There was nothing Tohre liked better than seeing him in pain, of any kind, and his wedding day would be no exception. "Aye, Kaileel, I swear," he said so softly only the High Priest could hear, and tears began to sparkle at the corner of his long lashes.

Tohre turned his face toward the King of Oceania. "Is this woman given freely to this man?"

Shaz raised his chin. He had also realized what the priest was trying to do and he sent Kaileel a look of spite. "Aye, she is given freely and without coercion."

An angry, grating sound came from behind the veil. "And I have accepted Prince Conar as my husband of my own free will, without coercion or duress." The husky voice turned softer. "He, I have chosen as my own. He and none other."

Spite darkened Kaileel Tohre's face as he held Conar's stare. Without taking his attention from the young Prince, he asked the final question that would seal Conar's fate. "Is there one among you who has reason to believe this Joining should not take place or that it would be invalid?"

Teal wanted to speak out. Legion wanted to cry out to the priest to stop. But neither man spoke.

When there was no answer from those assembled, Kaileel once more raised his hands, arms wide, palms down this time, and loudly proclaimed, "I declare this Joining can be made!"

Chapter Thirty Three

From his place in the far recesses of the Chancel, Legion watched as Kaileel Tohre sent daggers of hate toward the two young people standing before him. Even the slowest of wit could see how furious the High Priest was that the ceremony had not been stopped in some way. His thin body was quivering with rage.

Listening to the man chanting, only partially paying attention to his entreaties to Alel to give His blessing to the ceremony, Legion found himself looking at the girl standing beside his brother and wishing with all his heart that it was Liza who would be Joining with Conar this day.

Such thoughts, he knew, were dangerous. Not only to Conar, but to him, as well. A part of him had rejoiced at Conar's promise of betrothing Liza to him. He was too afraid to examine his love for the girl for he feared it would rival the love Conar had for her.

"You have come here to bear witness to this Joining," Kaileel said, breaking into Legion's thoughts. "Let those of you who see this ritual know: In the eyes of his god, through dispensation given to him by Tribunal Law, with the permission of his father and King, and the blessings of this woman's parents and sovereigns, in the presence of his peers, and at the jurisdiction of my hands given by authority as a prelate of the Brothers of the Wind, I declare His Royal Highness, Prince Conar Aleksandro McGregor, bound by laws both preternatural and temporal, to submit himself to this Joining." The High Priest's mouth eased into a leering grin of anticipation. "Disrobe him."

Legion saw Conar flinch. It was part of the ceremony, had been the reason Conar had left his tunic laces untied, but something other than proscribed ritual had made his brother start. He was staring at Kaileel Tohre with abject terror on his face.

"Are you well, my Prince?" Kaileel asked with concern, his smiling lips tight with malice.

"He's fine," Dyreil sneered as she stepped in front of her nephew. Her slender fingers went to the tincture of golden links around his waist and unhooked the heavy belt, handing it to Coron when the younger McGregor brother came to her side. She put her hands on the cuff bracelets and removed them as well, handing them to Dyllon.

As she reached up to draw the golden loop from Conar's earlobe, her eyes went to his face and she smiled, willing him to answer, but although his gaze held hers, the young man did not smile. His face was blank, and his lips, a thin, straight line. He blinked as the earring was removed, but showed no other emotion. Her smile wavered as she put her hands to either side of his neck and took hold of the heavy serpentine chain of the Wind Warrior necklace that dangled about his neck. Empress Dyreil gazed down at the top of his shining hair as he bent forward so she could remove the medallion. When he straightened and his eyes again locked with hers, she could see the sheen of tears in those blue depths. It hurt her deeply and she broke with tradition, standing on tiptoe to plant a light kiss on his cheek.

Conar's face twisted with pain. He wanted to bury his face in her shoulder, to sob, to wail, to do anything, say anything, that would stop this thing from happening. He tensed, opened his mouth to speak, but her soft words stopped him.

"Remember who you are, son," she told him, gently warning him that he was honor bound to go through with the ceremony.

Conar's lips closed. He felt her reassuring hand on his arm, squeezing softly in comfort, as she moved behind him once more. Then, he found his father in front of him. The King's face was devoid of expression.

Gerren put his hands on the front of his son's tunic and spread the laces further apart. He slid his fingers beneath the neck opening and pushed the soft material over his son's shoulders, down his arms and over his hips until it lay in a silken pool at his feet. He barely glanced at his youngest son as Dyllon bent down to retrieve the garment when Conar stepped out of it.

Looking at his son, the King saw the torture of this ordeal lurking behind lowered lashes. It cut him to the quick to view the pleading in those too bright orbs as Conar raised his eyes and fused his gaze with his father's. He looked away from the condemnation on his son's face and, as he did, he saw the thin strands of black braided silk around his son's right wrist.

No, not silk, he realized, but human hair! His mouth dropped open. Black human hair. His look flew to Conar's.

He held his father's shocked stare, daring him to touch the precious braid. The ritual called for him to be completely naked from the waist up, to be divested of all adornment since the marriage bracelet would have to be soldered around his arm and he could wear no other jewels until then. But this was no jewel, no adornment. No band of gold or silver or copper around his wrist. This was Liza's hair and he would not part with it. He stared back at his father, his King, with hot challenge.

Gerren saw the defiance emblazoned on his son's still face and knew if he so much as reached for the bracelet, Conar would end the ceremony then and there. With a slight shake of his head in admonishment, he reconciled himself to this impossible turn of events and stepped back.

Kaileel Tohre had not missed the exchange between father and son. He, too, had seen the bracelet and knew exactly what it was and to whom it belonged. He bit his tongue to keep from shouting at the King that it had to be removed. He ground his teeth, forcing himself to wait for the right moment to chastise Conar for breaking the law. His voice was almost pleasant as he commanded Conar to help his woman kneel.

Relieved that his father had not pressed the point, Conar didn't hesitate before offering his hand to the woman at his side. He barely glanced at her as she took his hand, but he couldn't help flinching at the coldness of her fingers as they nestled in his palm. With a mental shrug he reminded himself that toads were cold blooded anyway and was thankful her flesh wasn't slimy to the touch.

Conar kept his attention straight ahead, behind the altar where Kaileel stood. Kneeling beside his bride, he found his gaze locked with the fierce, avenging glare of the god Clere.

"This man and this woman now kneel before god and man in obedience to the wishes of Alel. Here, before god and man, they will pledge themselves only unto one another. One flesh, one inseparable entity, until the end of their lives."

Kaileel lowered his gaze to Conar's bleak face and a small smile of satisfaction touched his thin lips. Aye, my sweet Prince, he thought, for the rest of your miserable life. His voice was threaded with amusement as he looked up at those gathered and went on with the ritual.

Legion's attention was riveted to the woman at Conar's side. Her head was bowed as though she were at prayer and her slim right hand rested lightly on his brother's raised forearm, the fingers curving down over his flesh in a soft grip. Even from the distance at which he stood, Legion could see her thumb moving slowly on Conar's arm, stroking the side closest to her, and he knew his brother wasn't even aware the woman was caressing him.

Kaileel's unpleasant voice broke Legion's stare and he heard the words the man was saying, frowning as memories flooded his mind.

He saw the Blessed Waters of Purification sprinkled over them and thought back to that long gone day when he had thrown Conar into the pond near Lake Myria.

As the Oils of Chastity were marked upon their chests, he remembered the time when he and Conar were little and they had stolen some of the sacred oils from the Temple. They had set fire to their father's favorite chair in an effort to see if the consecrated oils would burn, for it was rumored they would not. The oil hadn't, but the chair had gone up in flames which also set fire to the carpet and drapes.

He couldn't help but smile as he thought of the spanking he had received from Hern while his brother was made to watch. Although Hern had not laid one finger on Conar, the little boy had seemed to feel every pass of the belt on his brother's bare behind.

Legion's wandering attention was brought back to the ceremony as Conar was handed a goblet containing the consecrated Wine of Union, signifying the heady blend of their two sexual natures, a reminder that they would henceforth partake of life's pleasures and sorrows together. He took a long draft of the heady wine and then passed it to his wife.

Custom during a true Serenian Joining Ritual would have had the groom hold the cup to his bride's lips, signifying his care of her and his subsequent protection. But since the woman at his side was heavily veiled, and would not raise the silver net from her face until the ceremony was complete, he allowed her to take it in her own hands and bring it under the veil to drink. She lifted the veil with the back of her left hand, moving the silver net only enough to accommodate the chalice. When she handed the wine cup back to Conar, the young Prince, according to tradition, drained the remaining wine signifying his right to all she possessed.

The memory of the day Teal stole the wine from the vintner near Dulwitch--the day they had all narrowly escaped capture--wiped the smile from Legion's face. Liza had been with them that day.

When his aunt and Queen Medea walked to opposite ends of the altar and took up votive cups to light the two side candles in the tall copper candelabrum, Legion tensed.

When he saw his brother rise and hold out his hand to the woman kneeling at his feet, when he saw the couple holding the candles their mothers had given them to the unlit candle in the middle of the candelabrum, Lord Legion A'Lex began to cry.

This one act alone was the most significant part of the Joining Ritual. It was the beginning of the end for Conar, and Legion could see how it was affecting his brother.

Two lives, two candles. One life, one candle. Fidelity and Chastity. There would be no others for either of them for the rest of their lives. Adultery brought with it a harsh punishment under Tribunal law.

Legion looked away from the couple, for he could not bear to see the carnage passing across his beloved brother's face as the third candle blazed to life. He walked to the far end of the sacristy where he leaned his forehead against the wall and wept. He did not see the single tear fall from Conar's face as he was forced to extinguish the candle he held in his trembling hand.

Kaileel rounded the altar and held up his hand for the two Kings to come forward. Another man, robed in the garments of the Royal Jeweler, also stepped forward with his assistant who carried on a black velvet pillow two circlets of banded gold, each flanged open so that they could be slipped onto the couples' arms with ease.

One bracelet bore the name and crest of the McGregor family and it was the bracelet the Princess Anya would wear from that day forward. The other bracelet bore only the Princess' name and the date of their Joining. It would be the band that would be placed on the young Prince.

"The outward sign of your union, your link to one another, your eternal reminder that you are now responsible to another for your actions, is the Band of Devotion that will be placed on each of you by your fathers. With this symbol, you will be joined for all time. Let all who witness the placement of these bands know: You are one to another, forever as one, never to be parted by anything, or anyone, under penalty of death."

Aye, Conar thought grimly. Either death by natural causes or, at least for his bride, the hangman's noose. As for himself, unfaithfulness would be rewarded by a heavy application of the lash to his bare back.

Gerren and Shaz took the bracelets offered them, walked to their children, and waited for their womenfolk to join them.

"As your mothers have held you safe from harm, nourishing you, cherishing you, teaching you, they will now hold your flesh as it is consecrated one to the other signifying the end of their guardianship of you and the transference of that right to your mate."

Dyreil and Medea stepped forward and Medea took her daughter's left arm, extending it and holding it away from Anya's body. She smiled at her husband as Shaz slipped the three-inch band of gold around his daughter's upper arm, placed it just above her elbow, and held the two pieces of the bracelet together tightly.

"As your fathers have held your lives together, providing for you, protecting you, seeing to your wise choice of a mate, they will now hold the two ends of your wedding bracelet together signifying their relinquishment of their obligation and placing it on the shoulders of your husband."

Conar stepped in behind his bride and had to force himself to bring up his hands to the woman's smooth shoulders. Ritual called for him to bring the woman against him, to brace her body with his chest, protect her, but his flesh crawled as he touched her, and it was all he could do to pull her to him. She smelled faintly of lavender and he inhaled the sweet, heady fragrance and his mouth hardened with distaste.

Kaileel turned as an acolyte stepped forward with a burning brazier pot hanging from a thick, wool-covered chain and held out the soldering wand to his master.

The glowing heat from the soldering wand was applied to the bracelet and held, melding the two ends together. There was a slight discomfort from the heat, but nothing unbearable. However, the young Princess could not stop the slight cry of pain as the soldering wand accidentally grazed her flesh as it was removed.

"I am sorry, Highness," Tohre said with feigned contrition, his gaze going to King Shaz.

Shaz was ignoring the priest. He was looking at Conar. "Outside of childbirth, this had better be the only pain my daughter will ever experience or suffer because of you, Conar!"

Conar barely heard the man. Although he found the ordeal and the marriage, itself, an abomination, his tender heart would not permit him to overlook pain caused in his behalf on another. He had firsthand knowledge of too much such agony in his lifetime. He bent his blond head to the woman and spoke softly over her shoulder. "Are you all right?" When she nodded, he asked again, "Are you sure?"

"Aye, Your Grace," she whispered. "I will be fine." She reached up to briefly pat his hand.

The Prince raised his head and the look he gave Tohre made the man take a step back.

Tohre's chin came up. "Kneel at your woman's feet so you may be bound to her," Kaileel sneered at his Prince, seething rage at Conar's look of warning turning the priest's face hard with revenge.

Conar stood there, staring intently at Tohre, hating him with every fiber in his being. His hands clenched into fists, a muscle jumped in his lean jaw, but he finally knelt, his legs spread wide as his bride placed herself behind him and put her icy hands on his flesh. He schooled himself not to flinch, not to let Tohre see how much the woman's touch bothered him. He shivered as she pulled him against her.

Dyreil came forward and brought up Conar's left arm, holding it against her hip to brace it as his father knelt beside him and slipped the wedding bracelet over his son's flesh.

Conar looked at his father. The King's eyes were misted, his lips trembled, but he held his son's gaze as the bracelet was soldered into place around the young man's flesh. Gerren knew his son felt the heat from the soldering wand, but he gave no outward sign that it hurt. Not even when Tohre held the wand in place far too long and the flesh around the bracelet began to turn red. Conar' lashes partially closed, his breathing stopped, but he didn't move.

Beneath her hands, the muscles of her husband's shoulders tensed, bunched and Anya felt a tremor go through him. Her grating voice from behind the veil was a hiss of warning as her hands tightened protectively on his flesh. "You are deliberately hurting him, Priest. Remove that wand. Now!"

King Gerren looked at the woman, struck with the possessive way she had spoken. His gaze went to Conar, and although there was pain and despair on Conar's face, there was something else. Admiration for the woman who had dared speak so to Kaileel Tohre.

The High Priest let his piercing glare settle on the woman's face behind the veil and he hissed back at her. "Do you presume to tell me my business, woman?"

"Aye, and I will presume even further. I will make you a promise, Tohre," she hissed, "if you ever lay hands to this man again to hurt him, you will answer to me!"

Conar's head snapped around and he stared at the woman whose hands were now painfully tight on his bare shoulders. Toad or not, his eyes glowed with respect. When he turned around, he found Kaileel's hot glower on him. The smile Conar gave him, one of pure delight, and the snorting laugh he added for insult, made Tohre snap off a long nail as he clenched his fist.

With his mouth a thin slit of rage, the priest stared at Conar and his words were filled with venom. "As this woman is now a part of you, and this man, a part of you, woman, so shall these bracelets be a part of you. As your wife and your husband may not be taken from you, so shall these bracelets never be removed. They are the symbols of eternal union blessed by the gods, sanctioned by Tribunal Law, acknowledged and accepted by your parents, witnessed by those gathered and placed by my own hands as a representative of Alel on this earth." His smile was evil as his voice lowered and the words became a seductive, insinuating caress. "Conar McGregor, you are bound to this woman for the rest of your life."

King Gerren cringed at the words, still another deviation from proscribed ritual. He watched as the smile on Conar's face slid away.

It was over, Legion thought. Done. Finished. No turning back.

Ever.

Conar was this woman's mate for life. The look on the young man's face told everybody that he thought it a pronouncement of eternal misery.

Tohre turned his fierce regard to the woman at Conar's side. "Anya Elizabeth Wynth, you will be the only woman for this man for as long as you live."

Legion shuddered. The two were now legally wed.

The King helped his son to rise and walked behind him and his bride. Now was the time for the unveiling. He glanced at his sister, Dyreil, and tried to smile.

Conar's thoughts were no longer on what was happening around him. His thoughts were far, far away in the big brass bed at Ivor Keep. He glanced briefly at his father's worried face as the King took his place at Conar's right side, could almost feel the anticipation flooding the room, but it no longer mattered.

Nothing mattered.

Not the smoldering pain along his left elbow, nor the blazing nag in his heart.

Not what his bride looked like beneath that infernal veil, nor what she was.

Not all the miserable years of unhappiness he saw before him.

Nothing would ever matter again.

He stepped back as Tohre advanced, waiting for the priest to lift the woman's veil, but when Tohre bent toward him and spoke, Conar's head jerked up and he stared at the High Priest. "Why now?" he asked.

"Do you wish for me to have my men escort you?"

"What is it?" the King inquired, stepping forward. "What's wrong?"

"Nothing is wrong, Highness," Kaileel assured him. "I must speak to our Prince privately regarding a matter that has come to my attention. There is no need for anyone else to be privy to personal matters regarding the royal family."

"What personal matters?" Gerren snarled. "He went through everything today at the Temple."

"With all due respect, Highness"--Tohre bowed--"it is a delicate matter between your son and the Temple."

Conar flinched. He looked at Tohre and he saw the warning in the man's thin face. He wanted to refuse, but fear, old and well-remembered, well-taught, shot through him and he lowered his head, nodding. "It's all right, Papa. I'll go with him."

"Conar, no!" the voice came hissing through the thick veil, but Conar didn't hear it. He followed Kaileel from the altar through the archway and into the sacristy. He vaguely heard the mumbles coming from those assembled guests, but paid no attention.

Kaileel led him out of sight of the wedding party and those assembled. He stopped, turned, and reached inside his robes to bring out a curved, jewel-handled dagger.

Conar's face stilled, then became infused with hate and fear. His arm still stung from the soldering wand. He had known Kaileel would hurt him, had expected it. It was why he had schooled himself not to show the pain when it came. Looking at the blade, he almost wished the insane fool would come at him with it. He would have enjoyed turning the man's own weapon against him and ridding himself of Tohre once and for all.

They stared at one another: Tohre with smug satisfaction; Conar with wariness and loathing. Neither spoke, but they were as aware of the other's feelings as if they were carrying on a conversation.

"Your carefree days are over, aren't they, sweet Prince?" Tohre cooed to him.

"What do you want, Tohre?" Conar asked, unable to bear looking at the man much longer.

A smile of pure malice touched Tohre's bloodless lips. His gaze lowered, and then moved up to Conar's and fused. "Give me your wrist."

Blazing fury entered Conar's face and he took a slight, protective step backwards, his gaze immediately lowering to the same place Kaileel's had--the black braided hair bracelet on his right wrist. He protectively covered his wrist with his other hand. Slowly, very slowly, the Prince's eyes came up to Tohre's. "No." It was a soft, quiet, and decisive denial.

"You knew better," Kaileel told him. "I let you save face before the wedding guests, but I demand you give me your wrist. Now, Conar." His voice was pleasant, charming as though he were reprimanding a slightly stubborn child.

"No." A single, firm, blunt reply.

"The King bows before the power of the Temple, Conar. Our word is law. When we speak, Kings obey. You will obey, Sweet Princeling." He held out his free hand. "You will obey me!"

"No!" A sharp, bitter snap of anger, bitten out from teeth grinding so hard it was audible.

Tohre quirked a brow at his Prince. "Give me your wrist, Conar. I will not tell you again."

Conar stepped as close to the High Priest as his lurching belly would allow. "And I told you no!" His jaw clenched into a hard, unforgiving line. "Why now, Kaileel? You must have seen the bracelet when I was disrobed. Why do this now?" He could barely speak for his rage.

"Conar," Kaileel said with exasperation, "I don't believe you want me to have my Temple Guards take hold of you and force you to your knees in order for me to cut that whore's filth from your flesh!" He saw Conar start. "Aye, my fine Princeling, I know of her. I know all there is to know of her, and because of her, and your illicit lusting after her, I will gladly call forth my men and have them drag you to the very steps of the altar for all to see me do this to you." His smile turned evil as the pits of hell. "If that is your wish."

Conar jerked his head away, tearing his sight from that hated smug and vile face. "I won't let you do it, Tohre. I won't."

"If you want to bring shame to your father, and yourself, bring shame to the McGregor name in front of all these witnesses, then so be it! But I will promise you this. If you force me to such an action, I will humiliate you before I am through with you, Conar." Tohre's voice was oily smooth. "Far worse than I ever have before."

Kaileel willed the young man to look to him and was not surprised that he obeyed. He held the prince's desperate stare and smiled. He took in Conar's bleak eyes, and knew the young man was being pushed to the edge of endurance.

Tohre's push became a vicious shove.

"How do you think your father will react to what I can tell him about you?" He cocked his head to one side. "Shall I introduce him to the friends you made at the Monastery, Conar?

"You would do that, wouldn't you?" Conar whispered.

Kaileel smiled. "With the greatest of pleasure, my Prince."

Conar lowered his head. "You enjoy hurting me, don't you, Kaileel?"

"Aye, sweet child, and you know why."

Conar flinched. He wasn't used to begging for anything, from anyone. It galled him to do so, especially with this man, but he looked into Tohre's waiting face and pleaded with the High Priest.

"Kaileel, please. Let me keep it. It's all I have left of her. What harm is it doing?"

True glee spread over Tohre's face. It did his black heart good to hear his greatest of enemies' agony. To hear Conar begging him as a man instead of a boy. It brought back fond memories. It made him glad he was able to dash all hope, to destroy that part of Conar McGregor that was willfully holding on to the last dregs of a happiness Tohre meant to see him live without.

"You need no reminders of your past indiscretions, Conar. You are bound to that woman in there. You are hers, now, and not that whore's." He held out his hand once more, the wicked, curved nails spiraling upward.

For a long time Conar held Kaileel's stare. He saw his own shame written there and he knew it would humiliate his father and aunt if he had to be forced to his knees in front of their friends, and there was no doubt in his mind that Kaileel would do just as he threatened. There would be no stopping the evil man once he began.

Through the grasp of his fingers over the braided silk, Conar could feel the warmth of Liza, could feel the silk of her hair and body, could feel the heart inside his chest aching, he caressed the black braid, squeezed it one last time. His hopes and dreams and future dissolved before him. There would be nothing left.

Painfully, agonizingly, he withdrew the protection of his fingers from his wrist. His eyes lowered beneath the sweep of his tawny brows and he looked at the black silk of Liza's hair for the last time. He sighed, his pain too great to bear.

Slowly, reluctantly, sorrowfully, he held out his arm to Tohre, flinching as the priest's hand shot out to grip his forearm in a steely clutch. The sight of the long, curving, red-tipped nails made him ill and he cast his sight to the recesses of the sacristy where Legion stood, a look of uncertainty on his bearded face.

"No!" Tohre commanded, snatching viciously on the young man's arm. "You look at me, Conar!" He tugged again. "I will see your face when I do this!"

The young Prince shook his head, unable to look at Tohre.

"Aye, Conar!" Tohre snarled, tightening his grip even more. "You will!"

"No," came the weak, whispered reply. "I can't."

"You can and you will!" Tohre's grip turned malicious on Conar's arm, the long nails gouging into his flesh. "Or else I shall have you taken before the altar for this to be done."

Kaileel felt a degree of supreme gratification when Conar reluctantly turned his gaze to him.

"Don't you ever get tired of this game, Kaileel?"

"You are mine, Conar." The thin lips parted. "And you always will be." A hateful smirk appeared on the lean face. "You will never truly belong to another on this side of hell!"

"Get on with it," Conar mumbled, his heart breaking, his soul bleak and barren of hope.

"Then, you keep your eyes on me. I want to see your reaction when I take away the last link you have with your past." Tohre smirked.

"No, you want to see me hurt, Kaileel. Call it what it is." Conar's words were broken, filled with suffering.

"Aye, you are right. There has never been any need for lies between us." Tohre's hand caressed Conar's forearm. "We understand one another."

The dagger slipped none too gently under the braid and slashed upward, severing the only tie Conar had left to the woman he loved.

* * * *

Legion had warned Conar to remove it when they were leaving the steaming chamber. Now it had been cut from him in a way meant to humble him. Watching his brother's shoulders sag, Legion could almost feel his despair.

Conar's eldest brother pushed away from the wall and took a few steps toward the two men. They were staring at one another, speaking in low tones he couldn't hear, and he wondered what the High Priest could be saying that would cause such fury on Conar's face, what could be so horrible that it would cause such a reaction. Wanting to help his brother, but not daring to interfere for fear of bringing further punishment down on Conar's head, Legion remained where he was.

\* \* \* \*

"It is past time you remembered who I am, Conar," Tohre reminded his Prince as he dropped the silken braid into the pocket of his robe. "I am the Master; you, my sweet Princeling, are the servant. I command; you obey."

His young eyes turned old as sin as Conar narrowed them at the High Priest. With a growl of hate, he leaned close and spat on the floor at Tohre's feet. "Go fuck yourself, Kaileel," Conar ground out, wiping his hand across his lips.

Tohre smiled and the smile was vicious and teasing as Conar turned away, his hands clenched into fists, not even waiting for the evil man to follow him as he stalked through the Chancel to his new bride.

Conar glanced at Legion as Tohre took his place in front of the altar and wondered if Legion had realized what had happened. From the pity on his brother's face, he knew he had.

"It is time for the unveiling," Tohre called, drawing the attention of those who had been whispering about the exchange between the young Prince and the High Priest.

Everyone present was exceedingly interested in what the young bride looked like. Speculation had been rampant concerning her deformities and those who had gathered were now sitting forward on their chairs to get a good look.

"No!" Medea shouted as Tohre reached for her daughter's veil.

The people jerked with surprise. All heads turned to her.

The Oceanian Queen walked to the High Priest and looked at him with authority. "It is the custom of our people that only the husband of the bride may see her unveiled on her wedding night, and only then in the privacy of their bridal chamber."

"What?" the elderly noble sitting next to Teal asked. "What did she say?"

"That is not our custom," Tohre snapped.

"My husband and I have adhered to your rituals, even brought the wedding here to your country, but in this we are adamant. No Oceanian bride is unveiled until after her groom has seen her."

"That isn't true," Dyllon's wife said as she leaned over to whisper to her husband. "I've been to several Oceanian weddings and not once has the bride not been unveiled at the ritual."

Dyllon shrugged. "If The Toad looks as bad as Conar suspects, it's just as well he doesn't unveil her here."

"Aye," Coron agreed as he leaned across his wife to speak with his brother. "I don't think he'd like to have our guests see what he really thought of the woman."

"Well, that may very well be the reason her mother doesn't want her unveiled," Coron's wife reminded them. "Perhaps she is concerned for Conar."

"One thing's for sure," Dyllon replied, "I'm gonna gods-be-damned well postpone our leaving until I see her!"

Kaileel turned to the bride. "Madame? Is this your desire, as well?"

"Leave it up to His Grace," came a grating whisper through the veil. "If he wants me unveiled here, then I shall allow it."

"Daughter!" her mother gasped, looking to Conar. "Not now!"

The young Prince could feel Tohre's expectant stare on him, but he refused to look at the bastard. "It matters not to me. If that is what the lady wants, then it shall be so." He could feel his wife's gaze on him and he turned his head and looked down at her. "I can wait if that is your wish."

"It is, Your Grace," she whispered.

"Then it shall be as you wish."

Kaileel was vastly disappointed. He had wanted to see the look of horror on the young man's face when he viewed his hideous, lifelong mate for the first time. "This is a break from our traditions--"

"As if you had not broken with our traditions," Conar interrupted. "I am Prince Regent, Tohre, and as such, I have granted my wife her wish. You must abide by my decision."

If looks could have killed, Kaileel Tohre's glower would have struck Conar down in agony. The man's thin lips turned prim and hard and his chin lifted as he looked down his thin nose.

"As you wish, my Prince." Tohre turned to the assemblage. "I present to you His Royal Highness Prince Conar Aleksandro McGregor of Serenia, and his bride, Her Royal Highness Princess Anya Elizabeth McGregor!"

The people stood, applauding as the couple began their walk down the ermine pathway. Anya's hand rested on Conar's right forearm, his left hand covering her fingers as was tradition.

If anyone noticed the scowling frown on the groom's face, they took no notice. Their attention was glued to the perfectly formed and voluptuous body of the woman limping beside him, wondering at what lay beneath the thick silver netting.

Conar met Teal's look as he passed and he smiled at his friend. It didn't matter any more if he was happy or sad about what had just taken place. It was a moot point. He was shackled to The Toad. He would need friends like du Mer to keep him sane and help him make the most of it.

Law said he had to live with the bitch, to mate with her, get children from her; but it didn't say he had to spend every waking hour with her. In fact, he planned on staying as far away from her as he could legally and morally afford to do, without being censured by his father or the

Tribunal. Once he had her belly big with child, he would have nine months of near freedom until it was time to fill her up again.

The thought of turning this lovely body beside him into a baby-making factory put a smile so sinister and so threatening on the young Prince's face people were stunned by it.

Teal didn't like the look he was seeing. He particularly didn't like that smile. He had seen that smile several times before and it usually boded ill for whoever had caused it. Glancing at the woman on Conar's arm, there was no doubt who the culprit was this time.

Thom Loure caught the young Princess' head turned his way as she walked past him. His thick, bushy black brows shot up as she dipped her head in greeting. He glanced at Storm and Marsh. "Did you see that?" he asked with amazement. "She acknowledged me!"

Marsh snorted. "She's probably as ugly as you, Loure, and like loves like."

"She can't be that ugly!" Storm chuckled.

Hern's angry voice hushed them. "Keep a civil tongue in your mouth, Edan! And that goes for you, too, Jale! That is your future Queen you malign!"

Conar could feel his wrist burning where the braid had been cut away, but he knew the priest had not so much as scratched his flesh. His wife's hand was near the place where Liza's braid had been for nearly a year. He glanced down, loss making his eyes turn harder still. He didn't look at the woman who limped beside him, but he measured his long stride to hers so that her disability would be less noticeable to those who lined the pathway into the narthex.

He slowed his pace as two Temple Guards hurried forward to throw wide the doors leading to the outside. He felt a cold blast of frigid air on his naked chest and shivered, feeling the woman's hand tighten on his arm.

"Don't let them keep us long in the courtyard, Your Grace," she whispered. "You will catch your death in this weather."

Conar frowned. Did the froglet think him incapable of knowing when he was cold? He glared at her as she tipped back her head and seemed to be looking him in the eye. "I do not intend to freeze my arse off out there, Madame, you can be sure of that, if nothing else!"

A long sigh came from the veil and the woman turned her head.

The people of Boreas were hovered around burning pots of pitch, shivered under flaming torches, rubbed their hands over the flames of burning candles. Some had come from as far away as Ionary to see the royal Joining of the two greatest royal households. Many had spent days on the road, slept in inns and under wagons, in hay mounds and in stables, to be at this ceremony. Some had even camped out in the soldier's compound so they would be here this night. Their cheers were excited and anxious as the couple came under the archway of the Temple and poised on the top step.

Taking a deep breath, Conar took his new wife's arm and held it up so the people could see her marriage bracelet. There was neither inflection in his voice nor expression on his handsome face as he introduced her to them. "I give you the Princess Anya Elizabeth McGregor!" he said, and wished he could give her to them. He sure as hell didn't want her or know what to do with her.

Loud cheering and applause greeted their new mistress, but so did side glances and whispers concerning the reason why she still wore her veil.

Conar saw pity for him and could not bear it. He held his head higher and brought his wife's fingers to his lips, planting the softest of kisses on her chilled hand.

"You are wondering why the lady is still veiled," he said, his voice carrying, for not a single sound was heard in the courtyard. Every ear was cocked to his words. "It is the custom of her family that only I may see her unveiled this night. She has asked me to abide by that custom and, reluctantly, I have."

From the corner of his eye, he saw her head tilt up to him once more. He ignored her. "If you will be here tomorrow morn, I shall be delighted to present my wife to you," he said through grinding teeth. He felt her stiffen beside him and an imp of malice brought a wicked gleam to his eyes. "She is as anxious as you are for you to see her."

A soft, husky whisper came to him from behind the veil and, with a look of vengeance, he bent his head to her. His face turned red, and he straightened up, squinting his white-hot irritation down at her. He had expected her to balk at the public unveiling, but that didn't matter. He was her husband now and he would carry her kicking and screaming to these very steps if need be, for when he made a promise to his people, he kept it.

But what she had said to him had not been a chastisement, no denial of what he had told his people, no refusal to be unveiled in public. Instead, she had turned the tables on his vicious, childish prank.

He turned to the crowd, his eyes flashing dangerously. "My lady-wife has reminded me 'tis already morn." He glanced at her. "If you will be here by noon?"--he saw her nod in agreement--"Then we will take off this stupid veil!"

Laughter rang out over the courtyard and behind him as his father tittered nervously and his aunt chuckled. He sent them a damning look and turned around. He felt his Lady-wife tug on his arm and snapped down his head, glowering at her.

"What, now?" he growled, put out with her husky, irritating voice. She tugged again and he lowered his head. "What?" he hissed.

She whispered to him and then nodded toward the far doors leading into the Banqueting Hall.

"She's got you on a leash, now, Your Grace!" a merry voice called from the crowd.

"She'll keep him right warm, I reckon!" another said with a chuckle.

"I know I would," some woman said and the crowd roared.

"You sure we should come at all tomorrow, Highness?" one of his Elite asked.

Conar's people were as used to teasing him as he was to teasing them. His wicked sense of humor and roving eye, his grand good luck with the fairer sex, had made him somewhat of a legend in Serenia, and even beyond Serenia's borders. It was the customary thing, this teasing, the remarks, the innuendoes; but the remarks tonight both angered and embarrassed Conar. His jaw went tight with fury and his face flamed in humiliation. Not that he cared a whit what the bitchlet at his side felt. The comments about chains and leashes hit too close to his already festering sense of imprisonment. He was about to make an angry retort when the woman at his side tugged sharply on his arm and spoke to him in an anxious, warning voice.

"They love you well, Your Grace. Let them not see how hateful you find this marriage."

Shock went through him at the woman's perception. He felt her hand lightly squeeze his arm. "I find their comments unwholesome, Madame!" he said.

"It is natural for them to tease you, for you have always encouraged it, Your Grace. Let them have their joy this night. Noon will give them more to jest about, I assure you." Her head dipped and he had to strain to hear the rest of what she said. "Please do not embarrass me this night, I beg you."

He let out a harsh sigh. "I had no intention of embarrassing you, woman."

"I know full well your intent, Your Grace," she replied softly, and with head held high, she let go his arm and limped forward, heedless if he followed or not.

Conar ground his teeth and stepped quickly to her side. He snatched up her hand, placed it on his forearm, and covered her fingers with his left hand, anchoring them to his cold flesh. "You will walk with me, Madame!"

Beneath the veil, the lady smiled wickedly. "As you wish, Your Grace."

Chapter Thirty Four

Weddings were not commonplace in the palace at Boreas. The only other Joining to have been performed there in over thirty years had been that of Conar's mother and father.

Neither Coron's nor Dyllon's Joining had occurred in Serenia, but in their Lady-wives' homelands since it was unlikely either young Prince would take the throne at the Court of the Wind.

Relatives from both sides of the royal families had assembled in the Great Hall along with visitors from the Principalities of Chale, Ionary, and Virago. A few hardy travelers had made the trek with the Emperor and Empress of Chrystallus and would be returning later that next day without her. Crossing the mountains in wintertime was not a trek many of them cared to make, and the snow had begun to fall heavily about the Great Palace of the Winds as the wedding meal started.

Hardy applause rang out as Conar entered the hall with his new bride. They walked amidst nods of greeting and the occasional wish for a good and long marriage.

Conar's face was closed and set as he walked past the smiling faces wishing him well. He let go of his wife's hand as soon as was decently acceptable. His hand closed about the filled wine goblet and he raised his it to make the traditional toast to his bride.

"My people," he said through clenched teeth, "I present my lady-wife, Princess Anya." He brought the goblet to his lips to wash down the unpleasant words he had been forced to speak.

"Long life and gentle births to Princess Anya!" Gerren saluted.

"To Princess Anya!" the crowd roared.

The voice of the bride's father rang out. "Long life and many sons to Prince Conar!"

"To Prince Conar!" the crowd agreed.

Conar held his wineglass out to the steward for a refill as soon as his new bride was seated at the table. "Keep it coming," he told the man.

"Milord?"

Conar looked around as Gezelle came to his side and laid a brightly wrapped package before him. "What is it?"

Gezelle could not look at him, nor could she look to the woman at his side. Her face was downcast, her fingers nervous as she twisted them at her waist. "It is a present from your bride, Milord." She didn't wait for him to give her leave before turning and fleeing, her sobs drifting behind her.

"What's wrong with you, 'Zelle?" he called after her.

"I fear her behavior may be my fault, Milord," his bride said.

He turned to look at her. "In what way?"

The answer from the veil was low and soft and filled with contrition. "I made the mistake of greeting her yesterday, Your Grace," came the sad confession. "I fear I have frightened her badly." There was deep apology in the words.

"Did she see you without the veil?" he asked, his forehead wrinkled.

"Aye, she did." The Princess' hand clutched the table edge until the knuckles bled of color. "I did not intend to cause her any...."

"Leave Gezelle alone," Conar interrupted. "She is under my protection. Is that clear?"

"Perfectly clear."

Conar felt a hand on his shoulder. He looked up to see Legion.

"Aren't you going to open the present your lady-wife brought to you from her homeland?" Legion asked.

Conar exhaled a long breath. "Aye," he agreed. He picked up the gift and removed the gold foil lid, pushing aside the fine tissue paper.

Legion smiled at the Princess but at Conar's "aah" of surprise, he glanced at what his brother was withdrawing from the box. In his hands, Conar held a tunic of the palest lavender, hand-stitched with silver thread, embroidered with a deep purple silk.

"I hope it is the right size, Your Grace," Conar's bride told him in her smoky whisper. "I wasn't sure."

Legion looked at the woman and realized there had been love, recognizable love, in her tone as she had spoken.

"Look at the work involved in that," Coron said to Dyllon.

"Conar!" his father called. "Hold it up so everyone can see!"

Conar glanced at his father and then stood, bringing the tunic up for the scrutiny of the wedding party. He heard the immediate patter of approving hands and sat back down, staring at the tunic in rapt wonder.

"I wasn't sure what color you would like, but with your coloring, I thought a pastel shade would suit." The grating whisper turned soft. "Do you have a shirt of this color?"

Conar turned his face to her and shook his head.

"Lavender is his favorite color," Dyllon remarked.

"Do you like it, then?" she asked, looking up at Legion as though for his approval as well.

"Very much, Your Grace," Legion assured her.

Conar looked down at the tunic. It was a delight to behold. Despite his dislike of the woman sitting beside him, Conar could find nothing wrong with the tunic. It was well-crafted and bore the effort of many hours of meticulous work and careful stitching.

"Conar?" Legion prompted, "your lady-wife has asked if you like her present."

"She embroidered it herself," Queen Medea informed him. "It took her over a year."

Gazing at the tunic with wonder, Conar touched the beautiful width of one silver leaf with the tip of his finger. He seemed to remember the woman at his side and looked down at her.

"You did this?" She nodded and he turned his head slightly to one side. "For me?" Again she nodded. He gave her a long look. "Thank you, Milady."

"You are most welcome, Milord," she whispered.

For over an hour Conar said nothing else nor did he eat the food placed before him. He simply continued to drink. His left hand toyed with his fork while his right rested on his upraised knee as he leaned back in his chair. Now and again, he would look at his new wife, but when she would turn to look inquiringly at him, he would look away.

"Have you a request, Your Grace?" one of the musicians called to him.

Conar started to shake his head, but stopped, thought a moment, and then his lips lifted with a grin. He looked straight at his new bride and answered the man. "Do you know the ballad, 'The Prince's Lost Lady'?"

The men began to play before King Gerren could object. He sent daggers of spite at his son, who smiled maliciously at him down the length of the table.

"A lovely song, Your Grace," the lady at his side commented as the balladeer sang in a rich baritone.

Conar turned the grin to his new bride. "Every Prince has his lost love. Did you know that?" He raised his goblet of wine to her in salute. "I have one."

"And where is this lady, now?"

"Gone. She left because of you," he said sorrowfully. He sent her a damning look. "She left because of *you*. Do you understand?"

The Princess folded her hands in her lap, and in a prim, clipped voice, she assured him, "I understand you better than you think, Milord."

Queen Medea and Empress Dyreil came down the table with graceful strides, their shoulders back, their faces stern and filled with reprimand as they glanced at Conar in passing.

"Come, daughter," Medea said. "It is time."

Conar frowned. "Time for what?"

A frosty glare down her nose was the only answer Conar received from Medea.

His aunt, on the other hand, answered him with a rather glacial snap to her usually warm voice. "To prepare your lady for bed, Conar." Dyreil looked around. "Legion, you, and Teal come see to your baby brother."

"I don't need any help getting myself to bed," Conar stated.

"Aye, but you do," his aunt said. She motioned Legion to pull Conar's chair out.

"Easy does it," Legion said, reaching out to steady Conar when the prince staggered. "I think you've had entirely too much wine, baby brother."

"Not enough to numb me," Conar mumbled. He was finding it hard to put one foot ahead of the other and he walked between Legion and Teal.

Dyreil held the door open for the men as they escorted Conar into his chambers. Queen Medea and her daughter stood beside the bathing room door as Gezelle folded back the covers on the huge oak bed.

"Lord Legion, his robe is on the chair," Medea told them. "Please strip him and see that he puts it on." Her mouth was tight with fury.

Legion glanced at the Queen as she motioned her daughter into the bathing chamber to give the men privacy to carry out her wishes.

"I can undress myself!" Conar muttered as his brother and friend deposited him on the edge of his bed.

"I would wager you can't," his aunt snapped and shooed Gezelle out of the room ahead of her, speaking over her shoulder as she closed the door. "Get him undressed, Legion. Don't let the fool try to do it on his own. He's liable to hurt himself."

"Don't need any help," Conar grumbled.

* * * *

Medea jumped as a resounding crash, followed by an equally resounding curse, accompanied the shutting of the bedchamber door. The tinkle of breaking glass made the Queen shake her head.

"Your new husband will have a lot to answer for, daughter," she snapped as she turned the young woman around to unbutton her bridal gown.

"I wonder what they're doing to him," Anya said, worried, as another expressive curse echoed through the door.

"Probably mauling him," Medea tittered, "and with good cause."

After helping her daughter out of her bridal gown, the Oceanian queen opened the bathing chamber door and stuck her head out. "Is he dressed?" she inquired.

"Almost, Your Highness," Teal answered for Legion who was trying to tie the belt on Conar's robe. "Will you stand still?" Teal asked with rancor and looked to Legion for help.

"I'm not going to touch the little bastard again!" Legion snarled.

"I'm no bastard!" Conar snapped. "You're the bastard, one among many my father got off one of his whores!"

Conar was so drunk he didn't see the look of intense hurt cross his brother's startled face. Not once in his entire life had Conar ever said such a thing to Legion. He had taken great pains not to, even when they were little and fighting and name-calling as brothers will. The humiliated look on Legion's face didn't register, nor did the deep wounded pride in the older man's eyes.

"He doesn't know what he's saying, Legion," Teal defended.

"Oh, but he does," was the stiff reply. "He knows perfectly well what he's saying."

"And he will apologize for having said it," the Princess said as she came into the room behind her mother.

## Chapter Thirty Five

Both men looked to her and stilled, their eyes going wide. She was gowned in a pale peach silk shift that accentuated the lush curves her bridal gown had only hinted at. Her face was hidden behind a matching net of thick gauze, but her hair now hung free and it was as blue-black as her mother's and hung well past her waist. Her tiny feet were bare, the delicate toes peeking from beneath the gown.

A faint scent of lavender drifted from her and, as she put out a slim arm to show her mother the broken pier glass in the corner, neither man could see what difference it would make if her face was the ugliest in the land. Her body certainly wasn't.

"How did that happen?" Medea asked, frowning at the broken glass.

"He stumbled into it," Legion answered. "He's had too much to drink, Your Grace. Ordinarily, he wouldn't be so--"

Medea put up a restraining hand. "My daughter understands how it is with him, Lord A'Lex. I think it is time we left the two of them alone." She took each man by the arm to propel them from the room.

Legion took one last look at his brother. "Perhaps you should just let him sleep it off," Legion suggested.

"I think not," the Princess said. "He is overdue for a set down, Lord Legion."

Legion frowned. He wasn't sure tonight was a good time to talk to Conar about anything. He seemed to be ignoring the woman standing next to him, her hands on her hips, her foot tapping out a dangerous rhythm on the carpet, instead of falling asleep as he should have from so much wine consumption.

"Why not wait to speak with him? He'll be in a better frame of mind tomorrow," Legion said, smiling.

"If he lives through the night, Lord Legion," she whispered in her grating voice.

Legion let the smile slip from his lips and turned cold and hard. "He is dearly loved, Madame. There are many who would take exception to the words you speak, even if they are in jest."

"Who said I was jesting, Sir?"

He stared at her, feeling her mother dragging on his arm. Not being able to see her face, to judge her eyes, he wasn't sure of her state of mind. For all he knew, the woman could be insane. Conar might well be in danger from the bitch. He politely shook his arm free of the Queen's hold.

"Perhaps I didn't make myself clear, Your Grace. If anything, anything at all, happens to my brother, you will have me to deal with." He heard her mother's gasp of outrage, but it didn't matter. He kept his eyes on his brother's new wife.

For a moment the young woman didn't speak, but then her words were low and deceptively polite. "Even after the insults he has thrust at you, you would defend him?"

"With my last breath, Madame."

"I see. And am I to take it you would actually do me harm should I harm him?"

Medea started to speak, but her daughter stopped her. The Queen snapped her mouth shut with a hiss of angry breath.

Legion nodded. "I would."

Stillness entered the room, but then the Princess laughed and her laugh was genuine, full of delight. Her voice cracked as she answered Legion's threat.

"If anything happens to your poggleheaded brother this night, Lord Legion, it will be at his own hands. Not mine. You have nothing to fear on that account. I love your brother dearly."

"You don't know my brother, Madame."

She turned her head to one side and regarded him. "Oh, I wouldn't be so sure, Milord."

"Come, Sirs," Medea insisted. "Let them be alone." She took Legion's arm and pulled hard enough to make him stumble into the hall. She shoved Teal out to join him. "Out, please."

Legion opened his mouth to protest, but the Queen stabbed him with a flint-like glare. "They will work it out between them." She stood just inside the doorway, blocking the men's reentry.

Just before the door closed, Legion saw the Princess lifting the edge of her veil. He could see her neck, slim and straight, smooth and creamy; her chin, flawless, slightly pointed, and he craned his neck to see more as the veil moved upwards, but the Queen slammed the door behind him.

Legion was about to knock, to demand the Queen open the door, when his brother's voice stopped him dead in his tracks. His hand froze in midair; his eyes widened; and the hair on his neck rose.

Teal grabbed Legion's arm to steady himself.

The last thing they heard was Conar's agonized shout through the oak portal. "Oh, Sweet merciful Alel! I'm gonna be sick!"

## Chapter Thirty Six

As his new bride began to lift her veil, Conar had tensed, his stomach heaving with all the wine and brandy he had consumed prior to and after the Joining. He had waited for the horror he knew lay beneath the thick peach-colored net, but as the veil cleared the lady's chin and he could see the tip of her nose, a violent wave of nausea surged up to his throat at a gallop. He turned, shouting out the words--words meant to ward off the bitch, words that had so upset Teal and Legion--and scrambled off the bed and dropped to his knees, frantically reaching for the porcelain chamber pot. Retching horribly, he lost the contents of his stomach into the gleaming white glare of the vessel. He was totally unaware of the furious young woman who glared at him with lethal intent.

Watching her new husband as he crouched over the pot, hugging it fiercely to him, relieving the sour bile that now permeated the room with a noxious stench, the young woman's face filled with the unholy light of battle.

"Do you wish for me to stay?" her mother asked.

The Princess silently shook her head, too angry to trust her tongue. She didn't look her mother's way as the door to the bedchamber closed silently behind the Queen.

Conar reached up, and behind him, to grab hold of the mattress to keep the room from spinning so crazily. Everything was tilting and he felt as though he were going to slide down the floor and splat against the far wall. His eyes were squeezed tightly closed. He swallowed and tasted the bitter acid of bile. He licked his lips, grimacing. "Water," he croaked, not even sure if she had heard his feeble cry. "Madame, please. I need water."

Her face stretched into a purely evil mask of revenge. "As you wish, Your Grace," she said sweetly.

Spinning on her heel, she made straight for the bathing chambers, just off Conar's room, and slammed the door hard against the wall as she entered. She heard him gasp in pain and her grin widened even more. Furiously looking around, she jerked open the door to the armoire and after pushing aside linens, oils, soaps and towels, she found what she was looking for. The spare chamber pot.

Bending over the copper tub filled with her used bath water, already turning cold and clammy, the top coated with soap scum, she dipped the chamber pot in the water, filling it to the brim. Slowly she made her way back to the bedchamber, careful not to slosh the soapy mess on the floor.

He heard her angry purr, a hiss of seething air, but he didn't pay heed to it. He was hurting too badly, his head throbbing like a million horse's hooves inside his brain. Her voice when she began to speak to him likewise set off a million iron gongs in his head and he winced in pain.

"Call me a toad, will you? Send another man to do your dirty work, eh? Get yourself drunk on our wedding night? Insult your own brother?" Her voice was shrill with disgust and anger as she threw the contents of the chamber pot into his face. "There's your water, Your Grace!"

The force of the water hit him like a rock. His eyelids flew open and he sputtered, shaking his head to fling the water from his sopping hair. A bad mistake, he realized, for his world went careening off into a multitude of directions.

"Oh, god!" he gasped then snorted, trying to dislodge the water from his nostrils, for his head had been thrown back along the edge of the bed.

"I hope you drown!" she screeched.

He tried to focus on her, but his vision was still doubling and tripling, the room, and her, skipping away from his view. What little he could see of her was a vision of a wild-haired harridan bent on killing him before he could bed her.

"Damn you, woman!" he shouted, immediately regretting the volume of his shout. "Damn you to the everlasting pit," he whispered fiercely as he brought up his hands to wipe at his streaming face. "You infernal tadpole!"

Turning himself over, mumbling what he intended to do to the bitch who had tried to drown him, he grabbed at the bed and tried several times to pull himself from the floor before actually being able to do so. At last, he heaved himself onto the edge of the bed and then wiggled his way like a child to the very center. Gasping, for it had cost him much in the effort, he lay clutching the bed covers as though his very life depended on his ability to keep himself from falling off the mattress.

"You insensitive lout! You insufferable, arrogant ass!" she named him.

His head throbbed unmercifully with each of her harsh words. "Peace, woman!" he whispered, blinding pain tearing through his body. "Peace!"

"Peace, hell!" she shouted.

"I am in pain."

"Good!" Her footsteps as she neared the bed were like the giant footfalls of a hell-wrought demon.

"Let me die in peace."

"You'll not die."

"My belly is--"

"I hope your belly is cramping like a woman in hard labor! I hope your head is thundering like the sound of an erupting volcano! I hope you wretch up everything you've ever drank in your entire life!" She put out her foot and set the bed to shaking beneath him.

"God!" he moaned and scrunched his face deeper into the covers to keep from retching again. His fingers dug into the coverlet, dragging it closer to his head. "Don't do that!"

"I hope your father has you cast into the deepest dungeon Boreas has to offer! I hope your aunt disowns you! I hope your friends ostracize you! I hope your people make you a laughingstock all over the Seven Kingdoms! I hope your brother never speaks to you again!" She shook the bed again.

"No," he moaned feebly into the covers.

"Don't you tell me no! I hope you live long enough to regret humiliating me in public!" Her hands clenched into fists as she placed them on her hips. "Of all the godawful things for you to have done to me! And in public, too! To get drunk on our ... my wedding night! I hope your intestines rot! I hope your head explodes! I hope you drown in your own puke! I hope ... I hope ... I hope....." She couldn't seem to think of the right word to say.

"I hope you're finished," he mumbled from beneath the covers he had now pulled over his head.

"Finished? *Finished*?" Behind him he heard the angry swish of silk as the bitch leaned over him. "I haven't even begun!"

Conar wished with all his might that the gods would take pity on him and strike the bitch speechless, if not entirely dead. He wished he could sink into the bed and be swallowed up so he could die in silence. He hurt all the way from the ends of his hair to the tips of his toenails and he was convinced he could feel those parts of him as they grew, shafts of hair and horny plates squealing as they erupted from his body.

"Woman, go away. My head is pounding like a--"

"I hope your head is splitting, Conar McGregor! I hope your belly turns inside out! If you ever, ever, get this drunk again, 'twill be the very last time you ever see me!"

"Then get yourself gone," he gasped as she kicked the bed once more. His fingers dug into the coverlet with renewed strength. "Get as far away from me as you can!"

"You will pay for this, Conar! I swear it by all that is holy. You will pay for your actions this eve!" She leaned over him and braced herself, shaking the bed with mighty pushes.

"Damn it, woman! Cease!" He drew into a fetal position and pushed his face as hard as he could into the mattress. "You're making me sicker!"

"I'm not kidding, Conar! If you dare do this again, I will leave you and never come back!"

"Then leave, damn it!" he gasped, his voice a mumble. "Leave and never, ever come back!"

"Oh, I don't think you'd like that, Conar McGregor!"

"Woman, it is my fondest wish!"

"Truly?" The grating whisper, the shrill drag was gone. "Who'd torture you if I left, you ego-inflated churl?" She shook the bed, her sensuous voice tight with reprimand. "Who'd save your hide from the were-tigers, then?"

Despite his agony, Conar's head popped up, shock, and disbelief stunning him. He knew that voice! Were-tigers? He thought with a gasp. His mouth dropped open and his face drained of what little color it had. With his eyes wide as saucers, he slowly turned to stare at the woman who was scampering onto the bed as she spoke.

"You're a pig, Conar McGregor. You're a slug. A slimy, slithering slug. Toads eat slugs, you know." She leaned over him and fixed him with an evil grin. "Shall I eat you, Milord?" She flicked out her tongue with a slurp and drew it back into her mouth, smacking her lips as if in great delight. "Shall I make lunch of you, dearling?"

"Liza?" he croaked feebly, unable to believe what he was seeing.

"And you had better pay heed to me, Conar McGregor. If you dare to ever humiliate me so again, I shall leave you and never come back." She folded her arms across her breasts and plopped down to sit beside him, her legs crossed under her.

"Liza!" he cried and grabbed her, dragging her down to his chest. He showered kisses on her face, her neck, and her shoulders. His arms were so tight around her body, she could barely breathe and was trying to push him away, but he was so overjoyed to see her, he didn't notice.

"You're suffocating me, Conar!" she protested, pushing at his shoulders. "And stop it. I'm mad at you! How can I curse you when you're doing that?"

He leaned back, a smile of wondrous joy on his face, swept his hungry gaze over her beautiful face then suddenly turned pale as realization set in.

"What are you doing here?" he asked. His head was aching as much as his heart was beginning to. His love was here. But where the hell was The Toad?

"I got rid of her."

With sudden, dawning suspicion, he grasped her arm. "Where is she, Liza?" He pushed himself up, disregarding his throbbing head. "What have you done with the Toad?"

"Who, Milord?" she said, her voice lowering in a warning he didn't hear.

Mumbling incoherently, he managed to scramble to his knees. He took her upper arms in his hands and shook her, despite the vomit that threatened to erupt from his throat.

"Where did you put The Toad?"

A strange light entered Liza's face and a slow, angelic, innocent smile spread over her lovely lips. "She's gone, Milord. Gone forever." Her voice was like a sweet caress.

"Gone? Gone where, Liza?"

"Out of your life, Milord. Aren't you pleased?"

"Oh, my god!" His eyes widened even more. "Papa will have my hide. Her papa will have my...." He shuddered. "Oh, sweet Merciful Alel!"

"You said you would rather have me than her, didn't you, Milord?" She grinned. "Well, here I am!"

"They'll kill me, Liza!" He screeched and regretted doing so, for he grabbed his head and moaned.

With a pout, Liza told him, "I said she was gone, Milord. You'll not be bothered by The Toad again." She giggled as he slowly raised his head.

"You killed her, didn't you?" He thought of the magic-saying in the dungeon at Norus, remembered the man she had killed at the Hound and Stag and the were-tiger she had dispatched with such ease and he shivered. "Liza?"

When she only smiled at him, one dark brow raised, he thought he understood. "You did, didn't you? You killed the bitch!"

"Let's just say I sent her on her way." Her smile puckered into a sensuous challenge. "Aren't you happy I am here instead of some ugly toadlet?"

"This is serious, Liza!" he shouted, wincing even as he did. He thrust his hand through his hair, tugging at the golden mass. "Can you bring her back?" He looked at her with a hopeful expression.

"I don't know...." She pretended to think.

"Bring her back, Liza! Bring her back, now! Bring the bitch back before they find out she's missing." He watched her face fall as though she had a terrible secret. His voice was barely a whisper. "You can bring her back, can't you?"

She looked away. "Well, I don't think I can, Milord."

Conar groaned. "You've killed her."

"Not exactly."

"What does that mean? Not exactly?" he shouted, flinching at the agony in his head.

"Well, you did tell me you didn't want to marry the beastlet, didn't you? You said if it weren't for her, you'd marry me. Isn't that what you said? So I sent her on her way and took her place. If I wear the veil all the time, as she does, and limp, as she does, no one will know it's me and not her!" She laughed and clapped her hands. "Aren't I clever, Conar?" She pushed her knees into the bed and began to bobble up and down.

Conar felt the bile rapidly rushing up his throat. The motion was playing hell with his battered belly. "Liza, stop it!"

She couldn't. The more she looked at the wretched man who crouched beside her, the more she bobbled. The more she bobbled, the more she laughed. The more she laughed, the more the bed shook. The more the bed shook, the more he begged her to stop. The more he begged her to stop, the less inclined she was to do so.

"Have pity on me, Liza! If you have ever loved me, have pity on me now and stop!"

"You dimwitted sot," she said lovingly, caressing his bare shoulder where the robe had fallen away. "You well deserve this, but I can't let you go on suffering."

She scooted off the bed and rummaged through her things until she found the green powder she knew would cure him. Giggling as she filled a tumbler with cool water from the pitcher on his night table, she poured in the powder and mixed it with her finger. She stuck her finger in her mouth and sucked away the wetness, grimacing at the taste.

Conar turned over on his back, his head hanging off the side, his hands covering his face.

"Here, my love," Liza said softly. She put her hand under his neck and gently raised his head to bring the elixir to his dry lips. " Drink it all down. Do you remember the taste? I sent it to you a few hours ago." She smiled as he gulped. "Well, actually The Toad sent it to you."

Curling his body into a tight knot, he clutched the pillow to him and flung it over his face, shutting out the light that was now flooding his chamber, for dawn had come at last.

"Thank you," he mumbled through the pillow.

"Even toads have some worth, Milord."

He pulled one corner of the pillow from his face and stared at her. "Who are you, Liza?"

She smiled, pulling the pillow from his face. She tweaked his nose. "Know you not your own wife, Milord?"

"You are The Toad?" he asked in wonder. "Truly?"

"Truly!"

He grinned, despite his pain. "My Toad?"

She laughed, caressing his cheek with her palm. "Yours and yours alone."

"Anya Elizabeth?"

"Liza is a nickname for Elizabeth, Milord. I was surprised you never realized that."

"Mine," he said softly. "You are truly mine."

"For all time, Milord."

"Mine." He smiled. "My Toad."

It was a short, flat statement and it was the last thing he said before he passed out.

Liza looked at him and shook her head. In sleep he always looked like a small boy, smiling to himself, his hands tucked under his chin.

She bent to plant a feather-soft kiss on his cheek. "Aye, Conar. Yours and yours alone." She kissed his nose. "Sleep well, my love," she cooed and touched his smiling lips with one fingertip.

Lying beside him, she watched him until sleep closed her own eyes and she slipped into dreams.

## Chapter Thirty Seven

Liza awakened slowly and looked into the calm, peaceful, loving face of the man who lay beside her. She smiled and he answered the smile. "Are you feeling better, Milord?" she asked, snuggling into the arm he opened to receive her. Her head went to his naked shoulder.

"I have never felt better." He touched her forehead with his lips. His lips moved to her ear. "Tis our wedding morn, my love."

"Aye, so it is."

"And the vows must be consummated, mustn't they?" he said, running his tongue along her ear.

Liza sucked in her breath as he captured her ear lobe with his teeth. "I suppose they must."

"And the sheets examined for … ah … the signs of the seal," he reminded her.

"I've a dagger on the dressing table, Milord." She giggled. "Your thigh or mine?"

Conar lifted his head and looked at her. "I suppose the sacrificial blood should be my own."

"I believe I can make it worth the offering, Milord."

"You do?"

She grinned. "I'm gods-be-damned sure I can."

Conar lifted up just enough to tear the unbelted robe from his body. He tossed it away, then put his hands on the bodice of her gown. He cocked one golden brow.

"If you must," Liza sighed.

"I must." His grin was evil. "By the gods, I must or I will explode, wench!"

The ripping of the silk gown was all the impetus either needed. He shredded the gown, tossed it aside and his hands were all over her-- touching, stroking, kneading, and lightly pinching. His lips locked onto her nipples and he suckled like a starving man as her hands roamed the thick waves of his hair.

Liza's arms went around his neck, his hands went under her bottom, and she brought her legs up around his waist as he hefted her against him. He pushed her against the wall and slanted his mouth across hers, their tongues dueling like gladiators of old. He ground himself against her and when she squeezed her legs together, he spun around and carried her to the bed, falling with her, digging his knees into the mattress to scoot them up farther in the bed. He rolled with her until she was above him and he lifted his head and captured her breast in his mouth. He drew on her nipples then flipped her over again, sliding over her, his knees pushing her thighs as far apart as he could open them. With one deft movement he was slithering down her body until his lips were on her sex and he was pulling on her clit, his tongue stabbing between her folds to lap at her juices. Two fingers went inside her waiting hot sheath, his thumb went into her anus, and Liza nearly vaulted from the bed. He had to clamp his free hand on her arm to keep her still as he used his fingers to penetrate her and his tongue and teeth to torture the swollen nub of her clitoris.

"Conar, damn it!" she hissed, trying to draw him up and over her. "I need you!"

The Prince of Serenia gave an evil, satisfied laugh and snatched his hands from her wetness. Ignoring her grunt of frustration, he was up and over her, his hands hooked under her thighs as he lifted her. In the flicker of an eye, Conar's ladylove was impaled on his thrusting shaft.

"Conar!" she cried out as he began rocking against her, slamming his body into hers, shaking the bed beneath the onslaught.

Her hands wrapped around his upper arms and she arched up to meet him thrust for thrust. What followed was an orgy of pleasure that left them both exhausted and asleep in each other's arms.

* * * *

"And are you happy with your Toad?" Her smile widened as she nestled into the warmth of his side.

He shrugged his unhampered shoulder. "Fairly well content with my Toad."

She looked up at him. "Only fairly well, Milord?"

Conar moved so that he hovered over her, his body barely touching hers as he braced himself on his elbows and knees. "As content as any man with a woman who plays the game by her own set of rules and neglects to warn him." He blew a stray wisp of hair from her cheek.

Liza's nose crinkled. "Faith, Milord!" she gasped. "Have a care! Your breath could scorch the quills from a porcupine!" She tried to shove him off, but he wouldn't budge. She saw his grin turn into a lecherous smirk.

"And whose fault is that?" He scooped her up in his arms and flipped over to his back, pulling her over him, holding her above him, her body stretched full length along his own. He shook his head in wonder. "First you get me mad; then you get me drunk; then you have me manhandled up here and stripped of my clothing; then you torture me as I lay dying in agony. I would venture to say my breath should be the least of your worries, Madame."

Liza's face held an innocent look. "I didn't make you mad, Milord. I didn't get you drunk. Your aunt had you brought upstairs and my mother had you stripped."

"But you tortured me by shaking the gods-be-damned bed!"

"True, but well you deserved it."

" 'Twas not the first time you've tortured me, Liza," he said in a soft voice.

"When did I hurt you?"

"When you left me. All the times you left me, but the last was the worst. Why? Why did you let me hurt so?"

"You sent another man to find out about me, Conar. You didn't come yourself; you sent Rayle. When time passed and you never came to meet me, my parents sent a spy here to ask questions and what they learned made them angry. They almost broke the contract because, in believing what Rayle told you about me, you had questioned my parent's honor."

"In what way?" He was puzzled by her remark.

"Papa was furious with you. I overheard him telling Mama that if I had been born with some horrible defect, he would have broken the contract then because it would not have been fair to you. But instead of asking him or my mother, you took Rayle's word without finding out for yourself, and in doing so, you made it seem as though my parents were trying to lie. Papa is one of the most honest men I know and you questioned that honesty."

"So, why didn't he just send a messenger telling me nothing was wrong with you? Why let me go on believing the worst?"

"They thought you deserved to suffer," she said with a sober smile.

"And you? What did you think?" His forehead crinkled with worry.

"It took all my begging and pleading and threatening to persuade them that I understood your reluctance to marry a woman you thought handicapped." She lowered her gaze. "I would not have wanted to marry you if I thought you were in a like way." She looked at him again. "They said you were a pompous, arrogant fool who did not deserve to know the truth. Papa was all for marrying me to another."

"Brelan Saur?" Conar sneered. His face hardened.

Liza grinned. "Someone told you?"

"So, why didn't he break the contract?" Conar asked, ignoring her question.

Liza shook her head. "I made a bargain, and a bet, with him. Papa loves to gamble and I wagered I could get to know the real Conar McGregor, not the high-and-mighty heir to the throne of Serenia, not the arrogant, egotistical man who had said such wicked things about me, but the man beneath that cold heart and exterior. He bet me I couldn't." She shrugged. "You see who won."

"That's when you came looking for me?"

"That's when I started following you all over Serenia," she replied. "I was never far from you when you were out and about."

"I've always thought of myself as a vigilant man but I wasn't aware I was being followed and watched," he said with a frown. "That doesn't say much about my warrior abilities, does it?"

"You were preoccupied with what you were doing," she replied. "It only means you are single minded in purpose although that isn't always a good thing, I'll admit."

"What do you mean?" he asked.

"That day at the Hound and Stag, you were so smug, so self-righteous. You were so cynical and condemning of women in genera, so determined my entire gender was out to make your life unbearable. That's a single mindedness I could well do without! I decided not to tell you who I was. I don't think you would have believed me, anyway." Her hand curled around his neck. "You seemed so distant and angry, but beneath all that, I saw something I don't think anyone else ever had. A terrible, terrible loneliness. I was determined to have you love me." Her free hand began to stroke the hair on his chest. "I wanted you to know the real Anya Elizabeth, not the Princess, nor your betrothed, nor the woman you thought deformed in some way, but the real woman, the woman who had fallen in love with you years ago."

"You're joking!" he grinned, his brows shooting up. "When was this? When you realized my reputation as a stud was so well-deserved?" He wagged his brows.

Liza looked at him with exasperation. "You conceited oaf!" She laughed. "No it was the first time I ever saw you, when I came with my brother Grice and Brelan Saur to a fair near Corinth."

His forehead wrinkled as he tried to remember. He shook his head.

"It was the summer festival there. Do you remember Grice winning one of the du Mer stallions? It was a big roan? You even joked about the stallion, telling Grice he was one of Seayearner's cousins and Grice decided to name him Sea Star?"

Conar's eyes lit. "I do remember! That was the day me and Grice and the baker's daughter--" He stopped, his face turning beet red.

"Aye, that day!" Liza giggled.

"But I don't remember you," he said, hoping she hadn't been a witness to what he and her brother had done with the baker's voluptuous daughter.

"Brelan kept me occupied while you two were enjoying the other pleasures of the festival." She laughed.

"Then we didn't actually meet?" He wanted to get her away from thoughts of the baker's daughter and Brelan Saur.

"Oh, but we did."

"When?"

"I was your second when you and Prince Chase Montyne had your little discussion on the jousting field."

"That was you?" he gasped, staring at her, remembering the slim boy who had gazed up at him with such moonstruck eyes. He had even made a rude, hateful, and extremely vulgar remark to the boy, telling him to find another of his own kind to ogle.

"You thought I was a boy and that was what Grice and Brelan wanted you to think."

"But you couldn't have been more than--"

"I was twelve, Milord. And I thought you were the handsomest boy I had ever seen. And so did every other female at the festival."

He shook his head. "And because of that, you fell in love with me?"

"No," she answered quickly. "It was an added incentive, but it was what you did that endeared you to me."

"What I did?" He couldn't remember doing anything out of the ordinary that day, except maybe with the baker's daughter, and he didn't think that would have endeared him to her.

"There was a little girl who was lost from her mother. Do you remember her?" When he shook his head, she added, "You took her up on your shoulders and walked all over the crowd until you found her mother, who was getting frantic trying to find the child. When you put down the little girl and the mother hugged her so fiercely, you smiled, and there was a sheen of tears in your eyes, Milord, when you told the woman no child should ever be separated from its mother. It was then I knew I loved you."

"Her name was Katie," he said, his memory returning.

"That you could remember her name after so many years is a wonder." Liza smiled, a catch in her voice.

"Not really. Her mother came here to work. Katie is one of the chambermaids here, as well." There was no way he could tell her that Katie, that little lost ten-year-old girl from so many years before, was now the mother of Tia, one of his children.

"When we finally met as man and woman, Milord, it was at the Hound and Stag. Your attitude surprised me. I was amazed that you would marry, sight unseen, without regard to your own personal happiness. Even though you were being forced to marry, I had always assumed you would try to find a way to break the contract." She grinned. "Not that I would have allowed that. I wasn't prepared for the man I found that day. I was stunned that you would honor a woman you found detestable. I was touched by your faithfulness to the Princess Anya Elizabeth when you defended her to me at Norus."

"But you set out to seduce me anyway," he reminded her.

"Aye, but it was my own husband I was seducing."

His hand came up to tangle in her thick tresses. "How did you know that Conar, the man, would love, Liza, the woman?"

She smiled against his chest. "I simply gave him the chance, Milord. How could you not? We were destined to belong to one another."

His hand stilled in her hair. "I tried not to love you. I didn't want to."

"I know, but you didn't count on Liza's tenacity, Milord." She gazed at him through her lowered lashes. "Or her willpower. I have yet to want something that I could not find a way to get."

He laughed a deep rumble in his wide chest. "And you decided you wanted me? Despite my churlishness and cynical outlook."

She raised her head and looked at him, her face serious. "Over the years I had watched you, I had seen such deep hurt in your eyes, Milord. I had seen pain so deep that you thought you had it buried, but I could see it. I could feel it. You needed me and I wanted you to need me. I refused to let what some other woman had done in the past cost me your love and affection for the future. If you could love Liza, you could love your wife, for they were two sides of the same coin. You just didn't know that."

"Maybe if I had known...."

"Would you have believed me if I had told you who I really was?" She cocked a brow at his uneasy look. "I didn't think so. That was why I never told you."

"And all the postponements? Why were there so many postponements even after you knew I had fallen in love with you?" There was a dull ache in his heart as he realized all the months of pain could have been avoided.

"The postponements were not our doing, Milord. It was the Oracle who set the wedding date, not me. Why, I don't know, but I can make a fairly good guess."

His brow rose in question.

"She was testing how well you truly did love me. There is an old saying in my homeland. What is gained without effort is lost without thought; but what is gained through difficulty, is kept with care."

His palm cupped her cheek. "Never doubt how much I love you, Liza. I will keep our love safe even with my last breath. That, I will promise you."

"And I shall promise you this, Milord. Never again will I ever be the cause of your hurt." She touched his lips with her fingertips. "Never again."

His eyes searched hers and he knew she meant what she said, but the ways of the gods and Their ladies are fickle and "never" was a word he knew not to trust.

"Do you doubt my love for you?" she asked, misunderstanding the look.

"Never."

"Then what brings such confusion to you, Milord?"

"Do your friends call you Liza?" he asked, changing the subject.

She giggled. "Aye. I guess Rayle didn't find that out."

"And that godawful veil?" He grinned at her impish expression.

"A rather bad case of pimples," she said, ducking her head in embarrassment.

"And you said I was vain. What about the limp?"

"My lady's maid, Liza? You've met her?"

"Aye, I've had the misfortune."

"She's not all that bad!" She giggled at his hard expression.

"She doesn't care for your husband," he said with rancor.

"She doesn't know you."

"The limp?" he insisted.

"You're going to laugh," she warned, not really sure if he would or not. She chewed on her lip, gazing at him from under her lashes.

"Go on."

"Well, Liza has a limp."

"I know." His face was stern.

"The day Rayle came in search of me, he saw Liza with my parents, not me." At his look of disbelief, she hurried on. "I didn't want to go to that street bizarre so Liza took my place. She wore my veil. Did you know she can talk just like me when she wants to?" His warning look made her smile waver. "Anyway, I told my parents--well I didn't tell them, Liza told them--that I had taken a nasty spill off my nag and that was why I was limping."

He tried to glower, but her grin turned his resolve to mush. He shook his head at her prank. "And they never suspected it wasn't you?"

"We did it all the time when I was younger. When Papa finally did catch us at it, he thought it quite funny, although he would never have admitted it. Liza impersonated me a lot while I was following you and then later out gallivanting with you and your men, Milord. Papa was even the one to suggest it so no one would suspect that Prince Conar's light-o'-love and the Princess Anya Elizabeth were one and the same. But they didn't know it was her that day Rayle came searching me out."

"Rayle heard your parents telling you not to remove your veil in public because you might cause a stampede. What was all that about?" He wasn't about to let her off the hook so easily.

Her lower lip thrust out in a pout. "They were teasing me, or rather Liza without knowing it. I was so sensitive about my face with all those ugly red blotches, I didn't want anyone to see me that way."

"Don't you ever accuse me of being conceited again," he said sternly.

"Are you angry that I played by my own set of rules, Conar?"

He chuckled. "No, but I am angry you kept up the pretense even after you had come to marry me."

"I caught you glaring at me those times we crossed each other's paths, Milord. You didn't even deign to speak to me but once, and even then rancor filled your voice. My pride would not allow me to go to you. I was rather annoyed."

"So you sought to punish me, eh?" He put his fingers on her chin and raised her face to his. "What would you have done if I had come looking for you in Oceania?" He grinned. "Or had broken the engagement?"

"I would have brought the heavens down about your ears if you had tried! As for the other, if you had come looking in the first place, none of this would have happened. And we would not have enjoyed our year of play, either."

He tugged on her chin. "You're lucky you didn't get with child."

"I was careful, Milord." She rolled off him and swung her legs over the side of the bed. "But when the time is right, I shall conceive your child. I shall have many of your children, Milord."

"The ones I already have are yours. You made sure of that." Her face turned to his and he could see the smug smile of victory on her pretty features.

"I told you long ago you should not be made to give up your children. What is yours is mine. I will see to them, Milord. With Wyn's help, of course." She laughed. "That boy is assuredly your son!"

"And most assuredly your conquest!" he teased, running his hand down her back. "He is very sensitive about his illegitimacy. You have made him feel worthy and that is something even I have been unable to do." He saw her face tighten with sadness. "What is it?"

She put her fingers on his cheek. "I was thinking of the bridal dinner, that's all."

"If you're thinking about my surliness and the drinking...."

She shushed him as her fingers moved to his lips. "You more than made up for that before when you had the musician's play, 'The Prince's Lost Lady.' Since my parent's knew all along how you'd react when you found out what was behind the veil, they were more shocked than angry by your behavior, but your father--" She wagged a finger at him. "You owe him an apology. It was what you did to Legion that hurt me."

"Legion?" He pushed himself up, his face crinkled with worry. "What did I do to him?"

"You don't remember?" she asked and when he shook his head, she touched his cheek. "Well, for one thing, you called him a bastardly by-blow."

He stared at her with horror. "Oh, Liza, no!"

"I could have slapped you silly, Conar." She got up, plucked his discarded robe from the floor, and put it on. She walked to the window and threw back the curtain to let in the morning light.

He turned at her gasp of shock and saw she was staring down into the courtyard, a look of pure horror on her face. He was on his feet in a second. "What's wrong?"

"You told our people you would present me at noon." There was hopelessness in her voice.

"So?"

"Conar! By the sundial it is nearing four in the afternoon!"

"What?" He came quickly to the window and, standing to one side to hide his nakedness, looked into the courtyard to see every available space of grass and gravel covered with people.

She stared at him. "They've been there for hours!"

"Quick!" he said, scooping up her veil and throwing it to her, "put that on." His eyes swept over her possessively. "Along with some clothes."

He didn't give her a chance to reply before he was rummaging through his armoire, tossing clothes left and right in his haste to find something, anything to wear.

She watched his clothes being flung and a vengeful light came into the green depths.

"That is a habit you will cease, Milord!" she murmured as she slipped into her bridal gown, stepping on Conar's discarded clothing to get to her slippers. "Come button me up," she said, clucking her tongue as she saw him trample a freshly ironed shirt.

"Hurry, Liza!" he said, his fingers flying through her buttons. "We don't have all day."

She started to put on her veil but stopped to watch him hopping about on one foot as he drew on a boot. She had to dig her nails into her palms to keep from screaming at him. His boot heels were making little half-moon tattoos on clean shirts scattered all over his floor. She winced as he kicked a pair of breeches into the bathing chamber, craning her neck to see them land in the scummy bath water.

"Liza! Hurry up!" he pleaded. "They'll think we've killed one another!" He hurried to the door and flung open the portal with a crash.

Liza looked away from the breeches that were disappearing beneath the grayish water.

"The day isn't over yet," she mumbled, sidestepping the mess he had made of their room.


## Chapter Thirty Eight


The courtyard was filled with as many people as could fit into it. Some were standing under the protection of the covered walkways, some hovered near the burning cans of pitch that had been hastily brought out when the time had dragged on. Men slapped their arms around themselves; women huddled deep into their shawls and woolen coats; children wrapped themselves within the folds of their mother's skirts. There were those who peeked out from the confines of blankets, shivered under the overhangs of the keep's high crenellatedlated walls, leaned out of windows, sat on tree branches.

Legion and Teal stood side by side with Thom, Storm Jale, and Marsh Edan. The men had tightly pulled their military great capes around them, but white plumes of steamy breath eased from them, giving evidence that they, too, were being chilled by the clear, wintry blast of icy December air flowing through the open courtyard.

For once Teal did not have a humorous look on his dimpled face and Thom's beady eyes were not intent. Storm was unusually quiet; Marsh was unusually talkative. Legion was sulking, his anger at Conar still festering with hurt.

Coron had waited to see his new sister-in-law. He stood with his wife held tightly against his chest to protect her from the cold. Dyllon sat on a stone lion at the base of the steps leading up to the portico. His feet dangled over the statue's ears. The young Prince was hunched down in his wool parka, the collar up over his ears. He cupped his hands and blew into them, then thrust them once more inside the pockets of his parka.

The Emperor and Empress of Chrystallus were stamping their feet in an effort to get warm and King Gerren was flanked by Dyllon's young, bored wife, Princess Grace, and Sir Hern. Gerren's scowl left no doubt in anyone's mind as to his displeasure. King Shaz and his lady-wife stood only a few feet from the main steps.

Gezelle, her green eyes blank and filled with speculation, kept staring up at the window of the Prince's room. She had seen what no others in the courtyard had--the Prince and Princess staring down into the courtyard. She knew it would be only a matter of moments before the couple came to greet those gathered. She cast a side look at the servant girl, Liza, and timidly smiled.

There was no answering smile on the other girl's face. Instead, a hard, brittle glower of dislike hovered over the Oceanian's lips before the girl deliberately looked away.

Galen and Kaileel Tohre stood side by side on the gallery that ran across the front of the Wind Temple. Both men sipped on hot mugs of spicy ale and stood close beside a burning brazier that had been brought out to keep them warm.

Hern leaned against the lion statue opposite the one on which Dyllon sat. His arms were folded across his wide chest and there was a look on his face that few, if any, men had ever seen. One of uncertainty. He chewed on his lower lip. He was edgy, nervous, confused and his scowling face was not a sight many wished to look long upon.

As the couple came onto the steps of the main keep, the buzzing talk, stamping feet and moaning hisses of very cold people stopped.

Liza's hand rested on Conar's arm as he stopped at the top of the steps. His hand covered her fingers, patting them reassuringly as she squeezed his arm. She glanced up to one of the covered walkway canopies and then she nudged her husband. She heard Conar grunt with surprise.

Scattered along the hastily swept canopy, dotting the wooden structure from one end to the other, their legs dangling over the side, were what she knew must be all of her husband's love-children. Their little cheeks and noses were red with cold and they were all huddled in such a way it looked as though they had been glued together. She saw their little faces break into wide grins because he had noticed them. She brought up her free hand and waved to them, grinning behind her veil when she heard them giggle as they returned her wave.

"Ready?" Conar asked.

"Aye, Milord."

His face became grave and he cleared his throat. He felt his wife's fingers tightening under his own and knew she was sending him encouragement and strength. He took a deep breath and then let it out in a rush.

"My people, I have something to say to you before I remove Her Grace's veil. First, I wish to apologize for keeping you waiting, but the lady and I had much to discuss."

A nervous titter went through the crowd.

"Second, I wish to apologize for my conduct over these last few days. It was deplorable and I can offer no excuse except for that of being a mindless drunk who was feeling sorry for himself. If I offended any of you, I offer my most sincere apology and ask your forgiveness.

"I dishonored this lady. I dishonored my father and King, my relatives, this lady's parents. I behaved like a spoiled child who had been denied what he coveted and could not have." He brought Liza's fingers to his lips and planted a light kiss on them. "I have asked this lady for her pardon and she was gracious enough to grant it. Now I ask my father's pardon, as well." He turned to the King. "Majesty, I shamed you and I would understand if you could not find it in your heart to forgive me. I dishonored the name of our fathers and there is no excuse I can give for that."

Gerren raised his chin. "It is your lady-wife and her kin who must be the ones to grant you absolution. It is she to whom you have done the most damage. If she has forgiven you, then so must I forgive you, but I will hear her say it in my presence!"

Conar held his father's stony stare for a moment and then sighed, realizing his King would see him humbled for his behavior of the night before even if his father would forgive him. He squeezed Liza's fingers, lowered himself to his knees, and knelt on the cold steps at his wife's feet. He touched his forehead to her fingertips, raised his head, and looked up at her veiled face.

"Before all those gathered here, Milady, I beg your forgiveness."

Liza spoke in as clear and carrying a voice as she could muster. "You have it, Milord."

Conar came to his feet and faced his wife's parents. "You, better than any others here, know why I behaved as I did. Can you forgive me for my actions?"

King Shaz glanced at his wife, saw her tiny, fleeting smile, and turned a grave face to his new son-in-law. "As long," he said with authority, "as you will promise to honor our daughter from this day forward and seek no others before her, we shall grant you pardon, Prince Conar."

Legion and Teal exchanged a quick look.

Conar smiled. "I will gladly promise you that, Highness."

"Then you have our forgiveness," Medea told him.

The Prince's blue eyes wandered the crowd until he found Legion's stony face. His older brother stared back at him with heat. Legion's stare never wavered from Conar, but the lean jaw jumped where a muscle ground. Conar could feel the disappointment in his brother's rigid form. He raised his head a fraction more and put true contrition into his words.

"If you can find it in your heart to forgive me, I would be most grateful, brother. What I said was inexcusable and I am deeply sorry for having insulted you last eve. Can you, will you forgive me?"

Legion's heart welled with tears. He couldn't speak. He couldn't move. All he could do was nod and that cost him, for a tear rolled slowly down his cheek. He, more than any man, knew what an effort it was for Conar to humble himself in front of these people.

"If there are any others among you whom I have offended or shamed, I humbly beg your pardon. It will not happen again."

King Gerren felt Hern's hand on his shoulder and he relaxed. Maybe it would be all right, after all.

"My people," Conar continued, "I have told this lady I will protect her, defend her, and keep her safe, for she has given me something no other woman could." He stepped in front of her and took the edge of the veil in his hands. "She has given me unconditional love."

Everywhere heads turned, necks craned, bodies shifted to get a better look at the young Prince and his veiled wife.

"This woman's name is Anya Elizabeth, but I don't like that name. I never have," he spoke over his shoulder, "so we'll have to find another name to call her." Lifting the veil, Conar blocked everyone's view with his broad back and raised arms as he pushed Liza's veil over her head and looked down into her smiling face.

He stepped back so the crowd could see her. "I will call her Liza."

An audible gasp went through the crowd. Whatever they had been expecting, it was certainly not this!

The afternoon sun shone on her blue-black hair as it tumbled down her back and shoulders. Her deep green eyes were sparkling with tears, but were alive and bright with warmth. Her pretty rose-tinted lips were lifted in a sweet, happy smile that melted nearly every heart in the courtyard.

Here was no ogress! No toad! Here was a stunning beauty whose breath-taking face matched the promise of the slim, curvaceous body they had seen the evening before. Here was the stuff of legends. Here was the Sea-Lady come to Join with the Wind-Prince! Here was the siren about whom sonnets would be written and songs sung for centuries. This was the woman of whom the ancients had spoken. Here was Serenia's Glory!

Conar looked to Legion and Teal and Thom who stood with their mouths open, not believing what they were seeing. "Legion! Teal du Mer! Won't you come forward and welcome my lady-wife?" Conar called to them, watching Legion flinch, laughing at his brother's shocked expression. Never once had he ever seen Legion speechless.

He looked into the frosty, furious gaze of his twin. A slow, cruel smile touched Conar's lips. "What about you, Galen? You, who have met my lost love. You, who vowed to find the lady and wed her yourself. Won't you come down and greet your new sister-in-law?"

Galen looked as though he had been kicked in the stomach. This was the woman he loved. This was the woman he had wanted. Seeing his brother with her, knowing they were truly wed, brought a pain deeper than anything he had ever known.

Conar laughed, hugging Liza to him before swooping down and claiming her lips in a kiss that brought a gasp of stunned surprise to the crowd. Silence stretched out as the Prince's full lips played seductively over the Princess', as their two bodies molded together as though a flash of intense heat had locked them together.

Galen whimpered, a heartsick groan, as he turned away, fleeing the sight, running from the gallery as fast as he could.

Conar released her lips and faced the crowd, though did not relinquish his hold on his wife.

Liza looked to the crowd and smiled. Her voice--soft and sweet-- carried to the outer reaches of the courtyard. "To bring the stag to ground, you must first get his attention. And Conar's attention was hard to capture, but I managed to do so well enough. If it wanders again, I'll tack his head to the Great Hall's collection!"

"And this is the woman who could." Conar laughed. "Her hand on a crossbow rivals mine." He grinned, his face smug and content. "What think you of the Prince's Lost Lady?" Conar called.

A gasp ran through the crowd and then pandemonium broke out. The people finally understood what he had said and their cheers were deafening, their hand claps, and foot stomping thunderous as they put the seal heir approval to their Prince's woman.

Coron slapped Dyllon on the back as the younger man slid down from the stone lion with a look of disbelief. "Here is a woman worthy of our big brother, wouldn't you say?" Coron asked.

"Our brother has the luck of the Chales," Dyllon agreed.

Empress Dyreil put her head on her husband's shoulder.

"You knew, didn't you," her husband, Tran, asked.

"Her mother told me last eve. Isn't she a beauty, Tran? She'll make him a fine mate, eh?"

Tran nodded. "Quite a pair," he said earnestly, looking at the blazing blond hair and deep midnight velvet blending in the bright sunlight. "Shall we go inside and toast the young couple?"

Dyreil looked up at her husband's beloved face and grinned. "I can think of a better way to get warm, Tran."

Sighing, the Emperor raised his eyes to the heavens. "Is that all you McGregors ever think about?" He looked down at her. "Well," he sighed, "if I have to, I have to."

All along the canopy, Conar's children were giggling and clapping. It wouldn't have mattered to them if she had not been the beauty she obviously was, for her heart and soul were beautiful and they knew that already.

Gerren was watching the couple as they walked about the crowd greeting their people and he was stunned. This was the girl he had almost had kidnapped and taken out of his son's life forever?

"Come, Gerren," Shaz said, draping an arm about his friend's shoulder. "Let us tell you all about our headstrong daughter and the man she was determined to have love her."

Legion sat on a bench and shook his head. "I can't believe this."

"Neither can I," Teal replied

"Liza is the Princess," Thom said, his voice filled with wonder. "The Toad is Conar's Liza!"

Cayn chuckled. He'd brought that little boy into the world twenty years ago, but looking at his smiling face now, was like looking back in time. That face had the look of having played the very best of practical jokes on everyone there.

Hern Arbra nodded. The smile on the brat's face was beatific. The girl was lovelier than he remembered. He dared not tell either father or son that he had known all along who Liza was. How did he explain not taking Rayle Loure's word for what the Princess looked like and going to Oceania himself? How did one go about explaining how a long talk with a certain young Princess had set an old warrior's mind to rest? And how did you explain giving directions to the young Princess so she could find her Prince at a certain tavern, on a certain day, at a certain time? Or how he had made sure Rayle Loure and his men had left them alone on their journey to Norus together? He saw the lady in question turn her pretty smile to him and he nodded in greeting, smiling with rare warmth to her. He watched her smile grow sweet and wide and he nodded again, knowing she understood his best wishes for her. As he turned, his eyes met those of a friend in the crowd and the smile on his friend's face mirrored Hern's.

"A good ending, eh, Hern?" the man asked.

"A good ending only if followed with a few quaffs of ale!" Hern said, slapping the man on his back.

"You buying?"

Hern slipped his arm around his friend's neck and got him in a hammerlock before the bigger man slipped away and feigned a punch at Hern's midsection.

Hern snorted, "How come I always wind up buying, Belvoir?" He shook his head. "You've got coins, too."

Sir Belvoir, Master-at-Arms of Norus Keep, spy for Her Majesty Queen Medea of Oceania, good friend and fellow conspirator of Hern Arbra, shoved his friend. "Come to Norus and I'll buy."

Hern's snort of disgust left no doubt in Belvoir's mind what he thought of Norus Keep. "I'll toss you for it."

Belvoir laughed, knowing Hern didn't mean coins. "You can try!"

A sneer puckered Kaileel Tohre's thin face as he saw Conar kissing the bitch again. His blood boiled, his breath coming in deep, shallow heaves of pure rage. He turned vicious eyes to the heavens and gnashed his teeth together. Spinning around, he started to leave, but jerked around.

"I will see you pay dearly for the love of that whore, Conar McGregor. I will make you wish you had never laid eyes on her. Mark me well, sweet Prince. That bitch will be the instrument of your well-deserved destruction!"

The End

Printed in the United States
73612LV00001B/13-45

9 781586 088361